D0773005

rar

97 98 09
/ 7 H /

'97

DON'T DREAM

THE COLLECTED HORROR AND FANTASY
OF DONALD WANDREI

Books by Donald Wandrei

Poetry

    ECSTASY
    DARK ODYSSEY
    POEMS FOR MIDNIGHT
    COLLECTED POEMS

Short Fiction

    THE EYE AND THE FINGER
    STRANGE HARVEST
    COLOSSUS
    DON'T DREAM

Novels

    THE WEB OF EASTER ISLAND
    INVISIBLE SUN (in preparation)

Mysteries

    FROST (in preparation)

DON'T DREAM

THE COLLECTED HORROR AND FANTASY
OF DONALD WANDREI

Edited by
Philip J. Rahman and Dennis E. Weiler

Illustrated by
Rodger Gerberding

Minneapolis, Minnesota
1997

Layout and design by Felix Bremer

ISBN:1-878252-27-5
Library of Congress Catalog Card Number: 97-60609

CONTENTS

Prose Poems, Essays, and Marginalia

Illustrations

EDITORS' NOTE

Even before *Colossus: the Collected Science Fiction of Donald Wandrei* was published, a companion volume, concentrating on the author's horror and fantasy writing, was in the planning stage. It has taken nearly eight years, but this project has culminated in the book before you. In the interim, a good deal of literary and biographic material on Donald Wandrei has been exhumed, including several new stories, prose poems and essays, many of which have been incorporated into this collection.

Don't Dream includes such traditional supernatural horror stories as "It Will Grow on You" and "Uneasy Lie the Drowned," grim pyschological horror and Poesque confessionals, including the previously unpublished "Delerium of the Dead," and an uncharacteristically light-hearted fantasy tale, "Don't Dream," reprinted here for the first time since its publication in *Unknown Worlds* fifty-eight years ago. Besides these supernatural and fantasy pieces, there are a number of science fiction tales which were left out of *Colossus* because they were more horror than science-oriented. Thus, along with sea monsters and the undead, you will find plenty of mad scientists, killer aliens, and amoebic monsters on the loose, as in "A Scientist Divides," "The Monster from Nowhere," and "The Destroying Horde."

A third category of Wandrei's fiction might be referred to as his "dream" stories. These short mood pieces, some of which were inspired by actual dreams, chain a series of fantastic or horrible images into a loose, poetic narrative to capture the essense of a nightmare or bizarre vision. Nearly plotless and characterless, but filled with rich imagery and a luxuriously decadent vocabulary, the best of these are reminiscent of the prose poems of Clark Ashton Smith and H. P. Lovecraft. A few of the longer pieces, "Fragment of a Dream," "Nightmare," and "The Crater," have been included in the fiction section of this book. The balance have been gathered together in a section devoted to prose poems, juvenile sketches, and essays.

As with *Colossus,* we have organized the fiction section chronologically by publication date. An exception was made for "When the Fire Creatures Came," a previously unpublished story which was positioned chronologically by the date it was originally submitted to *Weird Tales*. This story was later rewritten as "The Fire Vampires," also included in this volume.

Our approach was more encyclopedic than critical. We realise that this may not be the best way to showcase a writer, but it allows the reader to see the author's thematic and artistic development. On that matter, we should note plans to eventually reissue *Colossus* in a revised, expanded edition, making available essentially all of Wandrei's short fiction.

We would like to thank Harold Hughesdon and his daughter, Helen Mary Hughesdon, for their assistance in this publication. Likewise, our thanks to Dwayne H. Olson for his illuminating afterword, and for his advice on the preparation of this book. Much of Donald Wandrei's unpublished fiction had been dispersed before this collection could be assembled. Regathering this material was a challenge that could not have been met without the help of a number of people and organizations. Special thanks are offered to Stefan Dziemianowicz, Steven Behrends, Dwayne Olson, and Peder Wagtskjold for providing copies of rare published and unpublished stories and manuscripts. Mr. Behrends' bibliographic essay, "Something from Above," provided guidance for much of our initial research.

Glenn Rahman, Dwayne Olson, and Scott Wyatt deserve our gratitude for the daunting task of proofing the galleys. Special thanks also to Barbara Jensen for her skill and patience in transcribing Wandrei's difficult handwriting and the less than perfect copies of photocopies of other uncollected stories provided her.

The photograph of Donald Wandrei that graces the dustjacket of this volume was provided by Mr. Wyatt from the collection of the late Eric Carlson. Eric was an old friend of Don's and ours, and he will be missed. Thanks also to Jon Arfstrom and Rodger Gerberding for their artistic contributions to this volume, and to the cover designer, Robert T. Garcia.

We would also like to extend our appreciation to The Minnesota Historical Society for the use of materials from their collection, and to Steven Stillwell, S.T. Joshi, and Ferret Fantasy for providing various help in our research.

INTRODUCTION

In *A Summons to Memphis,* (New York: Knopf, 1987) Peter Taylor writes of "the kind of communication and imaginative interplay that can exist between a child and an adult acquainted with each other only as friends—not as child and parent or in any other kind of kinship. What it amounts to is the same sort of fulfillment that friends of any age are able to offer each other." Taylor's words describe my relationship with Donald Wandrei.

Our first conversation occurred on July 1, 1955, the day we became next-door neighbors: he was then 47, and I was 8. Our last conversation was on October 14, 1987, the day before Don died: he was then 79, and I was 41. In the 32 years intervening, we talked almost every day, sometimes for a few minutes, sometimes for several hours.

As I grew older, I became increasingly interested and involved in reading and writing: grade school and high school essay contests, college as an English major and newspaper editor, graduate school in comparative literature, a career teaching English and foreign languages, and finally law school. Don's gifts to me were always books or writing materials: a dictionary, an autographed copy of one of August Derleth's children's books, a book of poetry, a fine point pen, a typewriter table. Our conversation was often about the books I was reading or had read.

I knew that Don was, or had been, a writer: I read the poetry he wrote as a young man. But although he recommended many works to me, he did not suggest that I read his own fiction. He spoke of difficulties with publishers and of copyright problems, but never discussed the works themselves. At the time of his death, I had read very little of his work.

I approached this collection of fiction with the desire to see what traces I could find of the author in the stories. I expected only traces, because the most significant features of the stories belied the man I had known: Don never manifested a taste for the gruesome, the ghoulish, or the terrifying; he was invariably courteous, gentle and sensitive to beauty. Moreover, almost all, if not all, the stories had been written decades before we met, by a man much younger than the man I knew.

I found occasional obvious indications of his authorship, such as the references to "Haupers' original oil painting, July Moon" in "It Will Grow On You": "it was still a perfect and timeless abstraction, a captured moment of eternity, serene from its dark shadow masses and detached, remote, immortal to the gibbous moon beyond its mysteriously luminous sky." Don had taken me to visit his friend, the painter Clem Haupers, had shown me Haupers' portrait of Don surrounded by elements of his stories, and had given my parents a Haupers painting as a gift.

Another obvious indication was the language itself. Don did not cease to be a poet when he wrote prose. Language to him was almost sacred: he never rushed a phrase or spoke in other than complete, well-constructed sentences, and he very seldom resorted to nicknames or slang. He listened, even to children, as carefully as he spoke. Almost every page of this book reflects his highly sophisticated vocabulary and sentence structure. It is easy to imagine Don reading these stories aloud: his voice comes through them.

Many other, less obvious, features of the stories correspond to my memories of Don. His sensitivity to natural beauty and to color, his interest in natural and psychological phenomena, and his kindly and generally amicable nature are all in evidence.

Don Wandrei was acutely alive and responsive to natural beauty. He spent countless hours sitting on his back steps, looking into his garden or up at the sky. I joined him in examining the shading of a rose petal, in smelling the lilacs outside his back door, in sitting motionless as hummingbirds flitted around his flowers, in gazing at the stars, the planets, and the northern lights, in spotting a rainbow, in watching winter snow dissolve into spring, in feeling the breeze and speculating on the weather. None of the sights, sounds, or smells of a natural setting was lost on him.

This faculty for observation showed itself in many places in the stories, for example in "Uneasy Lie the Drowned": "The water itself, leaf-green at mid-afternoon, darkened as the sun disappeared. The green turned to a sodden blue, and went down to a dull black. . . . The constant, quiet slur of waters divided by the canoe became a slap, at irregular intervals, and with mounting force."

Color fascinated Don. He was very definite about colors he would and would not wear. He usually wore shades of green and brown, and very often burgundy, but never any shade of blue, from pale to navy. He was aware of subtle color differences, and used color as a guide in selecting honey or fresh fruits, and in brewing tea. His work is replete with color descriptions: in one paragraph of "The Woman at the Window," we read of "the youth of the crimson realm when the sun blazed in the bright red of its dawn . . . darker colors erased the orange reds of youth . . .the reds were all dark as old blood save for a moment at sunset when the window burned with ruddy scarlet."

The occasional reference to alcohol in the stories puzzled me: the physician in "It Will Grow on You" offers his patient a decanter of whiskey in lieu of anesthetic; the protagonist of "Don't Dream" wakes with the feeling that "he'd eaten a roast ox [and] washed it down with a barrel of beer." It seemed odd for Don to refer to alcohol or its effects, he observed a rigorous and total abstinence, even from baked goods made with rum. Then I remembered that this was not always the case. Don was drinking heavily at the time we became neighbors; as small children, we noticed only that sometimes he was very "different." These "different" periods began to disturb my youngest sister, to the point where my father told Don that if the drinking continued, we children would be told not to visit him. Don later recounted that, after their conversation, he set off to buy another bottle, decided he didn't want or need it, turned home, and never drank again. There was no back-sliding, no support group, no falling off the wagon: when Don made a decision, it was made. Later in life, he went from being almost a chain-smoker to being a non-smoker with similar determination.

Although no one else, to my knowledge, could change Don's mind, he could change it himself. The most significant change I remember was in regard to our dogs. He was vehemently opposed to our getting a dog, and said he would never feel comfortable in our house again. With the passage of time, however, he became extremely close to our various dogs, coming along on their daily walks, keeping biscuits for them on his porch, filling their water bucket, and ultimately writing commemorative poems when they died. As we walked the dogs each evening, he often speculated about their perception of the world.

I found an echo of this interest in "The Witch-Makers," where scientists find a means of transposing the bodies and spirits of animals, and contemplate doing the same for man. "And if we try and succeed, would you even attempt to estimate how much we'll enrich man's imagination and add to his knowledge? Think of what it would mean if we enabled man to look at the world through the eyes of his pets, a dog, or a cat, or a horse! Wouldn't he have a more tender feeling toward them and a more profound appreciation of his capacities? Isn't it possible that, in course of time, his pets would acquire a new intelligence of the order of humanity? Isn't it conceivable that they could then be trained to speak, with results in strange, unimaginable new friendships?"

Don used the "pseudo-scientific romance" to explore his own ideas on the nature of animals ("The Witch-Makers"), the nature of plant life ("Strange Harvest") the nature of identity ("The Painted Mirror"), the nature of time ("The Lives of Alfred Kramer" and "The Man Who Never Lived") and the nature of pain ("The Nerveless Man"). He identifies the "pseudo-scientific romance" as the third type of imaginative literature in the book's only critical essay, "The Imaginative Element in Modern Literature." The other two types are the ghost story and the horror story.

The essay is part academic discussion, part personal reflection. Don explains the reason for the popularity of ghost stories: readers "want to be, nay ask and beg to be, convinced that there is a life after this existence ceases." Although Don professed no religion, he shared that conviction. He contrasts this desire with the reluctance of the readers of horror stories to "be too strongly impressed with terror; hence, the writer must cope with this antagonism from the start, must build so cleverly that in spite of himself the reader is swept along in fascination."

Don cites Francis Marion Crawford's "The Upper Berth," which he classifies as both a ghost and a horror story. The influence of Crawford and other writers in his genre is clearly seen in Don's own ghost and horror stories, particularly those featuring descriptions of corpses: "The Lady in Gray," "Uneasy Lie the Drowned," "Chuckler." Don explores the elements of the horror story again in "The Shadow of a Nightmare:" "A tale of horror is one which begins on a low key of foreboding and rises steadily and rapidly like the howl of a wolf until words of awful imagery twist across the dead pages in a stream of terror; a tale that begins in shadow and passes into darkness until another blackness filled with Things surges about the reader; a tale that preys on the mind, that destroys all but one central part and wraps itself around that part on which to feed." The speaker goes on to cite Poe and Lovecraft as masters of the genre. By the time this story was published in 1929, Don already had both a personal and a professional relationship with Lovecraft; he definitely regarded himself as Lovecraft's disciple, not his equal.

But most of the stories in this book belong to the third genre, the"pseudo-scientific romance," of which Don regards H.G. Wells, "the one person in literature whom I most admire and worship," as the master. Pseudo-scientific romance gave Don an opportunity to create characters, and these characters reveal some of the amiability and expansiveness Don exemplified for much of his life. During his last years, particularly after his house was broken into and he himself cut and beaten, he became increasingly reclusive, almost the point of paranoia. But prior to that time, he had been inclined to see the good in most of those around him.

The characters fall easily into types: the highly intelligent explorers of ideas in "Shadow of a Nightmare," "The Lives of Alfred Kramer" "A Scientist Divides," "The Man Who Never Lived," "The Witch-Makers," and "The Destroying Horde;" the simple individuals affected by forces beyond their understanding in "Strange Harvest" "Don't Dream," "The Chuckler," and "The Destroying Horde;" the chance adventurers of "Uneasy Lie the Drowned," "It Will Grow on You" and "Spawn of the Sea." The evil in Don's stories is far more likely to result from a discovery gone wrong or a supernatural phenomenon than from human beings: most of his characters are attractive, and villains are rare. "The Green Flame" is a notable exception. Don would have found it easier to believe in disaster caused by a scientist whose effort to benefit humanity backfired than by an evil genius bent on destruction: intelligence almost equates to goodness in his characters. The only major attempt at deception in these stories is by the extra-terrestrials in "The Fire Vampires."

In the final analysis, though, it is not the characters, nor the outmoded pseudo-science, nor the ghoulish element that makes Don's fiction worth reading: it is the use of language. A few lines of W. H. Auden come to mind:

> Time that is intolerant
> Of the brave and innocent,
> And indifferent in a week
> To a beautiful physique,
> Worships language, and forgives
> Everyone by whom it lives.

Time has shown how far most of Don's pseudo-science was from real science, but time has not dulled the glow of his gift as a writer of English.

Helen Mary Hughesdon

DON'T DREAM

THE COLLECTED HORROR AND FANTASY OF DONALD WANDREI

A FRAGMENT OF A DREAM

ALL DAY LONG, under the dusky glare of a green sun that flamed across the sombre sky, he had been traversing a burnt and blackened wasteland in his quest of Loma. All day he had been crossing a dead and utterly lifeless land, and when the green sun set, he had not yet emerged from it. But even as it set with its dying emerald glow it had lit darkly for a moment a forest of some sort far ahead. And toward it he went.

The night around him, as the sun sank, deepened from a strange twilight to a darkness, and from the darkness to an ebon blackness that crouched upon the land. But the wanderer paused not; on he traveled toward the forest, guided by the faint and unfamiliar constellations of stars that burned coldly and whitely in the sky above.

For a long time he kept on through the thick darkness, ever pressing toward the forest ahead, and it was only when he had gone more than half way that the darkness lightened dimly when a huge blood-red sun swept up from the eastern sky and cast a livid, leprous glow on the land. In tremendous bounds it fled across the sky, all surrounded by a many colored rout of streaming satellites. The air hung heavy and listless, and in the unearthly light of the red sun seemed to ooze with a myriad globules of blood. The land, burnt before, took on a desolation and an aspect of solitude as if a red rot were creeping through its rocks and sand.

The wanderer kept on, and he had almost reached the forest when the rushing red sun sank with all its satellites. But from every side, from every one of the distant horizons, there rocketed upward a horde of twisting comets, and the suffering vault became alive with jagged streaks of light hurtling erratic and aimless from horizon to horizon.

Dank and dark loomed the forest; to the right and left it stretched in never-ending line until it faded and vanished in the distant gloom. The wanderer plunged forward. In a moment he was threading his way through gigantic trees that towered up and up. The darkness deepened and deepened as the branches of the trees interlocked more and more closely, until the entire sky was hidden from his sight and the sullen branches formed a solid roof over his head. He picked his way in and out through the gaunt trunks that rose around him, and all the while that he moved forward they became thicker and thicker. Creepers began to make their appearance. And on every side of the black forest he heard things chuckling in the darkness; ever and again faint whisperings reached him, and sometimes he saw shadows peering from behind the boles of the trees. The still air became pregnant with a thousand sounds of sibilant whispers moaning faintly through the forest.

But he pressed onward, always before his eyes a vision of the lithe and slender loveliness of his lost Loma. And the creepers thickened and thickened until he had to claw his way through them, until, finally, he drew forth the great sword that hung at his side and hacked his way through. And every creeper that he slashed shrieked aloud, and from the severed ends dripped a soft, warm substance. . . . The forest became suddenly malignant and malefic. The baleful creepers twined insidiously about his legs, and all along his path the wounded ones howled in swelling ululations that made the forest echo with waves of fiendish sound. Ever and again, thick vines clutched at him like the trailing talons of some huge and hairy arm. And when he cut them, they wailed like flayed children. . . . He lunged ahead faster, and the branches whipped at him. His face grew scratched and bloody from the flailing of the branches that ripped his clothes and flesh and twined around him. He beat them off and staggered on.

And suddenly the ground underfoot grew damp. He stopped—just in time. For in front of him, stretching until it vanished in the night ahead and on either side, lay a vast, slimy slough. The forest came down to its very edge, and even throughout it, here and there, stood gaunt dead trees, and in places half-submerged logs rotted. As far as he could look to his right and left, the swamp spread its interminable length. He debated for a moment; he looked again at the logs, the stumps, and the occasional unfallen trees that rose at intervals. Then he ran forward.

The going was easy for a time. He walked across great tree trunks lying in the ooze, or jumped from stump to stump, or swam through patches of stagnant water covered with a luminous green slime. Sometimes he dragged himself through mud that made a husky sucking sound when he pulled out his legs . . . like the sound of ghouls feeding. On one or two occasions it seemed to him that a shadow passed overhead, a sweeping shadow as of some huge nocturnal thing. . . . He shuddered as he stumbled on.

And he came to an open space, brown-covered. Unthinking, he plunged in and swam forward. The entire surface instantaneously lived with a million million wriggling shapes that swarmed in hellish motion. Hissing snakes moved from his path and collected on each side; cold vipers slithered across his back and neck and squirmed like fat worms in a carcass. He dived under the surface and swam as long as he could. When he rose, the water rippled with mounting waves of serpents, and great bunches of snakes thrashed on every side. The affrighted air trembled in one mighty hiss that ascended from the hordes.

When at last the water ended in mud and he pulled himself upon a rotting log, he lay for a long while regaining his strength. The seething mass of reptiles gradually subsided, and when he took up his way again was quiescent. Above, the comets had fled the sky, and the heavens were void and absolutely empty in a terrible blackness.

Hour after hour he ploughed through foul swamps and slimy water. The noisome odors of the place made him dizzy after a time, but he fought onward. He sometimes thought of casting away the sword which hung heavy and cumbersome at his side, but he kept it. He knew not what he might meet.

He must have travelled leagues before he staggered from the slough unexpectedly. He was on firm ground, but the forest had ceased. He lay down on the earth for a time to rest his weary body, and carelessly looked back across the slough. From far behind came a shuddering heave; as he watched, something gigantic and horrible rose out of the depths and mounted upward. And from the top of the soaring bulk he saw a head swaying from side to side with one huge central eye gleaming blindly.

In a moment he was on his feet and running forward until the slough and the monster were entombed in the deepening gloom behind.

The ground was level and covered with a tall grass or weed that rustled gently. And a soft night wind began to arise in fitful moans and whisper with the grass in a reedy rustling. The plaintive music came dimly from the sounding darkness, infinitely sombre, in strange, minor harmonics and chants of loneliness as if the drooping soul of misery itself were floating through the reeds. From every side as he passed came, low and elusive, the rhythmic cadences, a mournful litany from the whispering grass. All the plain seemed weeping at his passing, and he became filled with a desire to rush through the trackless extent and soothe the crying of the grass. But there rose before his eyes the shadowy, haunting beauty of his Loma: in one fearful second the sounds blended together and streamed in speeding waves to the utmost darkness. And the plain was as a thing that, having lived, had died.

Winding and tortuous his way became, shortly afterward, when the plain ceased abruptly near a range of hills. And even as he entered them, the darkness again began to lighten. By the time he had crossed the hills, a wan, immense moon was crossing the sky like a decaying thing that fled, shunned by the aloof, ebon depths of the heavens. It cast a pallor, sick and deathly, on the ground; it limned the gaunt trees pallidly against the sky; it laid a soft and fat covering of white rottenness on everything it touched. And under the ghastly paleness the wanderer's features took on the appearance of a walking corpse. A nameless fear began to creep through him, and he went on faster toward the mountains towering beyond the hills. An utter solitude and silence had settled over the dreary waste. The country the traveler had crossed crouched faintly luminous far behind, but he turned not. Once he looked at the vault above, but the entire concameration was completely and desolately empty of all save blackness and that westward-waning moon. Only the steady low fall of his steps broke the appalling silence; all things that lay on every side as far as he could see conspired to give him a sense of minuteness in an infinitude that extended, ceaseless, upward and outward through the vacua overhead.

And as the wanderer mounted the trail that was now winding through the base of the mountains, the rocks and trees in some indescribable way began to absorb the light that fell on them, until they moved stealthily in slow corruption. And as he continued, it seemed to him that they changed their positions . . . as if to block his path. He touched a stone. A shiver of fear ran through him, for the stone was *living* . . . panting like some monstrous toad. In a sudden anger, he grasped his sword and smote the rock. It was cleft, so that the halves fell apart. And even as the sword touched it, the rock shrieked. From its core poured forth a horde of worms. . . . And the rocks began to converge toward him, like crawling heaps of liquescence, and the trees began to walk. Gasping, he slashed about him. He could do nothing. Wet, cold things were gathering around his feet and creeping up his legs. . . . Dead horrors caressed his flesh. . . . And in his despair, he thought of Loma: There came to his mind the picture of her slim, willowy body and half-shut dreaming eyes. . . .

With a start, he came to himself. The rocks and trees were still and lifeless. The moon had sunk with all its pale deathliness.

For hours he wandered on. The path steadily rose and wound upward through tremendous mountains that towered on every side. Darkness reigned, but the path lay distinct.

It was only when he had ascended nearly to the top of the central range that the gloom again lightened. Ahead of him loomed a cup-shaped circle of giants over which hung a faint and almost impalpable phosphorescence that illuminated slightly the grandeur of stupendous and colossal peaks. But he paused not to survey the scene; he followed the path where it led through a rift in the cup to the hollow itself.

The phosphorescence shimmered everywhere, and, as he passed, seemed to be thickening. The air suddenly and indescribably became fraught with expectation. It was as if his arrival were awaited.

When he reached the center of the cup, he stopped; and when he stopped, it began. The slow-drifting phosphorescence leaped into life and rushed toward the walls of the mountains in a cataclysmic surge. There the sweeping luminosity collected and condensed, and around him, in a great circle, sprang up a low, running line of flame. In a moment, the circle was completed and the light rose upward. Almost before he could move, a solid wall of cold radiance burned about him, mounting in immense waves.

And all the light was flame; and all the flame was gold.

And now there began to come a sound, a faint sound, as of the moan of distant waters, while higher, higher, higher mounted the liquid waves of light around the circle.

And all the light was flame; and all the flame was red.

And the distant moaning came louder and louder, rising in the ever-growing roar of mighty, warring seas. The light began to converge in a funnel-shapen roof above his head, drawing after it the thicker waves.

And all the light was flame; and all the flame was green.

A titanic wash filled the air alive in quickening motion, and a thunderous roar as of all the billion billion waters of all the worlds boomed with a space-annihilating crash of sundering stars toward the funnel. And the sheeted flame above commenced a spinning motion until it whirled furiously and dizzily in a twisted wrack of shifting radiance.

And all the light was flame; and all the flame was black.

And a tremendous and terrible drumming of bellowing abysmal storms howled toward the funnel in roar on deafening roar. The funnel widened and lengthened suddenly, and swept apart to form a maelstrom around an immense vacancy that led to outer Space. Far above, the blackness of the sky was moving and streaming in mighty rivers of ebon that serpentined madly toward the funnel.

He stood dazed and deafened by the fearful thunder of the space-leaping winds and the uncontrollable forces lashing themselves to savage fury all around. And instinctively he cried:

"Loma! Loma!"

The flame flung itself together in a coalescing sweep. In one huge, solid pillar of fire it soared upward. He followed its lengthening league-long height far above. And it seemed to him that a greater glare gathered about its peak, and that Something had formed there.

"Loma! Loma!"

All the howling winds poured downward and fled in whirling rout around the pillar of flame, walling it with a speeding blackness. He tried to move but he could not. Yet all seemed awaiting him, and the pillar became motionless in the screaming winds as if expectant. *They* were waiting—waiting—

But he moved not.

And the tower of flame which had hung still for a moment leaped upward toward the eternal blackness overhead. But the wanderer stood motionless. And the thundering, madly rushing gales vengefully swept downward and about him. He felt torn by a million waters fighting, smashing, and the noise of all enormous washing seas filled his ears. And he stumbled, battered by angry pounding winds.

"Loma! Loma!"

But the mounting winds fled upward after the flying pillar of flame. Far above he saw a living stream of fire that rocketed outward. About him whirled and twisted the howling blasts, and all around was an ebon infinitude of shouting darkness that hurtled after the streaming flame.

"Loma! Loma!"

But there answered him only the fearful mockery of the vanishing hurricanes—the hiss of a mighty sea that washed farther and farther—the dying echo of a cosmic whisper that faded into nothingness.

THE SHADOW OF A NIGHTMARE

"**I** HAVE NEVER read," remarked Arthur Marl, "a true horror story."

We who were with him in a corner of the club-house looked at him in surprize.

"Why, you've been making a study of Gothic literature for twenty years or more. You surely must have read *some*," a member replied.

"Of course."

"Then why did you say you hadn't?"

"I didn't."

"For heaven's sake, will you kindly explain yourself?" someone demanded.

"The thing is obvious, or ought to be. I said I had read no true horror story, though I have read many which seemed so for a moment."

"What's the difference?"

"This: The best stories of the type called 'Gothic' may affect a person temporarily; some may even give him nightmares if he is of a nervous temperament, but this does not necessarily mean that they are true horror tales."

"It depends on what you mean by a 'horror' story," someone remarked.

"Exactly. And can you tell me what a tale of horror is?"

"One that makes your spine crawl—"

"One that, if read at night while alone, will make you jump for bed—"

"One that will make you afraid of the night—"

"One that you can't recall except with a shiver—"

"One that you won't want to recall—"

Arthur quelled the babel. "You all are partly right."

"What's your own definition?" asked somebody.

He thought for a moment; then he replied:

"What I say will apply only to those who have more than a passing acquaintance with Gothic literature. One who reads but little and has never come across more than one or two specimens of the macabre will naturally have received a much deeper impression from those stories than would one who is familiar with the type. The more tales of terror you read, the more inured you become. There is always the thrill of the first few horror stories, of course, but indifference comes quickly. Life is so comprehensive that little can be new; but the unknown, the utterly unknown, is the essence of terror.

"I have made a study of this field for twenty years or so. My collection of such books and manuscripts, as you know, is one of the best—perhaps the only ambitious one—in existence. A taste for the gruesome, once acquired, is unappeasable, but although my library contains thousands of these volumes, there is not one among them which I consider a true Gothic romance.

"A tale of horror is one which begins on a low key of foreboding and rises steadily and rapidly like the howl of a wolf until words of awful imagery twist across the dead pages in a stream of terror; a tale that begins in shadow and passes into darkness until an utter blackness filled with Things surges about the reader; a tale that preys on the mind, that destroys all but one central part and wraps itself around that part on which to feed.

"As I said, there is no such story in all my collection. I have obtained many books, famed as being horrible, but they all lack something, or at best have only a temporary effect. *The Monk* in reality does not belong to the class; *Melmoth* is more properly an adventure novel; *The Vampyre* is as good as its progeny *Dracula*, but vampires are becoming common; *Frankenstein* is famous mainly because it was one of the first Gothic romances; Benson is often too definite; Poe is the master, of course, though Lovecraft is now writing terrific tales.

"You see, if an author makes his story too definite, it descends to the ordinary or becomes either disgusting or ridiculous, depending on how far he goes. Thus, Wells' *The Cone* is disgusting, as are tales of cannibalism and torture. Physical pain is ephemeral; it comes to an end. The mind cannot be greatly affected by definite or material things, because it is acquainted with them. It needs a tale of hints and whispers that it can develop unlimitedly."

We were silent for a moment, but someone broke out, "Do you expect ever to read such a story?"

"Perhaps," was his only reply.

2

I believe it was two days later that Arthur took me into his confidence. He did not mention the tale to anyone else, but he told me about it because I myself was quite fond of Gothic literature.

"There is now on its way to me a manuscript from an agent in India," he said. "It was purchased from a native who had stolen it from a collection of ancient writings somewhere in the north; exactly where I don't know. My agent could make little of it, but the native claimed that it had passed into evil legend. I have found a reference to the manuscript in a Sanskrit fragment over three thousand years old. Even there it is described as being of unknown age.

"Think of it!" he half whispered to me. "It was written perhaps a hundred or more centuries ago! I believe, from the translation of the Sanskrit fragment, that it will be the key to the forgotten past. For, ages ago, the fragment states, there arose somewhere in the northern part of India, or beyond the Himalayas, a civilization of the highest type among a band of people completely isolated from the rest of their kind. But they all were madmen—maniacs! They lived in the days when the world was still young, and they had access to forces which have passed with the waning of the earth. And because they were mad, they had those forces more readily at their control."

His eyes were gleaming brighter. "They developed an advanced, but a mad and perverted, civilization with the aid of those evil forces. Their architecture was strange and fantastic; their art was a thing of shadows, the reflection of their madness and their servants'; their literature was the key to all ancient mysteries, the portal to the entities which have remained hidden for epochs and are now remembered only as myths, legends, and fabled lore. They had at their call terrific implements of power and destruction in those Evil Ones; they kept that secret in their literature. But with the coming of a now-unknown doom, the entire country was ravaged, the cities became heaps of dust, the inhabitants were wiped out, and all their work was obliterated, except one small group of books. And of that group the only manuscript extant is the one I shall receive, written by a madman whose every thought was inspired by the ravening Things inseparably connected with the Country of the Mad, and giving somewhere in it the key to what the world has forgotten!"

I was inflamed, of course, by this extraordinary narrative, and eager to know more. A torrent of questions burst from me, but Arthur had told me all he knew. He suggested that I come over, however, when the manuscript had arrived.

I did not see him in the meantime, but when he notified me a couple of weeks later that he had received the manuscript, I immediately hastened over.

Never before had I seen him so excited. His eyes shone and gleamed steadily. He was nervous, and not only were his old mannerisms intensified, but he had picked up a dozen new ones. His voice had an unusual tone, an unsteadiness.

"Come in. The manuscript's here."

I followed him inside and we walked to the rooms containing his library. A large table covered with books stood in the middle of one room. He motioned me toward it. All the volumes were ancient and musty; some were riddled with worm-holes, some had damp-stains and mold-spots, while others had faded or discolored leaves.

"Here it is," he said, pointing before him.

It was almost with awe that I looked at the manuscript. The leaves of it were fastened between old and worn covers of ivory that once had been inscribed with strange gold symbols. The characters within, on parchment of great age, were totally unfamiliar to me. Many of those near the margins had faded or had been thumbed to illegibility, but in the centers they were black and distinct. The writing was clear and in a fine hand. Yet the manuscript aroused in me an immediate distaste. Something about those ancient leaves with their black, unknown characters repelled me in a singular manner.

"In what language is it written?"

"I'm not sure," he replied slowly. "I have been comparing it with the oldest of the Indian tongues, but it doesn't agree with any of them. It resembles Sanskrit most closely, and seems to bear the relation to it that Anglo-Saxon does to Modern English."

"Whew! It must be one of the oldest works in existence! Have you begun to decipher it yet?"

"I am just commencing the task, which I may not finish for weeks. But what a find! I think I have my tale at last!"

3

I did not see him again until two months later, for I was out of town. The manuscript was not forgotten, however; on several occasions it came into my thoughts and I wondered how Arthur was progressing, or if it lived up to his hopes. But I heard nothing from him during the period, and it had faded somewhat into the background of memory by the time I returned.

The evening after I got back, I decided to call on Arthur. I dropped in at the club on my way to his home, thinking he might possibly be there. He wasn't. But I met an old friend and we chatted for a few minutes. As I left him, to continue my way, he remarked, "Sorry you're leaving so quickly. Is it a pressing engagement?"

"Well, not exactly," I replied. "I'm going to see if Arthur's home."

I have never seen the face of a man change as rapidly as his. For a brief instant his features altered, and there came into his face an expression of aversion, almost of fear. I looked at him in surprise. He pursed his lips as if to answer my unspoken question, but said nothing. Instead, he motioned me toward a corner.

For another minute he was silent, after we had seated ourselves, before asking, "When did you last see Arthur?"

"About two months ago. Why?"

He ignored my question and said half to himself, "And you have known him as long as I."

"Longer. But what are you driving at?"

Again he ignored my questions. "You will keep this to yourself?"

"Of course," I answered. I was beginning to feel slightly alarmed as well as puzzled. "But what's the matter?"

He seemed to be arranging his thoughts, when, in a moment, he began speaking. His face was almost expressionless, and he talked in a low tone which did not go beyond me, though I could hear him distinctly.

"Perhaps you can explain this. I can't, though I have spent a week on it. And I'm beginning to wonder if it will be explained. Well, I saw him a week ago. Tuesday to be exact. I had gone out to his house for the evening and intended to pass several hours there. Arthur lives alone, you know, and we would not be interrupted but should have the evening to ourselves, since it was the servant's night off.

"I arrived about half-past seven, and Arthur himself admitted me. One of the first things he did was to show me some recent additions to his queer library. He had acquired some Latin works on demonology, among them a rather gruesome Sixteenth Century volume that contained several of Brueghel the Elder's nightmare-compositions, engraved, I think, by Cock. There was also a manuscript of great age which evidently fascinated him. He handled it with a mixture of like and dislike for some minutes while we were looking at his new volumes, and seemed half reluctant, half glad, to leave it.

"When we left the books, we went to his den, or whatever he calls the room where he keeps his curios. And it was there that I was first struck by something—unusual—about his appearance. I had not noticed anything different before we looked at the manuscript and the books, but I did now. There was nothing *definitely* wrong, but his eyes—you have noticed them? their sunkennness and depth? —well, they were lit curiously in a —*frightened*—sort of way. And he was nervous; he had picked up a number of mannerisms, and was so restless that I thought he must be suffering from overwork, or in need of a change. At times he fell into an abstraction, or gazed steadily at some vacant spot as if he saw something. Once he jerked his head around unexpectedly as if he though someone was behind him. And that frightened look never left his eyes.

"'You ought to take a vacation,' I remarked suddenly. 'You're wearing yourself out.'

"'I know it,' he replied. 'Perhaps I will soon. I've been spending all my time translating the manuscript, and it was quite a strain. But I finished last night, so perhaps I won't need a rest.'"

He stopped, but almost immediately continued, as if anxious to complete his story.

"It was after ten, I believe, when Arthur stood up suddenly with an apology and a remark about books that I didn't quite catch and left the room. I amused myself glancing at some of the curios while I waited.

"Five minutes passed. I turned to the old guns on the wall and examined them. Ten minutes came, and I wondered at the delay. I looked at the curios another five minutes. Then I began to feel slighty puzzled. The room was silent, and my thoughts were coursing in strange channels. I began to listen in spite of myself, but no sound could be heard. Fancies began to intrude themselves into my mind and I became vaguely apprehensive. I could have sworn that the atmosphere of the room had changed. Then I felt oddly uncomfortable and restless. I began to imagine all kinds of things. I tried to forget them. I tried to discount them as mere imagination. I thrust them away. They kept coming back. There was absolutely no ground for fear or doubt, but I was really alarmed. Then I got angry with myself and stood still. But the silence oppressed me and I walked about the room again. I could not imagine what was wrong with me. I pulled out my watch. Over twenty minutes had elapsed, and Arthur was still gone.

"'I'm an ass,' I cursed to myself, 'but I can't stand this any longer. He said something about books. I'll glance in his library, where he must be.'

"I left the room immediately and walked to the library, calling myself a fool as I walked. A light shone through the open door and I stepped in. I had guessed right. Arthur was standing near the middle of the room, with his back half toward me.

"'I hope I'm not intruding,' I said, 'but I got restless and thought something might have happened to you.'

"He did not reply. Then I noticed that there was something curious in his attitude; he was swaying, as if about to fall. I saw him pass his arm across his forehead and eyes as I sprang to his side. As I reached him, he removed it. I met the full stare of eyes darkly liquid and suffering with a black horror.

"'For God's sake!' he whispered. 'Brush them off!'

"I looked at him blankly. His eyes were fastened on some point in the air between us. He knew I was near, but apparently did not see me. 'Brush what off?'

"'Quick!' he moaned, in a voice which had become husky and frantic. 'I can't do a thing! They won't obey me!'

"I stood motionless, too dumfounded for thought. His eyes had taken on an aspect of utter terror such as I have never believed possible in any human being.

"'My God!' he moaned in a low voice. He was silent for a moment. Then he caught his breath suddenly and gasped—and the gasp turned to a rising moan, the moan to one continuous terrible shriek. He clasped at his face. He whipped the air all around, taking short steps in every direction but stopping immediately as if he had hit something. His face was hellish and working convulsively—his hands now covered his head, now lashed about—and that fearful scream never ceased."

He paused, and his voice became steadier. After a few seconds, he continued.

"I got a basin of water, carried it back in a trice, and hurled it in his face. Why I did, I don't know, except that I had no physical strength compared with that then in him. But at the first shock of the cold water, he stood still, and his face changed. A puzzled look came into it; he abruptly became himself, and sank exhausted into a chair.

"'Thanks,' he said, with a faint, ghastly smile. 'My nerves are worse than I thought. I believe I shall take your advice.'"

4

I come now to the last stage of that strange affair. That I may explain all is possible; that it will, I am not so sure. Perhaps Arthur Marl was insane, with a latent malady that had always afflicted him, or a sudden attack. But I saw the manuscript, and perhaps. . . .

It was getting dark when I left the club, but I decided to go to Arthur's residence at once, and hailed a cab. I thought over what I had heard, as I was carried toward his home, but I could make little of it. The one thing I was sure of was that the manuscript had something to do with the matter.

We drew up to his house, and I dismissed the cab. It was quite dark by now. A light was burning in the house, but, although I pushed the bell-button, I could not hear it ring, and no one answered. Then I remembered that this was the servant's night off. I decided to presume on our friendship as I had done many times before, and hence opened the door myself.

Since Arthur was usually in his library at this time, I wasted no more time but immediately went toward it. A dim light was burning there, but I could see no one. However, I turned the light on full before leaving, in order to make sure, and—on the floor lay Arthur Marl, long dead, his face set in a look of the most unutterable horror I have ever seen. His hands were extended, and his entire body seemed to be thrusting something away. Scattered near him were several small leaves of writing which I glanced at briefly and stuffed into my pocket.

It was not until an hour later that I got a chance to read them. I did what I could for Arthur, and made arrangements for proper treatment of the body. Once at my rooms, however, I hesitated no longer. I settled myself in a chair and spread out the leaves. They were mixed up, but even when I had arranged them they did not form a complete record, for the first pages, and some of the later, were missing.

And there, before the drowsy warmth of the fire, the room behind me darkened save for its dull glow, I read the leaves.

. . . And so there was a Country of the Mad long ago. That first allusion, then, was true, and the author right.

7. I have now translated the rest of the ancient volume, and part of the history of that strange land lies before me. Was there ever a myth wilder than the tale of the Country of the Mad? Think of it! More than ten thousand years ago, that band of madmen was collected and carried to a secluded mountain valley, and the only entrance sealed behind them. Guards were placed around the valley, at first, but the years passed, the story became legendary, and the guards were withdrawn for wars and never returned. The legend itself faded in time, and the Country of the Mad far beyond the known ranges lay forgotten.

But in all the years that the valley had been sealed, the band had survived and increased. At first they found it difficult to exist, for they were all insane and could not unite. But the valley was fertile, and they found it easy to live on the wild fruits and vegetables there, and the various small animals that were in it. They were people of all stages of insanity, and of several races. For awhile they were antagonistic to each other, race to race and individual to individual. Their twisted minds could not work together; none could tell what the madness of another might lead him to do. Murder, fighting, plot and counterplot, outbursts that sent them raging up and down the valley were common at first. But years passed by, and the young grew up accustomed to each other's madness. The children were almost invariably insane from birth; normal ones were killed because they were not like the rest. The races themselves intermarried.

And so, in time, their madness became equalized, their insanity a thing which affected all alike. The Country of the Mad flourished, a nightmare of nightmares. And it flourished, not because of the madmen, but because of what had entered.

The volume tells no more. What entered, therefore, remains a mystery—but I can guess.

12.   Received a letter from Chelton saying he has acquired an ancient manuscript for me and is forwarding it. He says it is written in a dead Indian tongue. Hope it refers to the Country of the Mad.

25.   The manuscript has arrived and I am beginning the translation. It is priceless! A chronicle from the valley itself, written by one of the band! It seems to be the key to some rite.

29.   John has left. I may never finish the translation. They are beyond my control already, wild from their enforced absence of nearly ten thousand years. God! I *can't* live without sleep. And I was fool enough to search for the most horrible tale. . . .

Aug. 1. I have destroyed the manuscript and my translation. If only I had never seen the thing! For I know now what it is that comes to him who has opened the door that they discovered. It is three days since I have closed my eyes; I have not slept since the night . . . And drugs won't keep me awake longer.

11 P.M. These may be the last words I shall write. I can hardly keep my eyes open, though I—though I— ho-hum— though I— seem— though I seem to feel them—gathering—insane—that are insane—no shape save the shape of nightmare and horror and rottenness—shapes of corpses and staring skulls—shapes indescribable—shapes—shapes—I *can't* hold out any longer—I *must* sleep—I tell you, I *must*. What if they do come again! I tell you, I've *got* to sleep.

My God! They're coming—they're crawling up my legs—they're creeping up my face—my eyes—God save me!—and entering my brain!

THE GREEN FLAME

MOULTON'S GRANDSON WATCHED with covetous eyes the strange actions of the old man. Behind locked doors, the old man thought himself safe, and performed the ritual that had become the soul of his existence. But his precautions were useless, as they had been for weeks, and his grandson looked on.

Within, for all his eagerness, the old man raised the lid of the box as if he thought it was empty. And even when he saw the heap within, he tilted the lid slowly until it hung back. Not till then did he raise the lamp. The emeralds that had lain dark within the chest began to glow softly as the first rays of light fell upon them, and when the lamp was directly over the heap, those on the surface shone with a wondrous green fire, a fire that mingled the dark tones of the sea with the sinister duskiness that moves within the depths of absinthe, a radiance as of stars and phosphorus and polished jade all wrought into one color, glowing with a mystic and ineffable glow. He lowered the lamp closer to the heap, and the slumbering fire burst into a blaze of dark glory that flashed from center to center, from stone to stone, from facet to facet, kindling every jewel, melting and blending the shades into living splendor. He swayed the lamp back and forth above the hoard, and all the emeralds began an innumerable winking and twinkling in little green tongues of fire that played across the gems, that flickered from every jewel, that leaped and danced as they poured forth all together their deep beauty. And he set the lamp down at his side and plunged his hands into the pile, and drew forth great handfuls of emeralds. And he let them fall in a stream past the lamp so that every stone sparkled and scintillated mysteriously while it imprisoned within its depths that priceless, living glow. And the stream of stones flashed upon the walls dark shadows that shifted with the shifting of the lambent tints of the jewels. In an ecstasy, he threw a shower of emeralds into the air so that flaming jewels filled the room with a tinted darkness shot with sparkles of green.

Again he lifted the lamp above the chest, and the emeralds shone with a multitudinous fire that swayed, oddly rhythmical, as if the gems were chanting an unknown music, could he but translate the colors into sound, into a symphony in green.

His eyes were lighted and his face shone with rapture; as he turned away from the hoard to leave the chamber, green fires burned before his haunted eyes.

Moulton's grandson wanted those jewels. There was only one way to obtain them. Even the thought of murder did not appall him in their presence. His kinship had long passed from his mind. Since he could not open the safe himself, he would be forced to kill Moulton while the old man played with his sorcerous gems. One thing still delayed the grandson.

A week later, even that one thing no longer made him wait. He was watching Moulton the night his collection became complete, the night he unwrapped the hugest emerald in all the world, and the myriad other stones paled beside a blaze of fire that flared out from his last jewel. They called it "The Green Flame." It had come from the heart of India, and now, in this chamber, it seemed to foam and overflow and spill out a wicked torrent of light. But the fiery stream that enchanted the old man raised in the younger only greedy thoughts.

It was after one o'clock when Moulton's grandson left his room a couple of nights later. He carefully turned his flashlight around him. The house was of great age, and strange. All the panelling, the decorations and tapestries dated back to older years. There were many rooms, and the passageway rambled in all directions. Some of the doors looked as if they had never been opened. It was a good thing he had lived in the house, else he could only have found his way with difficulty.

He followed his course and halted at length before the heavy door. Before entering, he stood in dusk for a minute. The silence was unbroken, as before. Somehow, he wished it weren't quite so silent, or the house so gloomy. Still, everything must be all right. Moulton had entered more than an hour before, and a light still burned inside.

He cautiously inserted his duplicate key and turned the doorknob, taking pains to make no sound. Then he slowly pushed the door open.

On the threshold he halted aghast. In the center of the room lay the body of the old man, curiously shriveled and shrunken. Beside it, on a table, lay an emerald, an emerald such as the eyes of man had never beheld, a great jewel of monstrous size. But he knew that no gem of such size existed in all the world, that "The Green Flame" was not one-third so large. The entire room shone with light and more than light, and in that fire, the bright ray of his flashlight glimmered pale and feeble. For out of the center of the emerald shone a flame, and that elfin flame rose and fell and rose, and with its rising and falling, an awful fire streamed out upon the table, across to the walls and along the walls to all the corners of the room and back; and with the ebb and flow of that terrible flame, the fire in the jewel blazed anew, while the air burned with a strange, unearthly radiance. For the emerald was aflame, and its heart was aflame, and its surface was aflame, and inside it was all fire, and from it poured that dreadful wave of glory. And in the core of the jewel, a great burning stream arose, and with its rise and fall, the hellish fire shone forth and the sinister blaze burst out as if long pent up, to swell the ebb and flow of flame across the table. And the fire blazed from one emerald!

A shiver shook Moulton's grandson. Then a blind terror overwhelmed him, and, scarce knowing what he did, he swung up his revolver and fired. There came an angry *spat*, an answering *crack* as the gem shattered. He screamed; at the same time, the house rocked to its foundation—the air burst with thunder—a strange lightning flickered about—the entire heavens seemed to be falling—he groped vainly as a rushing wall of blackness swept upon him.

THE TREE-MEN OF M'BWA

"**S**O YOU'RE AFTER big game," said the legless man. "What's your route?"

"Generally speaking," I answered, "up the Congo to its head waters, then inland, across the Mountains of the Moon to Uganda, and—"

I paused in surprise. The legless man was glaring at me with a curious mixture of fear, hatred, and warning. The expression that fleeted across his face was so strange that I halted in the midst of my sentence.

"Change your route!" he abruptly broke in. "Don't cross the Mountains of the Moon—if you want to come back!"

"Nonsense! I've hunted tigers in India, black panthers in Indo-China, and rubies among the head-hunters of Papua. I'm not afraid of anything that walks."

"I am," said the legless man, and again that curious expression writhed across his features. "And you will be if you keep on. Look at me! Nothing but stumps left of my legs—that's all you'll have when you come back from the Mountains, providing you return at all."

I gingerly felt my leg as if to reassure myself that it was still sound. I was ready enough to scoff, but you never can tell how much to believe in Africa.

Why my boat had stopped in this filthy hell-hole on the Gold Coast, I don't know, but here we were overnight and I had gone ashore to break the monotony of scalding days at sea. It wasn't much improvement, even after sunset. Fierce, steamy heat that made you boil with sweat. An unpleasant smell, half-native, half-decayed vegetation, that every village seemed to have. And overhead, a huge red moon that was almost as hot as the sun.

As usual, I wound up in the town's one general store, which meant saloon. Drink in the tropics doesn't make you any cooler, but it takes your mind off other things.

Heaven knows it was a squalid enough hut, full of vermin. The only other white man in the place was the legless man. We had sized each other up instantly. It wasn't long before we were taking our drinks together, and gradually unloosening, until I had started to tell him the purpose of my trip—which was to collect museum specimens and look for traces of early man through Central Africa.

That was what set him off. He had looked bothered ever since I mentioned my trip. But I've picked up a lot of valuable information from chance acquaintances, and if there was some unexpected danger beyond the Mountains of the Moon, I wanted to know what it was.

"You evidently think it isn't safe to follow my proposed route. Why? Tell me about it," I urged, and ordered another round.

The eyes of the legless man were turned upon me with an intent, searching gaze. Whatever he found appeared to satisfy him.

"Ever hear of the Angley-Richards expedition?" he began.

"Yes. They started out on pretty much the same route I'm following several years ago, didn't they? Angley died of malaria, and Richards disappeared after some terrible experience. Lost both his—"

Abruptly I halted.

"Legs," finished my companion. "Your memory is good. I am Daniel Richards."

The name came as a shock to me though I had been half-prepared for it. No one had yet learned the whole story of that ill-fated expedition. All interest and attention now, I settled back to listen.

"Ours was really a dual expedition," he continued. "Angley, like your-self, was after all kinds of game for museums. I had government backing to chart the land formations and hunt for mineral deposits—a sort of geologist-prospector combined.

"We pooled resources for mutual protection. Most of the country we were going through was unexplored. Even today there's no telling what may turn up in some out of the way spot. They haven't begun to exhaust the mysteries of Africa.

"We made our way up the Congo all right, and a devilish trip it was. I've always hated jungles—everything unhealthy seems to grow in them—snakes that strike without warning, flesh-eating plants, and more poisonous insects and deadly vegetation than science yet knows about.

"Well, we got our last supplies at Kola, then struck out across the continent eastward. As we went farther in and higher up, we left the jungles behind and I felt better. We didn't make progress very fast. I had to map the country as we went though there wasn't much in the way of rare animals for Angley to bag.

"It must have been over two months from our start before we reached our real base at the foothills of the Mountains of the Moon. We had already entered one of the great unexplored tracts. We pitched camp and decided to split our party for a couple of weeks. Angley wanted to go after specimens along the plains. In the meantime, I wished to chart rock formations ahead.

"So we decided to split. In two weeks we would meet again at the camp. If either had not returned by the end of four weeks, the other would follow his trail to find out what was wrong.

"Early one morning, in accordance with our plan, I and my six Neguchi boys started off for the Mountains. The last I saw of Angley was when he and his six boys were heading southward for better game country.

"We crossed the Mountains of the Moon in three days, but we were lucky in finding a pass or it might have taken us much longer to detour. I noted one great igneous intrusion that looked good for diamonds, and several quartzite deposits that yielded gold, silver, and mercury. There's many a fortune back there in the heart of Africa for any man who thinks it's worth the risk.

"Beyond the Mountains of the Moon, I decided to keep on for a few days. The country was mostly grass land, with a twisted tree here and there and an occasional swamp. I saw a number of buzzards the first couple of days, and one small herd of antelope. But game was surprisingly scarce. And we hadn't met a native since we broke camp.

"On our sixth day out, I didn't see a solitary living thing. Nothing but the tall grass and the everlasting sun. The Neguchi boys had become suddenly quiet. It's a bad sign when you don't hear them jabber.

"That afternoon I sighted a low hill to the northeast and immediately struck off toward it.

"The Neguchi began to lag.

"'Keep going, you lazy devils!' I swore.

"One of them spoke in his dialect. 'No go on. This bad country. M'bwa there,' and he pointed toward the distant hill. 'See! Black men stay away. Birds, beasts, they no come. All 'fraid of M'bwa.'

"'M'bwa? What's that?'

"He shrugged his shoulders. I cursed, swore, offered him 'bait,' all but beat him. Not another word could I get. For that matter, it was all I could do to make the six Neguchi go on even with the offer of double pay.

"We camped that night at the foot of the hill. The Neguchi huddled close to a fire. The night was strangely silent for Africa. We might as well have been in a desert. I heard only the rustle of cane grass, nothing more. When you've become used to the big cats and roaring carnivores of Africa, silence hurts.

"I woke to a worse silence the next morning. A glance told me that the Neguchi had fled. My stuff was intact but I was pretty wild for a few minutes.

"I could have turned back but didn't. I made a cache of the stuff and decided to push on across the hill, be back by nightfall, then, on the eighth day, begin my return trek. My curiosity was aroused by the obvious fear of the black boys of what lay ahead and their desertion. I took with me only light rations, but stuffed my belt and pockets with cartridges.

"The stillness was getting on my nerves. I didn't like the looks of it at all. A cloudless sky—and not a bird anywhere. Rustling grass—and not the hum of an insect or the sound of any animal. There simply wasn't a living thing except myself within sight or hearing.

"But I went on. The hill was not far off. I had reached and climbed it before noon. There was a grassy space on its top and I could see another hill off in the distance, so I knew that a valley must lie below me. I walked across the flat hilltop till I stood on the downward slope.

"Right there I got a shock. A low, circular valley stretched below me with the hill closing it all around like a ring. Perfectly flat it was, perhaps two miles across or less, and not a blade of grass in it. The soil was a dirty gray. And in the midst of it stood a queer structure glinting red in the sun. I'd never seen anything like it. At first I thought it was a pyramid, then I could have sworn it was an obelisk, next moment it looked like a sphere. I rubbed my eyes and looked away, thought of what I knew about mirages, then looked back, and there was the thing, shining with metallic red and never looking the same.

"It was a rum sight but something else gave me a shock. All around it grew a row of trees, maybe twenty of them or more. The trees varied in height, the tallest one at my left graduating to the smallest at my right. And every last one of those trees looked like a man standing guard!

"The hair rose on my scalp. The tree farthest left stood like a clumsy giant a hundred feet high, the one on the right looked more like an ordinary man. Between them were the other trees in a rising scale. No branches or leaves like trees I knew—just one limb hanging down on each side and a round lump in the middle where a head would be.

"A ripple of cold wind seemed to creep upon me, but I went down the slope until I reached the valley and kept on across the powdery gray soil. I don't know why. Curiosity maybe. Or just the damn fool courage that won't let you be scared out of anything. If you once give in, you're gone.

"I stopped about a hundred yards from the trees where I had a good look at them. That was when I got panicky for the smallest tree *was looking back at me with the eyes of a living man!* The arms hung limply down. The other trees grew bigger toward the end one which hardly seemed human at all except for its huge limbs and gnarled five branches like fingers that trailed down from the end of each limb.

"And behind them was that strange reddish metal structure that shimmered dizzily—now like a pyramid, a cone, a ball—God knows what it was really like, I couldn't tell. I thought I saw writing on it but it wasn't the writing of any language I'd ever known.

"The impulse to flee came upon me, terror at some unknown evil gripped me, but somehow I went on, alert, wary.

"I didn't see him come. Maybe he was behind the trees or that wavering metallic structure. I don't know. But there he was all of a sudden, not fifty yards away, a horribly wrinkled old black, with a face as pasty as the gray ground, and a blank look in his eyes. What's more, he was coming straight at me, no mistake about it.

"'Halt!' I shouted and raised my rifle.

"There wasn't a pause in his stride. In complete, sheer terror I let him have it, both barrels full in the chest. I saw the bullets crash clear through him, but he didn't even falter, and not a drop of blood came from the livid flesh around the holes.

"Then I turned to run and he was on me like the wind. He was cold, his eyes were dead like a corpse's, and I knew I was up against something beyond the most frightful dream. Never a sound did he make, never a light of life or intelligence shone in his dead eyes, he moved like living death, soulless, stiff, and his flesh was like ice but his strength was terrific.

"He jumped me from behind but I doubled up and flung him forward over my back. I knew my gun was useless. I leaped clear over on top of him and sank my fingers in his throat. But it didn't make any difference. He paid no attention to my strangle-hold, but mechanically fumbled around with his hands and suddenly my wrists were bound.

"Sick with horror at this monster that nothing could destroy, I kicked, wrenched around, brought my arms down with a smash that raked his face, lunged head first into his stomach. He went down like a sack of flour, and immediately was back on his feet coming stiffly back.

"In ten minutes it was all over. I was firmly tied. The inhuman thing rose without a sign of emotion on its pasty gray face or a sound of breathing though my own lungs gulped for air. It walked jerkily toward and into the whirling red structure. In a minute it came out again and over to me. I saw gleaming knives in its hands, and other objects.

"'Well, it's the end,' I thought, and wondered foolishly if I would ever be found.

"But the knife didn't rip into me as I expected. The thing pried my teeth apart with its loathly fingers at whose touch I nearly vomited. Then down my throat trickled a sluggish liquor that seemed to burn and scald like fire and afterwards freeze and congeal the blood in my veins. As in a dream, I saw the pasty thing cut long slits in my legs and busy itself with other objects. But I felt no pain, only a great nausea, and gradually the most merciful sleep I ever knew descended upon me. My last recollection was of being lifted.

"I awoke with a heavy, sluggish feeling of torpor. I appeared to be standing but somehow couldn't move though I swayed a little. It required a herculean effort for me to open my weighted eyelids.

"Only a kind of dull inner shudder racked me at what I saw. My legs were rooted to the ground. I was one of that circle of Tree-men. How long I remained in a daze of horror I don't know. Something snapped finally and I waved arms that were ponderously stiff feebly around, screamed myself hoarse, wore myself out trying to move even an inch. I stopped only when the blackness of shock and exhaustion swept over me.

"I wakened again to an inarticulate whisper. Had my ears deceived me? I listened intently.

"'Stranger, can you hear me? My time is almost up and I have waited long.'

"Slowly, laboriously, I managed to open my eyes and twist around. The Tree-man nearest me was looking in my direction. Pity, despair, anguish all struggled in his eyes.

"'Yes,' I finally succeeded in answering, and my voice was thick, unnatural. 'Who or what are you? And in God's name, what nightmare is this?'

"He shook his head gravely, and whispered faintly, 'No nightmare, it is living death. We are the Tree-men of M'bwa.' And then, pleadingly, 'What year is this?'

"I told him—

"He sighed. 'Twenty long years, and now the end approaches. Oh, what I would not give for one sight of my native land and one kiss from lips that have waited in vain if they waited at all.'

"He seemed to dream of something far away for a long while, before he said, 'I tried to warn you, but it was too late, and M'bwa was waiting.'

"That name again—it echoed in my brain. 'M'bwa!' I hoarsely cried. 'Who is he? What is he?'

"But his mind drifted off again and another long period elapsed before he spoke. I knew he was going fast, that consciousness would soon leave him forever.

"'M'bwa,' he at last said thickly, 'is dead. He has been for centuries. But he moves at the bidding of the master in the Whirling Flux, and the dead walk when the master commands. So the Tree-man next me said, and he was told by the Tree-man beyond him, and thus the story has been passed on.'

"'Who is the master?'

"'I do not know,' came the slow response. 'No one has ever seen him. He came to earth in the days before Rome, before Egypt or Babylon. He is of a different universe, a different dimension, and he dwells in the Whirling Flux. I know not why he waits, or for what, he who has communion with entities older than earth and titans that strode across the stars before Mu had sunk or Atlantis risen.'

"I did not understand half of what he was saying. 'Who are the Tree-men? Has no one escaped from this valley?'

"'There is no escape,' he went on. 'The Tree-men are unfortunate adventurers like yourself and me who have stumbled on the valley. Those who trespass serve as warning to all others. Only at long intervals have the foolhardy and the brave ventured here where no animal comes and which the black tribes avoid. I was told that the first Tree-man was an Atlantean, and the next an ancient Egyptian, and the third a Roman exile. But I do not know. The master rules M'bwa who was the first ever to come and who has been dead for centuries beyond history but who comes forth as he will always come forth to protect the secret of the valley. It is M'bwa who gives the paralyzing drug and makes the incisions and bridges the gap between animal and vegetable kingdoms. But it is the master who directs, the Evil Old One who came down from the stars in years beyond reckoning.'

"His voice trailed off. I think the effort of speech after so long a silence cost him what was left of his mind. He never spoke again.

"No escape! The words burned in my memory. Then I thought of my agreement with Angley. I hoped he would come, yet hoped he would not. For neither he nor any other human being could combat an antagonist who was outside human laws or the known world. Was the story told by the Tree-man true or partly the result of brooding? I had no means of telling.

"So the days passed, heavy, monotonous. Only a dead gray expanse and a curving hill to look at. Only the silent Tree-men for companions. And behind, that Flux of unknown metal, acting by the laws of an unknown other dimension. And ever in my veins crept the sluggish flow, a flow that I knew would some day conquer me and drive out my awareness even as the other Tree-men had become inanimate, insensate things.

"Nothing lived in the valley. No bird flew overhead. Always silence, and the dreary routine of thinking, remembering, plotting, in order to avoid madness. Complete inaction, hopeless inertia. And there was no escape. I lost track of the days. Would Angley come? Would M'bwa capture him too? Where was M'bwa? But from the time of my own capture I had not seen him again. Many an hour I wasted shouting myself hoarse at the Tree-man nearest me. He did not answer. He swayed dumbly, already on the way to that hideous transformation which would leave him only the travesty of human form.

"Unconsciously I found myself hoping as the days piled up. I wanted desperately to hear a voice. It would mean death to Angley. Often I wore myself into a nervous exhaustion and stupor, writhing, squirming, struggling to free myself until sleep brought a short relief. And oh! the horror of years whose every day would be the same until madness or mindless oblivion descended!

"My thoughts became chaotic. I think I must have gone out of my head for long periods. The sight of what I was, the knowledge of what I was to become lay like a monstrous worm gnawing inside me.

"One day, I had a delirium. I thought that Angley, faithful Angley, had come to save me. I wept with happiness, watched him with pathetic relief.

"And then fright paralyzed me. *This was no dream!* Angley stood, as I had stood, not more than a hundred yards off, his face a mask of loathing and horror.

"'Angley!' I shrieked. 'It's Richards! Watch out for the black M'bwa! He can't be killed! Run, for God's sake, run for your life!'

"I saw a horrified look whiten his face. My warning came too late.

"The dead monster M'bwa was stiffly pacing toward him. Even as I, Angley raised his rifle and sent both barrels crashing into the hideous thing where gaping new holes appeared. But M'bwa went on without pause.

"I saw Angley's hand swoop to his side and as the marching horror approached him, a blade flashed high in his arm and with a terrific side-sweep he decapitated M'bwa.

"Almost in the same moment Angley had raced over to me and again the heavy machete flashed high and sang clear through my limbs. He caught me as I fell. I writhed in agony, shrieked, twisted, and thin trickles of blood and watery stuff oozed out of the stumps that remained of my legs.

"Angley slung me over his shoulder and began stumbling back, white-faced, machete still clutched in one hand. There came a strange, high whine from behind, and even in my pain I turned to see. The Red Flux had come to rest, and out of it issued the titanic lich that haunts my dreams, with its tatters of vaporous flesh and the flapping black streamers that whipped from it as it towered to the skies above and yet sprawled over to M'bwa and set the dead head back on the shoulders. Then it was gone, all in a flash, the Evil Old One who came down from the stars in the days when the world was young, and the Red Flux was in its sickening dimensional whirl, and there was M'bwa stiffly striding after us.

"'Drop me! Save yourself!' I cried through the spate of blood and foam that was forming on my lips. But Angley only ran faster in great leaping strides. Now we were at the hill's slope, panting up it, but the foul horror was closer, closer, racing like a fitful wind, tireless as a machine—

"Suddenly Angley whirled and swung the machete around and shot it hissing through the air. M'bwa, severed from neck to waist, rolled in two utterly abominable parts down the slope, and not a drop of clean blood appeared anywhere on the livid raw flesh of that frightful wound.

"With a terrific charge, Angley was over the hill and crashing down its far side, and then we were stumbling toward the distant Mountains of the Moon.

"I shall never know how we made it. I remember a phantasmagoria of endless pain and agony that racked my body, of thirst and hunger and raving delirium, and the endless ache of muscles that throbbed for rest in our almost incessant flight toward safety.

"Angley came down with malaria, somewhere on our trek to the coast. He was dead when I came to, weeks later, in a ship's sick-room. They had amputated my legs almost to the thigh. But I wouldn't go back to civilization looking like that. I debarked at Bordeaux and shipped back here on the first boat I could get."

A great silence fell. Somewhere afar a jackal barked.

"So you see," Richards ended, "why I said, don't go to the Mountains of the Moon."

I'll admit his story shook me pretty badly, but I was still game. After all—a wild yarn in a saloon on the Gold Coast—I couldn't let that interfere with all my plans.

"Well, we'll see," I hedged.

With a sudden nervous jerk, he ripped away the pad on his stumps.

"Now do you believe!" he almost screamed. "That's what I got—and every month they have to be cut off!"

Sick, shuddering, I went into the night. From the stumps of his legs, pale, thin feelers like young shoots of a tree hung limply down.

WHEN THE FIRE CREATURES CAME

"**W**E MAY AS** well quit for tonight. It's nearly two o'clock now and it will take us most of tomorrow to finish up anyway," Dave Harkness was saying to the older man. The light of enthusiasm burned in his young eyes, but his face was haggard from sleepless nights.

"Well, all right," the older man wearily agreed. "But I'm due at Washington with my report in two days. You'll have to make good your claim, by tomorrow, or the government is not likely to pay any attention to your demand for the final, secret tests."

"You'll have the proof," Harkness confidently answered. "As I told you, the explosive power of Erthorum is so terrific that we've got to take precautions to the nth degree. But tomorrow the stuff will be ready for its first real test."

Major Douglas Ritter, specialist in explosive testing, nodded his understanding and the two men prepared to leave Harkness' private laboratory on the shore of Lake Michigan.

Harkness claimed that he had discovered the most titanic weapon of war and peace yet invented by man. He called his invention Erthorum. It was a formulary chemical, released under enormous pressures. Immediately after being released, it broke down the pattern of any atomic structure and accelerated the vibration rate. Almost instantly, Harkness claimed, the result was a miniature earthquake and the total destruction of nearly a cubic mile of earth.

So important would this discovery be if Harkness could prove his claim that the War Department had sent its most noted expert to make a secret investigation and report. The mere possession of the formula would give whatever country held it absolute power for good or evil over all the other nations of the world.

Harkness set the time-lock on the doors which were the only entrance to his steel laboratory for nine o'clock, threw on the electrical protection current, and followed Major Ritter out as the doors automatically slid shut behind them.

They emerged on the lake shore and set out for Harkness' home half a mile distant.

There was no moon but it was such a brilliant warm August night that they had no trouble as they walked along.

"This cool lake breeze feels good after being cooped up in the lab all day," Harkness said with a sigh of relief. "Shall we walk around a bit before turning in? Might do us good."

"Well, no," the major hesitated. "We've got a lot to do tomorrow and ought to be up early. I think—why, what on earth is that?"

The waves lapped gently, a faint wind blew through the trees, but suddenly there had come an ominous hush. Even as they paused in startled surprise, Harkness saw too that the path before them was growing brighter, as if moonlit. But there was no moon.

Almost in unison they stared into the heavens.

High above them, from the southeast, a fiery ball was streaking across the sky. Brighter and brighter it blazed until the heavens flamed as though the sun shone.

"It's a comet!" the major cried aloud.

"No, it's a meteor—it looks like the biggest one that's ever fallen!" Harkness answered excitedly.

They watched it for a full minute as it rushed overhead and burned downward toward Lake Michigan. The lake, the shore, the entire countryside around them and all the skies were dazzling bright from the radiant ball. Suddenly, far out, a fountain of sparks like stars shot up and they could almost hear the hiss as the meteor plunged into the lake. A pall of blackness settled down. Then there came the roar of a mighty wind, and terrific detonation shook the earth.

The awesome beauty of the spectacular display held the two men silent for a time. Then they resumed their way, talking of the cosmic visitor.

"It's too bad the meteor fell into the lake," Harkness was regretting. "We could have learned a lot by studying it."

The major said nothing and conversation lagged. Somehow, the ominous tension that had come with the meteor remained. There was curious unrest in the air, as if even the Earth was disturbed by this new wanderer from space.

When they reached the house, Harkness and Ritter turned in, each bound up with his thoughts, after brief goodnights.

Considerably refreshed, Harkness awoke to the insistent clanging of a bell. He glanced at his watch, then sprang to his feet in dismay.

"Nine-thirty—and the laboratory's now open for anybody to enter," he muttered with irritation. "Where is that infernal servant? I left word to be called at eight. Funny. This is the first time he's failed me in three years."

He hastily dressed, ran to the major's room and awakened him, then flung a hasty excuse as he dashed out of the house. No one lived within a mile—but couldn't take any chances—knew the formula by heart but what good would that do if agents for another country got hold of it?—must arrive at the laboratory as quickly as possible—

A jumble of thoughts raced through his mind as he sped down the path. He turned to follow the seashore, then in the midst of his run came to a dead stop with a surge of astounded horror leaping into his heart.

Immediately in front of him lay the body of his servant! The body? It was rather the hideous parody of a body. Even in that brief instant of recognition of an odd watch his servant always carried, he was appalled by the charred and powdery ashes of clothing, by the calcined bones and fire-whitened skull. But nowhere near, nor up and down the beach as far as he could see, was there a sign of any kind of fire, and what baffled him most, beyond possible understanding, was how a man could burn to ashes in broad daylight without calling for help or without any visible cause. For the tragedy was very recent—as Harkness bent over, a wave of heat shimmered up from the bones, and he almost thought he could still see them glowing.

He dashed back to the house. "Ritter—Ritter!" he cried.

The major appeared at a window.

"My servant's been killed—down at the foot of the path—you take charge while I see if anything's wrong at the lab!" Harkness cried out. He did not wait for answer but turned again and raced on his way.

It had suddenly occurred to him that paid spies might have killed his servant before looting the laboratory. He shivered momentarily but did not pause as he passed the enigmatic heap of bones.

Gulping for breath and well-nigh exhausted, he arrived at his experiment station a few minutes later.

To his first quick glance from outside, nothing seemed amiss, except that the foreboding hush of the night before still lingered on. He sighed with relief as he walked up to the now automatically unlocked doors and swung them apart to enter.

Stars and blinding darkness sent him to the ground as some metal tool struck him a terrific smash down the side of his head. A rush of blood trickled along his cheek. He dimly saw a short, swarthy figure leap past him and speed up the beach.

The world swam. His dazed mind refused to function. Everything spun with a blurred and sickening motion. Then the dizzy whirl slackened and he slowly staggered to his feet. Lucky the blow hadn't landed squarely—if it had, he might never have risen.

A hundred yards or more distant, the short figure was racing toward a roadster half-hidden back among trees. Harkness wasted breath in one hoarse cry for help. Without delaying longer to find out if anything had been taken from the laboratory, he stumbled in pursuit, still weak from the blow.

He had hardly taken a dozen steps, knowing all the while that he could never catch the thief, when an incredible thing happened.

A thin wisp of smoke curled backward from the flying figure. A ripple of white flame sprang out of empty air. Apparently unaware that anything was wrong, the man raced a few steps farther. Then instantaneously his body burst into a dazzling flash of fire. One single hideous shriek split the morning air. Even as Harkness watched with spellbound eyes, the white flame disappeared, and he caught a glimpse of bare bones stripped of every vestige of flesh falling to the ground.

The horror of that strange, weird phenomenon was beyond anything he had ever felt. Few men were braver than Harkness who had the reckless courage of youth, but here was something that violated all the laws of reason and nature. The ominous hush he had already felt was now an active menace. Danger and death walked abroad on invisible steps. Weakened by the blow and white from this new shock, Harkness without thinking made a dash for the laboratory. A sixth sense had warned him that unseen powers lurked near. Were spies of a dozen countries already on his trail? Or did these mysterious happenings of the morning have some connection with the comet of the preceding night?

Harkness as yet could scarcely guess what the explanation might be. But baffling events had taken place and it was up to him to warn the major before anything else happened.

An odd sense of security came over him when the fireproof doors clanged shut. He wasted no time in idle speculation but walked to a corner and lifted a private telephone connected with another at the house. He waited impatiently while the bell rang insistently on the other end. A click followed by the brusque voice of Major Ritter came as welcome sounds.

Harkness spoke rapidly. "Major Ritter? This is Harkness calling from the laboratory. I was slugged when I got here—what? No, just a scalp wound. The thief almost escaped but was burned to death and—"

For a split second Harkness paused while lightning thoughts flashed into his mind. If he told what he had seen the Major might think him suffering from hallucinations. He couldn't prove that there was any actual danger, yet he felt the oppression of imminent disaster. The house wasn't safe. But whatever the cause of the two puzzling deaths, the major might run grave risks in walking to the laboratory. A picture of the dying man came to his eyes. And instantly he thought of a temporary solution, at least.

He resumed where he broke off.

"One of my experiments has gone wrong. I'll need your help immediately. I'm donning an airtight asbestos suit now—we'll be working in high temperatures. There's another of these suits in the wardrobe to my room—take it out and bring it here as fast as you can. And Major—put it on before you come—*before you come!*" Harkness emphasized. "Haste is important and the suit is absolutely necessary. We'll save time if you put it on there and come as quickly as possible. In half an hour? Splendid. Make it sooner if you can!" He rang off and set about examining the laboratory to find out what damage had been done.

So far as a hasty examination showed, none of his precious instruments had been damaged. The formula had disappeared, as he was certain it would be. But he could rewrite it from memory, and the stolen copy had been destroyed—he hoped—when the thief was killed.

Harkness next examined a mixture he had prepared the evening before. This mixture he carefully lifted and transferred to an elaborate, delicately adjusted high-pressure compressor from which the hitherto harmless ingredients would emerge as an explosive of earth-wrecking power.

Only then did his throbbing head remind him of the wound he had received. He washed it and made a rough bandage. This done, he hauled out the asbestos suit and climbed into it. His precautions might be useless—but the testimony of his eyes warned him to play safe.

Hardly had he completed the action and adjusted a small oxygen tank when the major banged on the door. Harkness threw off the locking current, then switched it on again the moment the major had entered.

"You made good time—I'm glad you're here," he commented briefly . He walked over to the older man to help him unfasten his bulky suit for a short respite before they left the laboratory. As Harkness approached him, a wave of heat as from a furnace beat into his face. The outside of the major's suit was almost incandescent. He seized the major's arm to prevent him from unfastening the suit as yet, at the same time throwing his own hood over his face for protection.

A long minute they waited before Harkness dared to uncover his face. He had developed these suits himself. They were supposed to resist the highest temperatures that any man-made garment had ever defeated, yet the major's suit had been close to the limit of its effectiveness. Again wonder surged over him. Surely such heat could not come from even the hottest August day. Then what could Major Ritter have met on his comparatively short walk?

Harkness helped him throw back his hood.

"What is all this tommyrot about?" the major swore irritably when his face was exposed. "Phew! But it's hot in here. You ought to have a cooling system installed."

Harkness stared at him incredulously. "But it *is* cool in here! The heat is coming from your own suit! That's why I prevented you from removing it a minute ago."

It was Ritter's turn to stare. With a swift motion he wriggled one hand free and felt the outside of the stuff. A look of surprise came into his face as his hand turned red from the hot surface.

"Why—why it's uncanny! I followed your directions and came straight here. I don't understand how this could have happened!"

"You saw and felt nothing on your way here?" Harkness queried.

"No, not a thing, except for a trifling incident and that could not have been responsible at all."

"What was it? I've learned in my work that trifles may count most."

"Why, only that, as I was walking along the path, I suddenly felt impelled to stop and rest. Have you ever had a hypo—morphine injection after an operation? Well, you know the sensation—a soothing numbness that steals over you. It was like that. It vanished as suddenly as it came just before I arrived here."

There was a short pause while Harkness did some fast thinking. If an unknown agent was at work, nothing was to be gained by silence. And if the events of the morning had a natural explanation, it was one that eluded him. In either case he needed the help of Major Ritter.

"Listen to this and tell me what you make of it," he suddenly burst out, and launched into an account of his finding the bones, of the incident at the laboratory, and of the mysterious death of his assailant. "That was why I asked you to wear the asbestos suit," he concluded. "I don't like the looks of things but I don't quite know what to do. Offhand I should say either that the nation's enemies are secretly plotting against us, or that these incidents have some connection with last night's meteor."

"Your first guess is probably right," the major bluntly replied. "What made you think of the meteor?"

"I'm not sure. But it was a huge mass that fell, you remember, and it may have brought with it some kind of electrical or cosmic energy that might be responsible for these mishaps."

The major looked frankly skeptical. "The simpler explanation is usually the better," he commented. "It seems a little far-fetched to make the meteor account for events. However, we'll keep our eyes open. Suppose we go ahead with your experiment—my time is growing short. There may be a place for private sleuthing or speculation later but the government's business comes first now."

"All right," Harkness answered. "However, I won't be ready for perhaps half an hour. While I am attending to preliminaries you can look around the laboratory or tune in on the radio as you prefer."

Leaving the major to his own devices for the time being, Harkness strode to the high-pressure compressor and carefully noted the various dial and indicator readings. Satisfied that the Erthorum mixture had "set," he turned to a work-table and brought back to the compressor two hemispheres of a small steel globe. He was adjusting these in a machine adjoining the compressor when the silence was broken by a voice from the radio which Major Ritter had switched on.

"—last night's comet," the voice was saying. "Unfortunately for science, it plunged into Lake Michigan, but not until it had been seen by hundreds of observers in Illinois, Indiana, Tennessee, and other nearby states. A number of deaths have already been reported over a considerable area. Apparently the meteor passed so close to earth before it fell that human beings in its direct path were burned to death.

"A wave of hysteria has swept over the more superstitious people who witnessed the fiery sight. There are wild rumors circulating that men, women, and even children have died suddenly in a kind of spontaneous combustion. So far we have had no verification of these rumors, though it is true that electrical disturbances of the usual sort accompanied the meteor.

"Religious fanatics and ignorant backwoodsmen in Kentucky and Tennessee are reported using the occasion to stir up mob frenzy. This is all the information now available but additional news will be given to you from time to time as it comes to the station."

Again Dave Harkness felt that ominous hush of apprehension which had first gripped him when he saw the meteor flame downward from the skies. Out of what unfathomable cosmic gulfs had it wandered, and what train of disaster was it bringing in its wake?

Acting on a sudden impulse, he walked to the telephone and put through a long distance call. "Hello—Seabeach 1474? This is Dave

Harkness speaking! May I talk to Helen? . . . Oh, I'm sorry. And she left no word about where she was going or when she'd return? . . . Well, no, it was nothing important. Have her call me as soon as she returns. At the lab."

He was oddly disquieted when he hung up. Pshaw, there was no need to worry. Yet after all he and Helen Boyd had plans . . . in case everything went well. . . . With a snap, he jerked himself out of gloomy thoughts to concentrate on the work at hand. The major joined him as he returned to the apparatus.

"We will be able to complete the demonstration in a few minutes," Harkness explained as they stood before the compressor. He made a few rapid adjustments, then continued, "The Erthorum compound, under tremendous pressure, has now been brought to the point of atomic disintegration. Still under terrific pressure, it is being hermetically sealed in the steel ball together with a quantity of ordinary explosive which acts as a detonator. The ball may be burst either by electricity or by percussion. In either case, when it explodes the pressure is released, disintegration immediately follows and is complete, and the energy suddenly released displaces a quantity of matter varying with the amount of the charge."

A faint drone came from the mechanism as the Erthorum was poured into the steel ball which was then sealed. Harkness turned a valve, there rose the hiss of escaping air, and a moment later he held the heavy globe in his hands. He carefully deposited it in a cushioned container.

"Whew! It's heavy," he commented. "But you can't take too many precautions with such dangerous stuff. Help me trundle this up to the observation tower."

The two of them gingerly carried their burden to the laboratory's topmost pinnacle. Here they set it in the bowl of what looked like a huge spoon.

"This is nothing but a simple type of catapult," Harkness explained, "with a range of about two miles. The Erthorum ball cannot be fired from a gun without considerable danger. Since time is lacking to rig up electric connections, I decided to use this elementary type of flinger for safety and convenience. Just behind the catapult you will notice a camera with telescopic lens. We will thus witness the experiment ourselves and have a photographic record to study at leisure."

He pressed a button and a large section of the metal dome slid aside. The two men examined the great sweep of lake but no boat was in sight. The water undulated slowly, like almost motionless oil. A vast quiet lay upon the world. Bright sunshine poured out of the brassy-hot August sky. And yet, there was something curiously disturbing about the scene. It was almost too peaceful.

Harkness shrugged his shoulders and concentrated on the experiment about to be made. He must have been working pretty hard of late, he thought, if little things could bother him so much. He was vaguely conscious of a distant buzz but his mind was occupied with more important matters of immediate concern.

He made his final adjustments. . . . The Erthorum ball would explode when it hit the lake a mile and a half from shore. . . . Even with its small charge, a cubic quarter-mile of water should be displaced. . . . But they could watch it in safety from this distance. . . . And the camera would provide a lasting record. . . .

"Everything's ready," he said to the major. "Watch closely."

Major Ritter tensed with interest as he gripped a pair of field glasses.

Harkness pressed a button on the electric camera and almost simultaneously released the catapult.

As the globe sailed out over Lake Michigan, the buzz which had been distracting Harkness swelled to a roar. He glanced sharply upward.

A white monoplane was slanting wildly from the sky. He knew the monoplane as familiarly as his own—it was Helen's. Galvanized into action, he opened his mouth to shout a futile warning; but the cry died in this throat. As the monoplane dove past the observatory, he glimpsed the terror-stricken face of a girl peering at him, saw a tell-tale wisp of thin smoke curl up from her jacket and stream outward from the cockpit. In one brief, split-second of horror, Harkness saw again the running figure of the morning and a wisp of smoke that burst into brilliant flame—and then a heap of incinerated bones.

Forgetful of everything save the danger to Helen, he flung an unintelligible order to the major and bounded down the stairs and out onto the beach. Even as he left his laboratory a vast mountain of water thundered skyward out of Lake Michigan, hung for an instant, and surged downward again with a deafening crash. What seemed like a torrential cloudburst of water drenched Harkness to the skin. But he scarcely had eyes for anything except a white monoplane that hurtled to the lake surface, straightened out, dipped, and then catapulted while a limp figure shot from the cockpit.

He had a confused memory of tearing his clothing off, of swimming faster than he had ever swum before, of furiously struggling in a tidal wave of savage waters that suddenly boiled around him, of gulping great quantities of air and water, of a superhuman effort to reach that helpless form, and then of a hopeless attempt to reach shore with an added burden . . . but the world darkened and went out like a candle.

Slightly nauseated and giddy, Harkness emerged from a profound darkness and opened his eyes to find the major lustily pumping water from his lungs.

"How is—" he began.

"Shut up!" said the major and squeezed another pint of water out of Harkness. "Helen's all right. Looks darned cute in your old clothing! No, she wasn't hurt much—just a few bruises, stunned, rather badly shocked, slightly scorched, and half-drowned seems to be the total damage. But she's pretty well recovered."

"Did you—"

"No, I didn't or maybe I did. Keep still while I remove the rest of Lake Michigan from you. Here, Helen, turn on the radio and soothe this inquisitive young Olympian swimmer."

The girl, subdued and still weak from her recent experience, stretched out a hand and tuned in the radio. At the first words that broke from it all peace and quiet vanished. The three sat in startled silence while the voice of an unknown continued rapidly, shaking with suppressed excitement.

"All people within a five hundred mile radius of Chicago are urged to remain indoors and to close tightly every slightest opening. In the most seriously affected area, martial law has already been established and everyone ordered off the streets.

"Every agent of science and the government is at work on the mystery which will undoubtedly be solved soon. In the meantime every precaution is necessary. So far, about six hundred deaths have been witnessed and more than four thousand heaps of bones reported. According to the most reliable accounts, the victim notices nothing wrong until a thin wisp of smoke arises. A lethargy overtakes him. Spontaneous combustion and a brief fierce pain ensue, after which only the bone structure of the body remains. These details are broadcast only so that you may take any necessary steps if the need arises.

"It is now definitely believed that the great meteor of last night has some connection with these deaths. Leading scientists at first suggested that some new type of cosmic energy or ray had been brought and released by the meteor, but the theory has now been advanced that there is intelligent guidance behind these amazing deaths. If this report be true, the mystery is darker than ever. Our official relations are not known to be strained with any country. It is not likely therefore that an enemy is employing some unknown method of destruction as the first step of warfare.

"Medical science records a few rare cases of death by spontaneous combustion, but an outbreak of this sort is unheard of.

"Here is a late bulletin just received by wire. New deaths are reported at the rate of more than a thousand per hour, and the rate is rapidly mounting. The area affected is spreading toward Chicago on the west, Cleveland on the east, and southward generally from the Great Lakes. No clue as to the cause of the fiery death has yet been found.

"Stand by and we will—God in Heaven, *my clothes are smoking*!"

For an instant there was silence. The hush was broken by a single terrible scream that poured through the room. And afterwards the radio stood soundless while the three listeners looked at each other in shocked horror. All too well they could visualize a mound of burnt bones crumpled beside a microphone.

It was the major who first threw off the spell. He rose to his feet and paced grimly back and forth for a few seconds. Then he turned to Harkness and asked, "Have you the facilities here for developing a film record of your experiment? I feel it my duty to return to Washington at the earliest possible moment. I may say that I am convinced of the value of Erthorum but should like to take visible evidence back with me."

"Yes, I can develop the film in a comparatively short time, even project it if you wish," Harkness answered. "I am anxious to do so anyway since I missed seeing the whole event because of the general excitement." As if glad to have an opportunity for working at something that would distract his attention momentarily from the catastrophe that had descended on the world outside, he shakily stood up and made his way to the recesses of his laboratory, after excusing himself to Helen.

Conversation was desultory during his absence. The major was thinking of a mysterious new peril to this country, of duty that called, and of an odd experience or two that had befallen him this very morning.

And Helen, with her clear gray eyes sober for once—she thought of how she had gaily started off in early afternoon for a surprise visit to Dave. She remembered what a perfect flying day it was though so many days were perfect in this drouth-stricken month. She saw herself winging high above the lake shore, scudding along like a bird of space. And then—she shuddered inwardly as her plane in retrospect dipped toward Dave's laboratory. For she had seen men at work in a grape vineyard, men who looked up and waved tiny hands at her from far below, men who waved hands and suddenly vanished one by one with a faint puff of smoke and a blinding flame. Next came a curious lethargy, and a sudden scorched odor to her nostrils and an impression of forthcoming pain—but the laboratory had flashed past, and whether in unreasoning fear or desperation or forgetfulness she had driven her monoplane with throttle wide open straight toward Lake Michigan.

The gloomy reveries of both were interrupted some time later by Harkness' return. When he saw their serious faces, he began gently humming "The Dead March."

"Sing something sad for a change," said the major testily.

"Sorry. I was trying to relieve the tension," Harkness replied a bit nettled.

"Don't mind me, I'm only the audience," Helen interrupted with a grimace.

The two men looked at each other somewhat abashed, and the strain was broken, for a while at least.

"The negative's ready," Harkness said, abruptly changing the subject. "Come to my projection room and we'll have a look at it."

They filed after him to a basement, one end of which had been partitioned off and turned into a projection chamber with a screen facing it. Helen and Major Ritter seated themselves on make-shift chairs while Harkness adjusted the film reel.

"Even if we had been able to watch the experiment closely from beginning to end, we probably would not have seen as much as the camera record will disclose," he commented. "My camera has a number of extras, and in the past has frequently caught details I did not previously see. However, you can see for yourselves—here goes!"

He threw a switch. They heard the hum of electricity, the flick of a reel unwinding. Upon the screen appeared the familiar setting of an hour or two earlier. They saw the Erthorum sphere at rest, then catapulted to go sailing a mile and more out over deserted waters. For a trice it was obscured as a white monoplane zoomed across the foreground and—

"God almighty!" cried the major.

A little moan issued from the lips of Helen and she swooned to the floor.

For as the airplane crossed before them, they saw Helen's white, fear-stricken face lean over the cockpit, and, horror beyond anything they had ever felt, *fastened to her neck and streaming crazily away was an appalling, an utterly loathsome and hideous nightmare entity such as only the ultimately evil gulfs beyond space could have produced, or ultimate madness imagined*. It was all talons like fiery ropes. It drifted through a hundred forms. It lashed out to inconceivable lengths and curled together like a dead million-legged spider. Only that sickening, sucker-like beak fastened to Helen remained constant. Every other part of the foul thing's body, if it could be called body that no eyes could see or hands feel, wavered forever through hideous lighting flashes of detestable motion.

As if fleeing from a pestilence that the clean earth had never harbored, Helen's plane swooped toward the lake waters. Farther out, the Ertho-rum detonated and a fluid cliff shot skyward mushrooming as it surged. Nothing could have turned Harkness' gaze from the scene. It was a nightmarish delirium, like a part out of some hellish drama. Gouts and splashes of water cascaded everywhere, deluging the plane as it struck.

Dave stared at the screen incredulously. Without apparent cause, and as mysteriously as it had appeared, the frightful creature vanished. He saw Helen's unconscious form hurtled out of the cockpit. But there was no ghastly beak fastened to her throat, nor any trace of the gigantic form which had made the picture hideous. Was it all a sickening dream? Neither in sky nor land nor boiling waters could he see a vestige of the fiendish entity.

Half an hour later, three sober and gloomy people sat talking fitfully in the main wing of Harkness' laboratory.

"And so the conclusion seems inescapable," Dave was saying, "that this threat to humanity arrived here by meteor."

The major raised a haggard face. "But good heaven, Harkness, what sort of thing is it that we can't see or feel while it mows men down by the thousand? Do you mean that it actually *thinks*, like ourselves, and is purposeful? Why, no power on earth can save mankind if what you say is true."

"I hardly know what to think. We saw nothing unusual when Helen's plane swept past us. But someone of the extra attachments on my camera caught with perfect vision what was beyond the range of our eyes. As to its nature—your guess is as good as mine. It might help if we only knew where the meteor came from.

"Somewhere out in the vast spaces between the stars or in those stupendous gulfs beyond the universe there may exist forms of life or intelligence that are unknown to us. Perhaps we are faced by such an entity, one that is of ultimate evil. I have a theory, major, but I am afraid our doom has come if I am right."

"I come of an old, war-hardened school," said the major with grim courage. "The only defeat I admit is death. What is your theory?"

"You probably have read something about recent investigations into electrical energy, cosmic rays, and potential origins of life. According to the latest discoveries, what we call life is a kind of electro-genetic flow or current, somewhat like that in a mechanical battery but vastly superior to anything that man himself has devised. We die just as a battery does when our cells wear out, or are smashed, or develop flaws, or are not replaced.

"Our own solar system is comparatively young. Our life has hardly more than begun. And it is my belief that in the ultimate ends of the universe life arose countless ages before ours and reached a stage immeasurably more developed. I think that those unknown beings discovered how to minimize the body, how to exploit the current of life.

"God help us, Major Ritter, if they have reached their goal. For they would be all electrical energy, the essence of life and the epitome of thought. They would be indestructible, immortal. They are fire creatures out of space, feeding on fire of energy as we feed on food."

"But why should they attack us?"

"To increase their own lives! They are cannibals of the soul. They are protected from our gaze so that we cannot detect them—and meanwhile they batten upon our very existence. Don't you see? They live upon cosmic energy. But just as we like some foods better than others, so they find the life-current of human beings super nourishing. That beak fastened to Helen's throat—somehow, it was about to draw the soul of life from her, and when the process was completed flaming death would follow."

"Ugh, it's horrible," said Helen shuddering.

"I'm sorry," Dave answered quickly, with a sad light in his eyes, "but it's necessary. If we expect to take any measures at all, we need to know the strength of our enemy."

"But what can we do?" Helen queried helplessly.

Dave shrugged his shoulders. For a minute he did not answer.

"Perhaps there is nothing we can do. We cannot see our antagonists until too late—and how could we destroy them if they were visible?"

Major Ritter sprang to his feet. "We'll be hailed as lunatics but it's our duty to communicate what we have discovered, and turn over the film, to the proper authorities." He strode to the telephone to ask for a connection with Washington and jangled the receiver. For a long minute he fretted and fumed.

There was no answer. And as he turned finally Dave and Helen saw by his eyes that the menace had spread farther. There was no telephone service. They were marooned from the world, and in the very heart of the region where blazing death out of the skies had come to challenge the supremacy of man.

"If you are willing to run the risk, I'll fly you back to Washington," Harkness volunteered. "It will require several hours but I see no way to establish contact with authorities from here."

"Good!" said the major briefly. With fatal determination to know the worst, he switched the radio on to find out what was happening before they left. There was no broadcast from any nearby station. The usual blaring programs were strangely missing—mute testimony to a cosmic plague. When they finally succeeded in tuning in a station hundreds of miles distant, it was only to find their worst fears realized.

"The number of lives lost is now beyond computation," the announcer was saying. "There are said to be a million dead in Chicago alone, with thousands more being claimed by the fiery death every hour. The entire mid-continental area has been ordered evacuated and martial law established. So far the nature of the terror is unknown. The army has been mobilized at all points near the danger region, and the air auxiliaries have been sent to patrol the territory. But there seems to be no way to prevent the spread of death.

"Passage on any kind of outgoing boat has rocketed to five, ten, and twenty thousand dollars a passenger. Major riots have begun in New York, New Orleans, San Francisco, and other large cities. Asbestos suits, which seem to be the only possible protection, are no longer available anywhere. Air proof vaults of banks have been jammed with refugees to the point of suffocation. This alarm is broadcast by official request so that all citizens may take whatever precautions they can to protect their lives.

"For some unknown reason, the Great Lakes have acted as a barrier on the north, and so far the scourge has not been reported on claiming any victims in Canada. Eastward, westward, and southward, however, this mysterious doom is spreading like wildfire literally on the wings of the wind, in a great and growing semicircle.

"Every government of the world has offered its assistance in a crisis that may mark the passing of civilization. The sea is specked with cruisers and speed destroyers, the sky darkened with bombers and transport planes rushed to America to halt the encroaching disaster if possible. But the flower of humanity, the great scientists and the most brilliant minds, are claimed alike with the common man in hideous, white-hot death whenever they pass the boundaries to investigate devastated regions. Neither man, woman, nor child is spared. Without warning and instantaneously the unknown pestilence consumes its victims.

"Listeners of the radio world, America has been crippled and demoralized by an attack more terrible than any war. And unless preventive measures are quickly discovered, unless effective methods of resistance are brought to light, the United States of America may be wiped off the maps of earth. And if this all-consuming invisible menace continues on its blazing course to other continents, civilization itself may perish and return to dust!"

The major, stunned at the ominous words, had halted in the midst of his preparations. The fate of his country and perhaps of the world had been sealed. Mankind was on the brink of annihilation.

Harkness too had paused to listen while preparing to don an asbestos suit. But that phrase about the Great Lakes struck a responsive chord in his mind and a strange new hopeful light all at once gleamed in his eyes. Could it be likely that—? Without daring to complete the thought, he dashed headlong for his project chamber.

"Major Ritter! Helen! Follow me!" he shouted but did not wait for an answer as he disappeared below. Wondering what crazy idea possessed him now, his two companions followed. They heard the whir of a film reel unwinding as they finally caught up with him, and saw the afternoon's disaster again being unfolded when they entered the chamber. Helen, nauseated though she was, nevertheless felt able to watch since she knew what to expect. They together saw the nerve-shattering scene through to its end, saw the airplane strike water approximately when the Erthorum bomb exploded, and saw the deluge of water sweep over everything. Helen stared in blank bewilderment when this time she witnessed the inexplicable disappearance of the terrific thing.

"See!" Harkness cried excitedly. "See how it disappears?"

"What of it?" answered the major slightly irritated. "I don't see that its disappearance proves anything except that it vanished from your camera's range."

"And why?" Harkness almost shouted. "Because water quenched it! Oh don't you see? Fire and water—the thing is all fire and electricity—and that cloudburst of water from my experiment simply extinguished it—and put it out—discharged it—call it what you will, the water killed it. There's our answer—fight fire with water and we've got the enemy licked!" He danced over to Helen in the first exuberance of success and whirled her around joyously.

Major Ritter made no comment while he thought for a moment. Then he turned with despairing eyes to Dave and said, "Of what use is the knowledge? We can't see the creatures. Even if we could photograph them we would be destroyed before the negative was developed, or else the monsters would have moved on. Where could water be found in sufficient quantities in prairie regions? How could it be used if it were available? No, Harkness, I'm afraid that long before any of these draw-backs are conquered, there will no longer exist people to be saved. You have probably hit on the solution—but there is no way to make use of it. It is beyond our power to thwart destiny—only divine providence can save us now."

The light in Dave's eyes died as cold logic added its weight to bitter truth and destroyed his illusion of triumph. Was there anything that could be done? In a few days at most the territory devastated by the fire creatures would have spread to include the entire continent. Apparently nothing could stop their inexorable progress, let alone obliterate them from Earth. In his mind's eye he reviewed the film, saw a storm of water drench an unclean thing.

"Rain!" he exclaimed. "I have it, Major, providence can wipe out these invaders with rain!"

But the gloomy expression did not lift from Major Ritter's face. "Rain?" he inquired. "You forget that we are in the midst of a worse drouth than that of 1930. The nation has been sweltering in fierce heat. There hasn't been any rain to speak of in weeks. The whole Mississippi Valley is a roaring furnace. No, Dave, I'm afraid it's all useless."

Silence settled upon them, and they wearily began to ascend again, defeat implicit in the listless ways they walked. Dave became aware of a persistent gnawing in his stomach, and remembered that neither he nor Major Ritter, and possibly Helen, had had anything to eat since breakfast. But time was precious, and a long flight to Washington remained before them. It would be many hours before the grateful taste of food satisfied their hunger.

Thoughts of danger in connection with their approaching trip held no terror. The day's excitement had nearly exhausted them. Harkness mechanically collected various objects he had planned to take with him. The three of them dispiritedly climbed into asbestos suits as a final precaution.

Evening had fallen as they filed out. In all the visible sky there was no faintest wisp of cloud. Molten, glaring, a brassy sun sank westward to close another day of abnormal heat. A great and unnatural hush blan-keted earth. Harkness wondered idly if it would be like this—ominous and lifeless and dead—when the sounds of man or of man's making passed away completely and forever.

They wheeled from its hangar Harkness' roomy four-passenger strato-gyroplane and relaxed in its closed cabin. The motor's roar was oddly comforting as they shot zenithward. Shut off from communication by their asbestos suits, they were left to dwell on their individual thoughts while they hurtled straight upward to the stratosphere, and then onward at full speed to Washington. Harkness had an Erthorum formula, an explanation of the death that was sweeping America, and a strip of film for proof that the fire-demons were responsible. But he had no feasible counter-attack to suggest. And he felt a brief pang of regret that his brilliant discovery had been made too late to be of any service to mankind. Erthorum could destroy anything on Earth, but there was no way to use it against the meteor-spawn.

At what point of his trip the most colossal scheme ever conceived by man suggested itself to Dave he was not able to tell afterwards. For a long, melancholy hour he flew through three hundred miles of once populated land. But now there was not a light in the cities except for the glare of occasional conflagrations, and airplane landing fields, highways, villages, the entire countryside, was in total darkness. He could guess what havoc had been brought, a population decimated, quartered, halved and worse, could almost see tragic heaps of bones whitening each open space down below. Not a powerhouse was operating, not an electric light burning in an area that already included more than two hundred and fifty thousand square miles of fertile land in the very heart of the United States.

He felt relieved when lights at last began to glimmer far ahead, and the ravaged territory to fade away in its concealing darkness behind. Even the knowledge that he was flying the borderline of greatest danger—that wide belt where fiery death flamed out of thin air as the fire-creatures swept onward—did not phase Harkness. He grimly sped to fulfill his mission.

The Alleghenies rose in sight.

Somewhere as he soared high over them a thought of such cosmic daring gripped Dave that he nearly lost control of his flyer.

He fumbled clumsily to remove his protective headgear. The ship rocked crazily. He was none too far beyond the danger belt but he had to know one thing now.

"Major Ritter!" he yelled above the engine's roar. "Can you arrange a visit for us with the President?"

His companion, who had barely got his own headpiece off in time to hear, looked queerly at Harkness as if he thought his mind had given way, but shouted, "Why, yes, I think it could be done tomorrow."

"No! Tonight! As soon as we land!"

"Impossible!"

"Listen!" Dave shrieked a few hoarse sentences. The major made no audible reply, but Dave saw a series of answers in his eyes and his face's changing expression.

"Sheer madness!

"What a tremendous thought!

"It might work!

"Why not try it?

"Not much chance of success—but it's gigantic—and if it works—

"We'll see the President!"

Argonauts of humanity they rushed onward as if their vessel was driven by fiends. Fast as they went, Harkness begrudged each precious minute. Gold was not being lost by delay—something far more valuable, life itself, was at stake.

Midnight had passed when Washington came in sight. The lights of the airport raced toward them and passed underneath. They circled above the city.

"You've overshot the field!" cried Major Ritter.

"I know it!" Harkness answered excitedly as he shut off the motor. "I'm landing on the Capitol grounds!"

The army man's eyes lighted with a feeling like pride as they swiftly dropped toward the Capitol's impressive dome under gyro power.

An instant more and they had piled out. Guards had surrounded them even as they touched earth, but the major's rank was sufficient passport.

A strange clamor rose above the city. They heard guns spitting fire. Soliders and civilians struggled like phantoms beyond the Capitol grounds. Looting and rioting had broken out everywhere. Army planes dropped flares from above. Detachments of infantry, squadrons armed with light machine guns shot looters on sight and struggled to preserve order. The streets were jammed with fear-crazed men blindly fighting whatever was within reach. The roads were a snarl of crawling vehicles, smashed automobiles, mangled bodies. A bedlam of cries, noises, horns, gunfire, and surging, swarming human beings crashed upon eardrums like waves of an invisible sea. Terror here and all over the world was beginning to give way to anarchy. Horror of the unknown, frenzied fear of a relentless, hideous, inescapable death sweeping out of the Mississippi valley had in one short day broken down the civilization of five thousand years. Wreckage, debris, personal possessions of every conceivable sort littered streets. Refugee fought with refugee in the struggle to reach boats and escape. It was every man for himself and every man against the rest. Washington, and cities the world over, was a miniature battleground with the lurid dazzle of flares and unchecked fires glaring upon scenes of wildest confusion and unparalleled chaos.

The Capitol building was a blaze of lights. Desperate, last minute conferences were being held to find some method of saving America. Orderlies and ensigns, messengers and attandants hurried about.

Struggling; shoving his way ahead; bawling commands when he could and bluffing authority where he had none, the major worked a way through for himself and his companions. He knew that he ran the risk of dishonorable discharge or even court-martial, but these were empty threats if Harkness' plan failed, and he played for the biggest stakes in history if he succeeded.

There was a long period of anxious waiting and nervous pacing when their goal was in sight. Had their hasty message been delivered? And if so, had it been read? Or was it tossed aside for later action? Perhaps it would be treated as the mere assertion of an irresponsible crank.

After interminable ages, a door suddenly opened. An attendant stepped aside, motioned them through, and murmured, "Major Ritter, Mr. Harkness, and Miss Boyd. President Williams is ready to receive you."

They were ushered into the presence of a man who had the eyes of a dreamer, the firm features of a practical builder, and the figure of an athlete. But now those eyes were tired, and the face haggard from loss of sleep, while worry had taken an additional toll.

Without wasting one moment or a single word, Harkness launched into an account of what he had discovered, and for proof held the film strip to a light. Major Ritter corroborated his story where necessary.

President Williams received their announcement of the discovery and filming of the fire-creatures with that self-possession for which he was famous. His only comment was, "What do you propose to do?"

Harkness told him, concisely, clearly. "I intend, Mr. President, *to blow up the Allegheny mountain range from Maine to the Carolinas, and the Rockies from Canada to Mexico, yes, down to the inner fires of Earth!*"

"And then—?"

"Let nature do the rest!"

For one of the few times in his career, President Williams gasped. "What titanic vision! Eternal daredevilry of youth!" His eyes seemed to look far away. He appeared to be weighing, judging, considering many things. At length, "What would you have me do?" he inquired.

"As Commander-in-Chief of the army and leader of your nation, you have authority to countersign requests for men, planes, supplies, and equipment. That is what we ask and need to carry out the plan! Immediate action is necessary—within thirty-six hours the vanguard of the fire-fiends will have reached Washington. Within forty-eight the United States of America will cease to exist! We do not promise success. But desperate measures are needed. There seems to be no other system of defense suggested."

The fate of a nation and a world rested in one man's power. Would he accede? He thought deeply while golden moments raced by.

When he answered, it was with a faint, almost bitter smile. "Major Ritter, Mr. Harkness, I left my cabinet and advisors in session to hear you. In there," and he waved toward a chamber, "great scientists are wrangling over theories, politicians are shouting nonsense on party lines about militant foreign powers.

"You, Mr. Harkness have brought me an incredible story with the ring of sincerity. I accept the validity of your film. I accept Major Ritter's corroboration of your Erthorum experiment. I am writing you a blanket order to draw any supplies you need from any part of the country, and all the military forces needed to put your scheme into operation. Your headquarters will be here. Communicate with me if you require further assistance.

"If you fail, we can lose no more than we already seem destined to lose. If you succeed—your country will never forget."

The President returned to his council.

In the remaining hours of that fateful night, a feverish bustle of activity, a continuous stream of orders, telegrams, messages poured from the Capitol. Sleeping men were summoned from their beds to heart-breaking work in great munitions factories. In this hour of national peril, secrecy was thrown to the winds, and the Erthorum formula was flashed to Wilmington, to San Francisco, to a dozen other focal cities. Another order went out and molten metal flowed into hastily built molds at steel plants. There came an electric summons— and huge navy bombers began to mass on the outskirts of Washington, New York, Seattle, Wilmington, San Francisco, and coastal cities along the Atlantic and Pacific seaboards. A request for volunteers on a mission of death was made, and a thousand pilots waited beside their planes.

And ever fiery death leapt onward out of the central valleys. Irresistible, steady, the meteor monsters burned their way across a continent, feeding on the flame of life. Already their toll was mounting by millions. Whoever and wherever they were, without warning and almost without realization, living beings vanished in puffs of blinding fire.

And all night men strove like demons against time and fate. Warnings, evacuation orders, commands went out over the radio stations still operating. Despairing eyes searched the heavens in vain for rain clouds. The nation sweltered in a night of heat only less terrific than that of day.

How could this last desperate attempt succeed in the few short hours of grace remaining to America? Hope had died out—but grimly, doggedly, the work went on.

At dawn, after wolfing a hasty meal, Dave and Major Ritter and Helen finally permitted themselves the sleep of exhaustion.

Noon found them once more hard at work.

Illinois, Indiana, Ohio, and ten surrounding states had been devastated. Westward the terror had swept across Wisconsin, Minnesota, the Dakotas, and was now racing to the desert lands. Iowa and Kansas were depopulated. Forest fires set by human torches raged in Michigan. Chicago was a shambles. A horrible nauseating odor had begun to corrupt the atmosphere. No effort was made to check the crackle of flames which spread a pall of smoke over burning cities. Strangely deserted, strangely devoid of human sounds and activity, more than one-fourth of the United States lay under control of the fire-creatures.

But in late afternoon, from a dozen cities, bombing planes roared into action and winged their way over mountain ranges with cargoes of Erthorum. Steel spheres hurtled to earth in a thousand places among the east and west coast mountain ranges. Accuracy of aim made low flying necessary. Yet not a pilot faltered as he went to death with a jest on his lips and the eternal fighting spirit of mankind shining through his eyes.

Earth groaned and rocked. Colossal masses of stone and dirt belched heavenward. Entire peaks were blasted away and titanic gashes split the ground. No war had ever approached this man-made hell. The wildest imagination could not have visualized the scene. Erthorum in its full strength was loosed, and the globe's crust was blown away down to the monster inner fires. In New York City men's ear-drums burst from the stupendous concussions. Buildings shook as in an earthquake. A vast screaming wind howled up as air stormed in from the oceans toward the Erthorum-created vacuums. The halls of the gods must have echoed with exploding mountains and blasted hills and sundered ground.

Out of a hundred enormous pits five miles deep and more, lava spewed skyward and volcanoes extinct since the dawn of history vomited flame and incandescent liquid masses. As night descended, the entire heavens were reddened with the glare of titanic forces at work. Gales of cyclonic proportion lashed sky and land. White-hot rivers serpentined away from newly-formed volcanic cones. A pall of ashes and smoke and gases turned the atmosphere murky.

And ever the fire-creatures ravened fiercely onward, with half a nation already ravaged, and upwards of ten million persons metamorphosed into heaps of scorched bones. Invisible, their presence unknown except when consuming death blazed high, the foul entities conquered at will. No one knew how many of them had come. Perhaps hundreds, perhaps thousands. Because of their extraordinary power of expansion and contraction, there was even no telling how much territory a single one could occupy, or how many human beings it could simultaneously annihilate.

On the Capitol grounds Harkness stood peering anxiously above him. All the horizon was spectacular with belching flame and smoke, thundering explosions blasted the air, mineral gases seared his lungs, and he felt the ground beneath buckle and heave in torment. A bloody radiance shone evilly on everything. The end of the world seemed to have come. There was no peace in the skies above, no quiet on the lands below, no calm on the waters about. And the fire monsters sped onward toward man-loosed eruptions of cosmic forces.

There came additional rumbles.

"Blasting again," muttered Dave.

A drop of hot, muddy fluid spattered him.

"Volcanic mud," he thought.

The winds roared higher, trees crashed, a lightning bolt sizzled and cracked and struck somewhere nearby. And then it came, on the wings of a hundred-mile-per-hour gale, rain in sheets, a cloudburst of water, a deluge of hot mud in huge drops.

Like a man insane, Harkness stretched his arms out with face uplifted and let the wild downpour beat its fiercest against him.

All up and down the coast, and in the far west, cyclones drove a wall of water inland. Streams that had dried up under drouth became raging rivers and the rivers became floods that burst all embankments. A cloud of steam capped the volcanoes as fast as gales blew it away. Streets became quagmires of thin mud, whole towns that lay in lowland were swept away. Countless people were drowned in juggernauts of water that thundered down every depression. History recorded no downpour like this; never had there been such fury of all the elements. Men trembled in the presence of power above them and forces beyond their control.

And then reports began to trickle in from the crippled, the stragglers in the vast exodus—torrential rains had come, and with their arrival, odd, sinister cracklings arose, and monstrous, bluish luminosities flashed momentarily where men had been bursting into flame and dying. The fire-creatures were the most dangerous threat ever made to human existence. Man had answered the challenge with a gigantic achievement.

And the fire-creatures were defeated! Deluged by the rain that alone could harm them, they met their destruction. As silently and mysteriously as they had come, they disappeared.

Harkness stood in his laboratory, on a cool, September morning a month later, looking dreamily out across the waters of Lake Michigan. It was a rare day for those earth convulsions had brought a perpetually warmer climate to America. The trees were becoming splashed with tawny tints and streaks of red. They reminded him symbolically of a danger that had passed.

Over all the nation men swarmed like industrious ants, toiling to reconstruct a country that had been ravaged by fire-creatures, storms, and explosives. Crippled and stricken though she was, a new America struggled to existence through the wreckage of the old.

From where she stood beside him, Helen, smartly dressed in a tweed sport suit, looked quizzically at Dave. "Still thinking of our little fire friends? And what more, sir, could you be interested in knowing about them?"

"Much that will probably never come to light," Dave answered slowly. "For instance, where did they originate? We can only surmise that it was some remote, obscure part of the universe, else we would have been visited by them long before this.

"And why did they come? Most scientists, you know, think accident brought them, that somehow they were trapped or marooned on the meteor until chance led them here. But I am not so sure, Helen. They conquered swiftly, systematically, once they arrived. It would not surprise me if the whole thing was planned. Perhaps they were raiders searching for sustenance after famine had struck their own part of the universe.

"And how did they spread so rapidly after their arrival? It is difficult to believe that the meteor, large as it was, could have held more than a few dozen. Perhaps I underestimate their capacity, but it seems more likely that they increased in number after they came. How did they do so? It may be that they had infinite powers of expansion. And it may be that after they reached a certain limit, they simply divided and subdivided like other forms of life we know and so multiplied faster and faster as they reaped their harvest of human life."

For a few seconds Helen made no reply as she looked at Dave with a half-amused, half-disgusted expression. Then she said in a mocking tone of pseudo-despair, "Ah me, the most famous man in America spends his time thinking about abstractions and past events when he could be—"

But she got no farther. Harkness was making up for lost time on a large scale as he suddenly found other and more satisfying things to do than day-dream.

THE LIVES OF ALFRED KRAMER

THOUGH MY TRAIN did not pull out till eleven P.M., I had boarded it at ten. While the berths were being made up I strolled around. There were few passengers this early in the week. Indeed, when I walked back and took a seat in the smoking car, I noticed but one other occupant. To my casual glance, he appeared singularly repulsive. His grayish face, an immobile setness of expression, burning black eyes in which no pupil was visible, his gloved hands folded stiffly in his lap, all combined to give me an immediate dislike.

I paid no further attention to him during the quarter of an hour or so that I sat smoking. Several times, however, I had an impression that he was intently watching me.

When I arose and began to walk toward my berth, I had an equally vivid impression that he addressed some remark to me in a low and extraordinarily husky voice just as I was passing him. So inaudible was his voice and so marked my aversion that I pretended I had not heard and continued on my way.

Dismissing the incident from mind, I prepared for slumber. A variety of noises kept me awake. I heard brakemen call, the train pull out, its wheels clack rhythmically.

An hour later I was still tossing restlessly.

At about twelve-thirty I gave up my futile effort to sleep, climbed from my berth, and slipped on a dressing gown. Cigar in hand, I again made my way back to the smoking-car. Its lone occupant had evidently not moved, for he was still sitting where I last saw him. I did not notice his lips move, but plainly this time I heard his abominable husky voice.

"Won't you join me for a few miles?" it said. "I am an invalid, you see."

Perhaps his appeal for sympathy touched me, or perhaps his obvious loneliness. At any rate, I suppressed my unpleasant reaction to his physical appearance and dropped into the chair opposite him.

I made some reference to my unconventional garb, and idly remarked, "I thought I'd have another smoke. Sleep was impossible."

"Yes," he responded, "there are times when one would like to sleep but cannot. It is worse," he added cryptically, "when one would prefer to remain awake, but cannot."

A bit puzzled, I waited for him to continue.

"I have not slept for three nights," he volunteered.

"Indeed? I am sorry if your illness prevents you from sleeping," I said politely.

"No, it is not that. My indisposition is of such a nature that slumber is dangerous. I have kept myself awake by stimulants. And the long night hours are monotonous when one is alone."

Casual though our conversation was thus far, and despite my friendly resolve, I had been becoming more uneasy. There was a kind of psychic chill in the air which early autumn could not entirely account for. My companion's repellent aspect was hardly modified by the soft lights around us. For all the expression on his grayish face, an automaton or ventriloquist might have been speaking. No muscular change had yet livened his countenance, his lips had made no perceptible movement. His unrelaxing gloved hands, the unnatural shine of his black eyes, and his rigid carriage were as disquieting at close range as they had been at a distance. Nor could I accustom myself to the throaty degeneracy of his speech. About his person there was in addition an odor that bothered me. It was quite indefinable, but had an element of the beast in it, and of corruption, and stagnant sea-water, and mildew.

I now noticed what had hitherto escaped me, that a pile of books lay beside him. The topmost was Strindmann's monograph, *Racial Memory in Dreams*. Other books underneath it dealt with abnormal psychology.

"Are you a student of psychology?" I asked.

"To some extent, yes, but I am more interested in dreams. You see, I have been troubled by nightmares for some time. I am on my way to Vienna to place myself under Strindmann's care.

"Allow me to introduce myself: I am Alfred Kramer."

"And I am Wallace Forbes. Your dreams must be rather upsetting to necessitate a trip half-way around the world."

I, who never dream, had always been fascinated by that phenomenon in other people. Kramer himself must have desired sympathetic ears to receive his story, because, hesitantly at first, then more directly and swiftly, he began to tell his narrative.

"From early childhood," he commenced, "I was inquisitive into the world around me. I seem to have been born with a scientific and inventive bent. At the same time I was a dreamy child. My nights were vivid with a constant stream of images. Sometimes these were pleasant, often they were terrifying. I saw scenes and had strange experiences that I could not explain on the basis of anything I had read, or witnessed, or heard.

"Because of these visions I acquired a profound interest in brain processes as I grew older. My studies dealt with dream psychology, racial memory, and mental inheritances.

"A certain dream kept recurring over a period of years: I stood in the midst of a somber glade. All around rose the vast and evil boles of monstrous trees. Long shadows lay athwart the sere grass of autumn at my feet. There were indistinct figures at a little distance which harmo nized curiously with the colossal trees. They were watching me intently. In my hand I held a wicked sacrificial knife. Before me was a great stone altar, stained with the blood of countless victims. It stood by the hugest of the trees, and it had a slanting trough so that the spilled blood would water those gnarled roots. A naked young girl, like a flower unfolding, tremulous and shaken lay upon this altar. Her gray eyes regarded me with a baffling mixture of religious ecstasy, terror, and love, as I slowly raised the knife to plunge it into her breast.

"Time after time that vision came to me as clearly as an episode from life. But I never dreamed of what preceded the scene, nor did I know what followed.

"Out of my wish to know the full episode, and from my belief that many dreams were memories of past events, I conceived a hypothesis. The unbroken stream of life had descended from parents to children throughout the ages. Why might not major experiences have been so deeply impressed upon the brain that they too were inherited? Perhaps they were latent, awaiting only a magic touch to awaken them into reconstructed pictures. If this were true, possibly it would account for hitherto unexplained dreams. My own persistent nightmare was like an inherited image, surviving in me, of some impressive episode in the life of a long-dead ancestor.

"Under proper conditions, why shouldn't it be possible to release these ancestral adventures?

"Fascinated by the thought, I plunged into years of labor. Mental therapy, psychiatry, brain surgery became my special studies. I ex- hausted all sources of information on every phase of the brain, in health and disease, infancy and maturity, life and death. I made elaborate inves- tigations into physiology, the nervous system, motor stimuli, 'why the wheels go round,' in other words. I began a thorough and detailed research into the structure, nature, function, purpose, and action of brain cells.

"Behind my wild idea and its resulting intense activity was a coldly logical plan. If past events could be retained in memory by descendants, they would be recorded somewhere in the brain itself. And among its component parts the source most likely to offer fruitful results was the cells. Of these there are several millions, a vast majority of which seem never to be used. In fact, the average human being requires the services of only a few thousand cells during his lifetime. The remaining cells apparently are capable of storing up facts but simply are not called on except by individuals who pursue knowledge inexhaustibly. It was my belief that this enormous number of unused cells retained, but ever so slightly, impressions of the dominant incidents which had affected the lives of all one's forebears.

"I next supposed that when a cell was required to store away a fact or event in one's life, its latent memory of ancestral experience was obliterated. But if it were not used, the latent memory continued to exist, sometimes never to be realized, sometimes, however, to flash forth vividly in sleep or subconscious dreams.

"For a long time I pursued a wrong path. I thought that the memory-impressions made a physical change in the cells, just as a particle of metal changes in shape when you strike it violently: and that all I needed to do was to invent some sort of sensitive electric device which would tap these cells by means of their specific differences.

"Vain delusion! I wasted two precious years pursuing a ghost, as it were.

"And like many another person who deals with complexities, I found simplicity the keynote to my riddle. It was in 1931, not long after the cosmic ray was discovered and the electrogenetic theory of life propounded, that a brilliant idea occurred to me. You are acquainted with this theory? Its assertion that the human system is somewhat like a battery, and that what we call life lasts while a positive-negative interaction of electricity continues, while death is the complete cessation of that activity? Well, the thought came to me that by increasing this electrical energy of the body, and more particularly by heightening this activity in the brain, each cell might release its individual retained fact or ancestral memory. Recent impressions, being nearer and therefore stronger, would be unloosed first; but by gradually building up activity, older and yet older events ought to permit of resurrection.

"I worked with new energy. Light, wave-lengths, rays occupied my attention. Weird and intricate machinery accumulated in my laboratory.

"And now at last I began to feel success approaching with my isolation of the Kappa-ray. I found it in minute quantities in the bright sunshine that poured down, found, too, that it directly supplied human beings with much of that electrical energy which gave them life.

"I toiled feverishly until I succeeded in crossing my last barrier. I constructed a sort of Kappa-battery that would isolate from sunshine and store up in concentrated form the Kappa-ray! Day after day, as my black metal box stood in the open glare of the sun, charging itself with precious invisible stuff, I watched it, fondly, jealously. I would have killed any one who chanced to come upon it.

"Then came that evening when its capacity was reached. Carefully I closed it and carried it to my quarters as gently as if it were nitroglycerin. Worn out and prematurely aged from my years of intense labor, tired in body yet wonderfully excited in spirit, I lay down on my bed with the black box beside me.

"With a strangely steady hand I reached out and opened its shutter and pressed a switch.

"An invisible warm radiance flowed and flooded and poured into me. My head swam with an indescribable nausea, a kind of opiate thickness combined with an increasingly rapid surge of extraordinarily lucid thoughts. My mind seemed to be working faster and clearer than it ever had before. But at the same time, that soothing warmth stole pleasantly over me. Lest there be danger, I extended my arm and closed the box.

"Almost instantaneously I slept.

"A panic-stricken mob, fleeing in terror, bore me along in its mad flight. I fought and struggled to prevent myself from being crushed to death. A confused roar deafened my ears. Cries of racing figures, groans of injured and dying men, crackle of flame and howl of wind blended into a hideous noise. Buildings appeared to speed by me as I forged ahead. I knew I must be in some large city.

"My bursting lungs gasped for clean air but only drew in acrid smoke. The sky glowed redly, flame-shot darkness swirled around me, from behind came the glare of a vast conflagration. I saw swaths of fire leap from building to building on the wings of a stiff wind. Clouds of smoke billowed up, drifted upon us, choked the lungs of refugees. Ever and again, some poor devil fell, and the sheeted flame raced inexorably over him.

"A lumbering brute crashed into me. I cursed savagely and plunged after him. He tripped. I saw him no more. A frail woman with two children, crying as the mob jostled past her, leaned helplessly against a door-stoop. I caught her in one arm and swung her along with me, the children folded to her. And all these people were dressed in the fashion of a full half-century ago!

"We struggled onward in the midst of this livid nightmare. The city's heart was an inferno, a raging furnace.

"But now we were approaching outskirts and less thickly populated districts. Gradually we forged ahead. Smoke and blistering heat still smote us, but the danger region lay farther behind.

"Then, abruptly, the scene changed.

"I was at a ship's wheel. Under full sail we scudded along at a fast clip. Stretching to every horizon, with no land visible anywhere, a white-capped sea surged under a strong trade wind. The sun poured warmly from a sky in which only a few clouds floated high.

"With terrifying suddenness came a cry from the lookout.

"*'Derelict dead ahead!'*

"I swung the wheel mightily. The ship skewed. Crash! She quivered a moment, began to sink. I saw a water-logged hulk, black, submerged, hover by our ripped bow. There was a pandemonium of leaping men, despairing shouts where boats fouled in their davits or capsized when badly launched, a bitter fight for positions in those that remained. One went down, overloaded. Another was drawn by suction and followed our ship as she sank.

"At the first shock I tore my clothing off and dived far overboard, swimming rapidly to escape the deadly suction. I was hauled aboard one of two boats that survived. In all there were eleven men left out of thirty-two.

"Then came tragedy in the days that ensued as thirst, starvation, and a blazing sun took their toll. We knew of no land closer than five hundred miles. Sometime during our second night adrift, the two boats became separated.

"Six survivors had manned our boat to begin with. At the end of the week we were four. This number was reduced to three on our tenth day afloat when Olaf went mad from drinking salt water and leaped over-board. That left Petri, Andrews, and myself. I think Petri recklessly committed suicide rather than suffer a lingering death of torment, but I cannot be sure, for I became delirious on the twelfth day.

"I returned to my senses strangely refreshed. A rain squall had evidently struck and passed. I greedily lapped up warm, fresh water from the boat's bottom and revived still more. I noticed that only one of my companions was now left—and he had been dead for I know not how long. I heaved his body overboard.

"Two days later a little palm-fringed island came in sight. With what desperate anxiety I watched it grow larger, and how eagerly I stumbled ashore to drag myself feebly up its beach! I was saved! Saved! And without warning the scene vanished.

"Then followed a couple of less interesting dreams with details I will not bother to tell.

"When I at length awakened at dawn, I could scarcely keep calm because of the excitement that possessed me. Columbus could not have been more thrilled when he found a new continent. I had made a discovery that might open up unguessable stores of knowledge to mankind, or that might clarify many obscure and forgotten pages of history. Yet I had no intention of announcing it publicly until I had first explored for myself in full its potentialities. I hoped that I would sooner or later have a complete representation of that persistent but fragmentary vision which I alluded to earlier. I speculated on what fascinating episodes from ancestral life might present themselves as I continued using the Kappa-ray. For insofar as I could tell, it left no ill effects. Indeed, I felt unusually energetic, my thoughts came with exceptional clarity.

"That day I spent much of my time obtaining books from libraries and dealers. These were mainly works on genealogy, history, costume, antiquities, biography, and sciences.

"I pored over these till late at night. Two items rewarded a tedious search. One brief record told how my father had escaped in his youth from the great fire of Chicago. The second excerpt, which I ran across in Cooper's *Maritime Disasters,* narrated that a whaler, the *Nancy R.*, disappeared in the South Seas, 1809 A.D.; and that her fate was not learned until two years later when the clipper *Seagull,* anchoring for repairs at an atoll southwest of Keaua, found the sole survivor of that tragedy, my grandfather, who had been living there ever since.

"I was happy as a child over this verification of my theory, even though I had strained my eyes by such intensive research. More than satisfied with my achievement, I again opened the Kappa-ray battery and felt its radiant-soporific energy pour through my head just before sleep came to me.

They were ready to burn a condemned witch in England. A wizened, half-demented old woman, she was already tied to the stake. A crowd of stupid faces and stern persecutors ringed her in. I had somehow been drawn there but now looked at her with compassion in my eyes and would have turned away, sick to my heart, if I could. Any movement was difficult, wedged in tightly as I was.

"A vicious mob shout arose as the executioner advanced, torch in hand. Above that babel the old woman's voice suddenly ascended.

"'Innocent! I am innocent!' she croaked. 'Burn me, will you? May your heart turn to the stone that it is!'

"A startled expression came into the executioner's eyes. He paused in his stride, clutched his breast, plunged to earth dead before he struck.

"Supernatural fear laid an absolute quiet on the crowd. One of the witch's relentless tormenters, bolder than his associates, walked forward and picked up the fallen torch.

"'Sorceress!' he cried. 'Prepare to meet thy God and be sentenced to eternal damnation!' And he flung the torch among the faggots heaped around her. It caught, a thin flame sprang up and raced from stick to stick.

"'Fools! Fools!' the old crone cursed. 'May the vengeance of God and Satan, for this day's work, pursue every one—*except you!* And she raised a withered hand toward me. 'Only you have pity—may you and your descendants be blessed, even unto the tenth generation. But after the tenth generation, beware! *We shall meet again, yea, three hundred years hence, and you will tell me you remember!*'

"Without willing it, I cried, 'I will remember!'—and awoke to hear my own voice, *'remember—remember,'* echo hollowly in my room and die away. I tossed fitfully, dropped into a sound sleep."

But this account is growing longer than I intended. I must omit many details, fascinating though they would be. Flying miles accompanied flying minutes while I listened spellbound to Kramer's husky voice, and looked into his fever-bright eyes, and wondered how he managed to speak with any distinctness when his lips had not yet visibly moved. His story flowed on—or shall I say continued backward?—through Henry the Eighth's court, the Spanish Inquisition, Constantinople at its fall, Paris of Villon's day, the Norman Conquest, weaving its way through earlier and yet earlier centuries.

"So I finally came to my puzzling dream," Kramer went on. "I do not know exactly what year it was, but from its place in my sleep-atavism, I would guess the Fifth or Sixth Century.

"Autumn had come. Dead leaves and withered grass marked the dying year. I was a high priest among the Druids. Each year, upon the last evening of fall, we sacrificed our loveliest virgin to the forest god so that her blood would appease him and cause him to let our sacred trees grow green again when spring returned. I, as high priest, must offer the sacrifice—and she whom they had chosen was Neridh, beloved of my heart.

"I had done everything in my power to save Neridh, until they had grown suspicious. One desperate hope of success remained, but the ritual had been chanted, Neridh lay upon the altar, and a semicircle of dark faces watched me from all around this woodland glade. I dragged out my invocation and supplication. The sun sank lower, and shadows crept longer on blown leaves and brown grass.

"There could be no further delay. Sacrifices must be made before sunset. I raised my arm slowly and held the knife high, poised for its downward plunge into my beloved's heart. Anguish, terror, love, resignation struggled for expression on her face. Already the sun's rim was dropping, and—

"Somewhere afar a tree gave forth a sharp crack. Fear leaped into those eyes that watched me. I heard a heavy groan, a series of sounds from rending boughs, then a booming crash as a giant tree toppled.

"'The wood-spirit is angry!' I shouted. 'Our sacrifice displeases him! To the Great Hill, fly! and witness the evidence of his wrath!'

"Terror gripped the Druids, they melted away like ghosts. I knew what they would find—a forest monarch half chopped in two, and a slow fire that had eaten its way in. My work, my secret efforts to rescue Neridh were triumphant.

"I bent over and slashed her bonds. Swiftly but gently I set her on her feet.

"'Follow me, there is not a moment to lose!' I whispered. 'Make haste before they return!'

"Hand in hand down the endless forest aisles we raced. Neridh ran like a wild faun, her graceful body flashing among the shadows. Night drew on, and I saw her shiver with the chill of early evening. So intent had I been on saving her that I had forgotten her lack of raiment. I unloosed my outer robe, and scarcely pausing in my stride threw it around her tawny shoulders as we sped onward. She gave me a quick glance of pleasure and clutched the warm ceremonial garment close to her.

"And so, deeper and deeper into the vast forest, through thickening darkness, by trails that only I knew, we ran toward safety, weaving our way past immemorial oaks and gigantic boles that had stood even before the coming of our people.

"There my dream ended. I can merely surmise that we escaped into the fastnesses of that forest. There too, since I had discovered what I sought, I could have ended my experiment and ceased energizing myself with Kappa-rays. Such self-denial was beyond either my will or my desire. I was caught in a maelstrom, farther goals lured me on, I succumbed to a magnetic spell which my own imagination had woven. How much more could I learn of what my forebears had lived? I wanted to carry my experiment to its limit. Night after night I therefore utilized the Kappa-ray in pursuit of those adventures which a part of me had long ago experienced.

"A year that I do not dare to guess. I must have been a merchant, and I had gone on some annual trip to a town far from my native land. It was a rambling town, a town of crowded, connected little clay and stone houses. It lay beneath the glare of a scorching sun, and farther out the shifting desert dunes melted into bleak, red wastelands. Its men were swarthy, bearded. They wore long and flowing robes and spoke a language that I could understand but little.

"As I walked down the narrow streets, I heard a sudden hubbub above the usual street cries. When I came to a sharp curve that had interrupted my view I halted abruptly. There was a crowd of the curious, the holy, rich and poor alike, following a stranger who paced along the sunbaked street. He was simply clad. On his face was an expression of such glory, and in his eyes a light of so divine a purity, that my first instinct was to recoil in humility. He was radiant, and the very air about his head seemed luminous with a light I have never seen elsewhere. Then I felt a great serenity come upon me, and my spirit was lifted out of me, cleansed as if I had bathed in some mystical, immortal essence.

"There came a woman who flung herself at the feet of the stranger. Her left hand was hooked like a claw, and splotched with ominous patches of white. The fingers of her right hand were withered away, and her face was disfigured. The crowd shrank back, muttering 'Unclean! Unclean!' But the woman heeded them not and pleaded to the stranger with sorrowing eyes.

"He paused. I saw an expression of infinite pity and compassion shine through his eyes. I was reverent in the presence of ineffable beauty and transcendent wonder.

"The stranger stretched out his arm, and blessed the woman in a voice melodious as distant bells. I saw the claw-shaped hand become firm and rosy, the withered arm fill out to its former symmetry, the mutilated face glow with the happiness of restored health.

"The stranger continued on his way. The woman transfigured knelt in the dust. . . .

"Day after day I kept drawing aside the veil of oblivion. Night upon night I lived again in my dreams my previous lives and ventured still farther back through vanished years. In Alexandria I traded for the imperial silks of Damascus and the musk of Tatary, the sandalwood of

Indh and the golden apes of Angkor. I sold the blue-black men of Ruwhili, bought the kohl-eyed girls of Ophir, patronized the courtesans from Lesbos and Samarkand and Nubia, the small, tawny damozels of Mix, the massive-bodied women of Khangiz, the sinuous dancers of Chen-Sha, the voluptuous four-breasted harlots from Shebeth whose ecstasies were beyond man's endurance. . . . In Thebes I witnessed the wakening of a mummy from its tomb of ten centuries, and saw the doubtful Egyptian gods arise from crypts older than civilization. I dwelt at a lamasery near Tibet when all my future was foretold to me by priests of a forgotten cult. And ever I pursued my ancestral life backward through mounting ages. There came a night whose dream no history records, the memory of an event that must have occurred more than ten thousand years B.C.

"My lives had turned away from Asia and gone westward, beyond Egypt, beyond Greece, beyond all Europe, to a vast island or little continent far out in the wastes of the Atlantic. It was a fertile country, a land of mists and sunshine, whose people were happy in the unbroken advance of their civilization. In bays of the murmuring sea, and on slopes of the central hills, golden spires rose high above cities of white and black marble. This continent was a world by itself. There were legends of lands that lay far east from which the ancestors of these inhabitants had come, and there were occasional voyages to nearer countries westward. But they were an indolent race, safe from attack, undisturbed by strife, living in plenty, and rarely venturing afar since there was no need to.

"So the fruitful years marched by, and now there came to this island kingdom the rumor of approaching disaster. In Ixenor, capital of Atlantis, Lekti, high priest of the sun-worshippers, made a prophecy of doom.

"'Our god is angry. The sun shall fail above Atlantis.'

"What did this strange forecast mean? The Atlanteans looked at their sun god smiling high in the heavens and could not understand. They asked of Lekti that he interpret the warning, or tell them how to appease Elik-Ra, god of the sun. But Lekti had spoken, and answered that he could only receive the message of Elik-Ra and that it was not for him to explain.

"'The sun shall fail above Atlantis.' A hundred virgins were sacrificed with prayers and supplications for mercy to Elik-Ra. The foundations of a great new temple facing east were laid. Days passed and there was no sign that the prophecy would come true. Gradually the Atlanteans regained their faith, and went about their usual tasks again, and believed that their sacrifice of a hundred virgins had satisfied Elik-Ra. Even the prophecy began to fade from their minds, and no one quite remembered why another temple was being erected.

"But superstitious fear had taken root in my heart. I felt that words of warning, however obscure, should be heeded. There was a legend that fertile hot countries lay far east of Atlantis, beyond where any of us living had gone, whence our ancient fathers were supposed to have come and where the home of the sun-god himself was said to be. I reasoned that some terrible menace might be threatening Atlantis the golden, while the gods bided their time. And if Elik-Ra was really angry, I could either save myself by fleeing westward, or take an offering with me and strike out east to seek the god's home across the great sea.

"I set to work and had a large new galley built for me. When the inhabitants of Atlantis heard of my undertaking, a few thought my mission could be successful, some said I was foolhardy, but the majority mocked, saying that I was mad or presumptuous since Elik-Ra had been appeased by the sacrifice of the hundred virgins. Their scorn raised momentary doubts in my mind, but I went ahead with my plans.

"Thus there came a day when sixteen slaves took their places at the sweep-oars and we set off across dark waters to seek legendary lands of the rising sun. My galley had one mast whose sail could be used in emergency or when the crew was exhausted. There was a great store of provisions aboard, and as much wealth as I owned. Beside me in silver chains lay the sacrifice I intended to offer Elik-Ra when the time came: a young girl, lovely as the fading spires of Ixenor, and with red-gold hair that flamed like the setting sun. I had bought her quite reasonably, for red hair was not prized so highly as black hair among us.

"We had left Atlantis at dawn. Hardly a breeze stirred. The ocean heaved undulantly in slow, sinister swells. By noon we were entering that trackless wilderness of waters where no living man had penetrated. Far behind, my island kingdom, the only land I knew, dwindled toward the horizon, becoming dream-like and misty and unreal.

"And now as the oars pulled rhythmically a strange thing happened. The waters around us changed from heavy green to a complete and frightful black. Thousands upon thousands of dead fish floated to their surface, whales, tarpon, swordfish, octopi, sailfish, and a dozen other varieties of monsters of the deep such as had never been seen, all dead. Bubbles oozed out, vapor and wisps of steam drifted up. The sea boiled with a vast and nauseating motion. All in one instant Atlantis vanished from the horizon as the ocean reclaimed its own.

"'The sun shall fail above Atlantis.'

"To me alone was given understanding of the prophecy, unless my slaves remembered. Blind terror had come upon them, and they shouted wildly. I followed the direction of their eyes. From sunken Atlantis a colossal, a mountainous plateau of water extending across the whole horizon hurtled toward us. We saw it coming and we were helpless. We saw it tower overhead and engulf our galley as if it were a fleck of sand. Something bumped me and I grabbed it unthinkingly. An infinite roaring deafened my ears, I was sucked under and flung violently ahead, furious forces raged everywhere. I crashed into something else, hung on, half-drowned, pulled myself and my burden up. A freak of the great wave had righted my galley. With two feet of water in its bottom it raced along with the sea wall. Not one of the sixteen slaves had been saved, only myself and Teoctel, the flame-haired, who had been thrown against me when we capsized, were left of all the millions that had dwelt in Atlantis. And Teoctel was dying.

"I dreamed again, in search of my ancestral lives, and for many nights my visions became increasingly barbaric. I wandered through hills in what is now Spain, where swart people dwelt in caves. I fought a woolly rhinoceros in the Balkans, ruled a tribe of blond giants in the Rhine valley. Time and again I brought down my prey with primitive weapons, or even made my kill with only my bare hands and sharp teeth. More than once I fought, like the savage I was, to get or to keep the female of my choice.

"When the fire people discovered again the lost art of building a fire, it was I who found that meat improved by being burnt. Then the great cold and the field of ice crept down from the north, and my lives were passed in a strange warm country far to the south where my tribe had fled. And always the faces around me became more bestial, the marks of civilization fewer, until finally the only law was the law of one's strength.

"There, more than fifty thousand years ago, I halted my dreams. Did I say halted them? No, that is not quite true.

"For a week I had been feverishly writing my observations during the daytime, and poring over piles of books in order to localize in time and place the substance of my released memories. I begrudged the moments necessary for eating; it was many days since I had shaven or paid any attention to myself.

"But, as I said, my visions were becoming more savage, primitive, less varied the farther back I went. My initial excitement had begun to wear off, and on this morning, despite a certain heaviness that appeared to possess me, I felt the need of attending to my long-neglected personal appearance.

"When I bent over to draw the water for my tub, some unexpressed thought vaguely puzzled me. That thought continued to bother me while I slipped from my clothing. There is, in my bathroom, a full-length mirror; and not till I was passing it did my feeling of unease receive expression.

"For I glanced at my naked body in the mirror, and such a shock of utter horror froze me as I can never again experience on earth.

"*What I saw in the mirror was a massive, shaggy, beastlike man of fifty thousand years ago!*

"I cannot relate the rest of that fateful day. I tried to convince myself that I was the victim of an optical illusion. Perhaps my dreams had become so vivid that they persisted even in my waking hours. My mind may have temporarily given way, I thought, and made me a victim of hallucination.

"But it was all in vain. The mirror did not lie. Each time that I returned to it, drawn by a morbid curiosity, the same appalling figure leered back at me, ape-like, brutish. Slowly the bitter truth forced its way in, though I tried to evade it. Some powerful element in the Kappa-ray, or some unknown organic change that it had influenced in my physical system, was causing my body to revert, to follow my brain as it went back through the ages in the trail of my ancestral lives. I had played with mysterious forces and I was paying the penalty. A physiological atavism or throwback kept pace with the transformation of my mind.

"Shuddering, sickened, I gave way to a frenzy. I raged and stormed around like a trapped animal. My hate concentrated on the Kappa-ray. That was the source of all my misfortune. But at least I could prevent this abominable devolution from going any farther. Perhaps I might even be able to regain my old self when the source of that malignant energy was destroyed. And so, hardly realizing what damage I did and caring less, I kicked the Kappa-ray box across the room, smashed it, trampled it under my feet and ground it into wreckage. Even though I could never again become as I was, yet I would check this degradation before it went farther and before it was too late.

"I do not know how long the madness ruled me. It must have been far into the night that I finally managed to drop into the deep slumber of exhaustion.

"*And that night I dreamed again!* I re-lived a fierce, nomadic life in southern Italy, followed an earlier glacier as it retreated north, hunted the mammoth, and then roamed anew through the valleys of central Europe in the warm days before the glaciers came.

"When I wakened at dawn, I was beyond any paroxysms of despair. An apathy came upon me. I walked with dull and heavy tread, listlessly pondered over my fate. I realized now that the Kappa-ray had done its fatal work, and that I had saturated myself in an energy which I no longer had power to control. Whatever changes the ray had begun to make in my brain and my body were proceeding as freely as if they were a natural part of me.

"I could only hope that the effect of the ray would wear off in time. Sedatives, drugs, opiates, stimulants—I tried them all and without success. Nightly I lived backward through obscure dawn ages. Daily I wakened to find hideous and subtle changes metamorphosing me into a prehistoric creature. And what faint hope I had held died in my heart when I discovered that the rate of my noctural return to former life was accelerating with ever-increasing rapidity. At first I had spanned a few decades in a night, then it became a few centuries, now I bridged thousands and tens of thousands of years each time that I slept.

"I followed primitive man when he crept out of Asia half a million years ago. I lived in a luxuriant land that is now the desert of Gobi. Earth itself underwent great transformations. A continent sank under the waves, another one rose from the Pacific deep. Beasts that no living man has seen appeared in growing numbers, the curious vegetation of vanished eras became my habitat. There were vast saurians on land, ferocious nightmares of air, gigantic marine reptiles and monsters that battled in the warm seas.

"And always, too, there came a hotter, damper climate upon earth. Swamps and marshes became more numerous. Tropical jungles flourished everywhere, with weird, conical trees and hundred-foot ferns and evil flowers growing to incredible heights.

"So the years mounted by millions and the geologic ages were born again in my dreams and drifted on like a camera film run backward. The Carboniferous Age became an era of the future, the giant beasts of land decreased in number, steaming jungles and poisonous marshes covered what ground lay above water. The seas grew almost boiling. Terrific storms and deluges of hissing rain swept the globe. Not a single vertebrate now roamed upon land, only a few ephemeral moths winged their brief way through air, moths far larger than any we know, soft, immense, and spotted with gold, scarlet, indigo. But even these passed away, and life swarmed only in the almost universal sea.

"How long I have retrogressed in years I do not know, but it must be millions upon millions, beyond any computation. And it has been not only a dream that came to me, but a reality overshadowed by abysmal terror.

My brain has tottered on the brink of madness and I am so far degener-
ated physically that for three nights I have been taking powerful injections to keep me awake. I fear another vision more than I fear death."

The husky choking voice trailed away in a low gurgle. Over me as the
hours waned there had been creeping a nausea, a kind of revulsion
against my loathsome acquaintance and his mad story. A perspiration had
broken out all over me, and I was about to make a hasty departure when
that disgusting voice continued, but in a more uncertain and throatily
tired way.

"That last dream—Ugh! I shall never forget it. It haunts all my
thoughts and hovers deep within me like an evil incubus ready to de-
scend whenever I weaken.

"Dim sunlight filtered down through water that was thick with sediment and vile with elementary life. In masses of subaqueous growths
lurked nasty pulpy things. The black ooze beneath heaved with soft,
wriggling forms—gastropods, univalves, protozoa, cephalopods, infusoria, animalcules, and gelatinous forms of a myriad other kinds. A shadow
enveloped me—I stared up. Not far above, a giant cephalopod settled
toward me, its beak open, innumerable suckers quivering on tentacles
that were mushy as worms. I moved slowly aside—and found myself
enveloped in the ichorous filaments of a gigantic and viscous jelly-fish. I
do not know what happened—I do not wish to know. Ugh! I cannot
convey the vertigo caused by that sticky stuff—and the clammy life-
forms that originally rose in the ancient seas that once covered earth."

The voice trailed away and died, and silence descended stealthily. It
seemed to me that the invalid's figure had relaxed, and I thought his head
fell back. I did not wait to make sure as I stiffly stood up, for I felt uneasy,
yes, and slightly afraid. I do not know why it was, but even as I recoiled
physically from the stranger, so my spirit shrank as from a thing unclean
or accursed. Trembling a little, I steadied myself and paced down the
aisle after the briefest of muttered phrases, to which I heard no answer,
if indeed my acquaintance made one.

I had about reached the vestibule when a peculiar sound impinged on
my consciousness. I paid no attention to it, and tried to quicken my step.
My hand was outstretched toward the door, I believe, when that primeval cry froze me in my place and brought me facing about. It was a
whispered scream that died away hideously; a sub-human, sub-animal
wordless gurgle, like the death rattle in the throat of a drowning person.

Alfred Kramer may have dreamed his last dream. Psychologists tell
us that the subconscious mind may work at abnormal speed when the
conscious mind is at rest; and it is at least possible that a lifetime's

visions paraded through the fitful slumber of Alfred Kramer during those long seconds that I required in approaching the door. I do not know. And it may be true also that I was temporarily insane. Again, I do not know. But the sight that met my eyes when I whirled about could have been merciful only to madness. One may preserve an equilibrium in a completely normal world; and a madman would find, I suppose, a certain unity in his completely abnormal world; but to face the abnormal in the midst of every-day life, to find the incredible exchanging place with the usual, that is to unite insanity with sanity and make one doubt whether normality exists at all.

For when I spun around, I saw that Alfred Kramer had somehow risen to his feet. And as I stared in his direction, a frightful change took place.

His hands dropped from his wrists and thudded to the floor. His face suddenly went awry, slipped, melted away. The clothing squirmed, bulged, ripped off.

And now I knew the meaning of those motionless lips and that pasty face. It was a mask that I had been watching.

Swaying horribly for an ageless second, what was left of Alfred Kramer shook convulsively and collapsed.

On the floor lay a writhing mass of protoplasmic slime.

THE FIRE VAMPIRES

THIS IS A tale of war, and terror, and tyranny, and flaming death. It is a story that begins in the bleak abysses of space and ends upon the earth. It is the story of all mankind over a period of two decades. Yet it is also the story of one man, and one devil out of monstrous voids—but I anticipate.

I, Alyn Marsdale, venerable historian to the United Federation of Nations, have been deputed in this, the year of our Lord 2341, to chronicle the coming of the comet; but I cannot set the facts down as dead history, for the very deeds burn before my eyes and the strangeness of it all lives again. No man now existing could tell this story and remain unmoved, nor can I, though my work lies with files that gather dust, and papers that brown with age.

I shall begin with the beginning—or as much of it as we are likely to know; and I shall unfold the events as they were unfolded to us who lived through the disaster. As we look back now, with wisdom bought at the dearest sacrifice man has ever made, we wonder how we could have been so blind, could not have put together matters that were linked. But we did not, nor are we sure how much it would have helped if we had.

The new comet was discovered by Norby—Gustav Norby, the authority on cosmic life forms. Men had laughed at some of his speculations in the old days, but they do not laugh now. It was Norby who saw the comet on July 7, 2321. It was Norby who plotted its course and sent out the news that it would pass closer to earth than any heavenly body had ever come. It was Norby who predicted that there might be danger, that attendant phenomena would be widespread, that the very existence of earth was conceivably imperiled. And it was Norby who, by right of discovery, gave his name to the new comet.

When first seen, Norby's comet lay approximately five light-years beyond the solar system. At its estimated speed of fifty thousand miles per second, it would require about eighteen years to reach Earth. Consequently, the prognostications of future danger weighed lightly on the public mind. Eighteen years? Why, that was too far ahead to worry about.

Astronomers watched the distant comet through all of July and part of August. It showed up clearly as a curved nucleus, with a fan-shaped tail streaming away millions upon millions of miles behind it. Aside from its phenomenal speed, it was noticeable chiefly for its faint coloring of reddish blue.

On August 10, as the new comet was nearing the region of Alpha Centauri astronomers were electrified by its mysterious disappearance. Not the slightest trace of it remained. It was gone, vanished as though it had never been. The public jeered. Scientists looked puzzled as they tried to explain and could not.

On August 14, the world was stunned by the information that Norby's comet lay less than a billion miles beyond Pluto, and was approaching the sun at its former speed of fifty thousand miles per second! Within sixteen hours it would be passing the earth! Had it crossed more than four light-years of space in four days? "Impossible!" answered the wise men.

The world stared. Scientists everywhere were in a frenzy. It must be another comet. But how could any comet approach so close without having been observed?

At midnight of August 14 came the famous bulletin from Norby at the Mount Wilson observatory. It deserves to be quoted in full:

> New comet is definitely Norby's comet, first observed on July 7. Speed again calculated to be fifty thousand miles per second. Reconstruction of theoretical path brings it to last point at which Norby's comet was seen on August 10. Only two possible explanations. One, faulty previous observation. Unacceptable because of number of independent observers and witnesses. Two, *comet suddenly increased its speed far beyond that of light and leaped across five light-years of space so fast that light-rays have not yet reached us and will not for years!* Hence mysterious apparent disappearance of comet. Comet was present but approaching so much faster than light that rays had not arrived. Intelligent control of comet by living organisms forecast. Its action otherwise unaccountable by any known laws.

> (Signed) GUSTAV NORBY.

Plainly visible without the aid of glasses, the new comet drew the attention of anxious eyes wherever weather conditions permitted. Men felt uneasy or apprehensive. This could be no ordinary comet. Even its peculiar reddish-blue tint was different. Where primitive beliefs still survived in Africa and India and the jungles of South America, the coming of the comet was attended by a sort of wild hysteria. And in great metropolises, men could not look at the newcomer without emotions of wonder and doubt and awe.

Hour by hour Norby's comet grew brighter, drew closer. It swung past Pluto, hurtling steadily toward the sun. Rapid calculations showed that it would come dangerously close to the earth. Its mass was not sufficient to disrupt the solar system, but there was the very gravest danger of collision, and the possibility that fatal gas would poison Earth's atmosphere. By dawn, the comet was traversing the orbit of Neptune.

Radio broadcasts and television had spread the news, but the morning papers of August 15 sold like gold bricks, so eager was the public to read every shred of information about the menacing invader. Full-page headlines and flaring streamers told the story. The prophecies of disaster, the warnings of catastrophe, were printed. Norby sprang into instant fame. But what good was fame, men asked, if this were the end? Who could predict what would happen next?

A strange hush brooded over the great cities, throughout a sultry day. When the shadows of twilight darkened on the ground, men went out singly and in groups, by millions, to watch the newcomer. And long before darkness came, long before the first star shone, Norby's comet blazed forth bluish and brilliant, terribly near in the zenith, its tail sweeping fanwise in a majestic but awe-inspiring streamer of tremendous length. It was a marvel of the heavens, an omen, a prodigy that men compared to the Dark Star which had swept out of space in the Twentieth Century.

Would it wreck the earth? Would it plunge onward in its wild rush and crash flaming down upon a continent? Would it weld with the sun and cause who knew what disasters of collision or immeasurable heat? Humanity shivered at the terrifying and menacing beauty of the comet—so near, so dreadfully near, and so radiant that all the stars were outshone, and the moon gleamed wan and feeble.

A murmur of voices swelled along city streets; in the open country was heard the restless rustle of animals, the shrill whinny of frantic horses. Night turned to a kind of day. Gigantic and supernal, the comet visibly drew nearer, grew brighter, shining like a second and larger sun with a swath of splendor trailing away millions of miles behind it.

The murmur of humanity was hushed for a minute—then swelled to a babel as television and newspapers broadcast the latest bulletin from Norby:

Unaccountable change in path of Norby's comet. At 10:41 P.M., W. S. T., comet turned at right angles from course toward Earth. Estimated distance less than half a million miles. Present course in direction opposite that of Earth's rotation. Too early to state whether it will become permanent satellite circling Earth, or continue on a new trajectory and pass out of solar system. *No explanation for sudden deviation except control by rational beings.*

NORBY

As night raced westward around the world, so raced the intruder. America was lighted as if by a dim day; the comet shone reflected from the Pacific like a sunken volcanic fire; it swept across Asia while priests and fakirs knelt in supplication; nothing else within memory brought out such vast crowds in the capitals of Europe. Livid and flaming, it hurtled ever westward. The passengers on trans-Atlantic liners saw it flare up from the east and blaze high overhead. It followed darkness around the world, and when it reached America again, anxious eyes saw it burn above—*but farther away.*

At midnight it was very faint over the Mississippi valley. People on the western plains could hardly discern it. They were not disappointed, for they had seen Norby's latest communication:

Comet swinging away from Earth after complete circling of globe. New path will carry it out of solar system toward region of Antares. Phenomenon inexplicable. Nothing in history of astronomy to parallel it. All danger past.

NORBY.

On the morning of August 16, two men were engaged in angry conversation at the Mount Wilson observatory. Gustav Norby wore a look of confidence. His young assistant, Hugh Arver, was alternately skeptical and irritated.

"It's preposterous!" he burst out. "Just because a comet acts as no comet ever has behaved you think that it is controlled by intelligent beings. Why, man can no more control his own world than—than I can wish myself onto Mars merely by wishing!"

"Perhaps man *will* control every movement of Earth some day, Hugh," answered the older man quietly. "Remember, our civilization is only five thousand years old. And our scientific achievements are the product of only six or seven hundred years. There is no reason for thinking that our world alone contains life."

"That may be, but the surface temperature of the comet you yourself placed at about 1100° Centigrade. Why, nothing could live in such heat!"

"Nothing that we know could. But what of things that we do not know? How do you explain these?"

Norby picked up a pile of newspapers, telegrams, and radiograms. "Here are the accounts of more than *fifteen thousand* mysterious deaths last night from every country that lay under the path of the comet: America, the Philippines, China, Russia, Germany, France, Spain—a dozen others. Every death was exactly alike—a flash in the air like lightning, a man or woman who suddenly burst into flames as though by spontaneous combustion—and then, only a heap of bones. There are fifteen thousand instances of that fiery death already known, and the reports are still coming in. How do you account for them, Hugh? Does it not seem strange that they all occurred precisely when the comet arrived?"

"What if they did? Every one expected danger if it came too close. It might easily have loosed gases or energy that somehow struck down those thousands of people."

"Did you ever hear of a gas that picked one man out of a crowd, killed him, and left the others unharmed? Did you ever hear of lightning that drifted toward a man, suddenly shot around him, and consumed him instantly, and then drifted on again? No, no, Hugh, there was method behind this, method and purpose."

"What? Whose?"

Norby shrugged. "I don't know. Wait and see."

"The comet's gone. You can't prove anything."

"The comet is gone, as you say. But suppose it returns?"

Hugh stared for a minute. Then he brightened. "It won't in our lifetime. History does not record its previous appearance. The course it followed as it left would not bring it back again for nearly a thousand years, if at all."

"If it proceeded according to natural laws. But it didn't. It crossed nearly five light-years of space in four days. It turned at right angles to its trajectory and circled Earth like a satellite. Then it shot off on a still different course. It behaved as one might imagine a space-ship from Mars would behave, increasing its speed to reach Earth, circling Earth to survey it, and then departed home, or continuing to other worlds—*after sampling the provisions of Earth!*"

"Norby! You're mad!" came Hugh's startled cry.

"I am not sure. Can you offer a better explanation?"

Hugh was silent. He was skeptical—as every one else was skeptical. Yet he thought—as hundreds of other far-sighted individuals thought, trying to understand this riddle of the skies. The comet was the greatest

news item of the year—of centuries. Its mysterious arrival and departure, the peculiar and terrifying death that slew thousands of human
beings in its wake, the lightning that was not lightning, exerted a spell on
the imagination and yet baffled the mind with facts that were not put
together. Who could put them together? It seems so easy now, and yet—

On another hot August day, six years later, Norby and Hugh were
descending from the observatory in early afternoon. They had taken
dozens of photographs by the new 800-inch reflector the preceding
night, and had spent the late morning in an examination of the pictures.

"That new telescope is certainly a marvel," Norby was saying. "Why,
its range is dozens of times that which the old telescope had. And
Pletzka's force-tube which creates a vacuum through Earth's atmosphere does away with heat waves and all the distortions which used to
trouble astronomers. Why, they would never have been able to see that
new star in the Antares cluster."

"It's strange that the star didn't appear in earlier photographs."

The two men had reached the outer door and emerged into daylight.
A couple of workmen were passing some hundred yards distant.

"We ought to be getting a storm tonight," remarked Hugh after gazing
at the sky. "There seems to be a lot of heat lightning around. Look at that
fire-ball over by those trees."

Norby was already staring intently at the trees. A bluish striated light
seemed to envelop them. Strictly speaking, it was not a fireball so much
as a curiously motionless network of electricity.

"There's something unnatural about that lightning," said Norby. "I've
never seen any—great God!"

The bluish network suddenly leaped across to the passing workmen
and flung itself around them in coils of fire with two fingers of light
crackling into each man's head.

A tortured shriek burst from them as from one man. A more intense
flicker momentarily irradiated the network. There came two spurts of
blinding, livid flame, two volumes of yellow smoke issuing up—and
where the men had stood lay two calcined skeletons. For only an instant
the odd lightning hung poised over the bones. Without warning it flashed
toward Norby and Hugh. But the door to the observatory was sealed
against it—some deep instinct had caused them to dash inside and fasten
the door even as the lightning flashed.

Hugh's face was white. "Good heavens!" he gasped. "What was it?
Why, that thing acted as if it were alive, like an animal springing after
prey! Those men—I'll never forget them!"

Norby had a strained, queer look in his eyes as he answered, "I'm afraid you're right, Hugh, horribly right. An animal after prey—"

"But it can't be, it *can't* be! That was lightning!"

"Was it? Did you ever see lightning act like that? Have you forgotten—"

Recognition flashed into Hugh's eyes. "Norby's comet!"

"Yes. Do you recall the epidemic of deaths that occurred when the comet came in '21? Thousands and thousands of them. And the reports—the deaths must have come about much in the same fashion as these two did. That comet has returned, Hugh, and I'm afraid for the worst. It departed toward Antares, you know, and last night we found—"

"A new star in the region of Antares!"

"Probably it was the comet. It may be within striking distance of the earth already—it must be!"

"What can we do? How can we escape if you are right?"

"We can do nothing but stay here so long as we are sealed in. The other deaths all occurred outdoors. I think we are safe for the present."

Throughout the afternoon they remained inside, yet they heard and saw the tragedy that swept its fantastic way around the world. Television brought them pictures of additional deaths. They heard the story of an electrical plague that seemed to have broken out everywhere. Hour by hour the total of lives lost mounted. Men, women, and children were stricken down in city streets, enveloped as they emerged from buildings, burned as they worked in fields, incinerated on public highways and aboard ships at sea, slain even in aircraft. Nowhere on sea or land or in the sky was there safety. Every country in the world from Alaska to Antarctica, from Europe to Australia, reported the fiery death. Not a city of any size escaped the striated networks and the consuming bolts.

But it was at nightfall that the accumulating panic and terror swept to a climax. It was at nightfall, beginning along the Atlantic coast, and following darkness ever westward around the earth, that the incredible, monstrous, appalling truth flamed in the heavens in mile-high letters of fire.

Norby and Hugh heard the broadcast which announced that Norby's comet had again been sighted, moving across China. They heard in stunned incredulity the account of that new phenomenon which had also made its first appearance over China. But they could not believe, they would not believe, until the afternoon had worn away, and nightfall came.

Then they saw it—the comet streaking up from the east, brilliant and bluish-red and strange, with a corona haloing it and its tail fanning away behind in a vast curve.

They saw the striations and streaks of lightning that moved innumerably through the entire heavens, so that the stars were outshone and freaked by lines of fire, *lines that moved and formed themselves into letters, words, and a message, a mile high, miles long, shining in terrible flame against the darkness behind!*

Awed and speechless, Norby stared while a strained look settled on Hugh's face. They watched the message spell itself out—a message so simple, and yet of such stupendous import to mankind.

"People of Earth," it began, "you are ours by right of conquest. Henceforth and forever you belong to us, of Ktynga, known to you as Norby's comet.

"You cannot fight us, nor defeat us, nor evade us. We are superior to you in every way.

"At irregular intervals we shall return and claim as our due from twenty to fifty thousand of your inhabitants.

"We desire nothing else. But we insist upon the payment, and we shall take it. If you resist, we shall take more.

"On our next visit, we shall claim John Hanby, the president of the Federated Nations; Axel Gruno, master scientist of the world; Tsin Lo Hoy, commander-in-chief of the international army; and Gustav Norby of the Mount Wilson observatory.

"These men must place themselves in the evening of August 27, 2332, at the peak of Mount Wilson. If they are not there, we shall take a hundred thousand lives instead of twenty.

"FTHAGGUA, LORD OF KTYNGA"

"What can it mean?" gasped Hugh. "It's mad! It's unbelievable! You—Norby! Why should you be chosen? It's all a hoax!"

"Easy, Hugh," answered Norby to his excited assistant. "The danger is apparently over for the present—and we have a full five years to talk. It is not a hoax."

"For God's sake, what is it?"

The older man looked tired as he replied gently, "What I have long feared and warned the public about has happened—we are threatened by invaders from outside. This may mark the passing of mankind."

"Impossible! We'll fight!"

"With what?"

Hugh was silent.

Norby continued, "We can't even reach the comet. And how are we going to fight a wholly alien form of life of which we so far know virtually nothing?"

"If it *is* life."

"It is—and life of a vicious and frightening kind."

"It *must* be a hoax, it must be! How could the creatures have known English? What sort of thing could they be? Why, there's nothing on Earth to account for them!"

"True, but you forget. The message we saw appeared in Spanish over Spain, French over France, Russian over Russia, and so on. Each country read the message in its own language. Was that a joke? It was a miraculously intelligent joke, if it was. Don't forget the earlier visit of the comet. I had a theory then that no one would accept. Briefly, Hugh, the comet is controlled by life of a sort with which we are unfamiliar, possessing knowledge and power far beyond ours. They are electrical things, pure energy that has an intelligence and reason.

"Somehow, they feed on human life, human energy. They killed thousands on their first visit. They sucked out life from living men. Vampires—Fire Vampires—that's what they are. And they sucked out knowledge, too, mind and soul and brain, so that they were able to study and master the nature of Earth before they returned a second time.

"Don't ask me how they did it, I can only look at the results and guess. Somehow they feed on our life-force, spirit, energy, call it what you will. In so doing, they also absorb the entire knowledge of the victim. From the tens of thousands of people that they have now slain, they have obtained new energy for themselves, and a great cross-section if not virtually all the knowledge of Earth. Man is doomed. Earth has been made into a slave planet, owned by Fire Vampires.

"God knows where the comet's headed now—out toward its other slave-planets, I suppose, or to explore for new, inhabited worlds to subjugate. It's easy to see why they picked out Hanby and Gruno and Hoy: they are three leading minds of Earth today, information that the Vampires could have sucked from almost any one of their victims. But it's also easy to see that they cannot seek out and find specific victims; otherwise they would not have ordered these three individuals to be segregated in an isolated place."

"But why you, Norby? I can't understand that!"

"I think it's because they fear me. No one believed my theories and warnings, Hugh, but many people read them. The Fire Vampires probably reasoned that if I was several jumps ahead of the world in knowing about them I might also find some means to thwart them. They could have waited while we four sacrifices were brought together, and claimed us now, but they must have had urgent reasons for departing, or else they are so confident of their power that they merely want our lives as a precaution, and can afford to wait a few years."

"What can be done? What is there to be done?"

"I don't know, Hugh, but I'm going to need you. We have five years—and a short enough time it is."

On August 27, 2332, Norby stood again in the observatory. The intervening years had been crowded with labors and plans and projects that seemed to get nowhere. The immediate panic created by the comet had worn off the world by now, and a myriad explanations had been advanced to account for the phenomenon. The eve of its return was approaching, and excitement swelled along all the highways and cities of the world once more, excitement and uncertainty and fear.

Norby peered out from the protection of a heavy green curtain as if he were expecting some one. He looked ten years older, and a grim weight had taken its place on his shoulders. His hair was fast whitening. Wrinkles furrowed his face and forehead.

All at once his countenance brightened faintly. A few minutes later, Hugh rapped cautiously on the unused storeroom that concealed Norby. The scientist admitted him.

"Did you carry it through successfully?" he asked anxiously.

"Yes. I spread word that you had fallen into the river while on an outing with me, that you had failed to come up, that I could not reach you because of the steep banks, and that all points were to be watched for your body. I was detained several hours by the police for questioning, which delayed me, but finally released on my own recognizance."

"Good work! You are sure that my death is firmly implanted in every one's mind?"

"Yes. The television broadcasts have already gone out."

"Did you learn anything further?"

"Hanby, Hoy, and Gruno are on their way. They will be at the appointed spot by noon, without you, and firmly convinced of your death."

"If there were anything to gain, Hugh, I would be out there with them, but there isn't. In five years, the world hasn't been able to accomplish one definite thing toward repelling the Fire Vampires. If the deaths of those three men will save a needless waste of life, their martyrdom will not be wasted. The whole race is periled, Hugh, and no one man can think of himself first. But I have hopes. It's a long shot I'm taking, and if I lose, the blood of thousands will stain my hands, but if I win the danger will be over. And your help is essential."

"You know you can count on me."

Hugh walked to the one window of their hiding-place and pulled back one edge of the curtain to peer outside. As he did so, it rolled up with a snap.

"Quick!" Norby shouted. "Pull it down again before some one sees us!"

He was too late. Hugh jerked at the recalcitrant curtain, but a member of the staff passing by outside glanced up. Norby dived for a dark corner hoping he had not been seen—vain hope! A smile of recognition lighted the face of the man outside, a smile that turned to a writhe of agony as a whirling network of fire flung itself in rippling striations around him.

"They've come again!" gasped Hugh.

"And the damage is done," said Norby with a tight hardening of the lines around his mouth. "But don't blame yourself," he added as he saw the downcast look on Hugh's face. "I should have known better than to rely on those antiquated curtains."

How terribly right he was he found out as the day wore on. Twenty thousand lives if Norby, Gruno, Hoy, and Hanby were sacrificed; so the message had said. A hundred thousand if the instructions were not obeyed. By nightfall, the hundred thousand and countless more had perished in America alone. The whole fury of the Fire Vampires seemed concentrated on the country where one of their intended victims lived. And Norby knew that the Fire Vampires, in absorbing the life of the man who recognized him, had absorbed also his last impression: the figures of Hugh and himself in the storeroom.

Fate had beaten him, but he would not yet give in, not even when, after nightfall, he saw another message flame in the sky, a message that announced the next return of the creatures on July 17, 2339, and threatened the extinction of all human life on the North American continent unless Norby were sacrificed. He was requested to go on that day to the same spot where Gruno and his companions had met death.

Norby regarded the message with cold, murderous eyes. With a deadly calm he called Hugh to him then, and they prepared for part of their work. They adjusted the giant reflector to follow the comet that now blazed triumphantly in the zenith. They released Pletzka's force-tube which created an 800-inch vacuum through the air-blanket above the telescope.

And when Norby finally looked at the comet, immeasurably magnified, and nearer by far than even the moon, he uttered a cry of surprise.

"Hugh! There's a vast structure of some sort on that white-hot surface!"

Together they stared. Dim through the aura of the comet gleamed its almost molten surface, and on it loomed a great darker spot, a fantastic architecture, dream-like, unreal, with curved angles and alien geometry of sinister beauty. But of other buildings there was no sign, and there was no trace of the Fire Vampires.

After long scrutiny, and after hundreds of photographs had been taken, Norby commented with a puzzled air, "There is something curious about this. I don't understand it. If only I could put things together!"

"What's the trouble?" asked Hugh.

"Why, there's only one building on the comet. It's as large as a city, of course, and could house many thousands of the Fire Vampires, but it seems strange. Again, isn't it rather odd that they would raid the earth and still leave no one behind, not even a guard?"

"Not so strange," said Hugh. "There may be a large number of the things still contained in the structure where of course we wouldn't be able to see them."

Norby shook his head doubtfully. Somewhere in these facts lay the weakness of the Fire Vampires, the weakness that they feared he would discover. But where? And for that matter, how could he tell, among the countless photographs of the Fire Vampires which had been taken in various parts of the world, which one was "Fthaggua, Lord of Ktynga?"

"I have it!" he suddenly shouted to Hugh. "I've found it!"

Hugh looked as if he thought his superior had gone mad under the strain. "Found what?" he queried.

"The weakness! All the Fire Vampires are reddish—except Fthaggua, the blue one that we ourselves saw!"

"Well?"

But more than that Norby refused to divulge.

I must leave to others the story of the social and economic collapse that disorganized the world between 2332 and 2339. It is safe to say generally that civilization was plunged half-way toward the mire out of which it had so painfully risen. Most people came to regard the next arrival of the comet as doomsday. A sense of fatalism combined with a desire to extract every possible pleasure from the remaining years and created a prevailing chaos in which lawlessness, disorder, crime, and vice of every sort were universal. Scientists, it is true, worked feverishly in efforts to devise new weapons of destruction, to break down the atom, to control the laws of stellar mechanics, to invent space transports which in a last resort might convey the population of Earth to another planet. But the time was too short. Throughout the period, a tremendous exodus from America was under way, resulting in serious overpopulation of the nearest countries, and causing almost continual riots, struggles, and intermittent warfare.

Norby had plans—secret plans, partly because he was gambling on a long chance, partly because secrecy was imperative to his success, and partly because his life was constantly in danger. Branded as a coward and a traitor for not sacrificing himself with Gruno, Hanby, and Loy, accused of being directly responsible for a hundred thousand deaths, he found his work seriously hampered.

Somehow, with that indomitable courage that man achieves in his deepest despair, and despite the white hair which now hung above his haggard face, he carried on. There were rumors of blasting operations around Mount Wilson—but the entire mountain was now forbidden territory by governmental decree. There were trainload after trainload of apparatus that wound their way toward the observatory—long-needed repairs were being made, was the official word.

But all the crowded events of those years must be left for other hands to record. I pass to that fateful day of July 17, 2339.

"Are you sure you have all the directions straight?" asked Norby anxiously as he and Hugh stood on the peak of Mount Wilson.

"Yes," and Hugh briefly repeated them.

The white-haired man nodded, and they went to their stations.

In the former peak of Mount Wilson now lay a deep crater, as though a volcanic explosion had blown its tip off. The careful dynamiting and patient camouflage that were man-made had succeeded in creating an illusion of natural eruption. Near the center of this pit was what looked like a large, flat boulder, upon which Norby took his stand.

The walls of the crater rose almost sheer for five hundred feet, and were lined to the top with a series of irregular projections and ledges. Toward the biggest of these, at the base, Hugh made his way. An observer would have been startled to watch him apparently walk through the solid rock and disappear.

From the shadow and protection of a cavern, Hugh looked out at Norby, who stood impassively on the boulder. Behind him was a labyrinth of machinery, including enormous dynamos that droned with a dull rhythm. In front of him were several instruments, an electro-interferometer for detecting the electrical charge of the atmosphere within a radius of ten miles and a "staggered" triple switch being the most important.

The hours crawled by. A hot sun beat down on the crater. The silent waiting wrought upon the tense nerves of both men. They felt the burden of this last attempt to defeat the Fire Vampires, felt it more because they were going so largely on deduction. One slip—and the human sacrifices, the living bait that was Norby—would meet flaming death. One error—and millions of human beings would perish as an entire continent was depopulated.

So the portentous day waned, and the sun drifted overhead and burned westward, and shadows crept out farther from the western walls of the crater and lengthened upon the jagged floor, and twilight approached. Still there had come no trace of the Fire Vampires. Into Hugh's thoughts came a hope.

Perhaps they would not come! Perhaps the comet had broken apart in the outer reaches of space—perhaps it had been defeated by a superior race somewhere in the cosmic voids—perhaps it had even put up a bluff and had never intended to return!

As darkness came on, Hugh's hope grew stronger. The strain of the day had been great, he felt very tired, and every passing minute meant an increasing chance of safety.

He glanced again at the mercury mirror, that, beneath tons of rock, still reflected the heavens.

And there shone the comet, flashing into sight huge and brilliant, as though it had materialized out of nothing.

"Norby! It's come!" he shouted. His weariness dropped from him like magic.

He looked at the electro-interferometer. Its pointer was jumping and swinging madly.

Then he looked up across the crater and his heart skipped a beat. A vast mass of bluish lightning drifted ominously above the pit, as though suspicious, yet hungry for prey. In the darkness, Hugh could not make out Norby's reaction, and if the worst happened, he did not want to witness Norby's fate.

The sinister thing poised far above its victim, contracted—and like light hurtled downward to fling coils of living fire around Norby.

Hugh's hand, already resting on the staggered switch, threw it shut with a convulsive movement that brought three sharp staccato clicks.

At the first click, Norby dropped from sight through a trap-door while streamers of bluish energy ravened furiously where their prey had vanished.

At the second click, a solid sheet of fire shot across the upper rim of the crater, closing it completely with a roof of blazing incandescence.

The bluish Fire Vampire suddenly sensed danger and leaped upward—too late. Like a trapped animal, it halted at the solid flame that shut it in. A sound like a piercing cry, a noise like a hiss, emanated from it.

At the third click, from a hundred points on those jagged ledges shot a hundred roaring bolts of electricity—ten-million-volt streams that thundered and spluttered and crackled, crisscrossing the entire crater with a hell of surging power. In that mad and frightful glare, to the deafening crash of giant bolts, Fthaggua, the blue Fire Vampire, twisted in a frantic effort to escape. Only for an instant were its thrashings visible—only till that moment when the roaring electricity crackled through it, and there came a titanic flash as of a cosmic short-circuit, and a blackness of blackness followed.

And all over the world there swept a flash in the skies and a flame on the ground, every Fire Vampire was seen to writhe in torment and disappear in a spurt of diffused incandescence.

Thus the Fire Vampires passed away—passed away forever, leaving behind them only the comet that is now a satellite of Earth, with an identical rotation period, so that every night it blazes above the eastern horizon and trails high across the heavens.

Before me, as I write, lies a communication from Norby, in answer to a request of mine. It seems most fitting to close this record by an extract from that missive.

"You ask me how the Fire Vampires were beaten," he replies.

"I can only say that it was by guesswork and good fortune as much as by knowledge.

"Several facts that I had gathered impressed me. Why was there only *one* building on the comet? Why where there no guards left behind? Why were all the Fire Vampires *red* except one that was *blue?*

"A thought came to me—one of those guesses in the dark. The answer is, I said to myself, that the blue Vampire is Fthaggua, Lord of Ktynga. And there is only *one* Fire Vampire in all! Somehow, this monstrous ab-human entity grew up as a unit composed of individuals, a disconnected organism that nevertheless might die if its main member were killed. That main member, I reasoned, must be Fthaggua. All the red Fire Vampires were limbs, tentacles, parts, as it were, able to behave like separate individuals within a limited territory, but bound by invisible ties of energy to the parent.

"If my speculations were true, then we would only need to destroy Fthaggua, and the other countless parts of this weird organism would of necessity likewise perish. And since the thing was pure energy, I reasoned that pure energy might short-circuit it, or diffuse it, "ground it," in the terms of earth science. Together, Hugh and I worked out the details concealing anodes and cathodes for carrying an enormous charge all around the crater. The results you know.

"The danger is past. Yet I cannot help feeling a certain respect for an entity that almost made good its huge bluff, that almost succeeded in its pretense that there were millions of Fire Vampires when there was really only one—Fthaggua, Lord of Ktynga."

SPAWN OF THE SEA

Том Gordon had never paid any undue attention to the bottle until the moment he stumbled and knocked it from its shelf to shatter upon the floor, but from that instant his interest became prodigious.

Tom had been making a comfortable income from his gift shop for several years. He made a specialty of odd things—Oriental jewelry, antique terra-cotta figurines, illuminated parchment leaves, African sculptures, old Java batiks, and a thousand other things that were both unusual and artistic.

Every summer, during the slack season, he went abroad for a month or so and wandered from place to place purchasing as he went whatever odds and ends appealed to him. The bottle was one of the acquisitions of his most recent trip. It came to his attention when he was idling on the shore of Fezd-El-Tuah one morning and saw an Arab urchin playing with it. Tom wanted the bottle because it was obviously the craftsmanship of a bygone century. It looked something like a decanter, something like a Greek amphora, and was perfectly blown, with a long, slender neck and a gracefully rounded base. At one time it must have been buried, for stains and iridescent colors made even more opaque its original coloring of brown. It was stoppered and sealed with wax that had partly weathered away but still seemed almost as hard as stone.

Tom bargained with the shrewd gamin and finally obtained the bottle for the equivalent of fifteen cents. His Arabic was as poor as the lad's French, so that the two had difficulty in understanding each other. All that Tom discovered about the history of the curious bottle was that the urchin had recently found it half buried in the sand.

The bottle made its way back to America with the rest of Tom's purchases, and in due time was placed upon a shelf. No one priced it during the months it stood there, but Tom didn't mind, since he had bought it primarily to add a touch of atmosphere to his shop. And on the shelf it remained, half forgotten, until the accident that destroyed it.

Tom had little opportunity to regret his loss. His annoyance vanished when he saw the yellowed paper lying among bits of broken glass. Despite its apparent age, the paper was still strong and covered with quaint, fine script, though the writing on the outer leaf had faded for the most part to illegibility.

He took the tightly rolled manuscript home with him that night with as considerable interest as he had ever had in any of his purchases; and the dawn of another day was breaking before he had fully deciphered it and transcribed it into modern English. Most of the first page was hopelessly dimmed; he could make nothing of the superscription; and even the date was ambiguous. He deciphered a "17" but whether the year intended was "17—" or "—17" it was impossible to decide. Tantalized by the unreadable introduction, he eventually proceeded with the body of a manuscript that was in many ways even more tantalizing; and the hours flew by with never a thought from him as he pored over the script. To be sure, he grasped an occasional word on the outer leaf whose writing had been largely effaced by the action of sunlight, but nothing like a continuous narrative became possible until he turned to the second page, which began in the middle of a sentence.

"—day out the storm broke. We passengers were all ordered below deck while the crew raced above hauling in sail and trying to save the ship.

"May God's grace protect the seven seas from another such gale. Out of a sooty sky the rain lashed in torrents, the wind screamed through the rigging, and the vastest waves that ever were boiled up around us. The ship lurched and tipped as though any minute it would turn over or sink, and not one of us but was bruised from head to foot after an hour of wild pitching to and fro. The women, poor things, were all the more terrified, for it was dangerous to risk lighting the lamps; so we huddled in the dark and could hardly hear the shouting of the crew above the terrible uproar, what with the waves pounding, and thunder crashing, and the wind howling in a kind of fury. But besides these, we heard ominous cracks, and heavy objects smash across the decks; yet we knew not what went on up there.

"There was little food to be found, and that little of course went to the women and children. The rest of us did what we could to tie them and ourselves to anything solid, or brace ourselves against sudden lurches. We got no sleep, neither did we talk, such was the fear upon us.

"Many hours passed with the ship staggering and thus being battered; yet I knew not at what time God's wrath descended. There was a long, sickening slide of the ship, a groaning and bursting of timbers, and then a sudden deafening crash. We heard running feet, and next the panic caught us, poor devils, for the hatches were unbattened and a voice roared down that the ship was sinking.

"All was noise and confusion, the air a sound and frenzy, every one bawling and struggling and fighting to get out, only a few of us remembering that we were gentlemen, such was the terror. Up on deck we found the wildest disorder, two of the masts down, the other sail blown to tatters, and one of the boats squarely smashed.

The crew were desperately trying to launch the seaworthy boats, but another was wrecked before it got clear. By the glare of lightning we saw the awful scene. The captain, God have mercy on his soul, stood by his post. He ordered the passengers off first. Gun in either hand, he shot down the cowards who tried to save themselves by leaving the women behind.

"I hastened toward the boat nearest me. That is the last I remembered save of hearing a sharp crack and receiving from behind a blow on my head. Pain numbed my limbs as total blackness blotted out the scene.

"For a very long time I must have lost my senses. I awakened with a throbbing headache and a thirst. I opened my eyes to the glare of sun. The sea was like a sapphire, smooth and motionless and bright as far as I could see, and no land anywhere.

"When I attempted to rise, my head throbbed so fiercely that I fell back. I felt it and discovered a swelling, with dried blood already caked into a scab, by which I judged that I must have lain unconscious for at least two days. I was weak, the pangs of hunger assailed me, and an intolerable thirst parched my mouth. With difficulty I finally dragged myself to a clogged scupper that retained some warm, dirty rainwater and drank it in gulps.

"Feeling considerably refreshed, I rested until my headache had subsided, then cautiously arose. I was still weak, but I needed to know the best—or the worst—about my predicament.

"The deck was swept clean of every movable object and the framework itself wrecked in places. Besides listing, the ship hung low. I surmised that it had sprung a leak or shipped a quantity of water. Not another soul appeared to be aboard.

"I made my way to a hatch and descended into gloom. The matches in my pocket were useless from having been soaked in the storm. I am no sailor, and knew little about the nature of ships, but I was acquainted with the general plan of this one and sloshed through a couple of inches of water to the galley. Long fumbling around in darkness was finally rewarded by the discovery of dry matches, one of which I promptly used to light a lamp. I satisfied my hunger with the first leftovers that came to hand—stale bread, a piece of salt cod, and some raw potatoes, washed down with a draft of English whisky that refreshed me greatly.

"I then set out to examine the ship. In the passengers' quarters I found three corpses, which I heaved overboard after brief prayers for the repose of their souls. I found two more bodies in the crew's quarters. And I discovered one living man.

"He must have been among those shot by the captain for disobeying the command to let the women and children escape first, and had crawled below later; for I came upon him hanging from a berth. At any rate, a ball had pierced his thigh and gone clean through. He suffered much from loss of blood, had a fever, and was delirious when I discovered him. But if gangrene did not set in, he had a fair chance to recover. I did what I could for him, glad of any companionship, even though it might not be of the best, and devoutly prayed that he would live. Whether the other passengers and the crew had taken to the boats or been claimed by the sea, I do not know. There was no one else aboard, and I can scarcely believe that anything human could have survived so terrific a storm.

"I next went over the remainder of the ship. The hold had filled with an amount of water that I considered dangerous, and I wondered how much longer the ship would last. I could not determine if it had sprung a leak and was still settling toward its grave, or if it had shipped an extraordinary amount of water in the gale. The hold was an evil-smelling place where the cargo had shifted and some boxes broken open, the others likewise being or becoming waterlogged. I do not know what the cargo was, but from as much as I could see of the shattered boxes, it appeared to consist equally of a greenish powder which I judged to be some chemical, a whitish salt that I also could not identify, a gummy, malodorous substance, and boxes simply marked 'seeds,' none of these latter being broken.

"My search then took me to the captain's quarters, which were a bitter disappointment. I hunted everywhere, but the ship's log was gone, including the sailing-chart. There were other maps and papers, but not a scrap that would indicate our position, even as it was at the height of the storm. Most of the instruments were hopelessly damaged and useless except to someone who might know how to repair them.

"In the galley I found a great many barrels of salt pork, salt cod, flour, potatoes, various condiments, five tubs of pickles, much liquor, and varying amounts of corn, nuts, rice, coconuts, venison, and so on, together with about two dozen live geese, chickens, and turkeys. Altogether there were ample provisions, upon which two men could subsist for many months, possibly a year even. The supply of fresh water was low, but I collected about two barrels more in different parts of the ship which retained rain-water from the recent blow.

"At intervals I ministered to the sick man. Toward evening he began to improve. A couple of days later, the fever left him and he thereafter grew rapidly better.

"I cannot convey the loneliness of the next month, and it would be idle to make the attempt. Bill—his full name was William Gehrety—and I wore out our eyes peering vainly for sails that never came, and land that we could not find. We had no conception of where we were, since the ship might have been blown hundreds of miles off her course during the gale. According to the last reckoning he had heard, we were approximately nine hundred miles from the nearest known land. Nine hundred? It might as well have been nine thousand. Yet we continued to hope, even though we knew we were far off the trade route which, God knows, was travelled by no more than three or four ships a year, in this sea remote from the Americas, and farther still from England.

"We spent weary days building a crude boat, calked it with tar, rigged out a clumsy sail, and tested it. I doubt whether a craft was ever more unseaworthy. We hadn't the heart to go to certain death in it, for it wouldn't steer true, it pitched crazily, and we couldn't put into it a fraction of the water and provisions that we would need. We learned much by this experience, but we were also discouraged. Nevertheless, disheartened by the alternatives of eventual starvation on our prison, or certain death by sea, we set to work slowly erecting a more substantial boat.

"So the days went by, and the sun shone in deep blue skies, and the water lapped softly against the sides, and at night the stars came out brilliantly except when the moon rode high. Yet never a sail hove in sight, and though we probably drifted with currents, there was nothing to tell us how rapidly, and we saw no land. By ourselves, we could not repair and raise and rig a mast large enough to do us any good, for the season of calms had come, and since what canvas we had was too small for any benefit short of a stiff blow, we saved it for our boat.

"There was furthermore around the ship a bad smell that got on our nerves. It became stronger as the days passed until we determined to investigate its source. We traced it to the hold. We tried bailing the water out but the stench was so sickening that we were compelled to cease. The water in the hold was queer stuff, unusually warm, thick and slimy and a pale green in color. The cargo had evidently gone bad, or the chemicals, if that's what they were, caused the smell. We decided that the odor would dissipate in time, but it was so bad below that we took to sleeping on deck and going down only for our meals.

"There were strange noises that also bothered us: not the usual creakings and strainings of an old ship, but something we couldn't quite place. We used to hear it, as though down in the hold, or far away, a stirring as of someone awakening and a simmer like water coming to a boil.

"The smell didn't vanish. It got worse, until even though it wasn't so bad in the daytime on deck, at night when we slept it seeped up and polluted the air. We tried closing the hatches but it did no good. Then it got into the food, and we not only had to smell the stench but taste it.

"I don't know when the combination of curious sounds and horrible odors became too much for our nerves. I think it was the forty-third day of our drifting, but it doesn't matter. All the preceding night, the stink had hung heavily like a smoke cloud, and the strange noise, almost like that of a heart, became a rhythmic pulse as the night wore on. I at first believed my nerves were beginning to give way, but since Bill had had the same impressions, I thought we couldn't both be wrong. Somehow, I felt uneasy. The monotony and solitude were bad enough. Now we had a rotten miasma and a singular noise to contend with besides.

"That morning we decided to make another investigation of the hold. Since we knew that the smell came from there, we suspected that the noises might have some connection with it. Perhaps a fermentation was going on. If worst came to worst, we might as well devote our time to carrying the bilge out or heaving the boxes and cargo overboard. I myself was rather sure that they were responsible for both the bad smell and the queer sounds.

"Going below was like walking into salt water, the odor was that strong, pushing and holding us back, a nauseating odor, filthy, abominable, and beast-like. I think I was faint when we reached the hold, for I cannot otherwise quite account for what happened. Bill was carrying a lighted candle while I unbattened the hatch and looked in.

"'Shut it! *Shut it!'* Bill screamed, and we hurled ourselves against the door, fastening it securely. Down in the hold we had seen a vast, shapeless mass of undulating greenish-white stuff, thick as skin, with a beating motion like a pulse. The revolting odor came from that mass, but what terrified us most was the way that pulpy substance leaped up at us when we opened the hatch! Leaped, like an unknown animal after prey, with a furious beating of the pulse, its surface writhing into tentacles that flung at us, and a hiss like an inarticulate cry.

"The candle went out when Bill jumped. Darkness dropped upon us like a shroud. We heard the thing undulating in the hold, and pounding against the hatch. Would the barrier hold? Or was the noise only that odd pulse beating? Or the hammering of our own hearts?

"Panic caught us. We dashed for the other hatchways and fought to get out. Once on deck, we felt a bit ashamed, with the morning sun shining hotly. We looked at each other, white and shaken, for all that. Then a wave of corruption eddied around us, and we knew it came from the thing in the hold.

"Tacitly, we avoided reference to the incident and made no further attempt to investigate. Who can say what we saw, or whether we really saw? Yet I was convinced that a sea-change had somehow come over the cargo, that a slow and abnormal and utterly loathsome transformation was taking place. How else account for it? The salt sea-water and the hot sun must have combined with the seeds and chemicals to germinate a hideous, perhaps unknown, form of life, down in the hold. Life? Not as I knew it, but something that was strangely and dreadfully alive.

"All that day we toiled, bringing food from the galley and stowing it on deck near the stump of the foremast. Every descent was a trip of unexpressed fear, for we could hear a distant heaving in the hold; but by nightfall we had carried everything that we would need above. Nothing could have persuaded us to leave the deck again. We battened the hatches and calked all places where the storm had smashed openings in the deck.

"It must have been long after sunset before our labors were ended. It is not strange, therefore, that when we retired, I quickly fell asleep, worn out from my exertions, despite the tension of peril that hung around, and the persistent throb which crept up from below, and the moldy reek that poisoned every breath I drew.

"I woke with a start, to hear a pulsing throb that made the whole ship quiver. But what brought me leaping to my feet in rage was the sight of Bill stealthily lowering himself over the side. The coward had filled our first crude boat with provisions and water. He was trying to steal away with our only means of escape, leaving me who had saved his life behind to face death and terror alone.

"I might have killed him, but I didn't. He was unprotected because he was lowering himself with both hands. I whipped out my pistol and had him covered before he could scramble back. He didn't risk dropping to the sea; for he knew that I could have and would have shot him before he could pull out of range. I made him haul back every scrap of food, and hoist the boat, after I had disarmed him. Then I tied him securely and went back to sleep. I knew he would be dangerous from now on, but I also knew he would be unnerved by that hellish pulse which sounded from the ship's hold and the commotion the shapeless thing made, and the stench that hung thicker than ever.

"Existence became a nightmare. I had long abandoned hope of rescue. The only recourse left was to finish the larger boat on which we were laboring, and trust that we made land. The stench on deck was horrible, and at night I heard that damnable pounding that became steadily more insistent. What if the thing broke out? I trembled at thought of the consequences. And now I had to watch Bill every second. His aid was essential to finishing the boat, but the rat would kill me and flee the minute that he received the opportunity. Each long second I was under the greatest strain, listening to that maddening beat, watching the moves that Bill made, and always faint with the putrescence which assailed my nostrils. Yet I toiled as strenuously as Bill to finish our boat. And as if all this was not disaster enough, the food began to spoil, under the hot rays of the sun. The pork and cod became wormy. The venison dried out until it was tough as leather. Hardtack, pickles, potatoes, and nuts were about all we had left, except the flour that we occasionally made into soggy bread over a carefully guarded fire and munched without appetite.

"At night I trussed Bill up and obtained what fitful sleep I could. At morning I released him and kept a hawk-like watch over his movements while we sweated over the boat. He didn't say much. He was sullen, and by the wicked look in his eyes I knew he was still planning to escape.

"All through the night he would talk and mumble and try to keep me awake.

"'You can't do this!' he would plead when the distant pounding became loud. 'What if that beast gets out? You'd run away and I'd get killed. It ain't fair. Damn you, take these ropes off—I won't try to escape,' on and on he would go until he fell asleep or I did.

"To make sure that he wouldn't try deserting again, I insisted on dismantling our first boat so that we could use the planks on our second one and progress faster. It took the heart out of him when he saw his way of escape disappear under his eyes, but I imagined he would work more willingly thereafter on the other boat. I realize now what a foolish action of mine that was, for I ought to have kept a means of escape in constant readiness. Bill suggested time after time that we draw lots to see who should win the first boat and take a chance on reaching land. I wouldn't listen to him. I felt in a way responsible for him, and I was determined that we would live or die together.

"Any one calamity would have been disheartening, and I had three battles to fight: the silent hostility of Bill, the eternal sea itself, and now this living creature that dwelt in the hold. Bill claimed that the thing was some sort of sea-monster that had been washed aboard during the storm and had kept on growing. I said and I still think that it was a fearful product of heat, seeds, and chemical action occurring in saline water, but no matter how rational our explanations were, they didn't help us keep a grip on ourselves. I remembered all too vividly that gluey, greenish mass quivering foully with a sub-human, less, and yet more, than animal life, and the hideously purposeful fashion in which it contracted and leaped at us.

"We raced against time trying to finish a seaworthy boat for our escape. It would have been an arduous task anywhere, even with adequate materials. Our nerves were ragged, our tools were inferior, and we had to employ any plank we could lay our hands on. It was a hopeless race from the beginning, and we knew it; but at any rate it kept us from brooding over our plight, and a kind of madness drove us on, to the heat of a tropical sun and the interminable sound of a heart beating with monotonous regularity.

"For three days we lived in a wretched hell. By the forty-sixth day, the far away throb had swelled to a thud that was weirdly alive, louder than the faint lapping of waves or the blood that coursed in my temples. At night it fairly drove us wild. We listened to it with a sort of dreadful fascination, hardly conscious that for hours our movements had been rhythmically actuated by its tempo.

"I didn't sleep well, and I didn't sleep long after we turned in, that evening. I dozed a bit, only to wake from insane dreams to insane reality, and then doze again while that accursed heart beat steadily. I came to a sudden, terrified wakening when a heavy crash drowned out the sound. Bill screamed and I leaped over to him, freeing his bonds at a slash. Together we crouched in the darkness, listening.

"A sucky gurgling came from down in the hold, we heard a commotion as of oil bubbling, and the stench settled round us worse than ever. And closer yet, louder still, came the pounding that was shattering our nerves.

"'My God! It's broken out!' whimpered Bill.

"'Oh shut up!' I answered angrily. 'Crying won't help. The thing's loose. Our only chance is to kill it or get away, as fast as we can.'

"'You can't kill a thing like that!' he mumbled.

"I knew he was right. There were plenty of balls for the guns, but most of the powder was ruined in the storm. Besides, what effect could the pellets have on a creature of such huge size and unfamiliar nature?

"'Come on!' I ordered. 'We'll have to hurry.'

"But we halted in dismay before our boat. At least a week would be needed to complete it, and we felt certain that we would not have anywhere near a week's time.

"The way that that monster moved around below us made us shiver. It must have flowed along, for it made a sticky noise, and every once in a while we heard a sort of plop as if it had swallowed something, or maybe felt around with some tentacle like an octopus's that gave out a sucking smack when it jerked away. And ever the pulse drummed louder, hellishly regular, shattering our nerves with each thud.

"'We'll have to dismantle the boat and make a raft,' I curtly told Bill.

"He started to complain.

"'Then stay here and rot, unless the thing gets you first,' I cursed. 'We won't have much chance of coming out alive on a raft, but we won't have any chance if we remain here. And we'll have to work fast. It's only a question of hours before the thing breaks on deck.'

"As if to confirm my words, we heard a faint, tentative slithering underneath us.

"'It's probably smelled us already,' I whispered. 'I think it's feeling around for a way to get at us. It may be able to slide through a crack, like water. Come on!'

"That was enough for Bill. Together we started our work all over again, tearing apart the half-finished dory.

"There was no moon, and the starlight was insufficient to see by. We set up a couple of tapers and labored as best we could in their feeble glow. Labored? It was a humid night. In ten minutes we were soaked with perspiration while we ripped the boards apart and began fastening them into a rude raft. And all the while, the thing throbbed in great beats underneath us, and made loathly noises that nauseated us. If it had been a definite kind of animal, we might have stood it better; but the beast was amorphous, or rather, protean; and the only sounds that it made were its movements and the pulse of its life, except once in long whiles when it emitted an inarticulate and dreadful unvocal cry. I could not help thinking of the beast as a disembodied stomach, expressing its hunger for food; and its audible desire was the more shocking for it implied neither the animal nor the organic, but the sub-vital, the sub-organic; as though the monster, God forgive me for the thought, belonged halfway between dead earth and living bodies.

"Desperate, anxious, fearing, and apprehensive, we worked in semi-darkness with reckless haste. The ship was ghostly on the dark waters, and the tapers shed a phantom glow; very close I heard the eery sounds of the thing below.

"I do not know how long we strove. An hour, perhaps two. The gray dawn was coming before our rough raft had been sufficiently completed to be launched.

"'Two more planks and she'll be ready,' I told Bill. 'It'll only take me a minute or so to finish. We'll save time if you go over to the stores and bring the food back while I put the planks on. Better hurry!'

"Bill nodded and left. I had barely got one of the planks in place when he returned, staggering under a load of miscellaneous provisions.

"'Good work!' I encouraged him. 'Now roll the keg of water here and we'll be set to leave.' I heard his steps move away while I prepared to finish my job.

"And I heard an ominous crack, a bursting smash that came without warning. I leaped to my feet and whirled around, suspecting treachery.

"Would God that it had been treachery—anything save the reality that stunned me into a momentary stupor!

"By the dim light of dawn, I saw the main hatch burst open; and out of it bubbled and flowed with torrential swiftness a mass of sickly green corruption, thick, horrible, noxious, suffocating by reason of its putrid stench, and sinisterly alive, and foully sentient with a purpose whose nature I could guess; a heap of crawling liquescence, formless yet held together and directed somehow by a rudimentary awareness; opaque, and yet with dark filaments like hairs or veins or vines weaving a webwork through it; moving swiftly and strangely, with a rhythmic advance and recession, a bloating expansion and contraction as the pulse that dominated the hellish mass rose and fell.

"Between it and me stood Bill, rigid with fright. Then he gave a strangled cry and bounded toward me.

"The scene that followed is burned forever on the unfortunate altar of my thoughts. Even as Bill sprang, the pudgy heap vented a rustling hiss and surged outward with a turbulent rush, and flung after Bill a swath of greenish viscidity. He could not help himself, in midair as he was from his leap, and down he came in the green ichor.

"And he kept going down, oh God, he kept going down! He dissolved inch by inch in that gluey puddle, his furious thrashings could not budge him a step. Fire cannot consume nor acid eat so rapidly as that thing consumed and ate and fed upon him and devoured him alive.

"When he first landed in it, he uttered a piercing shriek, shrill and terrible. I fired both my pistols at the monster, and saw the balls rip into the quivering jelly, but nothing indicated that they had had any effect. Then Bill screamed, a long series of uninterrupted screams, rising and falling, frenzied and tortured and insane, until his voice was raw and only a hoarse and hideous lowing came from his writhing mouth and convulsively cording throat.

"I prayed for blackest night, but the dawn grew lighter and the scene stood out with sickening clearness. I fumbled in haste to reload a pistol; then, with an arm that trembled, I took careful aim, and steadied myself, and fired true. The ball buried itself in Bill's heart.

"He sagged, and what was left of him fell. I hope that I was not wrong when I believed I saw the briefest shine of glad thanks in his eyes before they glazed and went blank.

"And the stuff welled interminably from the hatch, and the corpse dwindled while I watched. A rosy tint began to suffuse the webwork of the monstrous thing, a certain awful muscular distention and contraction shook it, its stench grew insufferable.

"A deep horror racked me with a shudder, then panic, ungovernable terror swept me and I dashed for the rail. I saw the glistening mass drive after me like a hurricane, and I knew that Bill's frightful fate would be mine before ever I could leap into the cleansing sea. And at that moment the sun's rim slid above the eastern horizon, and its golden rays slanted to the deck.

"The monster shrivelled as though tormented. A voiceless sibilance poured from it, it heaved and twisted and contracted madly down the hatch, leaving behind the back and part of the head of what ten minutes ago had been a man. Something in the monster's nature, or its long confinement in darkness, had made sunlight an agony which it could not endure.

"It is now mid-morning. I gave Bill a hasty sea-burial. I have written this narrative and am about to toss it overboard sealed in a bottle, so that if by chance it reaches a passing ship, a watch may be kept out for me, and this derelict if it be sighted sunk from a distance or wholly avoided. For the monster still is living below, and its dreadful pulse dins through my thoughts, and its disgusting smell defiles the air with charnel odors. Cheated by sunlight it will emerge again at nightfall.

"I do not know what my fate will be. The raft may capsize when I launch it. If it does not, I may escape, or perish at sea. If it does, I may drown, or make my way back aboard. But here the coming of darkness means certain death—by the thing in the ship, or by my own hand, for sooner suicide than the consuming loathsomeness of the monster.

"May God's grace protect me. There is death whichever course I choose."

THE LADY IN GRAY

DURING THE WHOLE of my life, the hours from sunset to sunrise, when other people sleep, have been oppressive with fear. Since early childhood, I have been subject to terrifying dreams, from which neither physicians nor psychologists have been able to offer me the slightest relief. Doctors could find no organic derangement save for a few minor troubles such as are common to all men. My life has been singularly free of accidents, shocks, tragedies, and misfortunes. Financial worries have never beset me. I have pursued my career, at which success came steadily. Psychiatrists have devoted months to analyzing me, probing my life, my emotional development, my conscious and subconscious minds, hypnotizing me, making innumerable tests, and searching for secret fears or obsessions that might account for my nightmares, but in vain. Sedatives, opiates, dieting, travel, rest: these have been urged upon me at one time or another, and I have tried them without success. To doctors, I am a healthy man of thirty-four. To psychiatrists, I am a mentally sound, normal, and balanced person whose extraordinary dreams they either discount or discredit.

This is no comfort for me. I have come to dread the hours when night approaches. I would gladly expend my fortune if I could be relieved of the visions that possess my nocturnal mind, but the great diagnosticians of America and the foremost psychiatrists of Europe have alike labored in vain.

As I sit here now, writing these last words, a calm and a despair burden me, though my head seems clear as seldom before, despite the horror, the loathing, the terror, the revulsion, and the fear that combined in the first, and I believe final, profound shock which annihilated only a few minutes ago, and in full daylight, what hopes I had of fulfilling my life. That dreadful thing is at my elbow while I write; and when I have written, I shall destroy.

Let me go back for many years. I have been, I repeat, subject since early childhood to hideous dreams. Disembodied heads that rolled after me; cities of colossal and alien statuary; fire that burned and beasts that leaped; falls downward from titanic precipices; falls skyward up from pits of ancient evil; the old ones, waiting and waiting; flights through eternal blackness from nothing or something I only sensed; the grind of infernal torture machines against my flesh; monsters all of flowers and animals, fish and birds and stones, wood and metal and gas united incredibly; the pale avengers; descent into necrophilic regions; the leering of a bodiless eye in the midst of vast and forlorn plains; a corpse that rose and turned upon me the visage of a friend, with tentacles and ribbons of tattered black flesh writhing outward as though blown by gusts of wind; the little ones who pattered toward me with strange supplications; sunlight upon an oak-covered hill, sunlight whose malignance, nameless color, pulse, and odor instilled in me the unreasoning hate that is allied with madness; orchids lifting blooms like children's faces, and sipping blood; the dead ones who came, and came again; that awful moment when I drowned, and a fat thing swam out of the sea-depths to nibble; mewing blades of grass which purred avidly as my feet trod upon them; these and countless other such nightmares, inflicted through slumber as far back as I can remember, bred in me a deep and rooted aversion to sleep. Yet sleep I must, like all mortal men. And what shall I say of those darker dreams, those fantasmal processions that did not and do not correspond with any knowledge I possess? What of the city beneath the sea, all of vermilion marble and corroded bronze, in whose queerly curved geometry rest the glowing configurations of things that earth never bore? What of the whisperer in darkness, and the call of Cthulhu? I saw the seven deaths of Commoriom, and the twenty-three sleepers where Hali raises its black spires in Carcosa. Who else has witnessed the dead titans waken, or the color out of space, or the ichor of stone gods?

These, these tormented me and wakened me to fever and to sweat in the hours past midnight, and the silence before the gray of dawn. But they were small things, old dreams, compared with those of late.

I can not now narrate the events leading up to my acquaintance with Miriam, nor the brief but boundless love that we enjoyed, the eternal marriage we planned, and her tragic death when the airplane in which she was nearing the city from a visit to her parents fell upon the eve of our wedding. Perhaps the shock of that waking nightmare completed the slow devastation to which sleeping nightmares had almost brought my mind. I am not the one to say. Miriam was dead, all her strange beauty, the gray of her eyes, the gray and subdued mood of her personality, the pallor of her cheeks, the haunted and roving spirit prisoned within her, gone. I thought of her as the lady in gray, as she lay in her bier, like a woman from Poe, or an eery creature out of *The Turn of the Screw*. So lovely, so unreal, so alien, and yet so eerily sweet. Dead, and not for me. Even the day was gray, that wild, autumnal afternoon, and the leaves that the wind blew rustled with a dry, sad sound, until the rain began falling later, and the world turned to a duller gray where the noise of slashing drops rivalled the sodden howl of gusts, and I was alone with my loneliness.

In the sanctuary of my chamber that night, I dreamed a dream. I dreamed that Miriam came to me, and took my hand, and led me forth. Now we came to a great and slimy sea, whose frightful color appalled me more than its stench.

The blackness of the sea, its viscidity, and the universal atmosphere of decay, made me sick before ever she led me into it, so that the touch of that fluid brought a double horror. Far out in the sea, as I struggled with choking lungs, the lady in gray, who floated luminous above its surface, turned without reason or warning, and guided me back.

I could not account, in the morning, for the awful stuff that coated me, or the mephitic smell in my chamber. Only after arduous labors was I able to remove it from my person, and I was compelled to burn every article that the slimy, sticky, nauseating stuff had stained.

That night, I dreamed merely of skies of flame, and lands whose sinister red masses of rock soared from sere valleys where nothing lived and no plant flourished toward a cyclopean metropolis suspended in the heavens; and thus, for many nights, my old dreams recurred, until there came a time when I visioned again the lady in gray; and in my sleep, she took me by the hand, and raised me from my bed. We walked across plains of dusty gray, and she led me to a pillar. Now there dwelt in this pillar a great white worm, yet not a worm; a fat thing, like a slug, all gray, and with the face, if I may call the hideous thing such, of a rational creature; a horned visage whose red, white and gray pulp sickened me; but Miriam commanded, and I obeyed. I strode to the pillar, and lo, it fell apart. Out of those shards rose the loathly worm, and I gathered it in my arms. It curled. Then my lady in gray led me across that tremendous and desolate plain to my chamber, where she left me, committing to my care the dweller of the pillar. Over me she bent, and the gray thing kissed the gray woman with its beaked mouth; and then she leaned above me and caressed my lips, and she drifted upon her way, like a fog, soundless, and without visible steps.

I was frightened in the morning when I discovered that huge and horrible slug beside me. As I remember, I leaped from bed and with the tongs from my fireplace I beat and crushed it to a froth. Then I wrapped the pulp in the stained sheets, and burned it in the furnace. Then I bathed. Then I found the gray dust on my shoes, as I was dressing, and fear came to me anew.

There is, indeed, in Afterglow Cemetery, where they had buried Miriam, a kind of ashy soil; and though the grass grows green, and tall grow the wild flowers, they have never conquered the soil; so that in spring the gray shows through, and in autumn the dust lies lightly upon dead leaf and dying blade.

But I would not go there to find my tracks; for if I found my prints, I would have the horror of somnambulism added to my delirium; and if I did not find my footsteps, I would have a more poignant fear. *Where had I been? Whence came the gigantic worm?*

Thereafter, for many nights, so many nights that the loss of Miriam became a dull ache partly obliterated in time and memory, I dreamed the old dreams, of falling and fleeing and cities beneath the sea; of torture, of unknown beasts, and of unsocketed eyes.

Then the lady in gray came again one night in early winter, when I was beginning to forget, as much as I could. That night was yesternight. All the day, the snow had been falling, and the northwest wind, with a prolonged wail, had driven it onward, and whipped it into drifts, while the branches of naked trees ground and soughed mournfully together, so that, as the bleakness of evening drew near, I became a prey to melancholy, and depressed by thoughts of Miriam, who was dead. The frozen scream of the wind shrilled higher, and to that far-away cry I fell asleep. And when I slept, she came to me, to lead me forth.

Through the desolate plains she led me, and into the shadows of a forest, whither we penetrated deeper and deeper with the boles of tremendous trees rising ever taller around us; and thus we reached the cavern that she entered; and I followed after, striving to approach her, yet unable to close by one inch the distance between us. Now a strange thing happened, for the cavern swept sharply downward, until it became vertical, plunging toward the bowels of earth; and now a stranger thing happened, for we sank, as though falling gently, and yet we must make an effort, as though we were walking normally, but the horizontal had become the vertical. And slowly I drew closer at last to Miriam, until after age-long falling, we came to rest far, far, incredibly far beneath the surface of earth. And now I found us in the midst of a vault whose ceiling swept onward in arches of ever vaster scope and huger curves, while the walls receded like the naves of a cosmic and buried cathedral; and so I followed her down the aisle of that spacious edifice; and ghostly tapers, rising like giant torches beside our way, cast, in the little damp gusts of wind which fretfully stirred them, grotesque and wavering shadows upon the floor; and the gray robes of Miriam, the gray death-garments, fluttered behind her, streaming almost to my face as the distance between us lessened. Thus we came to the blackwood door, which swung wide and silent upon its great hinges as we approached; and the lady in gray drifted within, and I followed. Now I found myself within a crypt, whose three red tapers, guttering to their end, cast a somber and sinister glow; one at her head, and one at her feet, and one dripping scarlet drops upon her breast. For there lay Miriam, my lady in gray, in repose upon everlasting marble. At her head, a bowl of the slime of the black sea; at her feet, the white worm resurrected; and in her hands, folded across her breast, one the taper, and one a gardenia, whose fragrance, spicy and virginal, overpowered the odor of the chamber of death.

Now in my dream, with the queer logic of dreams, I thought this natural and had no fear; so I went to my lady in gray, and lo, at my coming, the bowl spilled over, but I brushed it aside, and the great worm rose, but I trampled it under, while the candles guttered out, and the gardenia glowed weirdly phosphorescent. By that luminescence, faint as it was, I saw that Miriam stirred, and a sigh passed across her, and I lifted her in my arms. Now the gardenia palely lighted my way, and through the rustling darkness I carried her, and the gray of her robes swept downward and around my ankles as I walked; until I came to the gusty corridor, and the tapers that flared, and the stately march of arches in cathedralesque tiers. So, with the curious illogic of dreams, the vertical corridor disappeared, and I walked onward through the vast chamber, until I emerged upon the plain. The gray dust rose, but the gray robes of Miriam fell about me, and the dust passed away. The heavens were empty of stars. In blackness I walked, save for the single flower whose scent sweetened the air, and whose glow lighted a path. Thus I clung to Miriam, and carried my lady in gray to my chamber.

Only a little ago, I wakened from my dream.

I stared and stared for all eternity, with cycles of oppressive and wildly swirling circles of frozen blackness alternating with red holocausts of flame to shatter the tranquility of my mind, and forever. Not again for me the ways of man, or the mortal habitations of earth, or the transitory and ephemeral uncertainties of life. I have written, and now I shall die, of my own hand, and by my own choice.

For, when I wakened, I wakened to see the lady in gray seated beside my bed. In her face were the rotting vestiges of the grave, and her robes hung tattered and moldy; but these three things corrupted me from

being: the fresh gardenia in her hands; her finger-nails, long and yellow, as only the finger-nails of those dead and buried six months or more have ever grown; *and the dreadful way in which her hands were twirling the flower, while her black, liquescent eyes centered upon me!*

THE MAN WHO NEVER LIVED

O N MANY OCCASIONS I had discussed questions of metaphysics and ontology with Nicholas, but I never realized how deeply and afar his mind roved through all the reaches of time, space, matter, and thought, until tonight at the gray shrine in his home.

Nicholas van Allensteen is a strange man whose nationality and past life I have not known. I met him when he joined the faculty of Minnewaska University as assistant professor of philosophy. He was of striking appearance, from hair as long as a prophet's to aquiline nose and eyes of a deep and singular hue, from his gnarled hands to his loose, proud carriage. He knew many languages. He had made extensive studies into the physical sciences. To these he added a creative, intuitive power that led him into more abstract fields. Beyond the Einsteinian mathematics, he had evolved theorems and calculations of his own which I am sure no one else ever grasped.

The gray room was his temple of refuge. Drapes of dust gray covered its walls, and only one pallet, like a bier, relieved its quiet austerity. This low rest, resembling an altar, fronted a shield-shaped niche wherein an Easter Island sculpture gazed with conquering eyes across infinity. I liked that room for its repose, and I welcomed the chance to enjoy its serenity again tonight.

Nicholas was lying upon the pallet when I entered. He did not rise. I thought he was sleeping, as he lay there in shadow, but his eyes opened dreamily. The air held a fragrance most curious. I do not know its nature or origin.

I hastened to his side. "Are you ill?"

A flicker of the lids motioned me toward a chair, the only chair I ever saw in that gray chamber. I sat beside him.

"No, Paul; but my experiment has already begun. I am glad you came in time. Did you bring the notebooks?"

"Yes. Dictate all you wish."

"Later. I must speak fast. This is an experiment in mental monism, you know, along the time-space continuum that forms material totality."

I looked at Nicholas and, despite all my conversations with him, I did not comprehend. He was wearing robes of gray, which made him resemble more than ever a prophet, a mystic. His eyes burned from the sockets like coals in a dying shell. My face must have registered my bewilderment.

Nicholas looked fretful. "Last Monday, we were discussing mental monism, the theory that all matter and life can be understood in the conception of one mind of which the universe and all its works, past, present, and future, are only parts."

"I remember."

"Nothing is ever lost. Bodies that die change to other matter, and the breath of life inhabits each new child and every growing thing. There is an unbroken continuity along which, at this hour of this year, we have arrived at a specific point."

"Yes?"

"We recall what we have learned of the past, and it lives forever in the mind of the race. But the author of Revelations looked into the future and foretold some of the realities of today. Today, there are those who peer into the future and forecast the realities of tomorrow."

"Yes?"

"Who can say that these are not all manifestations of one mind, one whole, of which everything is part? That mind, wherein all time, all space, all matter, all life, and all thought are contained, may have implanted in one exceptional individual of biblical days a vision of the world to come. It may be implanting in unusual intellects today a vision of the future. And the prophet of the Bible and the scientist of today may be existing, each in his age or part, and yet simultaneously in the eternity or whole which comprises that mind. If we could develop our mental powers sufficiently, we might understand in a flash of supreme knowledge."

Nicholas' speculations outran the ability of my brain to follow. His voice, low, monotonous, continued unbroken, but fainter. "Any human intellect that understood each particle of Earth today could predict the entire future course of history and reconstruct all the past. The past behind us, and the future ahead, broaden from the focal point where we stand tonight.

"I am close to that all-encompassing mind, Paul. I have been working toward it my whole life long. I have been training to interpret its parts and to follow its design. Tonight I think I shall succeed for the first time, and I want you as witness to record my comments."

"What comments?"

The voice faded further still, and I bent low to catch his words. "I am pursuing that mind into those parts which form the past as we know it. My own mind will be divorced, in a sense, from my body, while it roams across the ages and approaches the monistic whole. But my consciousness will not be completely divorced. In other words, the conscious part of my mind will be questing away from here, but it will be linked to the physical part of my brain which remains behind. I think my brain will mechanically induce speech. I hope so. I want you to make notes on everything I may say. Do you understand?"

"Not altogether," I answered candidly. I was drowsy.

"No matter. All you need to do is to be a reporter. Will you do that? For me? And make no effort to interfere?"

"Yes." I hauled out notebooks and pencil.

His voice was barely audible. His eyes had closed. "I knew you would. Four-dimensional time-space continuum—the past is the definite and completed part of the whole—easier to follow—I shall go back—in time—and space—"

The phrases trailed off. His voice stopped. On any other occasion, I would have sworn he was dead. He lay, hands folded, as if for burial, and I could not detect a sign of breathing. The lids were shut over those mysterious eyes. A queer silence enveloped me. In the gray shadows of the room, I felt like a lone watcher of the dead. Eerily, faint light crept from the window upon Nicholas. The fading spice in the air still gave me an impression almost of dreaming. There was a long pause, during which I waited, like one relieved of mortal limitations, in a gray world beyond life.

A voice spoke. I swear it was not the voice of Nicholas, for his lips did not move. A voice spoke, clearly, but softly, and echoing as if across the centuries and aeons; a voice of excitement, interest, awe; a voice that marveled; a voice ringing with realities and yet divided from me by walls that I could never cross. A voice—it was the voice of one who slept to dream, but knew his dream reality.

"There are shells bursting all around and men die by thousands in gouts of flesh and blasts of flame," the alien voice murmured. "The world is at war. Now the war has not begun, and rumors are flying fast. There is a panic in Wall Street. There is a rebellion in China. A man is trying to fly a machine—it rises from the ground. A president is assassinated. Brothers kill each other in civil war."

The voice went on—or shall I say went back? This was history in reverse, and I listened, and I wrote, in a sort of automatic daze. The World War, the panic of 1907, the Boxer Rebellion, the Wright brothers' flight, these rose again. The tempo of the voice increased, and I found the years slipping backward, faster, through the Victorian era, the Georgian period, the age of Elizabeth, and Italian Renaissance. Shall I convey the myriad details of that voice —details which I have never found in any history? I could write dozens of volumes. I could add tenfold to known history, but I could only cite the voice for authority.

"A colony in the Western Hemisphere. Eadweard Arderic is fighting wolves on the coast of Labrador. Leif Ericson is pushing toward him with Vikings clad in mail. They are crossing the unknown sea. They are in Norseland, about to set forth."

Thus the story retrogressed, like a film run backward, producing pictures of earlier and ever earlier years. "There is a continent in the Pacific. The Murathians are building statues on Easter Island, upon Ranopon, and Alaku, and a thousand others. King Oale is being crowned. King Oale's father has been slain. Rebellion is brewing in Alaku. Alaku has risen from the waves. The sea rolls around Murathia, and the settlers from Asia rejoice in a fertile land from the sea. The sea boils. Murathia has not yet risen."

I found it puzzling to follow that voice backward. So accustomed are we to thinking in continuous terms that I was often perplexed, but I made notes even when the statements were obscure.

"Heliogabalus is slain. A thousand Goths fight a thousand beasts in the Colosseum. The streets of Rome run wild. The praetors and consuls lead the march to Heliogabalus' last feast. The flower girls dance ahead. Hundreds of thousands of citizens line the way."

There was a sacrifice in Mexico. "Spouting volcanoes subside. People terrified by doom hurl a virgin into the river of lava. At Lothai-Memsis, the priests bring news of a dark-skinned captive blown ashore out of the Eastern Sea."

So the queer, devolutionary narrative flowed backward. At first I had found it difficult to follow, but now my mind became attuned to the reversal.

"I am far away from you, Paul. You do not exist. You will not exist for ten thousand years, except as an eventual reality and a present conception of the universal mind. You are a part of the unfinished whole. You hear me, I hope, and I know that ten thousand years from now, you will be born and will live to await my coming.

I almost jumped at those words. Coming across the centuries and the leagues of space, yet from one beside me whom I knew, they gave me a sensation of bewilderment that I cannot express.

"I have gone far enough back, Paul. I am very tired. I have unlived a hundred lifetimes. I will retrace my way through the great mind and go forward to you."

There was silence for a long, long pause; how long, I do not know. I bent breathless over the marble form and watched the closed lids and the motionless lips for a sign of recognition, of returning animation. None came. This might have been a corpse that I stared at. Then the voice spoke again, but in oh, how strange a whisper!

"I cannot go forward to you, Paul!" In those words, there was a quality suggesting a sleeper faced with nightmare. "The universal mind has absorbed me and is forcing me to keep on. I am not the first to discover this secret, but like all who preceded me, I am compelled by the one whole to continue going back. I fear the end, but I cannot go forward!"

Again there was silence, and now the darkness of night lay over the gray chamber, and I could scarcely see the figure of my friend. The voice came anew, with a note of despair added to its breathless recapturing of oblivion.

"The glacier is retreating northward over Europe, and the hairy men are surging back from the south. Now they are roving eastward and into a vast, fertile plain in Asia. They are building huts. The mammoth and the saber-tooth tiger attack them. Wangh of the tribe of Lu is gored while defending his beloved. Wangh is striding through the mountains of Alai. Now Wangh's parents are deciding whether the child shall be sacrificed to Bud-ra or retained for the tribe.

"Paul, I cannot stop. I infringed on the supreme mind, and I am lost. Can you hear me? I will tell what I see for as long as I can. Everything happens in an instant. I can only give you the highlights. Swifter than I can speak, entire lives and events flow backward, tracing the completed parts of the mind. I am fighting it, but I cannot win. I am only a fragment, and it is all."

The resignation of Nicholas reached me across eternity. I could sense his struggle with a power beyond control.

"There are no men," Nicholas went on. "There are shaggy things shambling across Asia and Africa and Europe. A continent sinks beneath the Atlantic. Atlantic is unborn. I do not recognize some of the animals. There is one with enormous teeth and claws on a body as thin as a snake. And the trees are growing strange. They are like ferns. The beasts are getting larger. The shaggy apes are becoming one with the beasts. A great sea covers Central America. Greenland is drifting closer to England. I am trying to return, Paul. I want to go forward, I want to go ahead to my allotted life, but I cannot, I cannot! Mind greater than mine is forcing me back."

The voice of Nicholas sounded like a cry. I gripped the arms of my chair. The pungent atmosphere made me faint.

The voice went on:

"The seas are warm. Colossal monsters roam on land in forests I cannot describe. Conical trees. Tremendous fungi. Moss and ferns and slimy pools. Brontosaurus roaring against dinosaurus. South America and Africa are only a span apart. The Sun blazes larger and hotter. There are no apes. Volcanoes everywhere spout torrents of fire and ash.

"Such moths! And pterodactyls! There is a creature I shall never see in museums of my future. It resembles vaguely a diplosaurus, on smaller scale, but it has wings. It is sweeping at a triceratops. Now it is back in its nest in the cliffs of Olphar. The seas begin to steam. The land vegetation is decreasing. The coniferous trees are gone, and the ferns, and the vertebrates. A polypod is coming ashore in a continent where the Pacific will roll."

I lived each lifetime and saw each epoch as it unfolded to Nicholas, and as I am convinced he saw them. Geology and history and all the experience of my life never taught me as much as I learned from that prophetic voice in that apocalyptic hour.

"The Sun is hotter than I shall know it, Paul. It is incandescent. It blazes upon the soft, rank vegetation of primal land life. It is almost white-hot. The land is steaming and the seas—they boil. I am weary. I am still struggling against the universal mind. The will is greater than mine. I think I am being punished for tampering with secrets of the gods. No matter. It is more exciting than life. Lichens and mosses and scarlet slugs retreat across flat plains.

"Somewhere afar, the increasing number of volcanoes spout colossal stalks of flame into the heavens. The air is thick with moisture, rotten with decaying matter. A slime has come across the continents. Algae and moss alone exist. The moths and the birds and the beasts are yet to come. The seas are hot. Even the cephalopods and polypods are vanishing. The infusoria alone remain. All America is settling beneath the oceans. All Europe and Asia and mid-Pacific Mu are subsiding. There is no land. The sea seethes. The animalcules and infusoria are rapidly disappearing.

"Now the world-wide sea is too hot for life. It bubbles and boils, and a misty blanket enwraps Earth. Storms of steam and vapor howl incessantly. Deluges of rains alternate with steaming evaporation. The ocean shudders and heaves. It is murky with sediment. And still the Sun grows whiter and hotter, and closer. The temperature is frightful. There are no stars by night, so dense is the atmosphere. The Moon shows as a vague and immense sphere. There are only boiling seas and steaming air by day. And no life lives in the seas.

"The Moon is swinging closer to Earth! It is rushing downward night by night and day after day. It is larger than the Sun, larger than a hundred suns, and falling closer. The seas rise to mountainous heights. Terrific storms shriek around the world. All Earth is a hell of sound and an inferno of activity. The Moon is plunging into Earth! The break has come! With a noise like the blasting of worlds, the Moon has united with Earth from which it will part. The seas pass into steam, and in the red-gray glare of birth, Earth and Moon are swelling to the incandescent globe which will give birth to them both.

"I never saw such furious fire. Land and sea and sky are blazing to one white furnace. Earth is gone. Its solid parts become molten. A ball of incandescent and liquid fire flames where Earth will rise. The liquids turn to gas. Earth is as the Sun shall be.

"Paul, the Sun is speeding toward Earth!"

The voice was a tragic whisper in darkness. I heard it, and I yielded to its power. The lead of my pencil cracked, and beads of sweat gathered on my forchead from the intensity of my concentration.

"The Sun and Earth are plunging together. Earth is a ball of vapor. Its temperature is beyond measurement. Only a thousand miles separate Earth from the Sun. They swing closer. Earth and Sun collide. Tongues of flame like comets blaze forth.

"Now the planets are grouping together, narrowing their orbits as they circle. They are all larger and brighter and closer. Time must be retracing itself in strides of a million years. Mars plunges into the Sun! Again a gigantic flame as they crash. One by one, the planets are hurtling into that central hell. Jupiter, Saturn, Uranus, Neptune, and now Pluto, crash! The solar system is unborn. A nebulous star, blinding hot and terrific in fire, revolves alone.

"But all the skies are moving. I cannot convey the blackness of space nor the brilliant flare of stars and star-clusters. The sky grows steadily brighter. Time is retracing itself in leaps of millions upon millions of years. All the worlds of the galaxy are in motion. It is a cosmic parade. The spheres throng together. The Milky Way narrows. Out around Antares, a second star draws close. It crashes. The new star glows, an eighth the size of the Moon. Another star approaches, and still another. One by one, they plunge.

"Antares is swelling to immense girth and light brighter than the future Sun. I seem to be hanging inert in space. It is a strange sensation. I feel close to some invisible watcher of the process of creation, or rather uncreation; yet these events, separate in time, are coexisting parts of the universe in its full picture and totality from beginning to end.

"Now the crash of stars comes faster and faster, a rush, a brighter flare from the central sun, another rush, a vaster blaze. The Antares mass is a magnet drawing the far-flung suns of the Milky Way like iron filings.

"Only a huge and gaseous incandescence burns where the galaxy will be. Out in space are more of these gigantic patches, hordes of them. They, too, are moving. They withdraw from the utmost reaches of space. They cluster toward Antares. The nearest collides. The blaze is terrific. I can hardly bear to watch. The most blinding light of the Sun will be darkness compared to this.

"I am afraid, Paul. The smash of worlds in unbirth will be only a pageant. This is ecstasy; to watch masses, from each of which will erupt the millions of stars in each galaxy of years to come, fuse into ever-growing splendor is a sight for the gods alone to witness. Nebula by nebula, swifter than I can tell it, by thousands and millions, they are swelling the central nucleus.

"And now there exist only the nucleus and the first nebula. The nebula returns to that prime source of things. There is no universe. Space is a black and measureless void inclosing one stupendous core of gas, flame, and matter.

"But it, too, is changing. The core is mushrooming out. Its brightness lessens. Something dreadful is going to take place. The original nucleus spreads farther through space. It streams away in all directions like a universal gale. It dims as a dying candle. It is not yet blinding or even white-hot. The dissipation is complete. It is gray and dark, and all space has become a vastness, at rest, like a fog. There is absolutely no motion or world or light or—"

What happened, I shall never know. In his deific retrogression, I can only conclude that Nicholas was driven by the supreme mind before the beginning of time, for his voice halted in mid-sentence. At the same instant, I stood up with a cry. His body vanished from the pallet, leaving neither flesh, bones, dust, nor the slightest trace to indicate that any one had ever lain there, save the loose and crumpled robes whose sleeves were still folded.

THE NERVELESS MAN

(Extracts from the diary of Dr. E. J. Loris-Hayle,
M.D., Ph.D., Sc.D., etc.)

MARCH 14—Tried my new anaesthetic on rats. No external effects visible, but incision of skin and other tests indicated internal changes affecting nervous system. Diochloresthane would seem to cause complete anaesthesia or insensibility to pain but without loss of consciousness. Correction: rats have no consciousness. Must experiment further with diochloresthane.

March 20—Performed two appendectomies and removed one tumor today. Tumor patient a woman of sixty who had neglected tumor behind left eye for many years. Protrusion of eye, atrophy of optic nerves, sympathetic atrophy of left salivary glands, most pronounced symptoms. Advanced age of patient and weak heart made general anaesthetic impossible. Used local. Patient suffered great pain, but operation successful. Diochloresthane would be a blessing in such cases. Novocaine, morphine, ether, chloroform, *et cetera*, all have limitations. Urgent need for an anaesthetic that is one hundred per cent effective, but without attendant loss of consciousness.

April 3—To date, twenty-three intravenous injections of diochloresthane in rats, dogs, and cats have been completely successful. No loss of awareness evident, no sense of pain detectable in any of the experiments, in spite of incisions, excisions, vivisections, et cetera. New anaesthetic appears to paralyze all nerves. Wonder if human beings would give similar reaction? Complete anaesthesia without loss of consciousness has never occurred in medical history so far as I know, excepting of course, cases where hypnosis, dementia, shock, or other abnormal conditions were present.

April 6—Injected two cc diochloresthane into foreleg of dog. Tests for sensitivity to pain gave strong reaction at fifteen and thirty seconds, trace of response at forty-five, no reaction after sixty seconds, yet the animal walked, barked, exhibited full control of its muscular system. Confined it and amputated foreleg. Loss of blood surprisingly small. Blood circulation, pulse, et cetera, normal.

Explanation seems to be that the new anaesthetic not only paralyzes nerves but also causes intense molecular cohesion of blood on exposure to air, or else expedites coagulation. Further research necessary on this point. Proceeded with vivisection of animal. Finished in two hours, when animal died, with no indication of pain, after removal of heart.

Experiment an extraordinary success. Full vitality, liveliness, and animation present to moment of death. My new anaesthetic seems to cause not only complete and perfect insensibility to pain but also to last indefinitely. As a consequence, the subject lived well beyond the point where vivisection under the influence of other anaesthetics would have caused death. Possibilities of the discovery are tremendous.

I am so excited that I can hardly keep my mind on my practice. Could make a fortune from my discovery, but don't want it. Will broadcast my anaesthetic to the ends of the earth, give it free to humanity. The millions of sufferers from cancer, ulcers, rheumatism, leprosy, and all the other dreadful scourges of man will not be cured, but pain will be gone forever. Greatest medical discovery of the twentieth century. Only step left is to try diochloresthane on human subject to verify symptoms and properties indicated by experimental subjects.

April 11—Opportunity knocked, and I answered. It happened on the spur of the moment. Worked very late last night completing my laboratory studies of the effects of diochloresthane on animals. Used up my supply and prepared a fresh batch. Had the bottle in my hand when phone rang. Stuffed the vial in my pocket. Talked quite a while with Charlie over his leukæmia research. Almost mentioned my discovery, which might have subsidiary influence on white or red corpuscles, but decided to wait for final test. Felt tired and turned in.

At hospital this afternoon, emergency patient brought in for immediate operation. Attractive young man of about twenty-three, looked intelligent, good physique, victim of automobile accident. Diagnosis indicated punctured lung; severance of carotid artery; lacerations of scalp, fracture of skull, and probable concussion of brain; displacement of left kneecap; left leg broken in two places between knee and ankle; general body contusions and possible internal injuries.

Patient conscious when brought in. Total anaesthetic dangerous in his condition, locals inadvisable because of shock, time requirements, *et cetera*. Immediate operation essential. Remembered vial still in my pocket and acted at once. Injected five cc diochloresthane. Results splendid. Patient suffered acute pain up to time of injection, relaxed completely within a minute. Sutured artery. Trepanned where piece of skull was pressing on cortex. Removed splintered rib from lung and closed puncture. Set broken leg and taped it in splints. Spent whole afternoon working as I've never before worked on one patient. Not a sound, cry, or protest of any sort from him. Talked with him while I worked. Repeatedly asked if he felt any pain; he always replied, "Not a bit of it."

My new anaesthetic has met its last test. Diochloresthane in its first human application has proved itself everything that I dreamed. Pain, the dread specter always hovering over mankind, is gone forever. There need never again be the torture of nerves to any human being. Colin R. Leeds, track man, fencer, and star athlete of last season, has the honor of being the first to show humanity the efficiency of my anaesthetic.

April 12—Made thorough examination of Leeds for post-operative developments. Patient responding well, though condition still serious. Asked if he wished hypodermic. He declined with remark: "Thanks, doc, but I haven't felt a bit of pain since I was brought here." I was puzzled. After effects should include excruciating pain for two to seven days. Can it be—but no; that seems impossible.

April 14—I am becoming worried about Leeds. Recovery all that could be expected so far, but patient has not once complained of the least twinge or degree of pain. Pricked him with pins while examining his spinal column. No reaction. Either patient is under influence of persisting shock, which appears unlikely, or effect of diochloresthane has not worn off, which appears incredible.

Leeds has begun to inquire about his condition. He spilled hot broth on his hand yesterday, but felt nothing. He asked me the reason, and I evaded direct reply by telling him broth must have been cool and he was mistaken in thinking he saw it steam. Also, hinted he had been given sedatives in his food to prevent the occurrence of pain.

April 25—I can no longer deny the truth to myself or to Leeds. He is a nerveless man, may always be such. Diochloresthane was too perfect an anaesthetic agent. It paralyzed Leeds' nerves not only temporarily, but apparently for all time. Patient has full consciousness, muscular control, locomotory control, but complains that he cannot feel objects he touches, and is certainly insensible to pain. Told him the truth. The joy on his face made me miserable. He thought he had been given a great blessing. Didn't have heart to tell him the full implications. In any case, I may be wrong. Hope so.

Spent tonight going over my formulae in an effort to discover a neutralizing agent. The anaesthetic seems to have permanently deadened, numbed, or altered Leeds' nervous system so that he cannot experience pain. Yet he can see, hear, and smell as well as before. Says he tastes the difference between foods. I am not sure how much of this is true, and how much is merely memory—and experience-conditioning that makes him think he tastes and smells things when actually he does not.

May 15—Leeds recuperating in amazing fashion. I presume his splendid physical health up to the hour of accident has pulled him through. He looks cheerful, has stolen the heart of every nurse, and is liked by every one on the hospital staff. But I have noticed a thoughtful, almost puzzled, expression on his face once or twice. The queer look makes me uneasy. I know I am to blame, but it is doubtful whether he would even be alive if I had not used diochloresthane.

Still, Leeds is likely to remain the first and last human being upon whom it will ever be used. Have given up hope of its effects wearing off. Leeds is a nerveless man, absolutely insensible to pain. He will go through life, a pariah in one sense, free of physical agony, but in continual danger for that very reason. Must keep a careful watch over him after he is discharged. Feel personally responsible for his welfare. No progress with my efforts to discover a counter agent to diochloresthane.

May 29—Leeds discharged. Not completely recovered, but hospitalization no longer necessary. Wondered how to broach topic of check-ups, but he saved me the trouble by asking if I wouldn't drop in occasionally to see him.

May 31—After finishing charity cases yesterday, made a call on Leeds. "You know, doc," he said, "I've been thinking about this stuff you used on me. Will its effects last all my life?"

I faced the issue squarely. "I hope not, but so far as I know, they will. I am sorry to add that you will need to be under constant medical supervision."

"Why? For that matter, I have my own family doctor."

I may have flushed at the implication. "My practice is already so large that I am forced to limit the number of new patients. I do not care whom you see, nor will I ever send you a bill for any call I make upon you, but you must keep in close touch with a competent physician. Your life depends on it. Nature has always used pain as a warning that some part of the body is not functioning properly. You will no longer have that warning.

"In a sense, you are well off because you will never suffer. You cannot be physically hurt. But you could literally rot on your feet and never know it. You could die from any one of hundreds of injuries or diseases without realizing in the least degree that you needed attention. To avoid such a fate, you must take advantage of every prophylactic and preventive measure."

"I see," he answered slowly.

Again came that peculiar light in his eyes that has bothered me before. His glance strayed to the wall. We were sitting in his library, and above the fireplace two swords hung crossed.

"I am devoting all the time I can manage in search of a counteragent," I told him.

His gaze returned to me. I wonder what was in his mind. We talked a few minutes more before I left.

June 9—Where can Leeds be? I have stopped at his home daily since the first night I was there, but no lights show, and I have been unable to obtain any answer to my ringing. Can he have done away with himself? Or has he gone off on some wild adventure? I hope it is merely that he has consulted a good physician. Perhaps he has placed himself under expert care and retired somewhere.

Still no success in developing an antidote.

June 16—Just returned from Leeds' house. Drove by there as usual after completing the day's appointments. Had begun to give up hope of seeing him again, but the lights were on when I passed about eight-thirty. Leeds himself answered my ring. His attitude was strange, half aloof, half hostile.

"Well?" he remarked, lounging in the doorway.

"I came merely to make sure that nothing had gone wrong." I began.

"I'm all right," he said, eying me with that queer, hot, vacant look that was beginning to give me suspicions and apprehensions.

"You have been under good care?" He seemed healthier than when I last saw him.

"If you mean medical, no. Otherwise, yes. Spent two weeks with my family in the lodge up in the Catskills. Just got back today."

"Haven't you had an examination since you left?"

"I didn't need one. I can feel now. The effect of the stuff has worn off."

For a moment I felt relieved, then my natural skepticism asserted itself. Besides, his eyes were not sufficiently normal.

"How do you know the effects have worn off?" I demanded.

He thrust out his arm. The left forearm was scarred from elbow to wrist with cuts and half-healed knife wounds.

"I've been deliberately cutting myself every day," he replied. "A week ago, I began to feel twinges, now it actually hurts as it used to when I cut myself."

"I am delighted to hear this," I told him. "Do you mind if I make a thorough examination? Naturally, I am deeply concerned over your case, and I would like to satisfy myself that the operative work was a complete success."

He objected. I tried persuasion and insistence. At last he consented.

In the library, he stripped and lay on his stomach on the settee while I opened my kit. First I made a small incision in his shoulder. Then I used a probe to prick him in various spots. Not once did I receive a reaction. That was conclusive proof that the effects of the diochloresthane had not worn off.

When he cut his forearm, he only imagined he felt pain. It was purely psychological, a wish-fulfillment combined with memory-suggestion of past experience. He wanted to feel pain. A cut and flow of blood once signified hurt. Autosuggestion made him believe he again felt pain. My false elation subsided. Leeds had been a physiological phenomenon. Now he was on the way to becoming a psychopathic case as well.

I did not try to disillusion him. I suppose I hoped that I might foster his belief. Then I asked him to roll over. The slight swelling and feverish condition of his abdomen were grave symptoms. Perhaps it was already too late. I ordered him to lie still and hastily dipped my instruments in antiseptic solution.

"What are you going to do?" he demanded.

"I am preparing to operate. You have a burst appendix. There is not time enough to rush you to a hospital. It is a matter of life and death," I told him. "I can't tell how recently the appendix broke, but the condition of your skin indicates that it must have been several hours ago. Your system must be full of toxic poisons already. Since you felt no pain, the operation should also be painless."

I have never before seen on a human face so strange, dazed, and feral an expression as that which reddened his eyes then. But he lay without a quiver. Even his breathing was quiet. I opened the abdomen removed the ugly mess, cauterized, and stitched the incision.

All the while I worked, his hot, blank stare followed my motions. It must have been one of the weirdest operations yet recorded; an emergency appendectomy without anaesthetic, patient fully conscious and watching every move of the instruments, yet experiencing no real pain though he may have imagined some.

Suddenly his eyes flamed. "Damn you!" he shouted. "I can't feel; I don't hurt! Why don't you hurt me, why don't you do something? I'm all cold! It's living death!" he screamed.

Before I could prevent him, he seized the scalpel. I deflected his aim. The razor-sharp instrument cut my hand and ripped a deep gash across his right thigh. I knocked the scalpel away. He tensed as if to leap at me, then shuddered and shook.

"Lie quiet!" I commanded in as soothing a tone as I could muster. "You will be all right. The operation would have been agony to anyone else. It will be only a matter of time until I discover something to nullify the diochloresthane."

His feverish expression cooled. "Sorry I blew up," he muttered. "I guess the sight of blood and watching you and not feeling anything got me."

"You must remain quiet. Shall I have you removed to the hospital or would you prefer to have a nurse here?"

He decided to stay at home. After treating my cut and his, I made arrangements for both day and night attendants. By the time I left, his hysteria had subsided. His temperature was one hundred two, pulse above normal. Both were probably symptoms of toxic poisoning. I may have arrived too late. His condition is serious as a result of nature's inability to warn him through pain of appendicitis and the consequent developments. However, his general health was good, and he stands a fair chance of recovery. Hospitalization desirable, but he can summon his own physician if he wishes. Thought it best not to press the point in view of his resentment.

Mental phases of the case beginning to worry me. When Leeds is better, believe I'll ask Berger, the psychiatrist, to accompany me. I'll introduce him as a co-surgeon interested in trepan work. The pretext should enable him to obtain a general impression of whether Leeds needs mental hygiene. Can't help wondering if Leeds' reactions are merely psychological, or whether the anaesthetic, in some slow and concomitant metabolism, is altering the brain cells themselves, with a possible result in insanity of recognized or new type.

Tired from strain of day. No time to experiment tonight.

Later—Must record impressions. Tossed around for an hour after retiring. Passed into half-waking, half-sleeping condition where conscious thoughts and subconscious dreams intermingled.

Had terrifying vision. Vaguely aware of room, but also saw immense field in distance. Dreamed that vast army was attacking a city. Millions of men swarmed ahead, every soldier looking like Leeds. Machine-gun bullets raked them, but they drove onward irresistibly, without a cry of pain. Gases shriveled their skin and lungs, but they did not know it. They had all been inoculated with diochloresthane and were impervious to pain. The horror of war meant little to them. They might die, but they could not be hurt. So, though they fell by thousands, they rolled on, a horde that nothing could halt, except absolute annihilation to the last man.

This possible use of my anaesthetic which had not previously occurred to me has caused me to consider. Diochloresthane is revealed as one of the most potentially powerful and efficient agencies ever known in offensive warfare. Shall I turn my discovery over to the government? Shall I release it for use on those suffering from incurable afflictions? Or shall I adhere to my recent decision and destroy the formula because of its disastrous, antipreventive effects as in the case of Leeds?

June 24—Leeds almost recovered. Gave permission for him to move about, if he walked with care. He dismissed the nurses. His motions are mechanical. Sometimes he looks dull, half asleep, doped.

I have not yet been able to determine whether his hyperneurotic condition is physiological or psychological in origin; that is, whether it expresses a physical result of the anaesthetic or was induced by brooding over his situation. Tomorrow I will speak to Berger and ask him to accompany me to study the patient covertly.

June 25—No doubt they will be here soon. I have telephoned the police. I shall make a simple statement that will, presumably, be borne out by external facts, but I must let no hint of the real cause escape me. I have destroyed all the diochloresthane solution I had, together with the ingredients on hand, and the formula.

I spoke to Berger at the clinic this afternoon. He had a full day and could not find time enough between engagements to accompany me, but promised to do so tomorrow.

Operations, survey of patients recovering in various wards, dinner, and two emergency cases arriving successively, delayed me. It was nearly nine before I got away. The warm June evening, the young lawn of the boulevards, the greening oaks and poplars acted as a pleasant tonic. I enjoyed the cool feel of wind as I drove along Linwood Avenue and turned into Blair Street. I stopped at Leeds' place, No. 1432, a three-story stone house of the late Victorian period. There were lights on, a half-opened window, but I received no answer to my ring.

Then I smelled the smoke. It drifted out, just a wisp, but sickening. I tried the door. It was unlocked. I hurried in. The smoke was stronger. I called, but got no response. I followed the smoke. It grew thicker, more horrible. I came to the library door which stood ajar and pushed it open.

"Leeds!" I shouted, sick to my stomach as I ran forward.

It was all too plain—the half-open book, the cigarette tray. He had fallen asleep while reading, and a lighted cigarette did the rest.

I did not reach him. My cry must have wakened him. Out of the smoke and smoldering fire of the settee, the thing sprang, scorched, blackened, with smoking tatters of clothes and flesh peeling away, its eyes mad, hot coals. Before I was half to it, it leaped to the fireplace and snatched one of the swords.

Through swollen, seared lips, it gibbered: "You don't need to tell me; I can see it in your face! I'm dying, and I don't know it! I can't feel; I can't feel pain! But you're going to feel all the pain that I can't, and I'll watch you writhe and roast yourself, damn you!"

It bounded toward me through the evil smoke like a thing of nightmare horror. I crashed the table against it. It leaped around, covering the door so that I could not escape.

In defense, I jumped for the other sword. The thing plowed after me. I tried to make the telephone, but it slashed the wire.

Leeds was an expert fencer, but I received my training in Heidelberg. These were real swords. The smell in the air, the frightful appearance of the creature attacking me, may have helped to create something like frenzy in me also.

"Why don't you die!" I cried out.

The swords locked. Crash of steel. I parried, a lunge ripped open his cheek. Blood spattered his arm.

He mouthed in insane hatred: "Cut me, burn me, do anything, and you can't hurt me! But you will hurt, bit by bit, while I kill you and watch you suffer!"

He meant it.

I cannot describe that duel. The odor of smoke, the clangor of steel, the dreadful specter of living death that hurled itself at me, are memories I prefer to forget. Neither fire nor steel nor any known affliction could hurt that creature, half cooked and dying. Yet I sickened every time my sword slashed and sliced him, and I paused only to stamp out the fire after that scorched and bloody pulp sank in the final mercy of death, my sword in his heart. I flung a pail of water on the debris of the settee.

From my own residence, I telephoned the police. I shall plead self-defense. I think the hideous reality will bear out that part of my story. What else may come—

But they are knocking at my door.

THE CHUCKLER

I

7. All jewels of which I die possessed are to go to my daughter, Mary Walton, with the exception of the emerald known as "The Dark Flame," which is to be placed in my right hand and buried with me.

8. My entire collection of occult books, with the exception of four hereinafter named, is to be given to the public library of this city. These four are to be placed in my coffin: . . .

MARY WALTON LET the emerald be entombed for she was a dutiful child, and besides had no particular liking for the green jewel. And the four books she likewise had placed in the dead man's coffin; they were ancient manuscripts written in some unknown or forgotten tongue, and she did not know that each was the only one of its kind in existence. She was, moreover, utterly unaware of the forces they controlled and to which they were the key.

II

A shadow, black against the gloom of the moonless night, passed suddenly across the graveyard. It vanished in the deeper shadow around the great entrance to some family crypt. For a time faint rasping sounds came from there. Then they ceased. A part of the shadow swung outward a little, like a door; its position remained unchanged for a short time, but it swung in again. All was silent.

III

It was only by chance that he was returning home at that time. He had gone off duty at twelve but had remained at the station nearly an hour longer, talking with a couple of fellow policemen; one hour had not seemed of great importance to him. But it was, for it caused him to be late in passing the graveyard on his way home, late enough to hear the faint rasping sounds and see the black segment detach itself slightly from the entrance to the crypt and swing shut a little later.

He stopped, and in a moment was silently crossing the graveyard. Dim tombstones now and then flitted from the dusk ahead and vanished in the dark behind.

"The grave robber's at it again," he muttered to himself, "but he won't get away this time." He suddenly caught his breath. "Lord, if it isn't the Walton crypt! I'll bet he's after the emerald they say Walton liked so well that he had it buried with him!"

The monument loomed before him. The door leading to the vault beneath was closed, but the lock was broken; he had expected something of the sort. He listened for a moment. All was still and silent. He cast a look around at the array of tombstones that rose on every side, white and ghostly, at the cold, pallid stars in the sky above, and at the shut door in front of him. Occasionally he heard the eerie rustling of the night wind; except for that, all was deathly still.

He cautiously pulled at the door, and it swung open. An ebon blackness lay before him, from whose depths arose dank odors, noisome and evil. He shivered involuntarily and drew forth a gun.

He was undecided, and debated for a minute whether to enter or wait for the ghoul to come out. He listened again, but heard no sound. Once or twice he thought there were footsteps behind him, —it was only the faint breeze stirring the grass. He tried to see into the tomb, but the inky blackness disclosed nothing. The solitary loneliness of the graveyard never lightened. The minutes passed slowly, yet he was still undecided. Once more he cautiously put his head within the passageway and listened. And as he listened, his face went white in the darkness and he shuddered. For he had scarcely put his head in the entrance when from deep—deep within the tomb rose the dying echo of a long, high scream. And after it came a *sound,* an indescribable *sound,* immeasurably distant, as of something chuckling. The echoes of the scream faded away, but he still heard far below that throaty chuckling.

He paused no longer. He tore out his flashlight and snapped it on. In a moment he had entered the tomb and was passing rapidly downward. He had no fear of being seen; he knew that there were two turns in the passageway before the crypt itself was reached. The black walls slipped smoothly by. He watched his steps, but went as fast as possible. And all the while he heard that ghastly chuckling; and every moment it grew *louder.*

He came to the first turn, and the floor sloped more abruptly. He slowed down a little necessarily but he paused not. And since he was going slower, the pad of his steps became softer, so that he could hear better. And all the while he heard that ghastly chuckling; and every moment it grew *louder.*

Above, below, on either hand, the ebon walls silently slid by. Behind stretched the darkness of the passage he had traversed. Ahead lay the deeper darkness of the remaining passage and the tomb—and the Laugher. He came to the second turn, and though the floor became almost level, he continually slowed his pace: a door at the end of the passageway would lead directly into the crypt. Yet he pressed on. And all the while he heard that ghastly chuckling; and every moment it grew *louder.*

And when he reached the door, his flashlight carefully dimmed and shaded, his gun ready, the tittering came clear and distinct and terrible from the crypt, a loathly throaty sound which in some manner reminded him of plump drowned rats that gurgled. He trembled, and knowing that he could stand it no longer jerked open the door, flashlight pouring its full whiteness into the tomb before him.

For a moment he stood motionless. Then he turned and shrieked his way to the night above. For the entire chamber was lit with a pallid and hellish green glare that streamed in wave on livid wave from an emerald on the floor. Beside it lay the body of the dead ghoul, face twisted and distorted. And on the body, staring him full in the face, with its yellow graveclothes falling from its yellower flesh, with its gleaming eyes looking straight ahead, with its fat and bloated face wreathed in a leering grin, chuckling with a husky and throaty chuckle, sat a rotting, long-dead corpse.

A SCIENTIST DIVIDES

I SHALL ALWAYS remember him as he stood there by the slides and microscope that summer afternoon three years ago. His face was enkindled with the glow that is present only at the immediate moment of a great discovery. He held the beaker in his hands, and looked at it with all the loving pride of a mother studying the first babe. Yet it was characteristic of Doctor Weylith that his eyes wore a far-away look. It was never the discovery that mattered so much to him, as it was the potential and far-reaching effects that future generations might enjoy.

Doctor R. L. Weylith was then one of the country's brilliant biologists. He had made a name for himself by his exhaustive researches into the nature of cells and cell-structures, chromosomes, hemin, and more esoteric minutiae of the human organism. He was one of the men who developed the hyper-oxygenic treatment for schizophrenia. He successfully isolated, identified, and photographed the first of the non-filterable viruses. Yet he had scarcely reached thirty when he received the highest honor, the most distinguished medal, that science bestows on its own. And he was only thirty-five that afternoon three years ago.

A slender, quiet man, he carried himself with a curious and disconcerting air of alert detachment, as though he saw everything, but could not pause in his progress toward ultimate goals. Always tolerant, gracious, and generous, he encouraged and helped others even when his own work suffered. Gifted with a keen mind and a vivid imagination, he took advantage of every educational facility to specialize in the methods of science, making biology his particular field. He was no mere grubber of facts. His work was precise, elaborately documented, but also linked to the great dreams that lured him on. He was that rare and enviable type: the pure scientist in his technique, the pure visionary in his mind, the successful joiner of both in his work.

Does this sound as if I were writing his epitaph? I am. Or I hope I am, since I can not be positive.

Our relationship was somewhat unusual but readily understandable. I had long been interested in all phases of modern science, but without the aptitude or the interest in specializing in any given field. I was fascinated by the possibilities of new discoveries, and naturally turned to writing. Professor Weylith, on the other hand, confined his published work to material that would bear the strictest and most technical scrutiny. It was difficult for me to find laymen sufficiently versed in various categories of science to talk to, and it would have been suicidal for Weylith to expound some of his more fanciful ideas to his colleagues. But the two of us got along famously, for in him I found a man I could deeply admire, and in me I hope he at least enjoyed an enthusiastic listener. I advanced the idea that caught his imagination and set him off on the years of investigation which culminated that afternoon. Now I regret ever having mentioned it.

For the years that I knew him, I saw him regularly and discussed everything above the sun and beneath the clouds. I was the only person who did know the nature of his last experiment. It is just as well that he permitted no one else to share the secret. The world would be a less complacent globe.

Yet, in spite of our numerous conversations, I did not go with a full understanding of what might ensue that afternoon when Doctor Weylith telephoned and asked me to drop in at his laboratory. I had originally thrown off my suggestion as the germ for a fictional romance. "Science tells us," I had once remarked, "that the higher organisms all evolved from a single-celled animalcule or amoeba which represented the first life-bud aeons ago. From that humble beginning came vertebrates and man. Why may not man himself now be only a similar basic cell out of which even vaster and more complex organisms will evolve in the course of ages? Imagine what would happen if a super-scientist treated man as such a cell and then, in the laboratory, constructed from one or dozens of men a creature of the year one billion!"

That was the thought which fired Weylith's imagination, but not quite in the way I believed. Through nearly five years of work, he kept his real objective to himself, while discussing my suggestion as if he were making progress on it. Since the idea was merely fictional, and rather far-fetched, I did not seriously think he would turn it into reality. Then, too, he was noncommittal over the phone. He merely suggested that I drop around if I would like to see something interesting. From his casual tone, I suspected his request had to do with the topic we had often discussed. I decided he had probably made an important new discovery in the matter of cellular structure or an allied subject. I knew he had been making extensive researches of late in cosmic radiations, chlorophyll, hemin, hormones, and glandular secretions.

It was about three in the afternoon when I walked into his laboratory and saw him with the beaker in his hands. The westward-slanting sun poured a flood of light through the windows, hot light, molten light, but the air-conditioned laboratory was cool and dustless. The window-staves split the light into rectangles. They left a cross on the side of his smock. His face seemed a little tired, evidently from days and nights of arduous work, but weariness never prevented a quick smile of welcome.

"It's worth being half-cooked in that sun just to bask in the coolness here," I remarked.

"Is it hot out? I hadn't noticed. But come over and look at this."

I made my way between the tables of chemicals, slides, tissues, tinted specimens, microscopes, and other apparatus.

"What is it?" I asked when I reached his side.

He held the little beaker toward me. Inside it nestled a drop of opaque, reddish-gray stuff. There was only a drop, but nothing ever before gave me the creeps like that tiny nodule. It seemed to quiver with a strange and restless motion. It elongated, contracted, rested, made an abortive effort to roll up the side of the glass toward Weylith's hand. The reflected sunlight glistened on it. It looked pinkish, like an albino's eyes, slimy, like an angleworm's tip. It suggested in no single or specific way such diabolic and distorted anthropomorphic traits, so sinister a human nature in so subhuman a way, that I made no effort to take the beaker. The drop almost mesmerized me. I bent over and it slid up the side of the beaker so swiftly that I shrank away. The globule fell back, palpitated faintly and restlessly like a heart endlessly beating for a body to clothe it.

"What is it? I can tell you right now I don't like it, I won't touch it, and I refuse to have anything to do with it."

Weylith smiled. "That is why you write fiction. You romanticize things. I investigate them and find out their nature. Then they lose their mystery and neither repel nor attract. They are reduced to facts."

"Yes, but then you romanticize them by planning their ultimate possible use in the farthest future world. You haven't told me what this is?"

Weylith looked at the beaker thoughtfully. He shook it a trifle. The drop raced madly around the spot where his hand held the glass. "Hungry little devil, isn't it? It hasn't eaten since I made it."

"Made it? Out of what? What for? How?"

"Not so fast! I'll go back a little. Do you remember the day, years ago, when you suggested the idea that man might be only the basic cell of an immensely more complicated organism yet to develop?"

"Of course. I also said that it would be wonderful if some scientist could only speed up the cell and produce overnight the homunculus of the year one billion. Don't tell me that this is it?"

Weylith shook his head. "Hardly. No, that isn't quite the line I was following. Your suggestion captured my fancy but I went after it in a different way. After you left that time, I thought a good deal about the idea. Science has accepted as truth the evolution of multicellular organisms such as man from an ancient, original, single cell. You suggested that man himself might be, so to speak, only the real basic cell of which the primeval cell was only a part and that out of man might evolve a complex being almost beyond our power to envision. Right?"

"Yes. Then what?"

"It occurred to me that a reduction instead of expansion might be equally interesting for speculation. The simple cell produced, through countless mutations, man, and was itself changed. Why therefore might not man carry within himself a different kind of cell, substance, or essence, which was his full being expressed in its least compass? I don't mean sperm, of course; I mean something that was the minimum refinement of blood, bone, tissue, organs, glands, secretions, and so on; perhaps inert, but at least possessed of the capacity for life; a modern cell that was counterpart to the ancient, simple cell. Perhaps it might be found in extracts of each part of him, interfused into a unit. Perhaps he contained a hitherto undiscovered gland or secretion that had the latent capacity of summarizing his nature. Perhaps one could construct a centimeter model of man, from tiny parts of the brain, the nervous system, the skeleton, the muscles, the organs, the blood system, the glands, the hair, the cartilage, and imbue it with life. Perhaps one might take cells and subject them to enzymatic, metabolistic, biochemical, or other changes that would convert them into what might be called homoplasm."

"Homoplasm?" I queried.

"To distinguish it from protoplasm. And here it is."

I looked at the malignant little drop with intensified curiosity and dislike. To tell the truth, Doctor Weylith's comments had partly escaped me, I was so fascinated by the actions of the globule. I heard without comprehension. One graphic picture is mightier than a thousand words. I saw the result of his experiment, and I had only half-ears for the cause, the explanation.

But I managed to ask, simply for lack of any more intelligent comment that I might make, "What does it do?"

Weylith answered candidly. "I don't know. I isolated homoplasm this morning, and I haven't had time to go further. It appears to be sentient, animate, and locomotory, as you can see. What its other properties are, I don't know. I can't even say for sure that it is what I believe it is. It may be just a particularly voracious bit of protoplasm-plus, without any individual or special characteristics. I called you because I thought you would be interested in any case, since it was your suggestion that set me on my way. There are a good many tests yet to be made.

"For instance, how long will it last in its present state? Does it require food? If so, what kind? If not, why not? Are its actions spontaneous or deliberate? Instinctive or rational?

"Can it exist without air? And by what magic is it replacing the energy that it burns in its motions? It has hardly stayed still a minute in the last eight hours, yet it is as active as at creation. Is it directly converting natural or artificial light, or both, into energy? If so, it is the most wonderful little machine devised up to now and opens visions of immeasurable energies that can be harnessed for man. What everlasting dreams hover around this simple bit of homoplasm! Just to look at it, you wouldn't think that this one globule is the full complexity of man reduced to minimum, would you?"

"No," I said frankly. "I wouldn't, and I don't want to think so. My idea wasn't so hot after all, if this is what it boiled down to."

"On the contrary, it was a brilliant speculation. One thing you writers of science fiction possess that most scientists lack is freedom from fact. You can start out with almost any concept, expand it to its most imaginative limits, even take liberties with science, and produce a vision of the years to come. But we who work in the laboratory must always offer substantial proof, back every step with fact, and document our theories or claims by evidence that can stand the laboratory test. Domination by fact is both science's greatest safeguard and its worst drag. X discovers a cure for cancer. He knows it is a cure but can not prove it immediately. He tests it for years in every conceivable way on all sorts of animal tissues before he announces his results to the public and permits application to human sufferers. In the meantime, tens of thousands of victims die.

"Or take homoplasm. I know what it is. I've a good understanding of what it will do, and what its functions, properties, and actions are. That's why I keep it tightly stoppered. But I could no more announce its discovery to the world without perhaps irreparable loss of prestige now than I could make time run backward."

"It wouldn't surprise me if you even succeeded in doing that," I remarked, and sincerely. "All I can say about your homoplasm I've already said. I refuse to have anything to do with it. You could extol its virtues till doomsday and I still wouldn't like it. See how it's quivering? It's been squirting around the beaker like a crazy thing while you've been talking. It goes wild every time it gets near your fingers and that seems to be as often as it can. No. I'd get rid of it if it were my choice. My background of science may be weak, but there's nothing wrong with my eyesight and I don't like what I see."

"You may be even nearer the truth than you think," Doctor Weylith answered ambiguously. A ray of sunlight slanted through the glass of the beaker and turned the living stuff to a drop of scarlet flame, glistening like a bead of blood, beautiful in its own evil way. I shrugged my shoulders in dislike of it.

"Put it up on that shelf out of harm's way," Doctor Weylith suggested with a hint of the good-natured banter we often indulged in.

"Not I, thanks. I wouldn't touch that beaker for a million dollars. Or a thousand, anyway."

Doctor Weylith, his sensitive features again wearing a rapt expression as his dreaming mind was absorbed by the homoplasm and fascination over the endless fields of conjecture it opened, stood on tiptoe with bemused eyes and placed the beaker on a shelf.

I looked out the window and saw the sun burn across pavement with a glare that bubbled asphalt and sent the heat-waves dancing.

A faint tinkle and a heavier thud came from behind me. I whirled around.

Doctor Weylith sprawled on the floor, face up. A gash laid open his right forehead. I sprang to his side, saw that fragments of glass were embedded in the wound, decided instantly it was a case for medical care. He must have lost his balance in attempting to place the beaker on the shelf and it fell, shattering on his forehead and knocking him unconscious. I cursed myself for my reluctance to heed his request, even though it had been made in jest. The flow of blood was steady, but not large. For fear of driving the splinters of glass in deeper, I merely placed a clean handkerchief on the injury to act as a clotting agent while I raced to the phone in another room.

I called the office of Doctor Weylith's personal physician but was told he was in the midst of an operative case. To save time, I then called an ambulance and asked for immediate service. Weylith's name worked magic. I could expect the ambulance in fifteen minutes at most. I hurried back to the laboratory.

It does not seem to me that I could have been gone more than a half-minute but perhaps the telephone delayed me two or three minutes in all. It really makes no difference since there is nothing I might conceivably have done had I returned sooner.

When I entered the laboratory and rounded the tables obstructing my view, I received a shock of horror such as I hope may never be repeated. Weylith's head was gone. The upper half of his clothing sagged, but a squirming and hellish motion affected it from some amorphous substance within. Almost as fast as my eyes could follow, the rippling spread down the torso and limbs. I was paralyzed in my tracks. I remembered the pinkish nodule, but that dreadful thought only served to stun me more.

Then, out of that loose and shapeless heap of clothing slid a mass a million times the size of that original drop of ooze; a reddish-gray pulp of heaving and awful life which left not the tiniest bone behind, not the least particle except the glass splinters and the now flat clothing. The stuff quivered damnably, shivered as in a wind, split in two by simple fission. The sun imbued those two mounds of jelly with a smoky and sinister glow. And now they began to eddy and swirl and extend upward. They elongated here, contracted there, filled out elsewhere, assumed new form of terrifying significance.

"No! No!" I shrieked.

Before me stood two identical Weyliths, naked, each half the size of the original man. There was a duller luster on the faces. In the eyes there was nothing whatever of Weylith's intelligent and friendly gaze. They were dangerous, menacing, primeval eyes, and they stared at me. I wondered madly if each creature had only half the brain of Weylith, or no brain at all.

The homoplasmic drop, having absorbed every gram of Weylith's body, had divided, and each mass had built up a new body from the image of man that was inherent in it. That reproduction was faithful even to the cut on the forehead. And now a stranger occurrence deepened the spell upon me. The two Weyliths took a step forward, but out of the cuts oozed a rapidly swelling flood of the pink stuff that deliquesced the bodies almost as soon as they had been formed.

The sweat trickled from my face but my eyes burned and my forehead was hot, dry.

The two heaps quivered hellishly again, and I thanked the stars that no one else had witnessed the transformation. Or was I mad? Perhaps corroboration was the saving grace I needed lest I find this to be only a hideous hallucination. And still I stared, utterly incapable of motion.

The strange life-puddles stirred eerily. They narrowed in the middle and separated into four. They swirled into mounting shapes until four grisly phantoms, four pygmy Weyliths glared at me from eyes ferocious with basic, subhuman, food-desire. The four demons tottered toward me, their pink-white eyes blank of any intelligence. They were eyes neither of man nor vertebrate nor fish, neither insane nor sane; just hungry eyes.

I acted as I certainly did not wish to act. I wanted to leave that laboratory forever behind. Something drove me, some subconscious but lightning intuition of what might happen, some unreasoned desire to do what my dead friend would have preferred. I sprang to the door, locked it, whirled around. Already the four Weyliths were headless. They stood in their tracks like so many decapitated monstrosities, while the streams of ooze pouring down took with them the chests, torsos, limbs, every vestige of those abominable entities.

The speed of the cycle increased perceptibly and proportionately as the mass diminished. The two scientists had divided into four and the four into eight in only three-fourths the time that the scientist had first divided. The life of the eight little things was correspondingly shorter, but they moved a step closer.

Then, always more rapidly and horribly, the fission and reproduction of form, the deliquescence, and fission again, swept through the cycle. No nightmare was ever more gripping or terrifying by its distortion of the familiar than this travesty of the highest type human being. With every fission, the characteristics of the body became coarser, less human, more corrupt and devolutionary. Weylith, divided and re-divided, swept into the ceaselessly changing reduction of this appalling life cycle, became so many naked little animals ravening for food. They closed in on all sides. I lost my head. I kicked at one of the new knee-high creatures. My shoe ploughed into it and it clung like glue. Panic seized me, but the return to plasmic state caused the stuff to fall to the floor by gravity.

I dashed for the window and leaped on a radiator coil. It was two stories to the cement sidewalk.

I faced the laboratory. It swarmed with the ever-increasing horde of that ever-contracting spawn—128, 256, 512—I lost count of the doubling and redoubling. They were moaning now. They made wheening cries. A shrill and abysmal wail of hunger swept from their ranks when they assumed their momentary and minute imitation of man's estate. A sucking and univalvic sibilance filled the laboratory when they returned to their homoplasmic stage of their brief life cycle. Tummocks of reddish jelly. Little rat-like things of human semblance. Surge toward the radiator. Deliquescence. Smaller balls of homoplasm. Retreat into slime, advance into anthropoid form. I saw a million centuries bridged in seconds.

For a few moments, I felt comparatively safe. But I had only begun to consider the peril of my situation when a new menace rose. A great swarm of the viscous plasma turned into inch-high caricatures of Weylith at the foot of the radiator. Instantly they locked, scrambled up, shot a living pyramid toward me. The wriggling mass with all its thousands of intertwined limbs and pin-point eyes shining with a baleful lustre fell short of me by so small a distance that I was on the verge of leaping out the window. Then the column collapsed and I shivered, for I knew the next cycle would not fail of its objective.

What could I do? No matter what the cost, I could not escape from the laboratory, could not loose that demoniac horde upon the world. Somehow I must destroy it. Somehow I must save myself and obliterate every trace of these sub-human monsters. And every moment the task grew more difficult. I was still reasonably certain that the stuff could not get out. The laboratory had a concrete floor. The windows were weather-stripped, and the door sound-proofed. The ventilators were in the ceiling. But if the things became much smaller, they might seep out through invisible cracks and crevices.

The column of myriad, terrible little beasts, like human beetles, shot toward me again in a rising geyser. The nearest table was fifteen feet away. I leaped in panic. The column swerved instantly. Even terror did not give me strength enough. I landed on a cluster of the plasma and felt them squirt in all directions as if I had splashed in a puddle. I bounded to the table. A jar of hydrochloric acid stood on it. I sloshed the acid over my shoes, wiped it with a piece of waste cloth. My hands burned. I poured the container on the floor. The acid spread, ate its way in a widening pool. A thin but sharply reedy wail crept up. The whole laboratory was paved with a film of ceaselessly undulating slime that alternated with ant-like things, save where the acid lay.

There came a pounding on the door. "Ambulance for Doctor Weylith!"

"Just a minute!" I shouted, and made no effort to move.

In the stress of that moment, my senses must have become preternaturally keen, my mind clear as seldom before. I was in so tight a spot that no matter what happened, I must fail somewhere. My only choice lay between trying to save my own skin for what it was worth, or accepting all risks and doing what I could to annihilate every last mote of the homoplasm.

The beating on the door repeated. "Open!"

"Doctor Weylith has gone elsewhere! I'll be there in a few seconds if you want to wait!" I called.

On the next table lay an electric furnace, gas burners, thermite and cordite. And a blowtorch. I don't know what Weylith used them for. The moment I saw them, I sprang over, pumped the torch, and lighted it. The flame hissed forth with the roaring sound peculiar to gasoline blow-torches. And suddenly I felt protected.

I seared the floor. Foot by foot, I went over the laboratory. I burned my way ahead in swing swathes. I scorched the legs of every table, the base of each wall. All surfaces in contact with the floor, I subjected to that crisping flame. And a dim, hideous, murmuring cry squealed constantly in my ears, punctuated by the pounding on the door. There was a sickening smell in the air which the ventilators were powerless to cope with.

Nauseated, shaking like the jelly I had destroyed, and on the verge of collapse, I finally extinguished the blowtorch and tossed it on a table. I scarcely cared what happened now. Then I opened the door.

Probably most people are familiar with the incidents of the next six months. The circumstances were highly suspicious. I have no complaint against the authorities for trying to establish a case against me. It was out of the question for me to even hint at what I had seen. I took no one, not even the lawyer, into my confidence. The case became one of headlines through no fault of my own except the desire to protect the memory of Weylith, who was as dear a friend as I ever had. Perhaps I was foolish. I am in no position to say. But I feel absolutely certain that the case would have been far more notorious and given over to infinitely greater reams of speculation had I tried to explain exactly what happened.

So I botched the tragedy. I told the ambulance men that Doctor Weylith had already been taken away. I would not tell them where. The police became inquisitive, questioned me. They wanted to know why I had called a physician, then an ambulance, why the laboratory floor was seared. Weylith was listed as missing. Suspicion of murder developed. Doubts of my sanity arose when I gave confused explanations, or none at all. There were detentions, specialists, grillings, examinations. A grand jury investigated and handed up a presentment. But there were no witnesses, no proof of homicide, and no trace of a body. Eventually the indictment was quashed for lack of evidence. I was a free, but discredited, man.

That was nearly three years ago. And what saved me as much as anything was an occasional rumor that Weylith had been seen in other parts of the country.

To me, this is the most heart-breaking aspect of the tragedy. I did my best to give Weylith the absolute oblivion he would have wished, but I must have failed. I thought I was thorough, but evidently I was not thorough enough. The division and sub-division and fission of that strange plasm must have reached such minute degrees and such immense numbers that the blowtorch was inadequate. Perhaps some of the plasm adhered to my shoes in spite of the acid. Or it may have crept up the walls. Or a few flecks might have found some opening invisible to human eyes and thus made their way out of the laboratory. Even so, I think the stuff might have worn itself out—if vertebrate forms had not been susceptible to wounds and injuries; for the homoplasm would apparently never have spread had it not been for direct blood openings.

A child, scratched by brambles, was seen to cross a field near Greenwich one morning. She was never seen again. A caretaker pulling weeds claimed he looked up and saw a naked man, brutally resembling the missing Doctor Weylith, suddenly appear in a field. The child would have reached there about that time. But the caretaker unfortunately added that he was so shocked that he rubbed his eyes. When he looked again, there were two naked men, and they seemed smaller because they were making toward a clump of woods. His story would have been completely discounted except that the child's clothing was later found near the spot.

A butcher in Chillicothe left his store one noon to deliver an order around the corner. When he returned, he saw a strange little naked boy climbing out a window. He ran shouting toward his store and asserted that a gang of the brats swarmed from every opening. His narrative would also have been met with disbelief except for the fact that not an ounce of meat remained in his shop, with one exception. Cuts, loins, quarters, whole carcasses, liver, even suet, were stolen. Only sausage in the new, permanently protective casings was left. He thought he had recently seen a picture of the first youth, but he could not remember where.

At various times, in the years since, and in widely scattered parts not only of North America but of the world, the missing Doctor Weylith has been reported seen. A legend grew up about him, rivalling that of Ambrose Bierce. Sometimes the news dispatches carried items about his reappearance simultaneously in opposite countries of the globe, and in places thousands of mile apart. And with disturbing frequency, the press also carried accounts of phantom scavengers that looted food markets; of hordes of debased, naked, wild boys who vanished as suddenly as they were seen, leaving no trace behind them; of anthropoid, adult footprints that successively and mysteriously became youth's footprints, children's steps, the marks of babes, and finally ended in mid-fields.

A party of explorers came upon an African village where stew was still cooking over hot fire. But not a trace of any man, woman, child, or animal was found, nor were the villagers ever located. There were dwindling footprints, no other clue. I alone knew what had happened, and I preserved my silence.

To this lengthy and still growing list, I will add but one more incident, the incident that caused me to record these facts for the guidance of people, before I too disappear of my own choice.

The episode occurred last night. It had been a hot day, and I went for a long walk in the country. As evening drew near, I found myself sauntering down a narrow road that wound between pastures and fields and hills and an occasional farmhouse. The sun hung just above the horizon, and was already half-set, when I paused to rest against the wooden fence enclosing a pasture. Cows munched in the field. Most of them lay under the shade of trees on the far side of the field, but a couple of Jerseys grazed nearby, and lazily switched off the attack of flies and gnats. It was a peaceful, rural scene that I admired.

Then one of the Jerseys bellowed. The other moved away. The rest of the herd shifted uneasily. The first Jersey mooed plaintively. Sickness and nausea overcame me when I saw it melt down into a swelling puddle, but horror kept me watching though I could have predicted what was coming. The cow ceased struggling and its eyes glazed while the fore-half of its carcass still remained, but that, too, swiftly dissolved into the reddish heap.

Then that shapeless pile took form, and against the dark and lurid western sky stood outlined the gigantic and naked figure of a man. Man? It was a dreadful parody, a grotesque and misshapen monster, of bestial head, apelike hands, and animal feet, whose body was only faintly human in nature, and of a blackish hue. For seconds the giant stood there before plodding sluggishly toward the rest of the herd, and it lowered its head to utter a sound, a throatless and primeval food-howl, the like of which I never heard before. The huge shape collapsed into slime, and the slime fissioned, and I fled on my way while twin but smaller monsters rose behind.

There is nothing more to add. There is nothing that I or anyone can do, now. The homoplasm carries within it some instinctive or hereditary or vestigial image of man. Because its human manifestations are invariably cast in the likeness of Doctor Weylith, I must assume that he created the original stuff from his own body. So long as one drop of that now world-migrated homoplasm survives, so long will there be theft of animal food throughout the globe, and so long will the everlasting figure of Doctor Weylith be recreated, though it be till the end of time.

THE DESTROYING HORDE

OFFICER BERT WILLIAMS thought what a beautiful spring morning this was, as he attended to his usual duties. He had for some months been given a special assignment at the state university. It was he who tagged cars that had overparked the time limit of one hour, saw that student spirits did not become too combative, and kept watch for signs that the name of the Eighteenth Amendment was not being taken in vain.

As he strolled along the campus, which was situated near the geographical center of two adjacent cities, and distributed tags where he felt that they would improve the car owners' memories, he was also thinking what a comparatively monotonous life he led. The student body was a peaceful lot, hold-ups had been few, gangster and racketeering activities never approached the university grounds. So far as his work was concerned, he might just as well have been assigned to traffic duty.

Still, it was a warm, sunny morning, and he felt the fever of spring. A few students sauntered casually by. A squirrel frisked around the ornamental oak trees with lively purpose. Birds chatted excitedly where an unseen nest was probably about to be raided. The south wind blew gently with the breath of quickening life. The world was wakening from the long sleep of winter, and a drowsy restlessness pervaded all organic life.

Officer Williams continued his leisurely pace down the row of cars illegally parked in front of the chemistry building until he had reached the end of the line, which was also the end of the block. Across the street stood the animal biology building, toward which his duties would next take him. He waited while several automobiles and a streetcar clattered past, then took a step forward.

From the building came at that precise moment a shrill cry of torment, chilling and startling in the otherwise peaceful scene, a cry of nerve-tearing anguish.

"What the heck!" growled Officer Williams. "Sounds like somebody was gettin' killed." He dashed across the street—and at the very curb skidded to a sudden halt with his eyes bulging.

From an open window on the second floor, a great, roundish, jelly-like thing, the size of a bushel basket, had emerged and was clinging to the sill. As the policeman stared at it in consternation, it slid over the edge of the sill and half dropped, half crawled to the ground down the side of the building.

"That's a rum-lookin' animal," Officer Williams muttered. "Never saw anythin' like it before. What's it gonna do?" He eyed the object with a watchful and slightly apprehensive gaze.

He didn't have long to wait before obtaining an altogether too clear idea of what the curious beast was going to do. For barely an instant he was able to survey it while it lay supine a dozen yards away from him on the grass next to the animal biology building. It had a kind of iridescent shimmer, and seemed semi-liquid, or like a jelly-fish in consistency, thick and viscid. It was approximately spherical, seemed to possess no limbs or appendages, and looked a kind of pale, dirty gray in color, with a faint tinge of rose suffusing its mass.

Officer Williams had no time to pursue his scrutiny further. The object suddenly began rolling or crawling toward him, he couldn't decide which, at a disconcertingly rapid pace.

"Oh-ho, my fine beast, so that's your game?" he said. "Well, here's one for you and I hope you like it." He drew out his service gun, took quick aim, and fired.

The bullet plopped into and through the thing. The hole it had ripped promptly closed, and without a falter in its progress the mass flowed on toward the policeman. He emptied his gun into it vainly. The substance was only a couple of yards from him when it dawned on him that it might be wise to get out of its way.

His action was characteristic. Instead of turning to flee, he bounded high over and beyond the object, racing onward a dozen paces and reloading his gun as he ran. Then he cast a swift glance over his shoulder, and spun around with a gasp of horror.

Attracted by the sound of shots, people were craning out of windows, and passing autos slowed to a stop. But the policeman's eyes were fixed on the co-ed who had stepped around the corner of the animal biology building, unwittingly into the path of the spheroid mass at the moment when he had fired.

A blank look transformed her features and she fainted. The object rolled toward her, and upon her. There was a curious contraction and quivering of the heap. Visibly, before the policeman's eyes, the limp body was absorbed, consumed, digested, by the creature.

A kind of fury shook Williams and again he emptied his revolver into the heap. The bullets plowed through without effect. A crimson tint grew more pronounced in the gluey pile; it swelled to larger dimensions while a kindly darkness lay upon the unknown girl who had gone blankly to a hideous death.

The officer shook himself from his daze. Could this nightmare actually be happening in the broad light of day, and on the finest morning of spring? Automatically he reloaded his useless weapon—and gasped as an incredible thing happened.

The doubly large substance stirred and moved away, leaving a gruesomely white skeleton behind it. For a moment the thing shook strangely, contracted in its middle, and abruptly separated into two segments. Where there had been one object before, two spheres now rolled silently and grimly away.

As though that were the signal that released a general hypnotism of terror, babel broke out and wild confusion reigned. The heads disappeared from windows, automobiles roared into life, doors banged, excited cries pierced the air, and above all came another tormented scream.

A tremor of indecision held Williams motionless for an instant as the voices of humanity and duty both called. There were people inside the building who could help him who had cried out, he thought. Duty won.

He raced to the station box a block away and almost ripped the 'phone out in his haste. "Williams, No. 49, callin'," he stuttered. "Strange animal loose at the state university. Already killed one girl. Bullets don't stop it. Send out the radio cars and riot squads at once. Rope off the whole district and for God's sake hurry!" He banged the box-door shut without waiting for official confirmation or even hearing the bored voice that remarked, "Better lay off that stuff while you're on duty!"

There was no sight of the two sinister shapes as he sped back to the animal biology building. They had disappeared somewhere, nor had any courageous person yet come to cover the pitifully white skeleton lying on the grass. But the living demanded greater attention than the dead, and Williams tore around the building's corner and took the steps at a leap, almost bursting through the doors in his haste.

"Second floor!" someone shouted as he entered. He made his way toward the main stairway but he did not reach the second floor.

A little cavalcade was descending the stairs. Three students and a young instructor, all white-faced and shaken, bore a limp burden between them.

Before Williams could utter a word, one of the bearers spoke out. "No time to talk now, officer. This man is badly hurt and we've got to get him to the U. hospital before he dies from loss of blood."

"Who is he? What's happened?"

"Professor Anscot of the biology department. We don't know what happened."

Williams followed the group as it hastened toward the hospital two blocks distant. On the way he surveyed the burden that the men carried, and again he felt an inner turning of his stomach. Professor Anscot was a slender, gray-haired man of perhaps fifty, with the intellectual features of an ascetic, and yet with the finely-molded contours also which indicated a sensitivity to ultimate values. What sickened Williams were his legs. From the thigh down they had been stripped of every fragment of flesh. Only the bones remained, raw and starkly whitish. Above the knee they were stained by trickles of red that still oozed from the fleshy stumps around which rude tourniquets had been twisted.

The pallor on his face indicated how dangerous were his wounds and how much he suffered from loss of blood, but his head shook feebly, nervously, and he moaned unintelligible words although consciousness had left him. As Williams' eyes took in his slender hands that hung limp and his spare frame, he thought, "By the looks of it he's a goner. It'd take a pretty tough man to come out of *that* but I miss my guess if he's got any reserves."

All the while that he followed the gruesome burden, he kept a watch for further signs of the predatory beasts. Instinct held him in constant readiness for any emergency even though he knew that his revolver would be useless. Again he was torn by conflicting desires. His place was back there where the things were. Yet he had a hunch that the disaster would be explained if Anscot could be made to talk.

Williams had a good head for putting facts together and seeing how they formed a sequence. Animals the like of which no one on Earth so far as he knew had ever before seen do not as a general rule suddenly materialize out of nothing on spring mornings. The beast had unquestionably emerged from the animal biology building—with his own eyes he saw it come. Someone within must have possessed it or been responsible for it. The chances were that the owner was Anscot, because of his eminent position and because the building was under his supervision. It was Anscot who had screamed, and Williams knew to a certainty, as he looked at the fleshless legs, why he had screamed and what had caused the terrible mutilation.

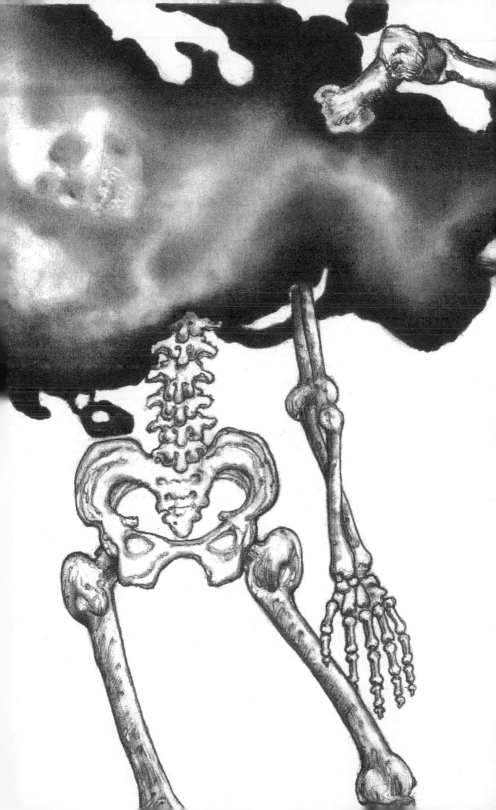

At any rate, Anscot was the likeliest person who might be able to explain the mystery—if he lived to talk. If he didn't, well . . . Williams shrugged his shoulders.

Were there more of the strange spheres? Or had he seen the only one? Was it capable of disjointing and rejoining itself, or had it split into halves for good?

Williams breathed easier when the group arrived at the hospital without having sighted the unknown creature. In the receiving-ward, a cluster of staff surgeons immediately surrounded the unconscious professor and rushed him to the operating rooms, in an almost hopeless attempt to save his life.

"How long will it be before they're through with him?" he asked the nurse in charge.

She looked up from the report that she was busily filling out. "Amputation of both legs, suture of veins and arteries, dressing and bandaging . . . With Doctors Colby and Warren together working on the case, an hour at the very earliest."

An hour was too precious to waste in waiting now. Williams grabbed a telephone and put through a call to headquarters.

"Williams callin' from the university hospital," he spoke rapidly. "Have the nearest radio squad stop and pick me up."

In barely two minutes the official car drew in.

"The police department is takin' charge. I'll be back in an hour. Allow Anscot no visitors until we've talked to him," he commanded the head nurse. With that he dashed out. Before the radio squad came to a full halt he had pulled open the door and entered. The car picked up speed and swung toward the center of the campus.

"What's going on here?" Jeffries, the driver, and Mulcahey asked in the same breath.

"I don't know, but it's sure bad. Some sort of animal's got loose. You can't kill it, at least with bullets. It got one girl that I know of and maybe more by this time."

Siren shrieking, the car squeezed through a space that opened up for it on Washington Avenue, one of the intercity traffic highways, which cut through a side of the campus.

Pandemonium reigned. The invisible wildfire that mysteriously warns people of danger had swept the district. A continual stream of automobiles left the territory which had already been closed to incoming traffic. Classes halted, buildings seemed to empty themselves, hundreds of students thronged the streets and lanes leading to safety, raucous horns and cries mingled confusedly with the shriller high notes of whistles.

"Where to?" inquired Jeffries.

"Toward the river. That's where they were headin' when I last saw them." The river was the Mississippi, which marked the western boundary of the campus.

The car leaped ahead. There wasn't a better driver on the force than Jeffries, who now proved his uncanny skill by dodging, threading, and twisting his way through a one-direction jam of traffic that extended from curb to curb.

They had scarcely gone a block when they heard a staccato burst of firing. Almost immediately afterward there came from somewhere ahead three sharp blasts of a policeman's whistle—and the chilling sound of a human scream.

"That's where we'll find them," said Williams grimly. "Keep yourselves ready—you've never been up against anythin' like this before."

Traffic thinned out, Jeffries drove the car as though it were an express train down Washington Avenue. A couple of blocks ahead hung the bridge that linked two cities. At the near end of the bridge they could make out a scattering group of men, some swiftly rolling objects, and two or three sinister white heaps. There was a truck lying on its side, too, and some squealing animals that ran madly in every direction.

"Pigs!" grunted Jeffries disgustedly. "So that's your strange animal, is it? Well you—"

His jaw hung open but he didn't finish his sentence. One of the rolling objects overtook a pig, there was a blurred thrashing, and with incredible swiftness the pig somehow dissolved into the ball that covered it.

A police captain was racing toward them with hand-signalling. Jeffries slammed on the brakes and the man piled in as the car decelerated to a screaming halt.

"Wait here for reinforcements!" the captain panted. "Can't do a thing with those brutes. Got three of our men already. I told 'em to get back in the cars where they can do their shooting in safety and at least have a chance to get away if necessary."

"What happened here since I sent the alarm in?"

"Are you Williams? Say, what do you know about these things?"

"Nothin' more than you do," and Williams told in a few brief sentences what had caused him to turn in the alarm, while all four kept their eyes warily glued on the scene half a block distant.

"God knows how we're going to stop them," said the worried captain, "but we've got to. I pulled in here less'n five minutes ago. Just after we came, a livestock truck somehow broke through the guard across the bridge. I sent one of the men down to head it off on this end, but before he was half-way there, one of those brutes rolled out of the trees by the river-bank and landed square in front of the truck. The driver must have lost his head. We saw his front wheels jerk sidewise and the truck crashed.

"He was thrown clear out and I hope instantly killed, for that big blob simply rolled over on him and ate him. The man I'd sent opened fire, and he's a crack shot, but his bullets didn't faze the brute.

"The pigs ran all over, squealing like mad. Five or six more of those blobs suddenly rolled out of the bushes and went after the pigs, hunting them down.

"There were six of us to begin with and we all opened fire, but we might as well have shot at the sky for all the good it did. The things went on eating and rolling, and I'd swear I saw one of them split in two and each half go sliding off.

"Then they started after us, and—well, there are only three of us now."

Only three of the spheres also were in sight, and they were occupied with the last of the pigs. As the captain concluded his brief account, they heard the weird wail of a siren, and a few moments later a riot squad car roared toward them. The captain hailed it.

"Got any grenades or bombs?"

"Yeah, but not many. I think there's four."

The captain took two of the grenades and passed the others to Williams, whom he apparently put special confidence in solely because Williams first had encountered the beasts.

The three huge spherical masses had finished with the pigs. For a moment they quivered uncertainly, then, as by a concerted movement, began rolling toward the policemen; but where three spheres had been, there were now six advancing swiftly.

"Try the guns on them again," ordered the captain. "We'll keep the grenades in reserve. Concentrate on the nearest one. Ready? Fire!"

A blast of shotgun, submachine gun and rifle fire literally tore the first mass to pieces, but the other five came on like the wind.

"Again!"

Another burst ripped to shreds a second mass, but the rest were within yards now.

"Two down!" shouted the captain exultantly. Simultaneously he and Williams heaved the grenades.

A third monster vanished, blown to minute particles. The other intended target slewed sidewise, and the grenade exploded harmlessly.

"Run for your lives!" someone bawled. "We can't get the guns reloaded fast enough!"

Then the creatures were upon them and all semblance of order vanished. A man yelled and went down before a sphere that got him from behind. The riot car began to pick up speed and the captain made a wild leap for its dashboard before it was too late.

In the first frenzied scramble Williams jumped crabwise. For a moment he had saved his life—at the expense of Mulcahey's. The Irishman who was standing by Williams believed that bullets would stop anything alive, and he stood his ground, emptying his revolver at the gray blob.

"You fool! Run!" screamed Williams.

And then the glucy mass was upon Mulcahey, and his limbs flailed vainly as he was sucked into it. A kind of horror seized Williams as he saw the body of his friend being hideously consumed. Hardly aware of what he did, he flipped the grenade. Man and beast vanished in the explosion that gave at any rate a clean death.

He heard another explosion follow close upon his and looked up. The captain had flung the last grenade at the monster that was devouring the first man to be overcome. But he flung it a second too late, and the monster finished and moved off just as he threw it.

Williams saw it coming and turned with a shout, "Come on, Jeff——"

But the radio car remained where it was, and Jeffries made no answer, since skeletons are for ever silent, and the sixth creature, glutted with the victim whom it had evidently trapped while he watched the main battle, dropped heavily out of the car, and likewise began hastening toward Williams.

If Williams ever felt the unnerving grip of fear, he felt it then, with the remaining two gray beasts driving toward him from opposite directions like balls of smoke. He knew that his gun was useless, that he could never outrace the devouring things.

There was only one remote possibility of escape. He sped toward the sphere between himself and the car and dived clear over it, sprawling to the ground. He was on his feet in a flash and bounded onward toward the car, but the gray beast had abruptly reversed its motion and was closing the gap with terrifying rapidity.

Williams won by a leap. He thanked God that the motor was running as he jumped in and crashed the door shut. The skeleton that was still huddled in the driver's seat crackled grotesquely as he shoved it aside. The pursuing animal plopped against the side of the car as Williams threw it into gear and almost wrecked the mechanism in trying to force it into instant high speed.

Just before he reached the bridge, he saw another cluster of the strange beasts emerge from the trees and begin rolling across the bridge toward the city beyond.

"Oh my God!" Williams muttered with a kind of despairing reverence. "There'll be no stoppin' them once they're on both sides of the river'!" But there was nothing that he alone could do to prevent them from reaching the opposite side.

As if by magic, another sphere materialized in the street. Williams didn't try to avoid it. Rather, with a savage delight he roared down upon the monster. The car thudded into it and skidded completely around as though on ice, and a shower of slimy stuff pattered the windshield, a substance greasy and malodorous.

"O. K. Back to the hospital and that Anscot fellow it is, then," he said softly, and sped up Washington Avenue.

An unnatural silence now lay over the campus. Not a human being nor a car was in sight, and all the busy sounds of activity that characterize the usual day in any city were strangely absent. Perhaps a few timid souls were still hidden in the apparently deserted university buildings, but if they were, they gave no sign of their presence.

"Can Anscot see any one yet?" Williams inquired breathlessly after he had hurried into the reception room of the hospital. "It's a matter of life and death."

"Well, if it's that important, yes, but only for a few minutes. He has just been returned from the operating-room and cannot be subjected to any strain. Room 27, left wing, ground floor."

Williams was already hurrying down the corridor before she had finished her statement. He paused for a perfunctory knock at Room 27 and was opening the door when he heard a faint "Come in."

Anscot, swathed in bandages, pale and emaciated of face, and with a feverish light brightening his eyes, barely turned to look as Williams entered.

"What is it you want?" The voice came, weak and tired.

Williams stated his purpose as briefly and quickly as possible. "And so you see," he concluded, "why it's necessary to find out all we can about the beasts. I am sorry to have to intrude upon you, but you can understand the danger. What are the things? Do you know anything about them? How did they get loose and where did they come from?"

A slight sigh issued from the wasted figure on the cot. A vague, far-away look appeared in his eyes and he seemed to be thinking of other things, or marshaling elusive thoughts.

"My worst fear has been proved true, then," Professor Anscot at length said slowly. "And the blame rests entirely on me, even though an accident was responsible. The 'beasts', as you call them, are not animals. They are protoplasm."

"They're—*what?*"

"Protoplasm, the primary stuff from which life developed. Or from another viewpoint, they are giant, one-celled amebas."

"Amebas?" echoed Williams foolishly, the conversation thus far having failed to convey much meaning to him.

"Yes, amebas. Artificial ones, or, if you prefer, manufactured ones."

"Manufactured?"

"Yes," answered the professor a bit irritably. "Or at least the first one was.

"I have realized the biologist's dream of creating life in a laboratory from man-made materials and with every step controlled. A sound knowledge of chemistry, physics, and biology, plus a little experimenting, were all that was necessary. You will find my notes and an account of my work among my papers in the laboratory. I would advise you to destroy them, as I most certainly shall do myself if I recover from these injuries.

"For many years, biologists have been on the verge of creating life. Undoubtedly someone else will rediscover my method even though I obliterate my results, but I am ready to close my inquiry, now that I have witnessed its disastrous results.

"All organic life, as you probably know, is based on the substance called protoplasm. The simplest form of such life is the one-celled ameba commonly found in stagnant water.

"I analyzed the ameba until I knew exactly what its chemical equivalents and constituents were. That was my first step. But one cannot merely mix a group of carefully weighed chemicals and expect an ameba to develop. Even that organism, low as it is in the evolutionary scale, is a system, infinitely less complex than the human body, to be sure, yet in its simple, unicellular nature offering almost insuperable difficulties to everyone who has tried to create it out of basic chemicals. The materials must be wrought into a pattern, a system, an organization.

"And when I had succeeded in this second step, still a third, and the most difficult of all, remained. I had fashioned something that was to all intents an ameba, except that it did not live. It was as dead matter as any corpse. The spark of life was lacking, the vital force that would activate the inanimate substance.

"It wasn't until Millikan discovered the cosmic rays that I was on anything like the right track. I then pursued my investigation along the lines suggested by his work, and was finally able to control cosmic rays. You will find that apparatus likewise in my laboratory.

"A week ago, under the stimulus of the cosmic rays, my artificial ameba came to life, stirred itself, absorbed food, and in general behaved like one of nature's amebas. That moment was the peak of my life, beyond which nothing can ever again rouse my enthusiasm. It was a discovery of greater significance to mankind than Columbus's showing the way to the Western Hemisphere was."

The glow of pride in successful accomplishment of a brilliant feat shone for an instant in the aged scientist's eyes, until it was replaced by a haunted look, and he resumed his account.

"An ameba, besides being a simple organism, is minute in size. Having solved the major difficulties, I now wanted to continue the experiment on a larger scale, so that I could watch every step with an eye unaided by microscopes or lenses. Furthermore, since my remaining years were likely to be few, I wanted to learn as much as possible in the shortest time possible.

"To that end, I deliberately changed the chemical constituents of my next ameba for two purposes. First, I wished to create one of large dimensions, which would not be dependent on water for its habitat. Second, I wished to speed up its natural functions so that I could study within a period of hours what would otherwise require days.

"Unfortunately, I succeeded. I created a giant new kind of ameba this morning."

A shudder of pain racked Professor Anscot and he bit his lips as the pain-deadening novocaine began to wear off.

"You created *one?*" interrupted Williams. "Then how does it happen that there are so many of them?"

The scientist smiled bitterly. "The answer is—fission. An ameba reproduces by the simple process of dividing itself into two individuals, a process technically known as fission. You yourself witnessed my ameba split into two parts after it had digested food. In some ways, it is like an animated stomach. The ameba is a viscous thing which absorbs and digests food directly. It moves by contractile projection of parts of its surface."

For a moment a frown of intense concentration wrinkled his forehead. "According to what you have told me, the first fission occurred about twenty minutes after I brought the ameba to life. We may assume then that so long as food is plentiful, fission will occur in each individual every twenty minutes. If all the individuals survived—and it is sadly evident that most of them have—there were eight at the end of the first hour;

there are sixty-four now, less those you killed; in an hour there will be five hundred and twelve. Within twelve hours, there will be millions of them!"

"Why did you let the first one out? Great God, how can they be stopped?" burst out Williams.

"I didn't let it escape," came the answer from pain-twisted lips. "It was an accident. About ten minutes of the cosmic ray were needed to animate the first ameba. I forgot, when I created one which would live at an abnormal pace, that the spark would also start it going more rapidly.

"My back was turned when it came to life. I received my first warning with a terrible pain in my legs as the thing began to—ugh!—digest me alive."

Anscot's countenance was white with suffering now, and his eyes burning with fever, as he tried in an almost inaudible whisper to finish his account.

"I suppose it was my scream you heard. I drove the brute off—would have killed it if it hadn't mutilated my legs. I—"

"You what?" Williams asked desperately, anxiously. "What did you do? Tell me, how were you goin' to kill it? How did you drive it off?"

But there was no answer to his frantic questions. Consciousness had slipped away from the wounded man, and a nurse hastened in with a morphine hypodermic to alleviate the searing pain that had been growing around the stumps of his legs.

"Sorry, but you'll have to go now," she told Williams. "The hypo will wear off in a couple of hours. You may return for a few minutes then, if you wish. There is no chance of his regaining consciousness earlier."

"A couple of hours!" muttered Williams in dismay as he retraced his steps down the corridor. Where there were only some sixty of the things now, there would be several thousand of them within two hours. Despite the warm day, a cold moisture dampened his face.

At the receiving-room desk he paused to telephone headquarters for orders. They were simple. Every available man was ordered to surround the district where the creatures had broken loose, except for Williams, who was to remain on guard at the hospital generally, and over Anscot specifically, until the precious information was divulged.

The next two hours were a nightmare for Williams. The radios in all rooms had been disconnected in order that patients would not be alarmed, but for the benefit of the staff, the key set in the reception room was kept on.

Minute by minute the scenes in a tragic drama were audibly unfolded. The destroying horde was multiplying even more rapidly than Anscot had predicted. Hundreds and hundreds, possibly thousands already, of the giant amebas were devastating an area of almost a square mile in the heart of the Twin Cities.

Low as the organisms were in the scale of life, their ferocity was unparalleled, their tenacity appalling. It seemed impossible to destroy them, except with high explosives whose use was restricted partly by the nature of the region infested, and partly by an actual shortage of dynamite.

The radio, newspapers, and whistles had broadcast a general alarm. All available men were asked to unite in attacking the danger, weapons of every sort came out of storerooms and hiding places. Two great streams worked at cross-purposes. Converging lines brought hundreds of volunteer fighters to resist the horde. Diverging lines carried the thousands who by all sorts of conveyances were evacuating the city.

Along a circular battle-front of about three miles comprising both sides of the river the battle was raging. And the line of struggle was steadily widening. Staccato of guns and the bursting of explosives were answered by cries of mortal agony when some fresh victim was caught and consumed.

There was no way of estimating how large the death list had grown. Undoubtedly dozens and perhaps hundreds of human beings had perished, with the total swiftly mounting. Any living organism, human or animal, seemed acceptable to the voracious amebas. And their astounding ability to multiply made the menace of their well-nigh indestructible nature doubly powerful.

Outside aid had already been requested. State troops were on their way now. Of manpower there was no shortage—as yet—but the nearest large supply of munitions was five hundred miles away. The local stores were on the point of exhaustion. Long before transport airplanes and fast express trains could arrive with additional explosives, the peril would be beyond control. Once the amebas were numbered in millions, or even thousands, mathematical reduplication and multiplication would result in their splitting and spreading faster than they could be destroyed.

Citizens could indeed barricade themselves in homes and buildings, sealed against entry by the organisms. But what good could be accomplished? Starvation would eventually force the occupants out, to be pursued by the prowling and ravenous monsters.

And when the amebas had multiplied beyond check in the Twin Cities, could there be any checking of them? They were likely to roll out in every direction, a circular tidal wave, engulfing whatever living creature lay in their path, protoplasmic, irresistible death racing across the country, devastating cities and devouring men with a cumulative rapidity.

Tense and restless from the excitement, Williams gripped his chair till his knuckles showed white, or paced back and forth. This inactivity was as great a strain as battling the amebas had been; but he had his orders and he was too loyal to disobey them.

There were moments when he cursed the biologist who lay dying as the result of his own work; yet it was not Anscot's fault that the first ameba escaped. If anything, he must be blamed for having been too thorough, having labored too well. The materials out of which he fashioned the giant unicell had also given it gastric activity of hitherto unknown power, efficiency, and nearly instantaneous absorption of food.

The radio continued to tell a story of disaster. All along the line, men were perishing and the line being forced back. From time to time, an ameba was slaughtered, and more slowly now their numbers increased; but the slight check was futile, for they still spread with a speed far greater than any possibility of restraint.

Williams was fidgety from inaction when a subconscious intuition that something else was wrong came to him. He had seen nothing to alarm him, his ears had not been startled by unfamiliar sounds. He sniffed the air inquisitively without being able to detect the trace of a foreign odor.

Whence came this intangible warning, this sense of imminent danger? He could not say, and although he looked around him and saw nothing unusual, the impression persisted.

"Say!" he suddenly addressed the girl at the reception desk. "Are you sure that all the windows and doors in this place were closed? Could anything get in?"

"Certainly not, at least without ringing a bell or smashing its way in," she replied crisply. "Everything was locked tight when we received the first warning."

Williams looked at her. She seemed about to make some further remark when her eyes gazed past him and opened wide. Her face went dead-white and she slumped to the floor in a faint.

Williams whirled around. From the corridor to the right wing a giant ameba was issuing.

All his faculties froze in that first instant of panicky horror and bewildered shock. The terrible possibilities that might come true with the thing loose in the hospital overwhelmed him. He knew not whether to flee or attack. Irrelevantly he wondered how the creature had gained entrance. Not till later did any one discover in Room 18 the skeleton which was all that remained of the delirious patient who had crawled from his bed and opened the window for fresh air.

The moment passed and Williams went into a whirlwind of action as the ameba emerged. He swept up the chair beside him and hurled it crashing at the viscid mass. The organism rolled sidewise but not quite quickly enough. The chair thudded against it, and for a second its progress was halted.

With the same motion, Williams had turned around and leaped for the corridor to the left wing. The monster disentangled itself from the chair and rolled after him.

There were few places within immediate access that promised safety, and of those few, almost without thinking, he chose Anscot's room. He raced down the corridor like a shot, knowing that at every step the ameba shortened the gap. He did not even try to look back and see how close the hungry organism was. He fled with the wings of fear and the desperate hope of safety. He reached the door of Room 27 with the furious patter of his running feet grimly echoed by a sinister and ugly gurgling rustle.

He burst into Room 27 and forced the door shut with the more than human strength lent by terror, closed it as a heavy weight thudded against it from the other side.

Trembling, shaken by the narrowness of his escape, he braced himself against the door for a long minute while he gulped in great lungfuls of air. He could hear the ominous sounds made by the monster on the other side as it prowled around and tried to find a way in. They ceased shortly, but without giving Williams any relief, for he did not know whether the thing had gone off in search of other prey or whether it had stationed itself for an indefinite wait.

He too might have prolonged his watch if his attention had not been diverted by an unintelligible muttering from the supine figure of Anscot, who tossed restlessly in the fever of delirium.

"Water?" asked Williams, and strode to a table where a pitcher stood. He forgot even the danger outside in the appeal of suffering to his humanity, and poured out a glass of water, which he raised to the patient's lips.

"Fire, fire," moaned Anscot faintly.

Williams felt his forehead. It was hot and dry. "Gosh, he sure is burnin' up all right," the policeman thought. "Here, drink this," he said aloud.

The dying man swallowed the fluid thirstily. Though his eyes were wild with the light of fever and his face wasted to emaciation, instinct helped him to what his wandering mind could not see. His body shook convulsively again, so that the remainder of the water spilled, but he continued to murmur, "Fire, fire."

"Out of his head . . . crazy," Williams thought. "What the heck does he want fire for?"

Anscot twisted aimlessly and the seconds flew by. It was obvious that he had not much longer to live. Suddenly an incoherent jumble of phrases poured out, faint and rapid, so that Williams had to bend low over him in order to hear.

"Fire, fire—burn it up—X-ray, take that, you spawn of hell—oh God, my legs!—now it's gone, I should have closed the window, but they'll catch it and burn it—help! help!—I'm done for—fatty tissue—if only I'd kept the blow-torch burning—"

The unguided voice went on, ever growing feebler, but Williams heard no more. He stood as one transfixed. The apparently meaningless words seared into his brain like flame, in a flash he saw it all—Anscot working in his laboratory with his back turned to the as yet lifeless protoplasm, the awakening of the mass and its silent attack on the scientist, his frantic manipulation of an X-ray machine that somehow drove the giant ameba away.

And all this precious information wasted, hopelessly wasted! If Williams tried to escape by the door, the ameba would devour him. He peered out the window, only to see more of the organisms coursing swiftly across the hospital grounds. There was no telephone in the room. If he pushed the night-bell, he would only summon a nurse to gruesome living death from the monster, if the bell was heeded at all.

He was ready to risk his own life in a futile dash when the simplest possible idea occurred to him together with the deepest disgust he had ever had for his occasional obtuseness. Swiftly he reached out and tore a sheet from the bed.

"Sorry, old man," he whispered gently, "it's our only chance."

With the sheet over one arm, he hurried to the door and listened intently. He could hear nothing. As noiselessly as possible, he whipped a pocket lighter from his trousers, flicked it, and touched it to the corners of the sheet. Spreading lines of flame began to race inward.

He jerked the door wide open and peered out. The huge ameba had been halfway down the corridor, on the point of pushing back a loosely-closed door to one of the wards. At the sound that Williams made, it turned and instantly began rolling toward him with its strange, swift motion.

There was a whiteness on his face but there was no shrinking away or trembling of his hands as he waited, even though the running lines of flame scorched him and licked around his fingers. He waited till the protoplasmic mass was less than ten feet distant; then, in a continuous, dual movement he flung the burning sheet over the creature and leaped backward toward safety.

Instinctively the giant tried to dodge; in vain, for the sheet billowed out and dropped squarely upon it. Williams saw a mad flurry and writhing for an instant, heard a weird, voiceless sibilance, and all at once the smoldering blaze flamed hotly brighter, with a greasy sputter.

Some people think that the narrative ends with the story of Williams' frenzied dash to a telephone, and of how headquarters sent out an excited message, and of how gasoline, wood, blow-torches, X-rays, gas, and acetylene torches were commandeered everywhere to fight the destroying horde, and of how for two entire days the relentless battle raged along a roughly circular front of approximately five miles before the amebas were checked and the last of their thousands destroyed.

But the real end of the story lies in a grave at Oakwood Cemetery whose headstone bears a simple inscription to the memory of George Anscot, "who half-solved the mystery of life. May he succeed as well in the mystery of death."

THE MONSTER FROM NOWHERE

I. The Lone Traveller

TWO DAYS OUT of New York, we met the autumnal equinox which arrived with heavy seas that made the *S.S. Mercury* roll. The stiff wind and the high waves were sufficient to keep most of the passengers off-deck, though the blow could hardly be called an equinoctial gale.

After dinner on the third evening out, I walked astern and watched the wake foam away behind us. The deck slanted from side to side with a slow motion that had made other passengers giddy. I enjoyed the rocking, partly because nature left seasickness out of my make-up, and partly because the deck for once was spaciously free of the usual crowd.

We lay somewhere off the coast of Florida, and ought to reach Havana for our first stop on the following day.

The last, sullen tip of the sun had set. Red and gray and flame-tipped clouds filled the western sky, mushrooming up as from some vast, mysterious conflagration. Eastward the waves pounded away into darkness, where the slate of the sky met the white-tipped turmoil of ocean. Ropes and wires hummed as the wind howled through them. Lifeboats creaked on their davits. The air was troubled with wild and lonely sounds. Salt spray stung me.

I lighted a cigarette. Sparks whipped off on the wind, and the smoke was gone as quickly as it formed.

While I stood there, absorbing, and absorbed in, all that sounding, immense turbulence of sky and wind and ocean, I became conscious of another figure. He stood at the starboard rail, about twenty feet from me, leaning upon it, and looking northwestward with an air of brooding abstraction.

I did not recall having seen him among the passengers; yet I felt immediately that I would like him, because he also seemed to find a kinship in that wilderness of unrest.

He clenched an unlighted pipe between his teeth. He wore a gray felt hat with the brim turned down in front. He was neatly dressed in a dark suit, but because of the gloom, I could only make out that he seemed to be well-built, a little on the lean side, and stood a couple of inches short of six feet.

As I watched him, he took out a penny box of matches and attempted to light his pipe. The matches flared in the breeze and went out. What prevented him from getting a light, though, was his shaking hands. After half a dozen matches, he hadn't succeeded once in bringing the flame to the tobacco.

I fished a handful of large matches from my pocket and walked over to him. "Try these," I said. "It's pretty hard to get a light in a wind like this, unless you use matches the size of a young tree."

I struck a match for him and cupped my hands about the bowl of his pipe. The tobacco glowed after two matches and he puffed, at first nervously, then with more composure. I saw, by the brief flashes of light, a face of determination and quiet strength. His mouth was firm, his chin blunt, his nose straight and slightly stubborn, his eyes wide-set with brows that turned a trifle up at the corners, giving his expression a somewhat quizzical appearance. And yet, for all the strength in his features, his eyes carried the spirit of a perplexed and haunted man.

"Thanks," he said briefly. "Going far?"

"All the way to Buenos Aires. It's a vacation cruise of sorts," I explained, and introduced myself. "I'm a writer by profession, but that's something I'm forgetting for the next month. This is purely a pleasure trip."

"I wish I could say the same. I am supposed to be taking a complete rest, but it isn't working out very well." He gave me a once-over in a way that at once marked him as a trained observer. I had tentatively classified him as a doctor or a psychiatrist, when he added, "My name is Steven R. Chalmer. I am the Commissioner of Public Safety in Woodfield."

"Woodfield—that's in the Midwest, isn't it? I seem to remember reading something about it in the papers recently, though I can't recall just what it was."

"Right." Chalmer inhaled deeply of his pipe. A film of ashes whirled from the top of the bowl and scattered upon the wind. Darkness had settled about us, a darkness oppressive with sound and the damp, wild wind and the roaring of waves. He made no motion to leave. His pipe glowed fitfully. I fell in with his moods and silences. For a long interval he peered off into the northern gloom, watched the wake foam and eddy behind the ship, before he turned his sombre, lead-gray eyes back to me and asked, "What kind of material do you write?"

"Oh, I've tried my hand at about everything," I told him. "I'm more interested in the strange and the weird than anything else. I don't mean the supernatural. I mean the curiosities of nature, the paradoxes of science, the freakish occurrences that cannot be readily explained on the basis of average experience. Like the red snow that fell in Minnesota some years ago, or the Loch Ness monster, if it exists, or the mysterious force that is said to wreck cars on a new road near Berlin. Why do you ask?"

Chalmer countered, "Do you happen to have read any of the books of Charles Fort?"

"Of course," I replied, with sudden interest. *The Book of the Damned, Lo, Wild Talents,* and *New Lands.* Fascinating reading, in spite of his irritating style, whether you believe his theories or not. There's a better-written novel by W. Olaf Stapledon, called *Last and First Men,* that's tremendous. It's a flight of cosmic imagination. Are you familiar with it?"

"I'm afraid not," he admitted, and looked at me in a curious way. "You're the only person I've met who's familiar with the Fort books."

"Do you have a special interest in the weird yourself?"

"I didn't until recently, a few weeks ago, to be exact. See here," he began abruptly, and I knew the instant of his brief pause that he was about to spill over. "I have something on my mind. I've had it on my mind for a month until I got a leave of absence for this cruise. It hasn't helped much so far. I suppose I always will have the thing on my mind. Like to listen?"

"I have plenty of matches and cigarettes."

He smiled faintly. "You were right in saying you thought you had read something recently about Woodfield. Could it have been the account of some rather grim murders? Or the disappearance under peculiar circumstances of a young man and woman? Or—"

"I remember now," I interrupted him. "I was much interested at the time. One of the news dispatches mentioned an aircraft of novel type seen in the vicinity. I hunted and hunted, but the stories ended abruptly with the old dodge, the police are investigating and arrests are expected shortly. I haven't seen anything more about it."

"You never will," Chalmer stated in a dry, tired voice.

I waited for some seconds, while he knocked the dottle of his pipe against the rail, and watched the sparks flash off. He let the bowl cool. When he filled it again, his hands still trembled.

"I can't quite see you as a Commissioner of Public Safety," I ventured. "You talk like a man of excellent education. You seem to have a sensitive nature. My guess would have been that you'd be more at home in a laboratory or a classroom than in a police department."

"Not more, but just as much. That was a pointed observation," he commented, "because the laboratory and classroom were responsible for my appointment. If it had not been for them—if the old type of Police Chief had been in charge—but let me go back a little.

"Woodfield has had an unsavoury reputation for years. One of its first Chiefs of Police turned it into a so-called 'protected' town. Out-of-town gangsters and criminals used it as a hideout, a layover place. They reported to the Chief of Police immediately upon their arrival. They were guaranteed freedom of molestation, so long as they did not pull anything in Woodfield. They raided neighboring towns, robbed upstate banks, looted and killed elsewhere, but in Woodfield they were safe. Woodfield had one of the cleanest crime records in the country. It was frequently cited as a model community. Actually, it fostered vice upon a large scale because it protected itself at the expense of every other community within a radius of five hundred miles. It became known finally from one end of the country to the other, and the scum of the underworld used it as a center of operations.

"The situation became so bad that a reform movement got under way, especially when the federal government developed its powerful new crime-fighting agency. The old political machine met defeat. The city council felt the voters' wrath. The state legislature forced through an option for charter revision. The voters approved, and the police department came under the direct control of a new official, the Commissioner of Public Safety.

"Woodfield is a small city of approximately seventy-five thousand population. The state university is situated there. I had been teaching at the university for fifteen years, in the fields of sociology and civics. One day, a committee representing businessmen and civic welfare organizations offered to back me for the new position. I suppose they chose me for my complete freedom from political affiliation and lack of contact with the intrenched organization. I accepted because I saw a public duty to perform.

"This," Chalmer murmured reflectively, "is simply background material. It has little to do with the story, except in so far as it explains how I reached office, and became vitally concerned with the series of incidents that you read about. It also explains how I happened to be vested with sweeping powers which enabled me to clamp down a comparatively rigid censorship."

"Censorship is hardly in the best tradition of American freedom."

"I agree with you, but there are exceptions to the principle. If a lynch-crazy mob was running wild, would you give them the name and location of your prisoner? If the government was planning an inflationary step, should the news be released in advance to speculators? Complete, constant, and immediate dissemination of news is never wholly to be desired, or approved. However, you do not yet know the peculiar circumstances which I believe justified my action."

II. Flame in the Sky, Blood on the Ground

"The suburbs of Woodfield," Chalmer continued, "lie to its south and east. Northward, beginning even within the city limits, stretches a rural area of farmlands, fields and pastures, second-growth timber, lakes and gently rolling hills. A new state highway runs northeast connecting with upstate towns and cities, but the district due north of Woodfield is not thickly settled, and the old country roads of dirt and macadam suffice for what little traffic there is. The largest farm in this area lies about eight miles north of Woodfield. It belongs to the King estate, and consists of a full half-section including greenhouses, truck gardens, a small lake, woods, and several buildings. It used to be a model farm with prize cattle and flower exhibits, but in recent years it has begun to run down. This summer it has been tended only by the caretaker, Kurt Jensen, and his family. I knew him because he had been janitor of one of the campus buildings for many years.

"The end of August brought a hot, dry spell. Day after day saw the thermometer climb to a hundred. Four days in a row, the mercury hit one hundred five or more. The air was like the air of a blast furnace. When I lay even in the shade, a breeze blew over me like a wind from hell. I watered the lawn each night; and each morning the grass was dusty and the soil powder-dry. The chairs and woodwork inside my house were so hot to the touch that I expected them to burst into spontaneous combustion. God knows where that breeze came from. It blew almost steadily, as scorching as the sun.

"On Saturday, August twenty-fourth, I expected to drive to one of the lake resorts to cool off. I left my office at one o'clock, and found my car an oven. The tar of the pavements was bubbling. Heatwaves shimmered and danced everywhere. It seemed to me a waste of effort to

drive for miles through that inferno for the pleasure of frying somewhere else.

"I went home and sat on the porch with an electric fan. In the late
afternoon, haze began to gather, and I thought that perhaps rain would
break the spell. Heat lightning flickered to the north and west.

"I remember that I ate a little potato salad and cold sausage at six. It
was too hot for a full dinner. I sat on the porch again, trying to cool off.

"About six-thirty, while I was sitting there, I saw a dazzling glare to
the north, a glare of such blinding and intolerable brilliance that it hurt
my eyes. The whole sky was lighted for a long instant with that white-
hot glare. Then came a sound, a gigantic sound like the roar of many
cataracts, a grinding blast as though a thunderclap kept prolonging itself.
The glare died out, and the roaring faded. The phenomenon interested
me a good deal, but it was too hot to do anything. I felt certain I had
witnessed the fall and explosion of a meteorite.

"About seven-thirty, the telephone began ringing. At first I didn't pay
any attention to it, but the ringing persisted, and finally I went inside.

"It was Kurt Jensen. 'Vill you come oop right ay-vay?' he asked, his
accent strong in his excitement. 'Somet'ing has yust happened. It iss a
fery strange t'ing.'

"I demurred, while seeking more information, but he kept lapsing into
Scandinavian terms that I couldn't follow. He was obviously upset; and
when I suggested that a radio squad car would be sufficient to cope with
the emergency, whatever it was, he reeled off a torrent of excited
protest. He insisted that I come in person for this very strange thing. My
curiosity aroused, I finally consented.

"The district around the King estate was out of our jurisdiction, of
course; but it lay within the county limits, and the custom had long
existed for Woodfield police to settle the extremely rare disturbances
which occurred there.

"I saw no reason to take any one from the force along with me. I am
glad that I did not. I drove my own car, and left almost immediately after
Jensen's call.

"Twilight was coming on when I crossed the city line. The sun still
hung above the horizon, obscured by haze, and glowing red like a monstrous, blood-shot eye. The scorching breeze had subsided. I passed a
couple of farm wagons and a few cars, but there was practically no
traffic. The trees along the road looked wilted and unreal. The film of dust
that covered them turned the leaves a silvery-gray; and this in turn
became suffused with crimson, reflecting the light of the setting sun.
Dust covered the wild grasses and bushes. It clung to the clover and

timothy. It hung upon the parched cornstalks, and the yellowing fields of wheat. There was no green anywhere; only the sunbaked fields and the dusty vegetation.

"About eight o'clock, I was driving between a tangle of second-growth wilderness on my right, and a fairly well kept patch of woods on my left, which was part of the King estate. I continued until I came to the driveway.

"I had just turned into the driveway when I heard a curious sound. It was like the explosive gasp that precedes a scream, but it ended abruptly while I strained my ears expecting a shriek that did not come. The sound had jangled my nerves. I do not know why. Nor could I tell how far distant was its source—perhaps a hundred yards, perhaps five hundred. The air was very still. Then I heard another sound, a crashing off in the woods. It continued for several seconds, growing fainter, and finally ceased entirely. I stepped on the gas and quickly slid my car to a stop in front of the farmhouse.

"Jensen had told me that his family was in Woodfield for the night, but that he would meet me on the porch of the main building. He was not there. I shouted but received no answer. Twilight deepened around me, and I became conscious of the peculiar evening hush of lonely places. Strictly speaking, it was not a stillness, for I heard the hum of mosquitoes, a whippoorwill mourned, and a meadowlark sang an evening song. I heard crickets chirp, then the call of a bobwhite, and the fireflies had begun to glow. Yet these things seemed only to call attention to the brooding quiet that prevailed.

"I skirted the house, without meeting anyone. A path ran along the edge of the woods to my left. I followed the path until it skirted around a big boulder. I was hurrying along and I tripped before I could save myself. The object that tripped me was the head of Kurt Jensen. It rolled a foot. The object upon which I fell must have been his body. But only a terrible pulp remained, and the clothing was mingled with flesh, and a great red splash extended for several yards in a swathe along the path."

III. Red Torpedo

Chalmer's pipe had long gone out. He held it clenched by the bowl in one hand as he leaned against the rail. He did not, for the moment, attempt to relight the half-burned dottle. He continued, and his deceptively calm voice affected me strangely against the roaring background of wind and whitecaps. "I have seen death a number of times, in different guises, but none that produced the shock of finding Jensen's corpse. The eyes were wide open, and it seemed that they still retained a gleam of life and of horror, but while I watched, they turned glassy. I will never be sure whether I actually saw the last ebb of his spirit, or whether the fading light deceived me.

"Blood oozed from his neck. The blood upon the ground was still bright and wet. His body lay as warm as if life inhabited it. Death must have come only seconds before my arrival, and his must have been the choked-off gasp that I had heard. But I could not imagine how he had been killed. His neck was sliced as keenly as though a sharp sword had whirled through it. No knife or any weapon of any sort lay near the corpse. Inconceivable pressure must have been applied to his body, but I was at a loss as to how and why. Even if he had fallen from a great height, that gruesome result would not have occurred. The only explanation that I could think of was that a giant boa constrictor must have somehow gotten into the woods. The most casual glance made it plain that every bone had been crushed and the body drained of blood in a matter of seconds only.

"Sickened by what I saw, I inspected the ground for footprints. I did not find any. Yet I distinctly remembered having heard a heavy body crash through the woods. I looked for further signs of a great reptile. Then, indented inch-deep in the dry soil, I found a wedge-shaped groove that entered the woods. There were no footprints. The furrow proceeded in an unbroken straight line. The bushes and undergrowth right of the line were slightly broken; but left of the line the growth was heavily damaged, even the tops of bushes several feet away having been crushed."

He lighted his pipe again and puffed strongly. "I followed this curious trail through the woods. It looked for all the world as if some large and heavy body, off-balance, and resting upon a wheel or groove or wedge, had progressed in a straight line, breaking even sturdy young trees that lay in its path. The furrow extended to the road, where it ceased.

Dusk was falling, but I made my way back to the body and followed the furrow in an effort to find its source. It ran along the path. The path wound past a barn, some fields, the private lake, then skirted a rock-strewn hill. A quarter of a mile from the body, I came into a dell behind the hill, and encountered another strange sight.

"For a radius of a hundred yards, the ground was blackened and charred. A faint smell of ozone lingered in the air, and recalling the bright flash I had seen in the sky about dinner time, I thought a bolt of lightning had struck here. But when I bent over to inspect the ground, I found the soil riddled with tiny pockmarks, and emitting a peculiar odor, analogous to burned gunpowder, but with a difference. I cannot explain the difference. If you have ever tried to describe a smell or odor, you know how difficult it is."

"I know," I agreed. "To say that a scent is like roses doesn't convey any impression unless the reader is familiar with roses. It is absolutely impossible to put into words any new, unique smell."

Chalmer nodded. "It was a pungent, irritating, fiery sort of scent—oh what's the use, I can't describe it because it wasn't like any smell I'd ever encountered before.

"But what got me after all was not so much the odor, as the huge, weird object that lay against the side of the hill. Shaped something like a torpedo, it reminded me of futuristic designs and plans for things like moon-rockets that I've seen pictures of in science magazines. Actually, it bore the appearance of two cones fitted base together. There was a heavy ring around the nose of the torpedo. The cone widened swiftly until, twenty feet from the nose, the craft was fifteen feet high. From this point, the body tapered off again, more gradually, for eighty feet. There were no wings or vanes, openings or doors, anywhere in that hundred-foot long projectile. In the tubing around its nose, however, I discovered eight small, blackened orifices, no bigger than pencils, and in the tail of the craft, eight similar vents. Around each of them clung the same musty, acrid odor I had detected in the pock-marked soil. The hull was balanced on its thickest section, and the tail hung seven and a half feet off the ground.

"I cannot convey to you the strangeness of my sensation. Only the rim of the sun lingered above the horizon. The evening hush had deepened. Amidst this heat and stillness and isolation, an alien and sinister craft had come to rest. And the unknown cruiser, with no large opening that I could find, was built of or covered entirely with a silvery-red metallic substance that glowed weirdly in the last rays of the dying day. I took out my penknife and broke its point without making the slightest scratch or indentation upon that surface. I rapped it sharply with a stone, and it gave off a deep, resonant, resounding *bong*, as though I had struck a gong of peculiar tonal qualities. The ringing did not die away for a full minute. The air quivered with soft percussions of sound, but I saw no change in the nature of the torpedo, and no one answered the challenge.

"Then the sun set, and in the swiftly gathering darkness, I all at once felt afraid. A little wind seemed to play across my scalp. Even in the half-gloom, the fabric or metal, tougher and more impervious than any metal with which I was familiar, continued to glow with a luminous, silvery-red lustre. I had the distinct and creepy impression that the shell of this thing, or the projectile itself, possessed a secret, mysterious life all its own.

"Frankly, I began to walk away. I could see nothing more to be done there. The body of Kurt Jensen must be taken care of. I had, however, come to some preliminary conclusions. A number of nations throughout the world have been experimenting with stratoplanes and high-altitude craft of various types, I knew from newspaper accounts. In my belief, this was just such a new invention, perhaps being tried out on an experimental trip, and compelled to make a forced landing here, or driven far off its course through some accident. It might even be an experiment of our own government, or at least of an inventor in our country. The flash like lightning which I had seen in the late afternoon was probably made by the descent of this very torpedo. Since it had no landing-gear or wings or other external parts, and showed no signs of wreckage, I made the obvious assumption that it relied upon some sort of explosive force, perhaps rockets, to check its fall; and that this force accounted for the burned and pock-marked nature of the soil in the vicinity.

"But there were several hurdles that I could not get over. I thought momentarily that Kurt Jensen had somehow met his death accidentally from the explosive force that checked the torpedo's descent. But he had phoned me after the craft landed. Again, there was no sign of any opening large enough for even a snake to pass. If anyone had been inside the torpedo, he could not get out. And if he had gotten out, I was faced with the mystery of how. Anything small enough to emerge through the aft or tail orifices certainly could not have made the heavy crashing I heard in the woods. As I reconstructed events, Kurt had seen the torpedo land, or had stumbled across it. He had then telephoned me, and while he awaited my arrival, something had distracted him. He had gone to investigate, and had met his death, at the hands of a killer or by means of a power unknown.

"When I reached the main farmhouse I telephoned to Gostad, Chief of Detectives, and told him to come out with a photographer and a finger-print man. Woodfield does not have the large staff of specialists that major cities do, but our men are trained in the all-round handling of murder cases. Even if I could have commanded a squad of experts, I would not have done so.

"I waited until they arrived. The darkness pressed around me. I passed a nervous, uncomfortable twenty minutes, because my imagination kept straying into disturbing paths. I had begun to realize that I might be up against something alien to average experience.

"When Gostad and the others came, I directed their operations. I explained that I had already thoroughly searched the grounds. I turned their attention to the furrow and swathe through the woods, and said the killer must have escaped in that direction. By then, utter darkness had arrived. In the gloom and trampling around, the men destroyed the odd characteristics of the trail, as I had hoped. The remains of Kurt Jensen were gathered up, and we returned to town. None of the others shared my knowledge of the silvery-red hull that lay beyond the lake."

IV. Black Horror

As he knocked the soggy tobacco from his pipe, refilled it, and lighted up, Chalmer's hands trembled. His face looked haggard. I made no comment. After puffing strongly, he inhaled deeply of the salt wind and said, "This occurred on a Saturday night. I returned to my home well after ten, and soon retired. I was fatigued, but did not sleep. The incidents of the evening drifted through my thoughts over and over again. I tossed around till midnight, and then slipped into a sort of half-slumber.

"I had nightmares, I dreamed of the gleaming long torpedo, queerly balanced upon its thickest section. I saw again the terribly crushed body of Jensen. I fled from shapeless monsters running wild in forests without end. I seldom dream, but my visions that night were of a sort to turn the hair white. This fitful slumber was broken by resonant bongs that prolonged themselves in musical thunderclaps through eternity. I struggled to slow wakefulness, and became conscious of the telephone ringing insistently.

"My wrist watch showed a little before six A.M. I could not imagine why anyone should be calling me at that absurd hour of a Sunday morning, and decided it must be a wrong number. I turned over, but the ringing persisted. I finally climbed out of bed.

"I was perhaps two-thirds awake when I reached the phone. A staccato voice came over the wire, 'Murphy speaking, Switchboard, Police Headquarters. Commissioner Chalmer? A call for the riot squad, corner of Cherry and Hilton Streets."

"For a moment I was annoyed. 'Well,' I complained, 'why waken me at this hour for a routine call?'

"Murphy said, 'You left orders with Chief of Detectives Gostad that you were to be notified immediately of anything unusual that happened. Gostad passed the order on to me. The call is a very queer one. It is to the affect that a large beast of some sort is prowling the district. I have already dispatched the riot squad.'

"That brought me wide awake in a hurry. The corner of Cherry and Hilton Streets was the heart of an exclusive residential district about three miles from Police Headquarters, but only a half-mile from my residence. Woodfield doesn't boast a radio unit. From the moment the call came in to the moment the riot squad reached the locale, three to five minutes would elapse. I had an even chance of getting there as fast as they did.

"I dressed with a speed that proved disastrous to buttons. I didn't try to do even a presentable job. I only took time to snatch my revolver and a small camera before I ran out. I lost a little time starting my car, but less than three minutes had gone when I was on the way. I didn't hear a siren, because one of the first orders I issued was that the siren should be used only in case of extreme necessity. Too many crooks have gotten away because they could check on police approach by that unmistakable sound.

"The streets were deserted. I saw only one boy delivering newspapers during the half-mile ride. I heard the noise of a car travelling up Cherry Avenue at high speed. It was the riot squad, arriving just before I did.

"A man in plain clothes was standing by a police call-box. I did not recognize him. He was white-faced, shaking, and stammered when he tried to speak. There were six men armed with rifles, submachine guns, revolvers, and teargas bombs in the squad. The captain had just started to interrogate the man when I got out of my car.

"What's going on here? Who are you?' I demanded.

"Captain Dollenbeck answered for the plainclothesman, who seemed unable to get a grip on himself. 'He's an honorary member of the staff. Employed as night watchman around here. The folks in this section mostly go away for the summer, and he sort of looks after things. His name's Reilly.' He turned to Reilly and spoke more roughly. 'Come on, shell out. We ain't got all day to hang around.'

"Reilly gulped and said, 'I never saw nothin' like it. I was makin' the rounds. Just as I got to the corner here I saw it tearin' down the avenue. Mother of Gawd! I jumped back behind the hedge. I took another look at it. It was all black and slimy like nothin' you ever dreamed of. It was bigger'n an elephant, but it didn't have no legs. It just rolled along. That was when I ducked over to the box and turned in a riot call. Then I ducked back and watched some more. The black devil had got as far as the next corner, tearin' along like—like—Gawd, I don't know what. Then it gave a funny little sort of jerk. It got off the road and slammed up the walk into the Martins' place, that big house down there on the corner. There ain't no one home. I don't know how it got in if it did. It ain't come out yet and I ain't seen it since.'

"Captain Dollenbeck's face was a study as he listened to this extraordinary recital. Rage, anger, and disgust successively swept across his features. His men eyed each other, and one of them openly snickered.

"Old Reilly almost wept when he heard that sound. His nerves must have been pretty well frayed. 'You think I'm drunk!' he burst out. 'Just wait till you see the damn beast yourself! Then you'll laugh—like hell you will! Now there ain't nothin' but—'

"He stopped suddenly and I thought he was going to faint. We were in a half-circle facing him. His eyes, looking up the street behind us, bulged with terror. He gaped and worked his jaws, but he was beyond speech. We all whirled around.

"Old Reilly had said there wasn't anything. But there was something.

"I don't know how long I remained in a sort of paralysis. There were eight of us, and we all stood there, simply gaping, while priceless seconds ticked by. We didn't move. We didn't yell. We didn't draw our guns. We didn't do anything. Utter surprise, like seeing a building explode before your eyes, will stop you for a second. The unexpected, like opening a closet door and having a corpse fall out on you, will paralyze you for a moment. Many kinds of shock will stun the human system for a brief interval, until the mind adjusts itself to the accident, and realizes that nothing in the matter is outside average experience, explainable by coincidence or the juxtaposition of incongruous events.

"But we faced, then, something that never before entered human experience. It had absolutely no relation to any ideas, any knowledge, any concepts, or any material of any sort that I had ever read or imagined. It was so utterly alien to everything I knew that I did not even feel horror in those first tense seconds. I experienced only astonishment, and a sort of wide-eyed, detached curiosity."

Chalmer took a long, deep, nervous breath. The memory of a tragic occasion affected him more strongly than the occurrence itself, if his words expressed the conviction that his voice carried. When he resumed, it was with a full and glowing pipe to steady him.

"From the sidewalk gate of the Martin residence, a block away, emerged a black, fantastic, and glistening mass which I will never comprehend. It spun out into the middle of the pavement, and there it paused. It had drifted out as a shapeless cloud, a solid shadow, a coherent body of ink. It seemed to flow, like a detached portion of a Hadean stream. In the street, it writhed and came together. It assumed a new and more sinister form. It stood upright, like an immense cylinder, at first, whirling at a feverish speed. It must have risen at least eight feet high and four thick. The shining black mass, ambiguous, gigantic, began to tilt, until it balanced upon one edge.

"In a flash came to me the explanation of that curious groove I had seen in the woods of the King estate, and the oddly broken bushes. This was the heavy body I had heard crashing through the forest.

"While I still waited in the grip of lethargy, the cylindrical thing ceased its tilting. In its way, it looked like a miniature version of the leaning tower of Pisa. But now its rotation increased, and all at once it hurtled toward us, a thunderbolt of malignant power. It was halfway to us before the spell of inertia snapped. Then chaos. I remember Reilly stumbling up Hilton Street with a green face and twitching hands. Dollenbeck pumped six bullets at the monster. All were directs hits. It did not even hesitate in its rush. Somebody gasped. Somebody yelled. Somebody swore in a mad, crazy rush of words. Somebody grabbed a submachine gun and ran forward. It coughed in a long spurt, and the flashes and fumes were dotted with the thud of slugs smashing home. Ten, thirty, fifty, I don't know how many ploughed into that plunging Juggernaut, without effect. There was no reason for anybody's action. We went by instinct. I leaped for my car and dragged out the camera. I sprung it open and began taking snapshots. The air was full of sound and explosions, gasps and powder-fumes.

"The man with the submachine gun stood a dozen feet in front of us. Somebody hurled a tear-gas bomb. It burst with a tinkling plop, but the white fumes that eddied around the black mass slowed it not at all, and faded behind as the thing sped on. It uttered no sound, aside from a slight whir caused by its friction on air and pavement.

"Then, in all that kaleidoscopic compression of furious developments, there came a new horror. The man with the submachine gun had begun to back and sidestep. Without warning, and in a motion so instantaneous that the eye could scarcely follow it, a tentacle like the finest of wire lashed out from the onrushing monster and whipped around the neck of the gunner. I cannot conceive of the power behind that long, thin loop. It contracted instantly and completely. The man's head fell to the street. A sheet of black doom shot forward from the thing and enveloped the man's body. Like the tentacle, it contracted, and a great, terrible fountain of blood spurted fifteen feet into the air. I knew how Kurt Jensen had met his death.

"The riot squad scattered in all directions. I do not blame them. I suppose I would have fled myself, if I hadn't had a kind of half-conviction that no matter what I did, this was the end. Or perhaps I was simply too frightened to move. Captain Dollenbeck held his ground. I don't know if he was foolhardy or brave. He had reloaded his revolver. He pressed the trigger as rapidly as he could. I distinctly heard the wham of the slugs.

"The thing turned aside at an angle toward us where we stood by the curb. Dollenbeck swung his pistol, and the motion threw him off-center. A bullet ricocheted from a fire hydrant. It struck a spark. The thing stopped dead in its tracks, but the sparked had leaped. A blinding, purple flash from the thing stunned me. It hung poised, for a fraction of a second. The air smelled of ozone and weariness. I remember hearing the *clippety-clop* of a milk-wagon's horse somewhere near by. The cylindrical monster toppled slowly forward and hit the pavement with a sort of flat, sucking thud."

V. The Captive

"Again, for a timeless second, we stood spellbound, staring at the inert mass. The noise and shooting must have frightened the horse. In the tense silence that gripped us, the wild *clippety-clop* of hooves and the bouncing rattle of the milk-wagon came with sharp clarity. In my thoughts, fleetingly, I gave thanks for the hour and the season and the district, the houses that were fortunately closed and shuttered, their owners away on vacation trips.

"I realized, as I came out of a daze, that I still held the camera. I had taken four snapshots. I had not reached for my pistol. I could not think clearly, under the shock of that unearthly experience. I looked down with awe and loathing at the mass on the pavement. I believed it to be dead. I walked over to it, and forced myself to touch it.

"A violent shudder shook me. The substance of the monster felt warm, tingling, and yet metallic. It was as though I had contacted living flesh; yet I beheld a formless thing, black, inhuman, inscrutable. You know the feel of quicksilver?"

I nodded silently.

"Imagine, if you can, warm quicksilver that will not dissolve into globules, and that retains extreme cohesive strength in spite of its fluid nature; a metallic mass charged with some sort of radiation, electrical or otherwise. Then you will have some idea of why I shivered when my hand touched it.

"Reilly had disappeared. One of the police had met a gruesome death. Six of us remained, and I took it for granted my face was just as white as theirs. They looked to me for orders, and while I did not care to go over Captain Dollenbeck's head, it was no time for petty formalities. I detailed one man to summon an ambulance, keep guard over the dead man until it arrived, and drive my car to headquarters.

"Two others held submachine guns and tear-gas bombs ready. It is odd how we rely upon weapons of long-standing, even when they have failed us.

"The rest of us tried to lift that sinister hulk, and to my great astonishment, we succeeded. Ugh! I will never forget the feel of the stuff which composed that alien monster. It came up as if we were lifting a heap of dough. It gave me a queer sensation of extreme weight counter-balanced by some other force. Once, when going through a steel plant, I saw an immense flywheel that I couldn't even budge. An electromagnet was hung over it, and the power turned part way on. I could lift the wheel with ease, but it still gave me the impression of enormous weight. Well, our inert nightmare was of a similar nature.

"The sweat dripped from my face, but I wasn't warm. I quaked in fear, the chilling fear that this monstrous distortion of life would suddenly arise and smite us with hideous doom. I knew of nothing we could do to stop it. I prayed that it was dead, and that its warmth resulted from exposure to the sun, or would gradually ebb away, with life departed. I thought of it in terms of life, though certainly it bore no relation to any conceivable life-form that ever existed upon earth.

"Somehow, we piled it into the squad car. It sagged upon the floor. I stared at it with a confusion of emotion all the way in. It fascinated me, with an almost hypnotic intensity, and yet produced a sort of ecstasy of horror. My hands sweated. I tried to convince myself that its reality and immediate presence removed it from the category of the bizarre or the supernormal. But its nature, its power, its ferocity, its incredible weird-ness, only roused in me apprehensions and conjectures of the gloomiest kind.

"The ride to Police Headquarters proved a nightmare. The only problem I solved concerned the temporary disposal of the captive.

"Police Headquarters adjoins a new Building of Municipal Affairs erected about two years ago. The City Jail comprises a separate unit, linked by underground passages to Police Headquarters, the Court House, and the Building of Municipal Affairs, the four units occupying an entire city block. The City Jail, modern in every respect, contains a group of four subcellar cells for the solitary confinement of dangerous prisoners. These cells are escape-proof. They have heavy steel doors with a small grille through which food can be passed. Another steel door stands at the bottom and at the top of the stairs leading to the cellar. The cellar, in addition to the different mechanical units which operate the building, contains storerooms and detention cells used mainly to sober off drunks overnight.

"We lugged the monster into a subcellar vault. We dumped it upon the floor. It lay there, a mound of gluey black glistening substance, roughly hemispherical, the strangest occupant those cells ever had.

"Then I pledged the men to silence for the time being. We didn't know what we were up against. Anything might happen. If the prisoner escaped, we wouldn't have anything tangible to support our explanations. If it didn't revive, we would have the devil of a time trying to tell what had happened. If it did become again as we had first seen it, people could form their own conclusions.

"One factor later turned out to be in our favor. Woodfield has a morning and an evening paper, but only the morning paper publishes a Sunday issue. Its next edition is not run off until two A.M. on Monday morning. Thus, while reporters frequent the buildings on weekdays, none is on hand during the Sabbath, until six o'clock, when the *Morning Courier* man shows up for his copy.

"We had about twelve hours in which to decide our course.

"I asked Dollenbeck and the others to wait for me in my office. After they left, I told the guard in the subcellar block to take it easy while I studied our captive through the slide in the cell-door.

"The guard gave me a curious look but walked off to smoke a cigarette. Hatless, coatless, and in a dither, I suppose I looked as if I myself ought to have been locked up. I tried to figure some plan of action, some preparation for whatever emergency arose.

"It's hard enough, arranging yourself an out for any situation likely to rise in ordinary life. I faced a menace of incalculable resourcefulness. I didn't know its nature. I didn't know its origin. I didn't know anything about it, or what it was, or what it could do. It was beyond experience.

"While I stood looking at it, it stirred, with an uneasy, gelatinous motion. I broke out in a cold sweat. I had been afraid that we merely stunned it, and now when it wakened into sluggish activity, I had neither defense nor attack ready.

"All at once it quivered and stiffened, as though gathering its energies for action.

"I yelled at the guard, *'Unlock the doors!'*

"I heard him run, open the lower door, race up the steps.

"The monster began a spinning that accelerated faster and faster until it revolved with the speed and hum of a dynamo. I didn't know how swiftly it turned, but it must have been thousands of revolutions per minute. A strong draught of air rushed past me. The black thing, a living

Juggernaut, hurled itself against the solid steel door of its cell. The door
burst from its hinges with a scream of tearing metal. The next few
moments are a blur of pure terror in memory. I fled up the stairs
somehow. My lungs burned from the fierce effort. I tore across the cellar
and risked a glance over my shoulder.

"The prisoner, having already flowed up out of the subcellar, made
itself a battering-ram. It crashed into the door of a detention cell, and the
door slammed clear across the cell to the wall opposite. I never before
saw such terrific driving power as that thing had. It didn't seem to want
revenge, or try to injure us, so long as we stayed out of its way. Escape,
for the moment, appeared to be its single goal.

"The cell that it hurled itself into had a small ventilation grille, no
more than a foot square, at ground level. Four lashes of fine-spun wire
flicked out of the black mass with a twang as of snapping piano-string.
They looped around the steel grille, and those inch-thick bars became so
much cheese. The whole grille, cleanly sliced, fell to the ground. The
delicate feelers returned to the main mass. This much I saw before
dashing to the first floor and running to a window that overlooked the
inner courtyard.

"The thing had assumed a new shape. I could visualize it in the cell
below, sliding across the floor, up the wall, and out through the opening
it had cleared. It emerged as a gigantic snake, a half-foot thick, flowing
out almost endlessly, hundreds of feet of it. In the center of the quadrangle, the coil began forming the original mass, which swelled in size
visibly and rapidly second by second until it quivered again, a roughly
hemispheric mound, glistening in the sunlight with a wetly black sheen.

"I realized with a shock that it was watching me.

"By what means it observed me, I do not know, for it lacked eyes and
all other senses and methods of vision as we are accustomed to them.
Yet I knew, instinctively and definitely, that that formless blob focussed
attention upon me. I felt a wave of hostility, of malignant, impending
doom—and all I did was snap pictures foolishly. They've been a hobby
with me for so long that I take them by habit.

"Then the tension passed, but I thought I detected in its place a
quality of surging, triumphal power. It is difficult to speak with precision
of such intangibles in reaction, and during a crisis of such unimaginable
strangeness.

"I believe I was the only witness to an astounding manifestation.

"The thing, having assembled itself in a compact mass once more,
underwent a violent writhing that lasted scarcely more than a second. It
blurred with amazing speed through a shifting focus. Its form and outline

changed. There stood before me, perfectly proportioned but upon a giant scale, twelve or fourteen feet high, the parody of man! Nose, fingers, hair, mouth, ears, teeth, everything characteristic of the external body was present in that plastic image; but the eyes were liquid jet, and the teeth gleaming black, and all other parts the same sinister hue. And it was quasi-human only in appearance; for its substance had not changed. Half in shadow, half in the early morning sunlight, it towered watching me with those cold, wet, metallic imitations of eyes. The depth of my loathing and horror left me powerless. Why the sight should have shaken me so profoundly and brought me so close to hysteria, I cannot say. Perhaps it was the abominable hue of the thing, or its immense size, or the essential grotesqueness in its attempt to duplicate Man.

"Again it trembled restlessly through a cycle of new mutation; and now there loomed in the quadrangle a figure of Cyclopean, hyper-geo-metric form; repellent, infinitely strange and complex, yet possessing a kind of terrible beauty. Hundreds of feet in height, it had become a subtly interlacing pattern of arcs and cubes and spheres, of pyramids and the projection of lines and forms, cubes and spheres, into tissue of many dimensions; the whole a fantastic, wonderfully voluted, and fluctuant materialization of abstract design; like a skeletal framework or extension of some invisible, otherworld being. And yet, amidst all that marvellous complexity, there wove oppressively disturbing tatters and ribbons and tentacles, suggestive of corruption, and swaying with a black, avid hunger.

"Then it came down from the sky, and the nightmarish vision, the many-dimensioned warp, subsided to its original shape. And while I watched, it continued to subside, melting and vanishing before my eyes; and the heap dwindled, shrank to smaller and smaller size, as though seeping into the very earth, or as though drawing about itself a mask of invisibility. I don't know how much time elapsed; perhaps ten seconds, perhaps thirty; before it was gone, leaving only the wrecked cells as proof that it had ever existed."

VI. A Couple of Specimens

I thought a flurry of raindrops would drive us below; but Chalmer ignored the shower, and it passed as suddenly as it came. The *S. S. Mercury* plunged steadily southward. The wind howled, banks of cloud scudded across the sky, and the sea swelled and crashed with incessant roaring. Briefly I discerned a monster that rose from the depths. Its back broke above the surface, but it submerged before I caught more than a glimpse of its ponderous bulk. Chalmer shivered. His eyes trailed away into the dark wilderness that had swallowed the sea creature.

Chalmer said, "When the black mass disappeared from the courtyard, I experienced a reaction that left me giddy. I trembled so badly that I clutched the window-bars to steady myself. When I did regain a measure of control, instinct rather than logic spurred me. I turned and ran out of the building.

"My car had just arrived, driven by the man left on guard over the body of the murdered policeman. I snatched the ignition key from his hands without a word of explanation. He looked at me queerly. I must have seemed out of my wits. I jumped into the car and tried so anxiously to get under way that I bungled everything. I jammed the gears, stalled the engine, flooded the carburetor, and made a number of other amateurish blunders. I scraped a fender while going out of the ramp, and drove over the curb in turning a corner.

"Then I stepped on the gas. I shot the marker up to seventy. There was almost no traffic. For two miles toward the northern city limits, Center Avenue is a wide, straight thoroughfare. The stop and go signs had begun to operate at seven A.M. I sailed through them without diminishing speed, horn blaring away. I remember a roadster that slammed to a quick stop with screeching brakes when we almost collided. I swerved and my car swung a crazy arc to the left of a sedan approaching me. Danger didn't matter. The exhilaration of speed, and more speed, helped steady my thoughts.

"I was racing, of course, toward the hundred-foot long torpedo that had landed upon the King farm. The black thing must have been aboard the reddish hull. There might be more of the entities, dozens of them, but I didn't think so.

"It was plain by now that I had come across a riddle beyond crime and society and human motivation. That peculiar space ship didn't originate on Earth. The monster bore no relation to life or evolutionary processes as we are familiar with them upon a terrestrial basis. It may have started from a planet of the solar system; or it may have traversed the great void of four light-years that separates our system from the nearest star. If this latter conjecture was true, I had before me a vista of such colossal scope as to strain imagination.

"I am not very well versed in astronomy. It is a science that I know only in a general way, from a course I took in college and cursory reading since. I do know that the planets of our system have much the same composition, in different stages of development; that the Sun is too incandescent to tolerate life as we know it, and the Moon too frigid, Venus too steaming and dank, Neptune too cold, bleak, and aged.

"Both the astroplane, if I may call it such, and the occupant were of a composition foreign to matter, energy, elements, and life in the earthly sense. Therein lay my dilemma. Two murders had been committed, according to our standards, but how can you accuse something, whose nature, system, and origin are unknown, over an action it took in self-preservation, upon a planet hostile to its presence? How would you communicate with it, try it, and imprison it? How would you carry out a sentence of death?

"I recalled its mutations in the quadrangle. What if it had been trying to draw a parallel? Suppose it had first depicted human life by assuming the shape of the two-legged beings it had encountered. Suppose, then, that having given me its concept of humanity, it tried to express its own habitual appearance in the world from which it came? I thought of the Cyclopean and eerie hypergeometric form it had assumed, but I merely got a headache when I attempted to conceive of such an existence.

"I have called the thing a monster. I said that it frightened and revolted me. But when I tried to comprehend it, to put myself in its place, another disagreeable thought occurred to me. The thing, if it possessed intelligence of an advanced order, probably regarded our life as something horrible, incomprehensible, and enigmatic. Our appearance and our characteristics probably astonished it, or scared it, just as much as its presence affected us. In its view, we were the monsters.

"Amid all this welter of doubt and perplexity, I was baffled by still another problem. How had the entity managed to vanish so completely before my very eyes? I could not believe that it had seeped into the ground, though such was the impression I got. I once read somewhere, in connection with one of Einstein's theories, as I recall, mention of a possible curvature of light. Perhaps the thing had knowledge that enabled it to bend light rays around itself, in which case it would of course be invisible. At best, this was a far-fetched and rather obscure hypothesis, but I couldn't think of any other explanation. I ought to have guessed the obvious, simple truth. My failure to do so is proof of my muddled state.

"I suppose it took about fifteen minutes for me to cover the distance from Police Headquarters to the King farm. I left my car in front of the main house. Then I followed the winding trail until I came again to the strange, silvery-red torpedo.

"So far as I could tell, no one had visited it, nor had it changed in any respect. It still balanced precariously on the edge of its thickest section.

I startled a rabbit into the clearing, but it fled from the reddish hull in great, frightened leaps.

"I had no plans in mind. I hadn't the slightest idea of what I'd do if the monster came along. Electricity affected the thing temporarily; but how are you going to carry bolts of lightning around with you? Heat of the order of incandescence might halt it; but how are you going to carry such flame in your pocket, and if you could, what chance would the monster leave you of using it? What's the use of thinking in earthly terms about an invader that lacks any connection with earthly laws? How are you going to destroy something that is indestructible?

"I didn't even have a hunch. I simply reasoned that the monster had arrived in the torpedo, and that sooner or later it would return. I think it was curiosity more than anything else that brought me there. I didn't know what would happen, but I had to be there and find out, even if I got killed in the process. It wasn't bravery, but a need to know.

"About forty feet from where the double-cone-shaped torpedo rested against the hillside, a clump of gooseberry bushes offered some concealment. When I settled there to watch, I found that I had an excellent view of the hull and the path.

"I expected a long vigil, but I doubt whether I had been there a quarter of an hour before I witnessed an extraordinary, blood-chilling sight.

"Some hundreds of yards distant, there suddenly emerged into view around the path's turn the body of a man, floating face upward a foot from the ground, and borne along as though in the grip of a swiftly running tide. Nothing supported him. He did not move or cry out. I could not determine whether he was unconscious or dead. He floated toward me head-first, hence I could at first make little out of his features or appearance.

"I had hardly recovered from the shock when there followed in his aerial wake the body of a woman, likewise drifting along off the ground, face to the sky, and head toward me. The two bodies were not more than twenty feet apart. Silently, mysteriously, supported by some invisible force, and propelled by I knew not what, they drifted toward the silvery-red hull at a faster pace than a man can walk.

"As I watched the uncanny spectacle, I saw that the man was dark-haired and dark-featured, a Latin type. He seemed to be in his late twenties, well-dressed, a little above average height. The woman I had seen somewhere before, though I didn't know her name. She had a Nordic kind of beauty, with flaxen-colored hair, blue eyes, and a fair, lovely skin. She was tall, taller than the man, and possessed a lush figure that made me think of pagan goddesses.

"Their features, I now saw as they drew near, bore expressions of repose, in the limpness of unconsciousness rather than the rigidity of death. I might have rushed out to intercept them, save for the fact that the phenomenon of their motion followed so many other eerie events. There in the solitude, the heat, the presence of the queerly-shaped torpedo, I felt the physical drag which makes us loath to act when we are confronted by a manifestation that violates reason and experience. I should have brought someone along with me. Heaven knows I was desperate but helpless at that crisis.

"Then, amidst the familiar sounds of nature, I became aware of a thin and insidious rustle, so faint as to be almost inaudible. If you have ever heard the low, ghostly sibilance of a snake gliding, you will know what I mean. Anywhere else, the sound would have passed unnoticed; and even here, I detected it mainly because my overwrought senses were in a condition to imagine or magnify anything.

"I saw a small black bead, glistening moistly in the sunlight, appear beside the silvery-red hull. One moment the area was vacant, then the globule materialized out of nowhere. It grew larger like a balloon being puffed. The bodies drifted with a more languid motion, and finally came to rest, parallel with the ground and poised upon invisible support.

"The tiny, gleaming button expanded to the size of a cowbell, a puffball, a bushel basket. Suddenly I knew the answer. I could not, at my distance, see the truth, but I knew what had happened.

"In the courtyard, when the black mass disappeared while I was looking at it, it didn't seep into the ground or assume a mask of invisibility. It simply attenuated to the thinnest of threads. In the shape of a thin creeper no more than a hair's thickness and miles long, it slid away unnoticed across town. Somewhere en route, it had caught a couple of human beings, perhaps already on the way to outings or to early church services. Still thinner strands then disengaged themselves from the substance of that Protean entity, and paralyzed the man and the young woman. Fine, tough, wire-like loops held them aloft and bore them along.

"The swelling, inky mound had become the size of the original mass in ticks of time. A tentacle shot out from it. The end of the feeler bulged to the shape of a pearl-drop. The extension whipped backward, lashed forward, and the pear-formed tip smote the tail of the torpedo a mighty blow.

"Instantly, a rising clangor swept up from the silvery-red hull. The sound, deep, musical, and sonorous to begin with, rose to the upper registers and passed out of hearing beyond a high, piercing wail.

"The external covering of the hull shivered. It withdrew from the tail. The metal of silvery-red retreated, ran swiftly toward the nose of the craft, where it bunched into a coil, stripping the torpedo of its protection.

"I had a glimpse of the exposed interior.

"Shapes of things and things of shapes. Colors unknown to Earth. Phantasmagoria of devices, machine objects, dial forms, hyper-mathematical realities. Four-dimensional creations perceived in a three-dimensional world. Living metals, incarnated gases, corridors of time and walls of space. Distortion of matter to concepts and materialization of ideas into static, inert forms. I don't know what I saw. If I were to see again, to study and analyze for years, I might attain a measure of understanding. Or I might not. How can you discard everything you have learned and try to develop a comprehension of a new order of reality?

"The black mass flowed into the ship's interior. It issued numerous creepers which arranged themselves at different devices and in different places. The bodies of the man and the woman followed the drift of the main mass, and came to rest in a receptacle of transparent walls. I realized with something of pity, something of futile rage, that the invader was about to depart, taking with it a couple of specimens of the bizarre form of life which it had discovered upon the planet."

VII. The Long Voyage

"Impulse drove me out of hiding, the obscure sort of impulse that makes us act at moments of gravest peril to save other mortals from impending doom. I crashed through the gooseberry bushes.

"As I did so, the black entity snapped its pear-shaped attachment against the roll of silvery-reddish metal which had accumulated at the nose of the ship. The flying weight smote with a thud of concussion. Out of inaudibility into the highest range of hearing came a twang of sound that slid down the scale, deepening sonorously and amplifying to an ever lower and louder pitch, until it rolled with the clangor of a heavy gong. While that prolonged resonance descended, the silvery-red substance quivered, began to creep and slide around the framework of the torpedo, encasing it again. I hadn't advanced ten feet before the projectile was sealed. If the monster saw me, it paid no attention.

"Then the rear conical section of the astroplane tilted downward until it rested upon the bottom of that eighty-foot length. It continued to tilt, the nose rising ever higher in the air, until it hung perpendicular, poised like a gigantic top. The projectile commenced a spinning, slow at first, that accelerated until it hummed from the speed of rotation. The sunlight glistened upon its luminously glowing surface. The metallic substance deepened in tone from a silvery-red hue to a dark blood color.

"Blinding flame discharged from the eight rear orifices with a roaring, shrieking, reverberating, explosion of power. The projectile skyrocketted, vanished instantly at a velocity so great and multiplying that I could not follow its departure. A blast scorched me. I felt a rush of wind sucked into the vacuum created by the take off. Beating percussions thundered in my ears, but I suppose it was merely the aftereffect of the first explosion.

"For a long while I stood there, staring up into the bright sky, until my eyes ached from its glare, and I began imagining I saw radiant flashes. But though I was shaken and exhausted from the night's occurrences, I didn't begin to get the real reaction until days later, when I had had time to digest it all, and after my thoughts had commenced sifting the phenomena in their wider implications.

"I watched the papers for a week in the vague hope that I might hear of peculiar happenings elsewhere that would signify the return of the invader. I felt a sense of guilt over not having prevented the thing from taking its captives along. I still do not see how I could have acted effectively, but I was the only person with opportunity to intercede. But I have seen and heard nothing further. The projectile is gone. I will never view it again.

"Somewhere out in the great black voids of space, the astroplane is rocketting onward to an unknown goal, or returning to whatever part of the cosmos spawned it. Perhaps it is already there. Perhaps the entity had knowledge of forces and powers that enabled it to warp through space or curve across time. I do not know. But I visualize it travelling down the nights and down the months and down the years upon its colossal Odyssey across the universe. And secretly I respect it, for its fearless courage, its resources, its titanic initiative, its thirst for knowledge, the magnitude of its voyage, and the sufficiency that urged it on, alone for an incalculable period on a journey that must have been beset by perils of unimaginable scope.

"I suppose the thing is as nearly timeless, deathless, and eternal as anything can be in a universe of change. If it is of a metallic nature, as I believe, it is nearly indestructible. And if its life is of an electrical kind, or of cosmic energy, I suppose it would never require food in our sense. It could absorb the radiations that are present at all times in all parts of the mathematical universe. It would be beyond fatigue and age, illness and pain, hatred and jealousy, the sorrows and weaknesses of the flesh.

"Is it possible that metallic substances under conditions and laws beyond human experience and in some other part of the cosmos could pass through an evolutionary development that produced life, intelligence, and entities of a kind wholly alien to our thinking? If the two passengers survive their stupendous voyage, what sort of world will they discover, in what dimension of space and what era of time, where in the immensity of the cosmos?

"On the basis of what I saw, I have no doubt that the silvery-red projectile can travel at a velocity far in excess of that of light. It must be the fastest thing that ever moved. I dream of it boring through space, hurtling the astronomical voids with suns and stars and galaxies for mileposts. But where journey's end lies, even the passengers may never know; yet who can say that the stranger may not come again, somewhere along the distant arches of the future?"

Chalmer's voice broke off, and in a momentary pause, he seemed to reach a decision. "Take a look at these. Not here—you can't see them. Study them closely by the nightlight at the top of the staircase well." He thrust his hand into a pocket and withdrew an envelope which I took.

I followed his suggestion. Inside the door, and protected from the wind, I removed a group of eight snapshots, together with the films. The light was none too strong, but I saw enough to make my scalp prickle. My thoughts whirled along macabre channels and unearthly mysteries during the glimpse I had of those weird photographs.

When I opened the door, the wind shrilled past. I walked astern with the envelope, clutching tightly.

No one was at the rail.

I ran with a sickening premonition. "Chalmer!" I shouted, and again. *"Chalmer!"* My voice went out in a scream across the tumult of waters and roaring wind.

Then, in the far wake of the ship, I thought I saw a figure upon the foaming crest of a wave, and an arm rise in a gesture of farewell. I leaned over the rail and answered the solitary figure. Deliberately, I opened my hand. The white pictures and the dark films streamed away upon the wind, joining in ocean that disappearing arm.

THE WITCH-MAKERS

I. Flight

ALWAYS THE DRUMS talked in the distance, ceasing neither by night nor day. He had lost track of time. He knew only that open country lay somewhere to the south. Toward it he drove himself by instinct, draining himself of last reserves of energy that should long ago have been exhausted. He fled from the drums and their prophecy of doom, but always they throbbed with a monotonous and maddening beat.

His face was haggard. A wild light shone in his deep-sunken eyes. Beard matted his cheeks, and his hair straggled unkempt. In his blind flight the jungle had tattered his clothing. His sun-baked skin bore the scratches of thorns and the weals of insect bite. Fever consumed him, but not even delirium could end the fear that forced him on to protect the treasure he carried.

He plunged through green nightmare. Only twilight filtered down from the roof of trees and creepers, the tangle of foliage and branches. The vegetation dripped moisture. His feet squashed sodden, decaying matter. The air steamed like a hothouse, with a wet and musty smell.

Amid the half-light, an evil beauty flourished upon death. Immense orchids, black as ebony or blood-scarlet, striped with golden green, purple, or waxy white, reared their fantastically gorgeous blossoms out of slime and rotting mold. Macaws squawked harshly. Hummingbirds and tanagers made streaks of brilliant color. There were mushrooms two feet tall, and mottled with scabrous pink. Malaria mosquitoes and carrion flies droned, while now and then the savage scream of a mandrill silenced the monkeys.

Crocodiles chased him when he splashed through a murky pool of the stream he was following. Later he floundered across a swamp, waist-deep in ooze. The slime-covered surface rippled. He felt the touch of soft and horrible things that wriggled.

No sane man could have survived so frightful a passage. He should have died a hundred deaths. He should have left his flesh and bones to rot with all that other decaying matter. He reeled onward.

He passed ancient ruins, engulfed by the tide of vegetation, but still preserving a basic outline. Upon colossal blocks of fallen masonry were incised symbols of a language unknown. He had heard legends of lost cities such as this, but he did not stop to investigate. He clambered across mounds and slippery walls.

And always the drums talked, throbbing afar, surrounding him with doom. The heavy revolver lay ever ready in his hand. He expected each moment to feel a poisoned dart or a spear, to meet a ring of painted and grotesquely-masked faces. He saw no one.

A tangible foe would have ended the persistent torture of his nerves. His was the terror of expectancy, of inevitable death postponed from minute to minute. He must keep going, keep going, with the stolen witch-charm his prize if he won out. He stumbled on blindly.

II. The Witch-Makers

Two white men looked down at the cot where the unconscious figure lay bandaged. The younger man, of square build and overweight for his five feet nine, asked in a deep quiet voice, "What are his chances, Burt?"

"He hasn't any. Oh, the proverbial one in a million at the outside," the older man answered in a dry, rather testy tone. Dr. Ezra L. Burton was a spare and bony scarecrow; his semi-bald head fringed with sandy hair. What was visible of his features looked ruddy, but mostly they were concealed by a black beard of full and alarming proportions. He added, "It's a miracle that the duffer ever got out of the jungle. I've done what I could, but he's dying.

"Travers, I sometimes think that medical science, so-called, is a brutal farce. What was the use of patching him up today so that he can die tomorrow? He's going to die. He should have died days ago, but some silly will to live kept him going until he stumbled into our camp. It would have been better for him if he died in delirium. Now he'll wake up just long enough to know he's dying and to hate himself for it and to hate us for giving him a lease on life just long enough to know he's through."

Travers filled a briar pipe and lighted it.

"There's nothing to identify him except his initials." Burton poked a blunt and gnarled forefinger among the collection removed from the stranger's pockets. It included a banana, cheap watch, magnifying glass, some coins and gold nuggets, pocket knife, cartridge belt, matches, and the .45, with the initials "L. A." carved on its butt. Amid these items lay a remarkable figurine about six or seven inches tall.

A little less than three inches of it represented a misshapen torso and spindly arms and legs of solid gold. The rest was an enormous emerald for its head. Of rectangular shape, it had been beveled to portray a two-faced monster of inhuman and unearthly attributes, suggesting abysmal antiquity, beyond history. The edges of the jewel had rounded from the wear of countless generations of hands.

Burton lifted the weird figurine. "He would seem to have been an itinerant trader. This idol probably is the key to the mystery. It looks like a fetish, some witch doctor's symbol of power or some tribe's emerald god. I suppose the chap stole it. It isn't exactly the kind of thing you expect stray visitors to carry around with them. As to who he is, my guess would be Leif Abbot, but it's only a guess."

"Leif Abbot?"

"I know of him by hearsay. A Yankee trader with a flair for digging into hidden places. In other words, a complete fool or trail blazer, depending on your point of view. Born in the Midwest, Minnesota or Wisconsin, as I recall, went to Africa a few years ago, fooled colonial officials, tricked the natives, played both ends against the middle, and became a sort of legend. An imaginative cuss with a heart of gold—fool's gold."

Travers asked, "I wonder if he had anything to do with the drums we heard a while back?"

"I meant to find out about them. I'll see what that black thief Mokoalli has to say."

After Burton stalked out of the tent, Travers dropped into a folding chair.

Growls, snarls, and chattering made an uproar outside the tent. It was always thus at nightfall when the jungle creatures could be heard afar, and the captured animals grew restless. Within the camp enclosure, rows of cages held specimens of the district's life. Lion, jackal, ape, and zebra; python and mamba; buzzard, ostrich, even eels and brightly striped fishes lurked in the tanks and cages.

Travers glanced at the stranger, who was breathing heavily with a rattle in his throat.

In the same tent, looking oddly out of place, stood modern scientific materials of obscure and specialized purpose. A metal operating table rested beside a curious device that had been assembled from numerous parts. These included a small dynamo, some queerly-shaped glass tubes and ovaloids reminiscent of X-ray apparatus, and two tiny plates with a mass of wires hanging from each like fine, golden hair.

Travers reached out and picked up the grotesque idol.

He hefted it reflectively, fascinated by its eyes in different colors, and the way glimmers of green flame welled from the heart of the great emerald. There might be fifty or a hundred dollars' worth of gold in the idol, but the jewel must be worth a thousand times as much, and the entire object even more as a curio or museum piece.

He continued to inspect the gem when Burton strode in, his black beard waving, while beads of sweat glistened on his ruddy forehead. "Mokoalli is a liar as well as a thief," Burton announced in the tone of a weather report. "He stole one of my best scalpels which I said he could keep if he told me the truth, whereupon he gave me nothing but the most outrageous lies. He said the drums were talking not because the jungle tribes were tracking the fugitive down, but to warn other tribes to keep out of his way! They thought he was bad medicine, driven by devils, and though he'd made off with a powerful charm they were afraid to touch him till the devils consumed him. They were just keeping an eye on him. That's Mokoalli's story. Moko is a liar. I took the scalpel back."

Travers removed the pipe from his mouth. "Did it occur to you that he might have been telling the truth?"

Burton looked surprised. "Why, no, it didn't."

"I think he earned the scalpel."

"He'll steal it again soon enough."

"The savage mind works in queer ways. The emerald that means a fortune to us wouldn't mean a thing to them except as a fetish or idol. If they were afraid of Abbot, they might well have waited until he died before reclaiming the charm. They might even have expected the emerald god to take vengeance and kill him. Then, when he stumbled toward our camp, the drums stopped."

"That's what Moko said. The natives seem to be pretty much afraid of us by now."

"Do you blame them?" Travers, with a glance at the fugitive, suggested, "Let's break camp as soon as he comes around or passes on. We've got our data. There isn't much more we could accomplish here. Our work's done. Another three months of this and I'll be fit for the booby hatch. Besides, the war zone seems to be creeping up on us. I've seen airplanes in the east twice in the past week. One of these days a bomber may pick us out for target practice or some fancy ground strafing."

Burton tugged at his beard reflectively. He felt the pulse of the patient, listened to his heartbeat, and took his temperature in the course of a careful examination. He shrugged as he turned away. "He's done for. A day or two at most. Even if he recovers consciousness, which is problematical, he's too far gone for recovery. We'll break camp as soon as possible."

"Good."

"But," added Burton with a new note of decision in his voice, "we will immortalize him by using him as our first human control."

Travers frowned. "Why? If he's on the way out? What good would it do?"

"It's his body that's broken down. If he regains consciousness, his mind and intelligence should be relatively unimpaired. It's only his life force, his vital spark, the unit of identity that is his mentality which we need. And we may be able to prolong his life somewhat. In any case, here is an outside chance to obtain data of immense, I might say priceless importance.

"As you say, we've successfully finished our work with the animal controls. The ape-jackal interchange simply corroborated earlier findings. There is nothing more to be learned by duplicating previous experiments. We need a human control. Our next step must involve a human control if we are to open up vast new fields for research."

Burton's accents had taken an introspective tone as though he expressed aloud a passionate inner conviction that drove him. "Thus far, we have only objective data. The lower vertebrates couldn't tell us their reactions and experiences in a new environment. Only man can do that for us. We've already made revolutionary discoveries, but we stand on the threshold of a greater miracle than anything we've yet seen or done.

"We interchanged the lives of a monkey and a fox. Do you remember how elated we were with the success of that first experiment? How we watched the fox in the monkey's body cling to the ground? How the monkey in the fox's body vainly tried to swing through the tree tops? We put the personality of a rhinoceros into the body of a zebra, and that gentle animal became a driving, tearing Juggernaut of death, while the great rhino inhabited by the zebra's spirit fled in fear from the lion it could have crushed.

"For weeks and months, Travers, we've torn spirit and flesh asunder. Here in fifty square miles that contain almost every kind of the climate and life of Africa, we've learned more about animal behavior during our three months than all mankind learned in three thousand years. We've stolen a march on evolution. We've knocked the natural selection of species into a cocked hat.

"Why can't we do the same with the spirit of man? Maybe we can't, but we won't know till we've tried. And if we try and succeed, would you even attempt to estimate how much we'll enrich man's imagination and add to his knowledge? Think of what it would mean if we enabled man to look at the world through the eyes of his pets, a dog, or a cat, or a horse! Wouldn't he have a more tender feeling toward them and a more profound appreciation of his capacities? Isn't it possible that, in course of time, his pets would acquire a new intelligence of the order of humanity? Isn't it conceivable that they could then be trained to speak, with results in strange, unimaginable new friendships?

"And after that, Travers—after that—the transference of intelligence from one man to another! It's a magnificent and terrifying thought, isn't it? If we made it possible, where would it end? In greater peace for mankind? Would he understand his fellow men better and comprehend more fully their weaknesses and follies, their dreams and nobilities? Would he spy upon his friends and try to benefit by what he learned? Would each man cease to be an individual as he gradually absorbed the characteristics and peculiarities of other men? Or would he become more rapacious than ever before, carried away by the thirst for knowledge, made drunk by the infinite capacity for unlimited power?

"I can't answer my own questions, Travers. They're beyond answer except in the fateful mold of experience. But we have it within our hands to take the first deliberate step, the step upon which all else hinges. We'll be tampering with the mysteries of life, yes, but it's life that's hopelessly doomed anyway. Abbot, if he is Abbot, can die unconscious and forgotten, or he can have experiences never dreamed of in his last hours. He can die with the certainty of a posthumous immortality that will never fade until Earth itself runs its course or man perishes in the eons of the far future."

"You might at least wait till he comes to. He ought to have his say about whether he wants to be a guinea pig. And there's the little matter of the emerald."

Burton shook his head decisively. His beard jerked like an erratic pendulum. "The emerald? We can donate it to a museum. He won't recover, and as for the experiment, perhaps he *would* object, if he could. I don't suppose he'll thank us for extending his life under altered circumstances. That is too much to expect. And he's apt to suffer a severe shock when and if he awakens, but he'll recover more quickly and adjust himself better than if he approached the experiment with all the fears his imagination could provide."

"Suppose the one chance in a million pulls him through? What if he survives? He could make it pretty hot for us. Society might not approve of our methods or our goals."

"That's why we're here instead of in a nice comfortable laboratory at home. If all experiments were subject to the whims and censorship of society, civilization would still be in the Dark Ages."

"That won't be answer enough if he survives."

"We'll find answers when the need arises. And while I stand here arguing with you, his hold on life grows thinner, and if we don't act immediately our great opportunity will be gone."

Burton walked over to the dynamo and started it. A low hum like the buzz of a persistent mosquito filled the tent. What looked like mist in one of the oddly shaped tubes glowed with a milky light. The mist became rapidly less opaque until only a softly shimmering radiance remained.

He slipped a metal band around his head. The band had a small bulb and reflector in front. He pressed the switch. A beam of light leaped out. He removed the unconscious man from the cot to the operating table, arranged a number of surgical tools, and pulled rubber gloves over his hands.

Then he left the tent. A few minutes after his return Mokoalli and another native, panting and grunting, brought a cage in. The beast in the cage snarled sullenly.

As the patter of footsteps receded, Burton with a dexterous motion plunged a hypodermic through the bars of the cage. The beast roared and lunged viciously at his arm.

"He almost got you that time," said Travers in a voice of regret.

The guide-light focused on the stranger's head. Burton took a pair of scissors and snipped the hair off the base of his skull.

One by one, the surgical implements grew red. The sound of a man's breathing became harsher, and magnified in the stillness. The air became uncomfortably hot.

The moon rose, and weird noises drifted from the jungle. The animals yowled in their cages. Within the tent, the dynamo droned like a relentless carrion fly.

III. Strange Awakening

Leif Abbot passed from one fantastic dream to another. In some he was a boy on the Midwestern prairies, chased by monsters foreign to all the continents. In others he wandered endlessly through forests and jungles, alone and hopelessly lost, or accompanied by dead friends and pursued by invisible terrors. There were periods of blankness and periods of skyrocketing flashes. At times he was almost on the verge of knowing that he dreamed, but then he slipped away again into the phantasmagoria of unconsciousness.

Pain entered his dreams. He was running, running, running, with leaden steps that took him forward more slowly than the progress of tortoises. Balanced upon his head was a great cube of gold that for some reason he could neither touch nor dislodge. He was compelled to stagger onward with that intolerable weight while his shadowy pursuers drew nearer with the speed of hawks. Knives flying in all directions impaled him.

Then the nightmare lay behind him. His head throbbed. He felt stifled and breathed unevenly, but he knew that the dream had ended. He lay still, his eyes closed as he half-remembered his last hours of consciousness. Buala, the witch doctor—the emerald god that had passed from tribe to tribe and from father to son through untold ages until it fell into Buala's custody—his days of haggling and cajoling, with Buala adamant in his superstitious faith in the emerald god's magic powers.

Leif Abbot had wanted that treasure. When he couldn't get it by more or less legitimate means, he took it by theft. In spite of his African adventures, however, he had underestimated the emerald's influence and prestige. He awoke one night to find his own carriers attacking him, and to hear the throb of drums. He escaped with the jewel, but his porters and guides deserted him, taking all his supplies.

He could have followed the river, which would have taken him downstream through hostile villages that he now could not pass through and live. He chose the southward course toward the headwaters and open country, where he had heard rumors about two white men whom the natives called "Witch-Makers." Then came the nightmare of his flight through the green hell, the insect hordes, fever, thirst, hunger, and finally delirium. He remembered nothing from that point on.

His thoughts growing clearer each moment, he opened his eyes. A roof lay curiously near, scarcely a yard above his head. He was lying on his side on the floor. Bars interfered with his vision, but he saw two white men in the interior of the tent, and—lying upon an operating table, his own body!

Leif Abbot closed his eyes in a daze. He must be dead or in the grip of delirium still. An odd panic filled him, a premonition.

He forced his eyes open again and stared at the figure on the table. He was unquestionably looking at his own emaciated, fever-ridden body, with a metallic gleam showing through bandages on its head!

Suddenly afraid, he strove to rise. Unable to balance on his legs, he toppled crazily and fell with a jarring thud. His head throbbed. A moan of pain came from his lips—*but to his ears it sounded like the whimper of an animal!*

The room reeled around in his vision as he fell. His head lowered, and his stunned gaze fastened upon the padded paws of a beast, and black-furred legs. They seemed part of him. He stretched out a hand, and stared in the hypnotism of horror as a paw scraped the floor where his hand should have been.

For a timeless drag of eternity he lay immobile, trying to figure some meaning out of the strange distortion of things. He was not dead, because he was not disembodied, yet he stood apart from his rightful body which lay beyond the bars. The cage inclosed a beast; and he was the beast.

As his thoughts skittered through this new, waking nightmare he became conscious of a voice. It sounded extraordinarily loud and shrill, like a thunderclap. He realized vaguely that he had difficulty understanding the words, and that the room was filled with a multitude of familiar sounds magnified in volume, while other sounds of which he had never before been aware assailed his hearing. His ears had acquired a preternatural sensitivity. In the amplified breathing of the speaker he heard the lungs expand and contract, the heart beat. He heard a fly crawl on the canvas of the tent. When the second man tilted his pipe, he heard fingers rasp on the bowl, and a rustle as of raindrops when some ashes fell to the floor.

"Leif Abbot, if you are Leif Abbot, can you hear me?" asked the booming voice.

The beast in the cage scrambled to all fours and swayed against the bars. Glaring sullenly out, he lowered and raised his head.

Before the speaker could continue, there came a wild interruption. Leif Abbot, looking through the bars, saw his body stiffen on the operating table. The eyes opened with an expression of animal ferocity. Ropes bound the body, but it burst the ropes with a surge of strength that Leif Abbot in all his life had not equaled.

The mouth parted, but from that human throat came a snarl born of the jungle. The body hurtled across the tent in the spring of an animal, teeth bared, arms outstretched like paws ready to rip and gouge. The white men scattered and for seconds a furious battle raged. The white men won, but only because Leif Abbot's body was too exhausted to endure the terrific strain put upon it by the untamed spirit within.

When the struggle ended, the body lay motionless under the influence of an opiate. The taller of the men, the one with the waving black beard, painted their scratches and wounds with iodine.

After he had finished, he turned again toward the cage. "I am Dr. Burton. My colleague is Dr. Travers, a physicist and biochemist. We have been engaged in experiments here for several months. When you staggered half dead into our camp, we were compelled to adopt extreme measures or you would already be dead.

"Do not be alarmed. Whatever seems incredible to you is really very simple. We have discovered how to separate the life-stream or consciousness or whatever you want to call it from the body to which it belongs, and to effect an exchange with some other body. Thus far we have worked only with the lower vertebrates. In your case, your chances for survival as Leif Abbot were so small that we operated upon the six layers of your cerebral cortex and transferred your identity to the body of a strong and healthy black panther. The panther's identity now occupies your own sick and weakened body. By this interchange we hope to strengthen your body sufficiently so that your identity can later be restored to it, with better chances for your recovery and survival.

"In the meantime the door to your cage is open behind you. Go into the jungle, if you like. You probably will be better off there. You have all the intelligence of man and all the senses and instincts of the big cats. You should be able to avoid any danger and survive any attack."

Leif Abbot attempted to answer, but only a rumbling growl issued from his throat. His new vocal cords either were not capable of speech or would require long practice.

The greenish yellow eyes of the panther glowered his mute hatred. Burton's glib explanation failed to satisfy him. Not for an instant did he believe Blackbeard and his companion. They wanted the emerald god for which he had risked his life. What poorly paid scientist would pass up such an opportunity for easy wealth? They didn't have courage enough to let him die or to kill him. But it would be murder just the same, in a different form, more protracted, and under the guise of science.

Neither Burton nor Travers spoke again. They watched him go in silence; and he in turn glared balefully from them to the emerald that still lay among his effects, its glitter matched by the smouldering flame in his eyes.

Turbulent emotions swept him. Hatred rankled at the back of his thoughts. He tried to adjust himself to his weird change of state. He plotted a dozen ways of tricking them in order to regain possession of his treasure, but he hopelessly confused his lost resources as man and his as yet unknown abilities as panther. Forgetting his new form momentarily, he tried to grasp the bars of the cage, but his paws merely slid along the bars. He had no fingers to help him now. He had never before appreciated so fully the infinite utility of hands.

Probably they were merely awaiting his departure into the jungle before killing the panther-spirit that now occupied his real body. And there was absolutely nothing he could do for the present, except take their advice before they changed their minds. He might be doomed to die in the jungle, but while he lived he could scheme ways of vengeance.

He stared for the last time at his captors, then turned and bounded into the darkness outside.

IV. The Black Marauder

The rest of the night, all the next day, and the following night the black panther remained away. Burton and Travers watched the body of Leif Abbot, which seemed to grow stronger under the drive of the fierce animal spirit that now dwelt within it.

Toward dawn of the second day, Burton awakened from a fitful sleep to hear a weight dragging on the ground. He sprang up and flashed a light on it. The panther, its right hind leg broken, and bleeding from numerous wounds, dragged itself forward. It did not whimper. Its glazing eyes still burned with sultry hatred and rebellion though death fast approached.

"Travers, quick!" Burton snapped. "Turn the switch! Get out adrenalin! Scopolamin!"

He leaped to the dying panther and gathered it in his arms. Its savage heart beat heavily. He carried it to the operating table and laid it beside the shackled body of Leif Abbot.

The hum of the dynamo had already begun. Pale, vaporous light shone in the vacuum tube. Burton fastened the silver plate in the panther's skull and the similar plate in Abbot's cranium to wires connected with the transference apparatus of the psychotransferometer.

It was not a torrid night, but sweat glistened on his face. He watched anxiously, tugging at his beard.

Travers shook his head in doubt. "Afraid it's too late. If he'd only come back an hour sooner—"

As though in mockery at his words, the gleam of animal ferocity suddenly returned to the panther's eyes. For a moment it snarled at them and made an effort to attack. It shuddered, while its eyes filmed more swiftly. The brute thirst faded from the eyes of Leif Abbot as his human identity re-entered his body. A gleam of sanity and intelligence lingered for seconds, gradually to be replaced by an expression of trance-like repose and suspended will power when the drugs took effect.

Burton heaved a deep sigh. "A close call, that. A few minutes more and our trouble would have gone for nothing. Too bad the panther died, but we have all the notes we need on its behavior while it occupied Lief Abbot's body. And now let's see if he can or will tell us what he did in the part of a black panther."

He bent over and looked into the subject's eyes. They were wide open, but the hypnotic blankness had grown complete.

"Leif Abbot, can you hear me?"

The lips hardly moved, to give a faint answer, "Yes."

"Last night in the body of a panther you left us. You have been gone for two nights and a day. Where did you go? What did you do? What happened to you after you left? How did you receive the wounds?"

Speaking as though from a distance, his unblinking eyes exhibiting no change of expression, Leif Abbot said, "When I crept out of the boma, the moon rode high. It was a red moon. It bathed the plain in blood. Black shadows and scarlet moonlight, all the world was strange. I have never seen so strange a world. It was like the land-scape of another planet.

"I heard sounds beyond the range of my normal ears, the wings of night birds, the gliding of a snake, an indescribable chorus of separate sounds around me and drifting from the distant jungle. I heard grass rustle in the faintest of winds. I saw colors that no man has ever watched. They are beyond the spectrum of his eyes, but my panther eyes saw them. I can't tell what they were like, any more than you could describe color to somebody blind from birth. You would have to see those eerie colors for yourselves.

"All my senses were immensely keener. I detected smells of hun-dreds of different plants, flowers, animals, insects, decaying matter, and other things, where before I had noticed only a sort of general dank mustiness in the air. I was queerly mixed up. As a panther I noticed all these impressions for what they were. As a man I couldn't identify more than a part of them. I had half-memories that didn't quite bridge the gap between my own knowledge and the panther's instincts and habits. Certain odors made me afraid. The panther knew that they came from poisonous plants.

"I didn't know what to do, at first. For a while I strode around, accustoming myself to going on all fours, and to the movements of unfamiliar muscles. Gradually I got a feeling of power, for there was the strength of several men in that long, sleek, and ripplingly muscled body.

I tried crouching and leaping, and found that pounces of twenty feet and more came effortlessly.

"I traveled northward, downhill, toward the jungle. I had some vague idea of hunting for Buala and taking vengeance on his tribe. It was a crazy idea because if any vengeance was to be taken it really belonged to him. At the edge of the jungle I stopped. I could see into it better than I could in the daytime with human vision. It was filled with a kind of grayish green light, more ghostly than twilight; the shadows were blackly green; and the patches of moonlight a sort of ghastly red.

"Maybe that's the way the jungle always looks to the great cats by night. I don't know. That's the way it looked to me and it gave me the creeps. My fears as man carried over into my life as panther. I shied at going into that monstrous tangle.

"Besides, I had an inner pull to travel eastward. I couldn't account for it, unless some latent instinct of the panther was asserting itself. Finally I began to ramble toward the east, keeping at the fringe of the jungle in a long, gliding run that I found easy to maintain.

"I put hours and miles behind me. I followed the instinct that urged me on. While doing so, I became more confident in myself and more sure of my pantherine body.

"Loping through broken, hilly country that was beginning to show a sharp upward rise some hours later, I felt a pull toward the northeast. I turned from my course into the hills and went back to the tangle. I found a dim spoor that lured me on. My surroundings looked as if they ought to be familiar. I almost remembered, but not quite.

"There came a turn in the faint trail I followed. I reached the base of a cluster of rocks. With no intention on my part, a kind of spitting growl broke from my throat. It was instantly answered by a yowl. From a black and cavernous opening that I now noticed, a panther emerged, a female, with a couple of cubs at her heels. I stopped in my tracks.

"For just an instant the creature was on the verge of greeting me home, and I knew that instinct had brought me to the mate of the black panther whose body I had taken possession of. She was deceived only for moments. By whatever subtle or primitive sense, she knew that I was an alien presence, a menace. She came through the air, a snarling fury, with claws raking in an attack that caught me by surprise.

"I suppose I could have put up a battle royal. I didn't. I don't know why. Probably some atavistic feeling of chivalry that was a hangover from my previous life made me turn tail and flee, as if all the devils in hell were yapping at my heels. That female cat was a demon if ever there was one. She ripped a shoulder wide open and took a chunk out of my neck before I got away. Those cursed cubs tumbled around and yowled in glee. I wish I'd knocked the whole litter into kingdom come.

"The sky was turning lighter. I left the denser thickets and ran toward higher ground.

"After that, I decided to go very easy about trusting instincts. I sniffed the air and got wind of a water hole.

"There I drank greedily and shook myself in the tepid water. It soothed the wounds I couldn't reach. There was a rocky ledge beside a trail that animals used in reaching the water hole. I bounded on top of it and lay down to await sunrise.

"While I rested, a deer came mincing along the trail. It was a beautiful creature, a doe. I watched it drink and admired its graceful motions as it frisked away toward the grazing country to the south; and when it was gone I found that I was ravenously hungry and that I had blithely let my dinner skip off.

"My human scruples did not mean a thing in this case. A panther's body supported me and I had to support it in the manner to which it was accustomed. I waited a half hour before I spotted a wild boar. I made short work of it. Eating meat still on the hoof didn't exactly appeal to me, but my substitute palate gorged itself.

"I felt drowsy then. I turned toward the fringe of the jungle in search of a safe nook for a nap. I was looking for a high ledge or a cave, but didn't find anything with suitable protection. I scouted farther away from the water hole, trekking toward thicker jungle. As I was prowling along the trail, a sudden crackle gave me warning, but not warning enough. The ground opened beneath me. I made a vain scramble but felt myself falling. When I hit bottom, the wind was knocked out of me.

V. The Panther Strikes

"Though I didn't fall a great distance, I landed on my neck and shoulders with stunning force. I lay there for perhaps a minute before I grew conscious of a pain in my right hind leg. I tried to get up. It was torture beyond me. I squirmed around, and in the dim light saw that the bottom of the pit held fire-hardened stakes imbedded point up. One of these had pierced the leg. It was only pure luck that others didn't impale me. I had fallen into an animal trap.

"A quick, careful jerk of the leg brought agony and freedom. I licked the wound. Looking around then, I estimated my chances of leaping from the pit at exactly zero. The stakes had been cleverly placed and the pit so constructed as to make it impossible for any beast to escape. Yet I escaped.

"How? It was absurdly simple for a creature who could think. I took a stake between my teeth and pulled it out. I turned the sharp point toward the earth wall and pushed it as far in as I could with my jaws. Holding the blunt end in my jaws, and pushing at the same time with two paws grasping the stake, I imbedded it for half its length.

"I removed another stake and drove it in beside the first. I continued the process until I had formed a ladder of stakes in pairs as high as I could reach. It took time, and every second I was desperately afraid that the hunters would come for the kill before I got out.

"My wounded leg hurt badly. I fell several times trying to climb the stakes, but on the fourth try I eased my weight onto the top pair. Then I rose in a swift half-turn on my hind legs. The stakes gave, but I had my forelegs over the edge of the pit and pulled myself out with my hind legs shoving and digging into the wall. The pain was intolerable. After I had regained freedom, I rested for several minutes, my ears listening for footsteps. I would have killed any human being that came in sight, if I could. My rage wore off, and I forgot the wound temporarily, when I thought of a sardonic jest.

"I went to work with a will and a vengeance. Ten minutes later I was crouching on the limb of a tree, hidden by foliage, and with the pit barely visible. The jungle steadily grew hotter as the sun mounted higher.

"I was feeling drowsy again when my ears pricked to the sounds of a party approaching. There were seven of them. I watched intently until the first, a strapping young buck with chest and cheeks cicatrized, came into view carrying a long lance. The only other thing he wore besides a loincloth was a crude bracelet of some sort twisted tightly around his left arm almost at the shoulder. I don't know what it signified or why he wore it there. I noticed it because his left arm flashed up in a signal and he let out a yell you could have heard a mile off.

"The six others gathered around him, all jabbering at once and all getting more pop-eyed by the second. I chose that instant to do the best I could on a loud laugh. Even to me the result was weird. They fled like so many rabbits.

"They looked scared silly. My jest had been a complete success. I had scraped a patch of ground smooth. Upon it, using my paw as a pen, I had scrawled, 'Yours Truly, The King of the Panthers,' and under the signature I had drawn the rough outline of a panther's head.

"The natives probably couldn't have read anything in any language, but they knew what writing was. They recognized the panther's head. They saw that there were no human tracks in the vicinity except their own. They saw how the panther had escaped from the trap. For the rest of their lives they'll be talking about the panther god or devil that left his signature.

"I drew back to a crotch in the tree and dozed there.

"The sun stood overhead when distant reports that seemed to come from the east wakened me. They sounded like gunshots. I leaped to the ground and limbered up the injured leg. After a first sharp pain, it became manageable, through it remained stiff and throbbed persistently, forcing me to limp a little.

"I kept to higher ground, where I had good vision in all directions. From time to time I saw small parties of natives. Once I heard and saw a squadron of airplanes to the northeast.

"In a couple of hours or so I reached a region of sheer rock escarpments, hills, deep ravines, and narrow passes. There were patches of dense, semi-tropical jungle around water holes. Elsewhere grew thickets of thorn, stunted trees, and sometimes sparse brown grass. I heard the movements of a considerable force ahead. Guided by the sounds, I struck off at a tangent and hid in the shadow of a large boulder atop a dolomite.

"Over the crest of a hill came native scouts, in advance of a detachment of white infantry and native troops. In all, the raiding party consisted of about two hundred, of whom three-fourths were native troops. They looked like Somalis to me.

"The white men, except for the officers, weren't tanned enough or lean enough to have been hardened by long fighting in the tropics. I judged them to be fairly recent arrivals. All were heavily armed.

"Suddenly a rifle cracked, then another. Intermittent shots poured from an ambush ahead. One of the white men fell. A couple of natives staggered when they were hit. The rest was merely efficient slaughter. Two machine guns went into action like magic and peppered the hillside thicket. There were a few answering shots. A few of the black defenders charged into the open. Mowed down by the fusillade, none of them escaped. About a dozen seemed to have been posted in the ambush.

"Red rage seethed inside of me. You have to see things like that in the wild, unknown places of the world to know the seamy side of colonial wars and imperial aggression. Twelve against two hundred—twelve armed with 1876 Springfields and muskets so ancient and rusty that they couldn't tell whether the pin would hit or the cartridge explode when they pulled the trigger—twelve against modern rifles, machine guns and grenades.

"It didn't make any difference that I'd stolen a treasure from Buala when I couldn't get it otherwise. At least I hadn't tried to kick him off of his own land or put a bullet through him when he couldn't see the deal my way. I was mad enough to start a one-man, or rather a one-panther, campaign against the whole detachment. Idiotic? Sure. But here's how it worked out.

"I crept down from the dolomite and detoured ahead until I found a suitable spot for my purposes. At a V-neck that the column must pass and where the legend could not possibly be missed, I scratched on the ground:

Warning! Go Back!
The King of the Panthers.

"A quarter-mile beyond the V-neck, I jumped to the top of a great pile of fallen rocks, where I could easily be seen silhouetted against the sky. I had not waited long before the scouts found my message and my tracks. One of them ran back to the main body in great excitement. The others noticed me and stared at me. I stared at them. The moment I saw sunlight gleam on a rifle barrel swinging up, I dropped behind the rocks. Bullets whined past. I took a quick peek and saw a cluster of troops gesticulating and waving over my message.

"The native troops had obviously received a scare and the whites were trying to quiet their fears. It seemed as though they all saw me and turned toward me at once. There was a moment's complete silence, while I looked down toward them. Then I slipped away among the fallen masses of rock and the scrub thorn as more lead hornets buzzed.

"I doubled back by much the same route until I was well behind the raiders. Then I started catching up with them again.

"I singled out a victim at the very tail of the column. Keeping well to the rear, I took advantage of every possible concealment until the right moment came, when he was temporarily cut off from the rest by a twist in the defile. He saw me just before I hit him. His eyes popped. He didn't have time to squawk. I landed on his shoulders, he slammed against rock, and when his skull hit there came the sharp snap of a neck breaking. I lifted his rifle between my teeth and got back in the brush. Then I let out a terrific screech. I watched just long enough to see several white and native troops rush back. Morale took another blow.

"I had the devil of a time lugging that rifle in a circuitous detour toward the head of the column. I had to stay well covered and at a distance or light gleaming on a barrel would have betrayed me. When I reached a vantage point, my leg was throbbing worse. I was striking for the last time in my one-panther campaign, and I determined to make it a telling shot.

"Beyond the V-neck stretched a valley that lay between rock bluffs. A number of mud holes extended along the valley like beads on a string, each surrounded by grass, dwarf palms, and scrub. I got wind of a village somewhere ahead but the tribe had either moved on or taken to the hills for the time being. I set up shop, so to speak, on the highest of a series of broken and tumbled masses from the cliffs a couple of miles from the V-neck.

"The sun was westering and the heat had begun to abate. The valley, at least to my eyes, had acquired a sinister reddish hue. In the quiet air, the sounds of the oncoming force gave an effect like the motions of puppets.

"I had laid the rifle between two rocks so that no gleam would show its presence. The rifle, the shadow, and I blended into one. I was amused to notice the newly acquired caution with which the raiding party advanced. I marked the figure which I hoped was the commanding officer.

"Getting ready to fire that rifle was one of the hardest jobs I've ever tackled. I had no finger to squeeze the trigger. I could not hold the rifle against my shoulder. I couldn't use the sights. But I'd thought about all the difficulties when I was toting it, and I solved them after a sort. I drew back from the rifle and sighted along the rock groove in which it rested. Then I crawled up to it, shifted its angle, and drew back for another estimate until I had it aimed at a spot below a shoulder-high rock that the column would pass. I made these preparations, of course, before the detachment was in range. Then I lay on my side with the stock against my chest and the nail of a paw hooked around the trigger.

"When the man I had marked stepped into range, I fired. The recoil gave a wallop to my ribs. The officer finished his step, raised a hand toward his ribs, and collapsed. I grabbed the rifle in my teeth and stepped into full view.

"The results were electrical. Silhouetted against the setting sun, I must have presented an awesome appearance. The whole column halted as one, then pandemonium broke out. The Somalis turned retreat into rout. Brave as they were, they couldn't face a panther-devil that wrote warnings and backed them up with deadly marksmanship.

"Shouted commands were ignored. The officers shot down their own men in an effort to stop the panic. They fired at where I had been, but I had ducked.

"For months to come the survivors of that raiding party will, I hope, break into a cold sweat every time they hear a panther howl.

"My lone campaign struck me as a success, but I was weary, my leg ached severely, and night drew near. I decided to return to camp and see what I could do there. Further foraging in my present condition would have been simply suicidal.

"When the sun was ready to drop below the horizon, I had put several miles of the return trip behind me. I traveled clear of the jungle to make better time. Even so, my injured leg hindered me badly. I tried to keep my weight off it by trotting along hippity-hop in a sort of three-legged gait. In this manner I was limping toward camp when the ground shook to thundering hooves.

"The plateau and plains region south of the jungle was rich in game. Single animals, groups, and herds grazed there or browsed along. From time to time during the day I had noticed antelope, zebras, lions, giraffes, mountain goats, eland, and other species. At first I had been wary, until I found that most of them were more anxious to keep out of my way than I of theirs.

"Eventually I paid little attention to them, for which neglect I now paid the penalty.

"I glanced around when I heard the rush of hooves. A one-horned rhinoceros was charging me like a runaway express train. That squat-legged, ponderous ugly brute drove on with appalling speed. I jumped aside. The rhino slid to a jarring stop in almost no time, whirled, and thundered toward me again. I ran as best I could, but even using my injured leg I could not hold my own. Why it attacked me I don't know except out of sheer, spiteful, vicious meanness.

"My only hope lay in reaching the jungle where I could take refuge in the tree tops, but the nearest trees were a good half-mile off. I headed for them, jumping sidewise, and then had to change my course when the rhino came back snorting with its chubby stumps of legs driving like pistons. It was a losing battle. I might have outrun it if the injured hind leg hadn't hampered me. Flight, charge, dodge, retreat—the same pattern over and over until I was gasping and exhausted, but the rhino wouldn't let up. Its pursuit was as relentless and unyielding as any manhunter ever made on the trail of a criminal. I knew what it meant then to be run down and cornered with no quarter given.

"The end came when I reached the shadow of the jungle. The rhino charged and I dodged. The rhino whirled and charged again. I started to leap, the injured leg gave way. I only had time to get up and barely commence a short spring when the rhino struck. At the moment of impact it flung its lowered head skyward. Its horn, hooked around me, hurled me high in the air and backward. That terrific heave both saved my life and lost it. I went through the air in an arc and crashed among the branches I had been trying to reach. I was knocked unconscious.

"When I opened my eyes, night had fallen. I was draped over a limb. The rhino had departed. Its horn had opened a gash in my side, the branches had cut and bruised me, and my right leg which had already taken punishment enough was broken.

"As I jumped to earth I gave a screech that would have brought my friend the rhino back in double-quick time if he had heard it. I couldn't help it, so fierce was the agony. All the rest of the night I spent in hopping and dragging my way back to camp. Only the memory of the emerald drove me on. Growing fainter with every step, and losing blood steadily, it was all I could do not to yield to the temptation to crawl into a thicket and die.

"Almost any creature that walked could have beaten me then. The jungle and all its noises, its mysterious life, the strange greenish dusk within it, and the scarlet moonlight filled me with terror. The way back seemed endless. The air smelled sulphurous. I sweltered in that infernal heat. Or perhaps it was only fever that crept over me as I toiled on the long route, fever and the slow finger of death."

In the silence that ensued, Burton, who had taken copious notes on the story, sat brooding for the period in which a man could smoke a pipe. Finally he sighed deeply. "I resent it after a fashion, that he should be first to have so remarkable an experience," he murmured. "By rights you or I should have been elect."

Travers said flatly, "I haven't your skill at surgery. I can't perform the operation and turn you loose, and I won't let you do the job on me."

"I'm afraid you haven't the true instincts of the martyr, Travers. Fame, adventure, pioneering—they mean nothing to you. If I were dependent upon your inclinations, doubtless we might never have passed this milestone on the road of human achievement. It was a stroke of genius, no less, the scientific genius that is today tearing apart the secrets of life, mind, and matter."

"And now that the milestone has been reached?"

"On to the next!" Burton tugged at his beard as he glanced at the sleeper. His expression was curious: a mixture of envy, of regret, and of inhumanly calculating intent.

He rose and began to make preparations.

Travers did not finish the involuntary phrase that came to his lips. "You mean—?"

VI. The End of the Emerald God

From fever and the slow finger of death, from dreams and memories and lost realities hidden in mists afar, Leif Abbot slowly returned to consciousness. He was afraid to open his eyes through fear of what he would find, through fear that it would not be what he hoped to find.

He recalled Buala, the emerald, flight through jungle. The recollection was mixed up with fever and the impression of a nightmare in which he had somehow been imprisoned in the body of a panther. It had been a harrowing nightmare, too graphic and vivid. Among his haze of thoughts drifted the faces of two white men who proclaimed themselves scientists but who mastered demoniac arts. Leif Abbot had an uncertain feeling that he had talked to them at considerable length, but he could not imagine what he had talked to them about. It was all hopelessly involved. He tried vainly to force the pictures into a consecutive sequence.

When he blinked his eyes open and saw his own body still lying upon the operating table, he felt only the dull unhappiness of one who has already been shocked into numbness. Assailed by forebodings, he looked down. His head moved with singularly abrupt and sudden jerks. When he saw the talons, the thin, horny legs, and the feathered body of a bird of prey, he screamed his fury. The result was a croak, harsh and forbidding.

Travers had left the tent. Burton, who was taking the pulse of the body, looked around when the eagle screamed.

"Awake?" he queried, his eyes alight with excitement. "Another triumph, a complete success! Leif Abbot, your body is mending but it still is not out of danger. You unfortunately destroyed the black panther by putting its body to excessive strain. You have a very courageous nature, but you let it run away with your better judgment. We have given you a second temporary body. You have wings. You can fly. The skyways are open to you, while the spirit of the eagle is earthbound in your body. When you return, I trust that recovery has progressed sufficiently so that the identity of each can be restored to its rightful abode. The cage door is not locked. If you can hear me you are at liberty to open the door and depart. Return when you will, but I would advise you not to remain away for any extended period."

Leif Abbot had an insensate urge to fly straight at that ruddy face, hook his talons in the bushy black beard, and peck at the man's eyes. But out of the turmoil of his emotions, out of the need for radically readjusting himself to his environment, one thought stood clear. An opportunity other than the one specified had been unintentionally given him.

With mental prayers that Burton would not divine his purpose, he used his beak to push the cage door aside. He strutted forth and stretched his wings experimentally to get the feel of them. By the easy response, he knew that the bird's natural motions and habits carried over.

He struck instantly. A swoop brought him over the emerald figurine that lay among his belongings. He hovered, clutched it in his talons, and sailed for the tent flap. Burton lunged after him, shouting, "Come back here! Drop that, you idiot!"

His wing-tips grazed the canvas and deflected his course. Burton almost caught up with him, but his outstretched hands just missed the eagle's tail feathers.

Then the bird soared.

A bullet buzzed by. Leif Abbot heard a loud report. He squinted earthward. Travers had appeared from nowhere.

Running toward the tent, he whipped out his revolver and was emptying it at the flying target. There could be no doubt of his purpose. Only the emerald could have brought such greed to his eyes. He was willing to kill the eagle and the mortal spirit of Leif Abbot if necessary to prevent the loss of that treasure.

Leif Abbot swooped, swerved, darted in erratic arcs, mounted suddenly, sideslipped, nose-dived, and straightened out. No ordinary marksman could have hit so crazily veering a target. Only a miracle could have enabled even a superb shot to halt the eagle. Travers was not the marksman, and chance did not provide him the miracle. His bullets went wide of the bird. With his last triumphant glance and a scream of mirthless mockery, Abbot saw Burton struggling to wrest the pistol from Travers, a useless struggle now that the weapon was empty.

The figurine did not weigh enough to prove a hindrance. After the first thrill of flight and escape, he forgot about his prize. He felt a stronger emotion. A rapture gripped him, an ecstasy unlike anything he had yet known.

Many times during his life, when watching the wild ducks fly south on the Midwestern prairies in autumn, while staring at seagulls as they circled a ship, or admiring the lightning-like speed of hummingbirds as they darted toward honey-flowers, he had envied the birds their winged freedom. He reveled in that freedom now. He rose ever higher, his strong wings beating the way aloft. It took less effort than he had imagined, for his wings slanted automatically to receive the full lifting power of every gust of wind and utilize each upward eddy.

He felt like a spirit liberated from all earthly ties. The jungle became only a dark mass below him. The landscape unfolded toward farther horizons. Trees, rocks, and water holes lost their individuality.

The ground evolved into masses and areas, a darker carpet for the jungle, a lighter area for the plain, a sun-capped, shadow-filled mass for the mountains.

He found himself flying toward those distant peaks that rimmed the northeastern horizon. In the midst of his breathless enjoyment and elation, he wondered why his course came so easily. Then he remembered a previous experience and guessed that the nest of the eagle lay somewhere among those towering crags and gorges. He was about to change his line of flight when his far-sighting gaze was drawn to the puzzling actions of three birds. The birds swooped to earth in single file, rose, looped over, and dipped again. It dawned on him that the birds were airplanes miles distant; and their maneuvers could best be explained if they were indulging in the luxury of ground-strafing.

Fifteen minutes later, drifting at an altitude of approximately a mile, he found his surmise correct. The airplanes, fast bombers equipped with machine guns, had evidently resorted to ground-strafing for lack of any considerable target worth bombing. He estimated the region to lie twenty miles north of where he had met the raiding column the day before. But it was only a guess, for small landmarks could not be distinguished at all from his height, and the large ones he viewed from a different perspective.

Gorges, basaltic extrusions, lava flows, and jagged hills formed the terrain, as though a giant hand had built turrets and scattered massive blocks in random formation. Why any nation should want that lonely, unlovely land mystified him. Even from his height, however, he detected tiny ants here and there on the hilltops, or crawling from bush to bush in the valley bottoms. He heard the stutter of machine guns and saw answering wisps of smoke puff up from the ground. Now and then one of the ants stopped crawling.

He spiraled lower, the peril from stray shots forgotten in the anger that again welled inside of him. Leif Abbot had more than one contradiction in his make-up. As a footloose adventurer and trader, he had always been alert to strike a shrewd bargain when he could; but he was just as eager to leap into fray on the side of the underdog when someone else was taking an unfair advantage.

Still circling downward, he wondered if there was anything he could do about the one-sided battle. His intentness on getting a closer view and his preoccupation with means of counterattack brought him to the danger zone before he realized it. The song of a sky-riding slug passed too close for comfort. He was about to seek altitude again when the problem solved itself. Eventually he would have figured out a solution and maneuvered to make it practicable. He would also have taken precautions for his own skin. As it was, the whole thing happened and his reactions occurred so swiftly that he had no time to foresee the results.

One of the bombers completed its power dive and its burst of firing. It zoomed upward for position. Its nose was tilted toward the eagle. Leif Abbot clearly saw the leather helmets of its crew, and a surprised expression behind the pilot's goggles as he noticed the eagle. Leif Abbot dropped the emerald figurine. It fell straight to its target.

There was a crash and a zing. Glittering green fragments and a flash of gold streaked the air. It was as though the propeller had rammed a stone wall.

The bomber leaped under its own momentum, lost speed, and went into a tailspin. It plunged toward the ground from its altitude of only a few hundred feet. The pilot frantically worked the controls and had just got the craft straightened out when it crashed.

All its bombs must have exploded at the instant of impact. A gigantic fountain of flame roared up. Grass and bushes flattened as a wall of wind rushed in. The concussion numbed Leif Abbot even before he felt the skyward surge. The air filled with blasted objects, debris, shards of metal, bits of flesh. The second bomber, diving to do its own ground-strafing in the wake of the first was caught over that inferno, tossed as by invisible hands. Some hurtling missile must have struck the bomb rack, for the machine disintegrated in another great geyser of flame and smoke and erupting metal.

He never knew the fate of the third bomber. Tossed around in the violent currents from those blasts, he fought for control. Fragments, each bearing potential death, shot past him in all directions. He knew he had been hit. He didn't know how many times or where. One wing responded slowly. He felt suddenly numb and weary. He had a vague impression of the third bomber, its wings and fuselage ripped, tattered, and torn by debris, heading toward a forced landing. He did not stay to watch. He was terribly sick. He had long miles to fly to the only men who could help him. Every stroke he took for altitude made the next effort more labored. He must have altitude so that he could slant down on the wind and be seen if he fell before he reached camp.

The world was curiously quiet. It seemed to reel and grow fuzzy. His thoughts began to wander. How had he managed to hear at all? So far as he knew, birds were not equipped with auditory apparatus akin to man's, yet he had distinctly heard Burton address him, to say nothing of the holocaust he had created. Had he only mentally heard sounds because he expected to hear them? Or had sound waves been transformed by some function peculiar to the bird?

The wings felt sticky. He wanted to fold them in and plummet to earth. It would be so easy. He could straighten out just before he crashed—but he wouldn't straighten out any more than the bomber. He didn't even know if he was flying in the right direction, but he kept to a straight line. The emerald was gone. Why should he go on, with the treasure for which he had endured so much shattered into a million irrecoverable bits? What insane impulse had made him throw it away? At least *they* wouldn't be able to take it away from him now.

It had been a weird dream. It would always be a nightmare without end—fever, visions, jungle, beasts, birds, phantoms black and white in a green hell, an ever-recurring theme of pain, flying, falling—falling—

Leif Abbot awakened from a dream that he had been flying through the air and sinking toward the green shadows of the jungle. He was not at all sure that he had wakened. Instead of flying, he found himself in suspension. He floated, not in air, but amid a denser medium. He saw the shadowy green twilight, but it was the obscurity of water, not of forests.

Beast, bird, fish—what did it matter? One nightmare was no worse than another. He had survived the others, and he would live through this, until the delirium left him and he opened his eyes again upon the world as he knew it.

The illusion, however, persisted. The realization came with a keener terror because it built up gradually. From the misty hinterlands of fantasy he passed through disbelief and reached the inexorable truth.

He resorted to speculation in a frantic effort to ignore his surroundings. He had winged his way toward camp—had he reached it? He retained an impression of fatal injury—had he survived? He nearly remembered a period of lucidity, and of talking for a long while—but what had he said? Did this represent a single half-memory or two? Had he talked to Burton and Travers when he returned from his panther-life, or when he fluttered down from his eagle-state, or after both?

Try as he might, he could not close his eyes, now that a measure of awareness had returned. While he was brooding, he was conscious of somber twilight. As his thoughts became coherent, he was forced to abandon evasions. He could not substitute wishes for bitter facts.

Travers and Burton had cheated and betrayed him. They had used their fiendish discovery to deprive him of his rightful body for the third time. They had locked him up in the guise of a fish.

He tried to turn his head to see what sort of finny creature he had become, but his head would not turn. A flip of the fins and he faced the opposite direction. He rose, dived, circled, wriggled, and spun around until he was dizzy with exasperation. His eyes could see only forward and upward. He could not turn his head.

Had they placed him in the headwaters, the ground springs, that formed the source of the river he had followed in his original flight? He became aware of a gentle, lazy current, and allowed himself to drift along.

The water swarmed with life. He was appalled by what his human eyes had missed when he had drunk of necessity at tepid pools and streams during his years in the tropics. Millions of tiny insects and water-bugs lived on the scum-covered surface.

A great horror of these strange depths overcame him. He could not follow the stream to the sea. He could never watch beneath or behind. He had no weapon to fight lurking monsters. He had no desire to find out what terrifying life-forms infested the deeper parts of the river, or what rotting hulks and bones littered the sea-bottoms. Once he left his present position, he would never be able to find his way back.

A flip of the tail brought him face about. A fiercer horror assailed him, but he had no voice to cry out, no time to flee. A sort of dumb and paralyzing madness quaked through him as he saw the jaws of the crocodile close—

Burton looked worried. He watched the body of Leif Abbot which was twitching grotesquely. The arms and legs made spasmodic movements. The mouth gapped like that of a fish out of water.

The body flopped weakly all at once, with a quiver and a horrible finality.

Burton sprang to his kit, seized drugs, and worked for an hour in sweating anxiety. His efforts produced no results.

"What happened?" asked Travers.

"I don't know. I'm afraid the vitality of the fish was of too low an order to direct a highly-developed and complicated organism."

Travers filled his pipe irritably. "He was done for, no matter what. Why the devil couldn't he have left the emerald?"

THE EYE AND THE FINGER

HE WAS NEITHER contented nor unhappy as he plodded up the five flights of stairs toward his room. His eyes felt weary. They always ached a little at evening after he had finished his day's work, for the bright lights of the department store bothered him. Not the shrill voices of women, which swept into his ears for eight hours like a thin, far scream. Not the mask of calmness that rules compelled him to wear. Not the standing on his feet, the smirking, bowing, directing, explaining, and approving. He had long become used to these. They varied. Their relative values changed. But the glare of the lights was a tireless, implacable enemy.

He reached the second floor. The half-gloom of the staircase-well soothed him.

Tomorrow he would draw his salary check. The twenty-five dollars would guarantee his existence a week longer. If the fatal pink slip came with his salary, he could last about three weeks by scrimping and letting the rent slide. He was vaguely conscious of these possibilities, but they didn't prey on his mind. Five years of steady employment had fitted him into routine.

Passing the third floor, he smiled politely at a woman. He had seen her before, and was often on the point of speaking, but didn't know her name.

At the fourth floor he hesitated. He had a notion that he had forgotten something. He checked off the evening newspaper under his arm, the toothpaste in his pocket, the laundry that would arrive later. Halted there under the bulb on the landing, he showed no distinguishing features. No one would notice him in a crowd. Away from the store he was diffident, mild-mannered, and he himself found it hard to characterize his appearance whenever he faced a mirror.

He climbed on to the fifth floor. His room had an old lock on the door, which he had never yet succeeded in opening on the first try. He worked the key back and forth until the lock turned.

As soon as the door stood open he felt for the wall switch, and when the light came on, he closed the door with a backward kick of his foot.

An eye was lying on the top of his bureau.

He saw it instantly, for the eye was staring at him.

He grew ill at ease, for he had few friends and did not like practical jokes. Or perhaps one of the children in the building had thoughtlessly played a prank upon him. That must be the explanation. He felt relieved, though he couldn't imagine how the locked door had been overcome. He walked over to the bureau and picked up the eye.

A strange, colossal silence all at once enveloped him, in which he distinctly heard the tiny paws of a mouse scampering through the walls. Then a great roaring swept up, so that his eardrums throbbed to the hammer of gigantic poundings.

The eye was living, humid, and horrible to feel.

He dropped it. The eye made a soft, dull plop as it hit the bureau. It rolled and came to a stop staring unwinkingly at him. A moist film clung to his thumb and forefinger.

He backed away from the bureau, his gaze glued to the eye. Surges of thunder and blankets of incredible silence alternately shook him and numbed him.

The eye watched him retreat.

He backed into a chair and jumped nervously from the contact. The room whirled. Among the shifting objects, a cup crossed his vision. He remembered a piece of cardboard in a box of stationery.

He got the cup and the cardboard, but was loath to approach the eye. It continued to look at him with a singularly intense, compelling, and mournful fixity, as though it wished to convey a message.

He turned the cup upside down and dropped it over the eye. The cardboard rustled as it slid across the cloth spread that covered the bureau, and slid under the cup. Something rolled around inside the small area of the prison. He lifted the cup and cardboard, walked to the door, and went out, down to the street. A terrifying motion, like the slow progress of a slug, took place between the pasteboard and the cup. The faint warmth that seeped through seemed searing flame upon his palm.

He deposited the cup in a waste can, and weighted it with a brick so that whatever was on the inside of it could not escape.

He returned to the main entrance of the building where he lived. The threshold blocked him by an invisible barrier that he could not force

himself to cross. Walking on, he felt better when the doorway receded behind him.

Passersby did not register upon his consciousness. He had no memory of streets, nor of pavements flowing beneath his measured tread. It startled him to discover that he walked indeed with solemn paces, instead of strolling at random as he had planned. He was tramping through night, but the street lamps at spaced intervals broke the darkness with rings of light. They measured in time to the beating of his footsteps, in rhythm with the far roaring and alternate silences that divided his ears.

If he had been walking in a funeral procession, he could not have chosen a more appropriate gait.

He paid no attention to the lapse of hours, until he looked up and found himself again in front of the entrance. Aching weariness made him realize the miles he must have covered during his half-stupor. The shock, the grip of horrific nightmare, only now waned. And as it passed away, he began to wonder what had caused him so vivid an illusion of living through an experience that had no connection with any previous part of his life.

He began climbing the stairs, the five flights. His hand, clutching the banister, helped pull him along. The wood felt clammy as though sweating to damp air. The atmosphere must have been saturated, for beads of moisture collected upon his forehead.

The heavy pounding of his heart commenced upon the third floor. He went on, a sense of constriction and of doom accompanying him.

Arrived at last in front of his door, he listened, and heard the creaking sounds of the building. What else could he have heard? he wondered, breathing audibly.

The key wouldn't work, until he remembered that he had forgotten to lock the door. He pushed it open, slowly, and the light in the room gave him a moment's panic until he remembered that he had forgotten to press the switch when he carried the eye out.

He entered. Frozen into immediate paralysis, he jerked only when the door swung shut, of its own accord, upon its ill-balanced hinges. The click came to his ears like a detonation in the midst of a desert of solitudes.

A hand hung in mid-air, a hand that pointed at the open window.

Where it should have been attached to an arm, he clearly saw blood, veins, flesh, muscular tissue, and bone. But it did not bleed. And there was no body. And the nap of the rug underneath it remained erect.

He stared at the hand with blind, unreasoning, raging horror. The hand curled, so that the forefinger pointed directly at him. It curled in no haste, but as inexorably as the tick of time.

His first instinct, to flee forever from the room, he suppressed. He heard the rumble of wheels upon a street, and in the presence of that familiar reality, he could not yield to this visitation that had no right to afflict him. For if he rushed out, not to return, he could never through all years to come efface the haunting of events that he could not explain.

His breath came in deep gulps, and trembling fits of exhalation, as he advanced.

The hand, hanging without support, pointed straight toward him. He drew nearer, and nearer, but could detect no change in its position. The room fell away from his vision, light and darkness departed, leaving to him a universe composed only of a disembodied hand, and himself.

He seized the hand, intending to hurl it far out the open window.

The fingers instantly curled around his own, not fiercely, but tugging him along, pulling him toward the window. For a step he followed, hypnotized and unnerved. The hand felt neither living nor dead, neither hot nor cold. Its touch brought unrelieved terror, because it resembled nothing that he knew. It seemed most like the clasp of some fantastic alien, not of this or of any other imaginable world, but of a solidity beyond. It felt like a marginal thing, trapped midway between stone oblivion and tissue of life.

He pulled, and the hand reluctantly, with heavy drag, yielded, drifting away from the window as upon the surface of an unseen ocean. The fingers retained their firm clasp, all save the forefinger which opened like an unfolding worm. He fought the hand. He seized the forefinger with a tug that tore the other fingers loose. The forefinger began to curl inward upon his left palm. His right fist hit and hammered it. He freed himself wholly from that corrupt touch, and backed away, a salt taste upon his lips.

The hand relaxed. It drifted over to the spot at which he had first observed it. His own hands were shaking, shaking incessantly, and yet all the rest of him seemed ice. Not until the marginal thing had resumed its former position did he manage to overcome his paralysis, but the palsy of his hands continued. If the marginal thing had only attacked him—if it would try to overtake him, track him down, hound him deliberately—he could have coped with physical, tangible horror in action. The fiendish element was the thing's confidence. It urged, without threatening him, and waited because it had the whole of time till doomsday.

A towel caught his glance. Not once letting the hand out of his sight, he took the towel from its rack by the washbowl.

The forefinger curled up in a dreadfully wagging gesture as he drew near again.

The towel trembled even before he flung it over the marginal thing. He grabbed the four ends, wondering if the prisoner had escaped. With the corners of the towel clutched, he distinctly felt a weight, heard and saw a gruesome scrabbling within the bulge.

His descent was nightmare. He twisted the ends of the towel, and held the bag that imprisoned the creature under his arm. There it squirmed, nudging him with fingers that prodded inquisitively. Toward the ground floor, the forefinger began a diabolic tapping in measure with the beating of his heart, and when his heart skipped, the tap did not come.

At the refuse receptacle, he had a compulsion to lift the cup, and find if the eye had escaped. But the fear of knowing proved greater than the fear of not knowing. He knotted the towel to a mass of iron. He walked away rapidly, then, to escape the scuttling flurry that threshed the cloth.

The one man who could help him was Dr. Behn, the psychiatrist, who lived nearby. The psychiatrist did not like being called from bed. At first gruff, then skeptical, impatient, soothing, and interested in turn, he finally agreed to accompany the patient.

"It will at least help to settle your nerves for the night when I've proved that nothing unusual is present," said Dr. Behn reassuringly. "The hallucination may return, of course, but you'll be better prepared because you'll understand that it is a hallucination. I almost wish you were right, though. What an uproar it would create among my colleagues! But, of course, such things simply can't be, can they?"

"Not, they can't be, but they are. Why do they happen to me? Why not somebody else? Why not you?"

Dr. Behn did not answer.

The street, now dark and long deserted, echoed their tread as they entered the building. The echoes had a dismal, reverberating sound as forlorn, as final, as footsteps toward the grave.

The psychiatrist breathed a trifle more heavily by the time he had reached the fifth floor. He was not used to such effort. He waited for the door to be opened.

His companion, however, had difficulty with the key and the lock, partly because of the palsy, partly because he had again forgotten that the door was merely closed. When he finally opened it, the light in the room likewise made him rigid for a moment. The pattern of his life had been swept away. Twice he had forgotten to extinguish the lights and to unlock the door.

The eye—an eye—was lying on top of the bureau.

He saw it instantly, for it was staring at him. He pointed at it, cried out—but not even a whisper issued from his lips. He tried once more to speak, but the breath rattled around in his throat below the level of an audible murmur.

Dr. Behn half-turned his head, a strange expression on his face. He seemed to be looking at his patient, but his pupils remained fixed upon the eye.

The psychiatrist strode forward positively, and yet with a frown. "Hmmm!" he exclaimed. "I don't wonder you got a shock. That's the most convincingly real artificial eye that I've seen. Whoever made it is a remarkable craftsman."

He picked the eye off the bureau.

An expression of utter loathing altered his features until they were as dustily gray as those of a corpse. He felt the eye quiver. A sickness, a nausea added itself to the gray. He opened his fingers mechanically. The eye fell with a dull plop. Its pupil returned its gaze toward the other man, ignoring Dr. Behn.

The psychiatrist stood dazed, his glance crawling toward the eye and back to the film of moisture on his thumb and forefinger. His breathing became more rapid. All at once he turned, began walking, hurrying, running for the door.

A voice harried him. "Wait! *Wait!* What is it?"

The psychiatrist paused briefly, his face twisted into detestable ferocity and hatred. "What is it? I don't know. I don't want to know.

"My province is psychology and mental hygiene. This is wholly outside my field. I know nothing about it. I do not care to have anything more to do with it. When I leave I shall forget that I listened to you. I shall forget that I came here. I shall forget that anything happened. I shall leave instructions with my secretary that under no circumstances will any appointment whatsoever be made with you at any time hereafter. I refuse to accept your patronage. My practice is, and will be, confined to mental cases, not physical impossibilities.

"I can't help you. There's nothing that anyone can do to help you. This is your own problem. Work it out any way you see fit. Goodnight, and goodby."

The door slammed.

Even through the walls, he could hear Behn's receding tread, hurrying farther and farther below. The sound, fading swiftly, died away among the remote world.

When he turned around, he uttered a whistling sigh.

The eye upon the bureau still watched him unwaveringly.

And in mid-air hung the hand, forefinger pointed toward the open window.

He took a step in the direction of the hand. It began to swing toward him, leisurely. Its supreme indifference, the impersonal confidence of that horrible, marginal thing obsessed him even more than the eye. And the eye with its cold, implacable stare had already initiated him into the brotherhood of the blind.

The curtains gently swayed as he walked toward them. He did not look behind at the hand or the eye.

The drapes rippled from the eddy of his plunge through the open window.

THE PAINTED MIRROR

WHEN PAPA KHEVI moved to a new city and began again in another old shop that he had bought, Nicholas knew before he saw them that three faded golden balls would hang outside the door. It had been so nearly as long as he could remember. A year here—sell and move. Two years there—sell and move on to another shop, a different town.

It had not been so when Mama Khevi lived. But of her little Nicholas had only a vague dream that grew fainter each year. Then, long past, the three of them had dwelt in the place of strange, curious things, had always dwelt there; but after Mama Khevi died, a change came. Not many months later, Papa Khevi grew restless. He took the lad westward. And westward they went, from year to year, while Papa Khevi seemed ever more silent, with the odd, puzzled expression that troubled Nicholas showing more often in his eyes.

Like the others, this shop flaunted an array of objects that enthralled Nicholas for days—marvelous watches, magic cameras, guns, musical instruments, a rack of clothing, rings and bracelets, medals, paper currency and golden foreign coins, tarnished silver plate, oil-cracked paintings, an immense array of articles ranging from small treasure to junk.

But Nicholas saw it all as treasure-trove. Each piece told a tale of adventure among the inhabitants of far places. Nicholas learned every story merely by looking at the object. It was as simple as imagination.

While Papa Khevi puttered around the shop, straightening the showcases, dusting shelves, polishing a vase, or picking odds and ends for removal, Nicholas would take himself to a corner with his latest find. Nicholas had a knack of unobtrusively fading into the dark, shadowy spots where no one noticed him.

Not that there were many intruders. Papa Khevi was always gruff, or surly, with clients who came to buy. He put ridiculously high prices, which he refused to lower, upon even the most tawdry jewelry. He discouraged sales. Once in a while, despite his efforts, a purchaser met his asking price without quibble and walked away with the loot. Then Papa Khevi was cross the rest of the day. But he welcomed those who brought however little to pawn. He appraised the article, appraised the victim, estimated the need, and offered a trifle more.

Sometimes the police came, searching for stolen goods. Then Papa Khevi was all smiles. But at such times Nicholas stayed out of sight, because his father hated police, he never knew why, and after they had gone went around mumbling to himself.

It was on one of those occasions, when the measured tread of the police sounded through the opening door, that Nicholas discovered the mirror.

He scampered to the back of the store and the two tiny rooms that they lived in. He usually remained there until the police left, but he thought that the heavy steps followed him. He dashed to the stairway, forgetting that Papa Khevi kept it locked, and that he had yet to find the door open. It opened readily this time. He was up the first flight before he remembered that it should have been locked. He listened, listened, his heart a-flutter, but the heavy tread died out far away.

At the top of the second flight there was a single window. He peered through its grimy glass, and rubbed it hard with his hand. He cleaned an oval spot. The soot outside kept him from seeing more than the outline of one- and two-story buildings, brick rows, beyond them the bluffs, and below them the river.

The gloomy light that filtered in showed him, when he turned, an attic crammed with bundles. Yellowed papers wrapped them and covered the barrels standing around. There were boxes filled to the brim. A whole new wonderland of stacked books, picture-frames, trunks, hanging shrouded wraps, bureaus, tin cartons, and scattered unsorted heaps of stuff lay before him. He came across rolls of wallpaper, streaked cans of paint, brushes whose bristles had dried into a tightly cemented mass. A workbench was littered with dull, rusty tools.

Nicholas poked among these heaps of new treasure. It would take weeks to explore the attic thoroughly. It must have been accumulating its hoard from the day that the building was finished. The successive owners must have added to the collection without disturbing it. What few cobwebs he found sagged with the dust of years.

The roof, from its apex over the exact middle of the attic, slanted down to make an acute angle with the floor on all four sides. Uncovered beams, dry and fissured, formed the ribs of the roof. Resting on the floor, and tipped against these beams in one corner, stood a thick pile of screens and windows. At the very back of the pile, however, leaned an object of a different sort. It seemed to be a large, heavy pane of glass, a mirror.

Nicholas patiently dragged the screens and windows aside in order to get at the mirror. It must be a very special mirror or it would not have been so well concealed.

With the last of the frames removed, he felt a pang of disappointment.

A coat of black paint covered the entire face of the mirror.

Nicholas remembered that a can of black paint, partly used, and a brush caked with black paint lay in another part of the attic. Some previous occupant, then, had taken pains to render the mirror useless. Why? It would have been much simpler to shatter the glass. Why had someone avoided breaking the mirror, but at the same time destroyed its value?

Here was mystery, adventure, beckoning him. He went back to the workbench and picked out a chisel. The chisel had an almost blunt edge, but it served well enough for scraping the paint off the mirror.

The black coating cracked away in tiny flakes. At the end of an hour's hard work, he had cleaned an area somewhat larger than his two hands. He toiled for another hour before his arms grew tired.

A feeling of excitement had come over him, for this was, indeed, a magic mirror. He knew that already by the surface he had exposed, now as big around as a plate.

The mirror, as all mirrors should, reflected an image. But that image was not Nicholas, nor any object in the attic, nor any part of the attic! He could not make out more. He could not determine the true nature of the image. He had only a tantalizing glimpse of a portion of that imprisoned reflection.

Weary from his activity, and in a state of high anxiety, Nicholas pulled a couple of screens over to hide the mirror.

He tiptoed downstairs. When he heard Papa Khevi stomping around in the pawnshop, he felt better, but unrelieved. In the attic lay the road to the dark heart of mystery, or the shining eyes of fortune, if the door was not barred to him.

He tossed through a restless night, and worried in the hours of morning, his fancy gripped by the lure of the mirror. He put himself at the feet of Papa Khevi until he was brusquely told to go behave himself. Nicholas pattered from the display room in an agony of apprehension lest the attic door be locked.

The door swung open. Papa Khevi had evidently forgotten about it. With luck, providing Nicholas was cautious, he might be able to keep the door open for a long time. There was no reason for the attic to be used, now that Papa Khevi had looked it over or stored the bric-a-brac that he had removed from stock.

Nicholas climbed, his heart pounding so that his ears heard, and hurriedly slid the screens aside from the mirror.

His heart stopped pounding. The mirror reposed as he had left it. The plate-sized opening that he had made in the coat of paint showed the same baffling reflection as before. He seized the chisel and began to chip at the black film.

The layer grated loose with maddening slowness. It fractured in flakes too small to be measured. The particles dusted the floor at the base of the mirror, and sometimes whirled into his eyes with a sting. But he became more accustomed to the work, more intent on discovering what the magic mirror concealed. He scraped twice as long and cleaned three times as much surface as the day before, nearly a third of the mirror.

Still the scene hovered beyond definition. There were hints—no more than hints—of a bleak landscape; an entrance, hole, tunnel, cave, or hill of some sort rising stark from the plain; and the limbs of a fugitive.

A captive fleeing—from what? Away from a pursuer—a monster, an ogre? Toward refuge in the great spaces, the fringes yet hidden by the black paint—

His thoughts fleeted over the ways in which the full scene might manifest itself. He wondered what far place was mirrored in the glass. Since it was a magic mirror, obviously it wouldn't act like an ordinary mirror. Instead of reflecting what lay close to it, it reflected something at a great distance; and if at too great a distance, very likely Nicholas would never know or find the exact spot. Even after he stopped working, his mind remained nervously alert under the stimulus of the image, vibrant to its potentialities, quivering with the fever of anticipation.

When he opened the door for the third time, and climbed again to the attic, and found the mirror as he had left it, he hunted around until he brought to light an old file. With this he sharpened the chisel. His eagerness could tolerate no further delay in exposing the secret of the mirror.

The paint flaked off in the same tiny chips as before, but faster, much faster. The boundaries of the brooding landscape became wider, the dark cave stood out starkly upon the desert. Nicholas grew conscious of a

glow, an aura of pallor that reflected into his eyes from the figure at the entrance to the cavern.

The mirror, stripped of the coating of black paint, disclosed a flat desert, a wilderness unbroken by stone, dune, bush, stream, or creature, a void that stretched endlessly in all directions. Upon that desolation stood only the cave, a horseshoe in shape, tunneling to the far distance. And from the cavern emerged a figure, dimly outlined save for its face which reflected the luminous pallor.

That diminutive figure seemed to be running out of the cave. The figure looked tiny, like a toy, a mere doll, because it was so remote in the depths of the mirror. Its eyes were closed. Its face showed terror, as though it fled blindly—from what? What footsteps following faster down that infinitely long corridor caused the child, the girl, the doll to keep its eyes shut with fear?

Nicholas watched the image for hours, marveling at the illusion of three-dimensional depth in the mirror; the glass acted like a telescope seen through the wrong end, and multiplied by many times the distance to the object under focus.

He found himself unable to banish the picture from his mind. It stayed with him when he left. It preoccupied him during his waking hours. It persisted in his dreams, vividly, hauntingly alive.

Not without trepidation, he tugged at the screens upon his next ascent. The phantoms of sleep had lingered on, and deep within him quaked a bell that tolled unease.

But the marvelous mirror beckoned stronger, and Nicholas knew why when it lay exposed.

The eyes of the distant doll were wide open and fixed compellingly upon him!

A strange giddiness swept over him, like a wind that wafted all familiar things away. Knowledge smote him with its evil curse, knowledge that he had half guessed, half feared, and entirely denied—the knowledge that the mirror did *not* reflect a scene from some far corner of the world, but contained within itself a world of its own.

And the light, so pale, so unearthly, continued to glimmer from the elfin features of the doll, light originating in whatever sun or moon coursed the sky of that internal world above and beyond the frame of the mirror. Under the glow, the opened eyes of the figurine possessed a hypnotic brilliance, issued a silent message across all those intervening leagues.

A message—what message? Nicholas stared at the boundless, silent world—the vast plain, the cavern tunneling into distance beyond sight, the girl-doll emerging and fleeing from whatever terror lurked behind her. The vestiges of that terror dwelt on her face, in the pallor of her cheeks, and her lips parted to gasp for breath. But hope, all but fled, had returned to her, fleeing still, as she opened her eyes and saw Nicholas.

Electrical tingles fired him, turned him hot and cold. He could only watch, unable to help, forced to wait, because of the barrier that separated their two worlds, a veil that neither of them could tear asunder. But there was a hope, if time would favor them. In all the days that he had labored, the distant doll had advanced only by a step, to open its eyes. The other world moved far more slowly than the world of Nicholas. She was safe a little while longer, because of the slow, almost imperceptible life of the land of the mirror.

She was a lovely thing, a golden toy, invested with perilous beauty. She had emerged fully from the cavern, Nicholas noted with a start. Turning, he saw that the shadows of evening had crept into the attic. The day had passed, and she had moved without his awareness. He wondered about the trance into which he must have fallen, but not yet was he able to tear himself away.

He looked at the mirror again. In spite of the darkness that had fallen, the mirror stood out with ghostly luminance, and principally from the figurine came that impalpable glow. A tremor of excitement shook Nicholas. All fear had banished itself from the face of the golden doll, golden-green, rather, under that unearthly light; an elfin princess with body as enchanting and perfectly-molded as the features that had first bewitched him. She was wholly free of the cavern. She was running toward him. She had forgotten the terror that lurked in the depths of the cave.

As he backed away slowly, a state of abnormal ecstasy and dream-suspension enveloped him. So intensely vivid was the drama unfolding within the world of the mirror that he could not cast off its spell, nor did he wish to. He was unaware of descending the steps. His mind's eye had vision only for the golden-green captive; teasing him, tantalizing him, keeping him aquiver, the sculptured beauty of the figure of the tiny fugitive.

Sleep abandoned Nicholas all night long. He listened for a voice, for a bell-like call in the attic afar, for the murmur of the crystal maiden. He lay half in a panic lest she escape during the night and become lost, leaving to him only the unseen terror that had not yet burrowed its way out of the tunnel.

The hectic tautness, combined with the state of suspension, outlasted night. The anxiety of waiting through the dawn hours fostered a flame within him, like an invisible sun, whose glare gave him no peace and permitted him no restful descent into slumber.

And when at last he began again the climb up the attic stairs, he tiptoed while his ears strained for a sound from above—the shatter of glass—the tinkle of a crystalline voice—fugitive footsteps—

But silence deepened curiously, until he fancied a roaring in his ears from the strain of attempting to hear. Was it the surge of blood in his veins, violent over the scuffle of his ascent?

He stood upon the attic floor, now, and all speculation ebbed away. A torrent of reflected radiance like moonlight upon quicksilver issued from the mirror. Far larger in size, looming to almost full-grown human proportions, gigantic against the background of interminable desert, the golden-green captive seemed on the verge of stepping through the mirror. Her eyes summoned him, her arms were raised in supplication for escape.

Nicholas ran to the mirror, his hands outstretched. They touched hers, dissolved, blended. He hurtled headlong, pulled and catapulted and twisted fantastically. He was rigid, frozen, unable to press his way out of a solid sea of glass.

Far away, upon the other side of the mirror, beyond the crystal cliff that imprisoned him inside a timeless world, he saw his own rightful body, Nicholas, peering down at him, at this alien figure he had become, this elfin form of the creature of the mirror. Behind him stretched the tunnel with its hidden terror.

Upon the face of that Nicholas far away spread a fiendish smile. The other Nicholas receded, only to return with a can of black paint and a brush. Stroke by stroke, that other Nicholas began to cover the mirror.

Nicholas tried in vain to make this alien figure move or shout or beat its way through the cliff of glass.

He was trapped. Night deepened around him, and became blackness. He was imprisoned forever in this golden-green figure. His despairing gaze watched that distant Nicholas, an unholy light of joy in its eyes, while it finished painting the entire surface of the mirror. He was captive in a soundless, boundless, motionless realm of black.

UNEASY LIE THE DROWNED

H E WATCHED THE graying sky anxiously, but without fear, and
kept his ears attuned to the gusts of wind that pulled the waves
higher. He had made many direct crossings of lakes in the past,
alone, both in high-riding and heavily-laden canoes. This lake was new to
him. It was miles across. He did not know its depths and shallows, its lily
clusters, beds of weeds, or the way it responded to squalls.

The sky had been clear when he started out. A deep, rhythmic stroke
of the paddle, and a twist of the blade. Out and forward. Down and back
again. Each time that he brought the paddle astern, an expert drag on the
blade kept the canoe on its straight course. It was a simple trick. He
could go on for hours, stroking steadily on the right, but midway to his
goal, and still unwearied, he switched over to the left.

As often happened in fall along the border lakes, a squall was brewing.
A mass of slate-black clouds bloomed out of Canada and swallowed the
setting sun. He changed his pace, increased the power of his thrust and
pull, sent the canoe skimming more swiftly across the waters.

The lake, hitherto calm, began to spawn groups of nervously racing
ripples. The wind chased them in all directions over the surface They
vanished, and left a deceptive tranquility, until more of the uneasy whirls
and lines skittered along. A swell gradually made its presence, in slow
undulations, then in an occasional small wave that broke, and always
higher swells, and more strongly marked crests.

The water itself, leaf-green at mid-afternoon, darkened as the sun
disappeared. The green turned to a sodden blue, and went down to a dull
black. And far under that black, four hundred feet and more, lay the solid
rock that formed the deep-gouged bed of all these northern lakes. Rock,
and the sediment of centuries, saturated logs, perhaps the wrecks of
sunken boats and bodies of the drowned for the pike and the muskel-
lunge to forget.

Even the stillness had given way to disturbing sound. The constant, quiet slur of waters divided by the canoe became a slap, at irregular intervals, and with mounting force. The canoe, no longer gliding at even balance, began to rise a little, dip a little, and the lake smacked the fore keel. From the far distance came the advance echo of a mighty rushing howl. The dark mass of pine and spruce that lined the shore, now less than two miles ahead, stirred with a mournful unrest. The air grew colder.

During all the summers that Morse Calkins had spent canoeing and hunting, camping and fishing through the lakes and forests of northern Minnesota, he had not until now experienced a doubt in his mastery. His alarm crept up from his heart to his brain because he could not account for the apprehension. He had been lost in the woods, had rescued himself from a capsized canoe, outdistanced forest fires, escaped the charge of a full-grown moose. He had survived many a squall. Yet the germ of an obscure panic haunted him. Less than two miles, a mile and a half, to the camp where the three companions of this expedition awaited his arrival.

There came a lull.

As though a gigantic, invisible hand closed over the canoe, it lost momentum.

Instantly aware of the drag, he could not understand it. None of the possible causes that he was familiar with seemed adequate reason. A bed of weeds—there was no shallow here, only bottom hundreds of feet down. An added weight—he had not yet shipped water. The pressure of wind—the wind blew fitfully, not steadily, not enough to retard him. A drift of current—perhaps, but currents were more common to rivers than lakes.

The canoe lagged further. His senses, alert to every mood of the craft, warned him of pressure astern. For some strange, incomprehensible motive, he kept his eyes glued on the dark forest and the black mountains of clouds ahead. The prow of the canoe tilted upward higher than it should rise to crest a wave.

He stroked suddenly, deeply, the muscles knotting at his shoulders, and the veins rising on his arms, while his knuckles stood out in naked, bony lumps.

The canoe slowed to a standstill. The bow rode still higher. All his strength and power, his hardest paddling, could not move the canoe. He saw the sweat seep from wrinkles at his wrist, but the swart hairs were half-erect. Odd. Hot and cold—he couldn't be both.

Morse turned and glared all at once, as if expecting to find someone else in the canoe, someone to curse.

There was no one else in the canoe—yet.

But there was a hand clutching the stern, and the fingers of another hand crawled into sight, sliding over the rim. Morse watched them with an expression of detachment. It was almost a silly expression, for the anesthetic of shock had paralyzed him in one instantaneous flood.

A pair of hands—well, why not? A swimmer whom he hadn't noticed—or the exhausted survivor from a boat that had foundered—but the hands wouldn't have inched their way up with so stealthy an approach. These thoughts floated vaguely somewhere in back of his reeling consciousness. No swimmer, no living human being, ever possessed hands of such soapy fatness.

They slid along the side, those plump, bloated fingers, and found a grip. He couldn't make out a trace of knuckles or joints or veins. The nails were entirely missing. Only thick coils remained, like enormously pudgy, gray-white worms.

Above the stern rose a tangle of hair. It was wet, matted. Then the forehead and eyes and face, except that of these there existed only a swollen, fissured blob, the features of one drowned and immersed for months.

To Morse, it seemed that his arms and legs would never carry out his command, that his body drifted through lazy gestures akin to a slow-motion picture. Yet he found himself bringing the oar blade down again and again on those horrific hands. He was not aware of having made a mad lunge forward that almost capsized his craft, or of whirling around and lifting the oar above his head. Only his hammering upon the fingers and head of the corpse, there in all that tumult of wind and waters, formed a positive reality.

He could not pound or pry them loose.

The lips curled around the distended, protruding tongue—an illusion bred of darkness and terror. It couldn't be. Nor the gasped whistle of an inarticulate attempt at speech, like the hiss of steam escaping. He didn't hear it. He couldn't hear it above the rumble and boom of thunder.

Thunder—of course. In the old days, cannon had been fired to roil quiet waters and bring to the surface bodies of the drowned. The thunder, the roaring, reverberating claps and wild wind over the lake had raised this dead thing from its lodging. The rest was imagination. Mustn't let his nerves go.

He heard a husky, gurgling rattle. Once he had listened to a dying soldier whose message bubbled away upon the bullets that had punc-

tured his lungs. This was a sound more appalling, because of its delibera-
tion, and the words choked on the wind, "Don't, Morse. I came up to see
you. I had to see you. I was Pete LaRoy."

Morse didn't know that he shouted. There was frenzy in his voice. It
rode the storm. "Go back where you came from! I don't care who you
are! I've got to make camp—a storm's coming up— get away from here,
damn you! Why don't you go back?" The oar thudded, slipped off those
fat fingers. Morse wondered what insane impulse drove him to talk
aloud. You can't talk to the drowned.

"I can't go back, Morse. I've got to know you. I've got to talk to you. I
had to come up. You see, my canoe sank and I drowned—"

"No! No! Go down where you belong!" Was that crazed babble his?
What made him answer ghost-words that he dreamed?

"I will. But not yet. I drowned by accident, Morse. It shouldn't have
happened. I wasn't prepared. I hadn't lived as long as I was supposed to.
I ought to have gone on living. If I had, I'd have met you. I'd have become
a friend of yours. We would have made plans together. We would have
seen a lot of each other."

The thick, blurry speech submerged the gusts that now began to lash
the rising waters. Morse wished that the gale would scream down a
million-fold louder and blast into oblivion those corrupt words and that
hoarse voice.

Morse panted—and he himself found time to doubt if he made such
soft, persuasive answer—"I don't want to know you, whatever you are."

"But I want to know you, Morse Calkins. You see, if I hadn't drowned
months ago—was it months? I don't remember. Time doesn't mean
anything to me now. If I hadn't drowned, if I had managed to get across
the lake safely, I'd have known you well by now. So when I felt you pass
over me, something tugged me. You pulled me up where I could see
you—"

"No! No! I didn't have anything to do with it! Get the hell back!"

"Oh yes, you did, Morse. You compelled me to come up. Pete
LaRoy—you never heard the name before, did you?"

"I don't want to hear it again. Let me go. I've got to reach camp before
the storm breaks at its worst. Why don't you just let go and drop back?"

"I will. But not yet. I have something to do that I didn't have time to
do when I was Pete LaRoy and living. I'm dead now. Maybe I'm not Pete
LaRoy. But the part of me that remembers Pete LaRoy knows what he
would have done if he'd kept on living. That part of me felt you coming
over the surface of the lake. I had to rise up. I had to come as I am, and
I'm here as I am, because there's a mission I've got to carry out. It's the

same mission that I couldn't carry out when I drowned, but that I must have carried out if I'd gone on living."

Morse was hitting, slashing, jabbing again with the oar. The flat of the blade struck the monstrous head with sickening, mushy thuds. He pried at the rotten fingers, but they slid along the side and clung as though glued to the withes. He was breathing harshly. The spray that had begun to blow made his own hands slippery, and glistened wetly on the gray-white thing at the stern.

"Please," Morse said thickly, and again, "Go away, go down," and then suddenly his voice went screeching up a high, thin crescendo, "Let go, God damn you! You're dead and drowned! Get the hell down and rot where you belong!"

The fingers, bashed into loathsome pulp by the blows from the oar, curled over like talons. What was left of Pete LaRoy said in the same guttural drawl as before, "Yes, Morse, I'll go when I've accomplished my mission. I've got to go down where I belong, then. I haven't told you why I came. Don't you want to know?"

"You said you had to see me. You've seen me. Isn't that enough? Are you going to hang on till doomsday?"

"Don't you know why I came? What my mission is?"

"For God's sake, let go!" Morse's voice was getting raw. His howl ended on a sort of piping whistle. His eyes were beginning to glare. He had forgotten the storm. He didn't realize how dark it had become, how blackness came rushing across the lake to merge with the rioting waters. His whole world had narrowed to those pulpy hands and the fat, feature-less face that lay under the tangle of hair.

The horrible voice gurgled again, with a noise of drowning, a rattle of death. "It's a strange destiny that drives me, Morse. I don't understand it any more than you do. Sometimes I think I almost know. Then it slips away from me. In the life that I should have lived, I would be here now to kill you."

"To—to—kill—" Morse choked. There was a gagging in his throat that he couldn't gulp away.

"Yes, to kill you. You see, Morse, if I'd gone on living my natural life, I'd have got to know you. We'd have been friends for awhile. And then we'd have quarreled and turned bitter enemies. We'd have hated each other as much as we liked each other before. But we'd have tried to suppress our hatred, because we'd have been on this long camping trip. And then today we'd have started across this lake, and our hatred would have flared into the open, and you'd have made a dive for me, and I'd have knocked you overboard and paddled away, leaving you to drown.

"It's *you* who should have gone down, Morse Calkins, and *I* who should have gone on living."

The slow, creepy speech died away. Morse saw tiny rivers running down the face and the hands from the torrents of rain that now deluged the lake. The wind had stormed up to a gale, and the waves had begun to crash in foaming white caps. Into the dips dropped the canoe, and slid up the six-foot crests, and shipped the breaking spume.

Morse lurched drunkenly. His eyes felt like flaming coals. His own hair was plastered to his scalp. Streams of rain trickled down his face, sloshed down his back, squished into his boots.

The gray-white visitor bobbed with the rise and fall of the canoe. The soft, fat hands did not relinquish their grip. The dead, decaying head stayed always at the stern.

With a cry that was more like a hoarse bleat, Morse dived for the fingers, yammering as he tried to pull them loose. Their touch was a dreadful sensation that made him gag in crazed horror. He beat and pounded them while the rain glistened like tears on his yellow face.

The double weight on the stern stood the canoe straight on end as it started to mount a roaring white-cap. It plunged beneath the surface. Morse pitched out. The pudgy hands, oddly, seemed to be clinging to his. And then they had somehow enfolded him and he was beating frenziedly at something that had long been pulp.

His last upward glance showed him only raging blackness and the drive of rain.

He was still fighting when the waters closed over his head.

GIANT-PLASM

I. The Seaquake

TODAY WAS THE eighth in the open dory. We doled out the last of our water and provisions this noon. The sun continues to flame across an absolutely frightful sky. It is useless to seek protection under the tarp. The heat comes through, bounces off the bottom, and makes an oven between the canvas and the planks. The only thing to do is sit up. Then we can roast in what comfort there is from the breath of wind created by our slow progress.

There must be a breeze on the Pacific. God knows where. Certainly not here, the ocean a blinding blue mirror except for faint swells that are hardly noticeable.

Eight days gone, and only six of us left out of the eleven who started when the *Reva* sank. Three or four weeks more before we can reach the nearest land. We'll never make it. If there had been time to use the radio—but there wasn't. And we're far off the regular cargo lanes. Maybe Captain Bligh *did* steer an open boat for over forty days and reach shore safely after the mutiny on the *Bounty,* but I'm damned if I can see how.

Santos has started croaking about land again. I'm glad his voice is nearly gone. The first few days he hollered every time he saw a cloud, or thought he saw something. He drove us all frantic. There does seem to be some sort of blob on the horizon. It's straight against the setting sun. But we all know there's no land within five or six hundred miles yet. It's probably a cloud or just an illusion. Or maybe a ship. If it's a ship it'll pass on in the night without seeing us so we might as well forget it.

The only way to forget all this hell is to keep on writing, Diary. You're getting to be my best friend, a good substitute for the travel articles I was going to do at the end of this ill-fated trip. I wish you could talk back to me instead of this bunch of scum. Pablo Santos, a stoker, is short, thick, and oily, with the long arms of an ape. The *Reva's* second mate, Sam Glenk, is a fat lunkhead. Anybody with a name like that would be. Pete Lapous, the cook, is a scrawny, dour duck who looks as if he had a nest of mice in his tummy. He'd likely pitch me overboard if he could read.

Dave Anderson, one of the two passengers surviving besides myself, has a big body and a small head. He doesn't talk much. The other passenger saved when that tramp steamer nose-dived is a woman who goes by the name of Wanda Hall.

I don't know what her real name is but I'm sure that isn't. She looks a little like an adventuress, talks a little like a trouper, and acts as if she'd been in tight spots before. I can't quite make her out. I rather like her, though you couldn't possibly call her a knockout for beauty right now. At that she's easier on the eyes than the rest of these lugs. She has black hair that glistens and a dark complexion that makes her look Spanish, but I know she comes from the States.

It's a queer business, the way the *Reva* went down. We've been talking about it ever since. We haven't yet been able to figure it out. All I remember is being slammed out of my bunk in the middle of the night. I had the devil's own job getting to the deck. It was like bouncing around in a plane that went through loops, siderolls, and tailspins.

The sudden lurches threw me half a dozen times, but I managed to stagger out. Somewhere along the way I took the Hall dame in tow, I don't remember where, anyway we reached the starboard rail just as the first boat was launched. Right then the *Reva* stuck her nose down, and slid out of sight, and that was the end of her along with the rest of the passengers and crew.

The sea boiled and stewed in huge bulges of waves. I've never seen anything like it before. I didn't notice any wind, and yet by the dim light of the waning crescent moon the Pacific looked as if somebody down below had lighted a whopping big fire and the whole damned ocean was beginning to boil. But the water didn't feel any too warm when I got dunked. I came up beside the Hall woman, and somebody hauled both of us into the dory after we yelled awhile.

So that's all I'll ever know about it, except the stink—phooey, what a stink! Enormous bubbles kept floating up to the surface and going *plop!* Then we'd get a whiff of what smelled like a mixture of sulphur fumes and rotten eggs.

I suppose Glenk's guess is as good as anybody's. He thinks a submarine explosion of some sort created a tidal wave or a series of conflicting tidal waves that caught the *Reva* in the heart of the disturbance. The first push was the one that tossed me out of my bunk. Then the others rocked the ship, stood her on end so that the cargo shifted, and started her down. Probably the boilers blew at that stage and finished her.

The dory bobbed for an hour on walls and avalanches and whirlpools of crazy water, the air filled with the stench of gaseous fumes, and down below, far down, the glow of murky fires. We kept bumping into things. Dead sharks, dead tuna, dead tarpon, thousands of dead fish floated up to the surface. They helped out on the food stores the first couple of days.

Santos is still mumbling about land. The sun will pop out of sight in a minute or two, suddenly, the way it always does in these latitudes. I felt a thrill now when I took another look in the direction that Santos was jabbering toward, because I almost believe there *is* land ahead. But that's impossible unless the marine earthquake threw up an island. It can't be a ship for there isn't any smoke.

Santos and Dave Anderson have been handling the oars this shift. Santos continues to poke his head around to look at his imaginary island.

"Hey, you!" He just squawked at me. "Why don't you look? It's land, land! We're saved!"

It got under my skin. I stopped writing. "Why should I look? I'll believe it's land when we reach it. Anyway, the sun's going down. In the morning we'll probably find it was only a cloud. Then it'll be my turn at the oars and you can spend all your time squinting for land."

As I started to go on with my notes, I had a premonition. I raised my head, attempted to get up and dodge. Santos, fever-mad, had yanked the oar out. I saw the blade smash toward my head. I saw Dave Anderson rise and lunge, his hands clawing to bring Santos down. I saw the cankers that the sun and thirst and exposure had raised on Santo's face. They made him look like a Gargoyle, a leering ogre, in that wilderness of smooth waters, heat, torment, and loneliness.

I felt sorry for him. The sun vanished, stars rioted, and suffocating blackness swallowed me up when the oar bounced off my skull. I remember how utterly absurd it all seemed, Santos in a rage and trying to kill me merely because I didn't happen to agree with him that there was land ahead.

II. For The Benefit of Sharks

The coolness of night surrounded me when I regained consciousness. The process took time, a half hour, or an hour, I don't know how long. The blackness would grow soupy, and start swimming, and out of it would emerge the stars, the dory, the sound of oars dipping. My head felt wet. Somebody was holding it. I guessed that Wanda had washed the cut with salt water. The cut hurt like fire. When I tried to sit up, a blasting headache and waves of pain washed me away again into that blankness of darkness.

"Easy. You took a nasty blow," I heard her murmur the last time I came out of fog. Her voice sounded sweet and husky, but that must have been the softening effect of night on the moonless, vast undulation of water. I knew well enough that her throat was as parched as mine.

The advice was good. I followed it. I didn't try to get up. I lay there staring at the stars in the sky, millions and millions of them, clusters and hordes and torrents flaming coldly out there in the far gulfs of space. For some reason, I didn't feel small or insignificant, the way I was supposed to be impressed according to all the stories I'd read. The dory was bobbing around on an ocean that seemed just as limitless as space, and the feeling I really got was one of friendliness toward the stars.

I raised my right arm to wave at the stars. My hand hit a soft substance. Wanda gasped, "What's the big idea trying to knock me out?"

"Sorry, I didn't mean to. I was just waving at the stars." That time I managed to sit up and stay up though the stars went through some wild loops that would have brought cheers from an astronomer.

"Waving at the stars? You're still raving," I heard her mutter.

"No, I'm not," I insisted. She stopped rubbing her chin where I had unintentionally slapped her. From what I could see of her face, she didn't look any too convinced. I changed the subject. "I'm all right now. Who pulled Santos off? Did Anderson manage to get him calmed down?"

She didn't answer.

"What's the matter?"

She shuddered. I could feel her shake for a brief second, but when she spoke, her voice sounded perfectly normal. "Santos isn't with us any more. He and Dave Anderson went overboard."

That gave me a jolt. "How did it happen?"

"After Santos crowned you with the oar, Dave jumped up and grabbed him. It threw them both off balance. When they pitched overboard, the boat rocked so badly I thought we'd all go in. Glenk headed the dory around but only Anderson came up. They were pulling him back when I thought I saw Santos rise, but it must have been an illusion. He never did come up."

"People don't simply go down once—sharks!" I blurted.

She didn't say anything.

Suddenly I was tired, bitter. "What a rotten excuse for dying! We're going to die anyway, toasted black by the sun, or tortured by sight of water we can't drink, or famished for food we haven't got. But for a man to feed the sharks just because somebody else disagreed with him about land being in sight—it sounds as insane as the idiotic things that wars are fought over."

"It wasn't your fault. We're all on the ragged edge. Santos simply went berserk. He thought there was land ahead, he wanted to be saved, and he couldn't bear the thought of anyone to the contrary."

"Is land in sight?"

"We don't know. Pete says there isn't even a speck of land for five hundred miles yet. Easter Island is closest, whatever that is. I never heard of it before."

"Easter Island?" The name puzzled me—then I remembered. "That's an island several square miles in area lying a couple of thousand miles westnorthwest of Chile. It has some volcanic peaks and a lot of big stone images that nobody knows much about. We'll never make it."

"Glenk claims that maybe we won't need to. He says islands have been known to appear and disappear in the South Pacific and elsewhere. He says that the same submarine earthquake that sank the *Reva* might have tossed a mountain peak above the surface. Santos could have been right about sighting an island."

"Sure he could, and a lot of good it will do him now. Or us. A nice big peak fresh from the sea-bottom. Covered with lovely grade A mud and slime. Some sea-weeds—try and eat them. Possibly a few puddles of salt water—have a drink."

I might have gone on with the sarcasm but a voice bellowed, "Shut up, you, or take the oars!"

Curious, how you get used to things so that they don't register even when they're only a few feet away. Glenk and Pete had been rowing while we talked.

So there were only five of us left—one less mouth to feed, if there had been anything to feed it. Four men and a girl—a tough enough combination in an open boat, but at least we were bound by a common ordeal. I wasn't sure that I wanted us to land. Of course, I didn't have anything but a casual interest for Wanda's safety, but I'd expect anything from those other three cutthroats. I saw only trouble ahead whether dawn broke upon a deserted ocean or upon a forgotten or newly risen island.

III. Perilous Land

A shout wakened me before the sun came up. My eyes felt coated with sand. I heard excited voices. Truth to tell, I hadn't slept much or soundly. I kept dozing on and off, becoming drowsily aware of Wanda or the canopy of brilliant stars, then dropping back into nausea and a nightmare-ridden half-sleep. I don't dream much as a rule, but the ones I had that night would have scared hell out of a brass monkey.

I pushed myself up. I wondered how a man could live with so many aches—swollen tongue, long hunger, sun-baked skin, sun-blinded eyes, the steel-hard ribs and planks of the dory, and a splitting headache. Then I saw Wanda again, and it irked me to think that she could take it better than I. Maybe she couldn't, but she didn't let it show.

There was a pale immensity of dawn from the tinge of rose above the eastern horizon to the fleeing wall of night toward the west. The sea remained almost glassily calm. Just a low gurgle of water, and the creak and dip of oars, told me that we moved. It was already sultry, with no breeze. Another frantic day crawled on.

I couldn't believe it when I saw the shadowy hump of land ahead. I stroked my sore eyes, but that only made them feel worse. They smarted like acid burns. When I looked again, I saw the island still there, a dark mass coming into sharper focus as the sun rose.

The jabber of voices brought me really awake. Sam Glenk was croaking, "Look! Look! I told you so! I said the same quake might toss an island up! It did, there it is!"

Pete Lapous asked, "How'd it grow trees overnight?"

"Shut up, you half-baked scum of a cook. Some earthquake threw that land up. What the hell difference does it make if it came up last week or last century? It's here—"

"Oh, stop your everlasting gab!" Wanda said tartly. "You make me sicker than I am. This man is injured. He—"

"Who, that guy? He's only another passenger and a rotten one at that," Glenk rumbled. "Any time he could help, he sits and scribbles in that damn notebook. Who's going to read it? What use is it? You can't eat it. You know what's in it. The sap—lugging a notebook of all things out of his cabin—"

"What of it? He instinctively got what meant most to him when the ship went down. You're a bully and a would-be Napoleon, so you grabbed a gun and a pocketful of bullets. Pete is a cook. He swept up as much food as he could. If it wasn't for that, we wouldn't be here now. As for me, I brought my handbag and a bunch of press clippings. Now go ahead and land, that's what *you* are supposed to be good for."

I gave a silent cheer. Dave Anderson looked off across the waters. The other two men glowered at Wanda and me, then went ahead beaching the dory. I thought then that Wanda looked like an angel, but there was too much excitement the next few hours for further thought along those lines.

An hour after sunrise, we ran ashore on a sandy ledge. The island is of volcanic origin, rising straight out of the sea, with only a few short stretches of beach. In most places the cliffs drop precipitously. It advances by a series of terraces and slopes toward a central peak or crater. I wouldn't be surprised if it is part of a chain of mountains that extends under the sea.

This island, where no island should be, is a queer one. It is the queerest I ever saw. It is a ghost island. I got a spooky feeling when I first saw it by daylight, and the feeling grew after we landed and explored it a little.

It is a dark island, a black island, with rocks and hard, clayey silt underfoot. There is a good deal of grass, fairly thick underbrush and a sprinkling of young trees. They include some coconuts, mangoes, bananas, wild raspberries, oranges—a medley of stuff from seeds blown by the wind or washed ashore from the refuse of distant steamers, I suppose. There are also a couple of small, barely adequate springs. We could subsist here for a few weeks.

This island can't have been here for more than a few years, five or ten at most to judge by the vegetation. And yet—

Dead trees cover it, the trunks of trees that grew God alone knows how long ago. Beyond all doubt, this island existed at some past time, perhaps a couple of hundred years ago, perhaps much farther back in the dawn of time. I remember reading once about an old Dutch navigator who claimed to have seen a considerable stretch of land a thousand miles off the coast of Chile back in the seventeenth or eighteenth century. Maybe this is part of that lost land, maybe it isn't.

An earthquake sent it down, an earthquake brought it back. And here the old stumps stand, naked, stripped of leaves and bark, now dried out and rotting, amid the new growths. Those old trunks loom like dead giants, fifty feet high and more. It is impossible to describe the sinister effect that they have, rising as they do in such striking but desolate array far above even the tallest of the young vegetation.

It is a silent island, save for the sea washing against the cliffs. There are a few gulls that have sought it out, but no other birds, no insects, no animals whatsoever. And there are mysteries upon it—like the mystery of the great stone statue.

The statue faces west, its back to the sea. It stands a hundred yards beyond the inlet where we landed.

The inlet is under the handle of the cup. By which I mean that the whole island is roughly two miles long and a mile wide, shaped very much like a cup lying sidewise. A lagoon at one end, surrounded by a curving rim of land, is similar to the handle of the cup. Under the handle, where it joins the cup or main body of the island, is the ledge where we landed. Beyond that ledge, left toward the mainland, towers the colossal fragment of statuary. We noticed it when we first landed, but we didn't go back to examine it closely until after we had scouted for food and water.

The part of the statue still erect is at least forty feet tall. Originally it must have stood a hundred feet high. The head and upper torso toppled during one of those older earthquakes, leaving the legs and trunk. The shattered fragments that lie partly buried have weathered. The whole must have been a weird colossus. I cannot imagine what it is supposed to represent. It bears some human resemblance, but looks more like a grotesque, immense suit of armor or encasement for a faceless robot. When first erected hundreds or thousands of years ago, it must have dominated all else upon the island, and even now it overshadows the vestiges of the ancient forest.

"It's an ugly thing! Let's leave it alone," Wanda exclaimed as we looked at the fallen monarch.

"Sure, we'll find out what else is on the island," Glenk rumbled. "We got to climb the peak and name it and take possession anyway."

Dave Anderson, who had a curiously small voice for so big a frame, objected mildly. "That's easy for you to say. What about the rest of us who don't have shoes? We aren't fit for tramping around."

It was true. I realized again how strangely dressed a group we were— Dave Anderson and I barefoot, in the pajamas we wore when tumbled out of our bunks. Pete Lapous looked ridiculous in a suit of atrocious flannel underwear. Wanda, awake reading at the time of the disaster, came out with a scarlet blouse, white slacks, and scarlet sandals. She flaunted a good figure. Only Sam Glenk who had been strolling idly around the deck was fully dressed.

Glenk grinned. "Stay here then. Wanda and I'll name the island."

"The name is Miss Hall," she retorted. "Go climb a peak yourself. I'll loaf around with the others."

"Let's all go," I suggested. "Shoes or no shoes, I'm puzzled, though I don't care a hoot about claiming the island. I'd like to know if it has any more mysteries like the dead forest and this mammoth of a statue. We could make the climb in easy stages."

In the end we all went. Glenk swaggered ahead, but Wanda dropped back with us who walked barefoot. Glenk didn't like that, and finally lagged until we caught up with him. He gave me a mean scowl, since Wanda happened to be strolling alongside me at that moment.

I asked the second mate, "How long do you expect to stop, here?"

"A day or two. Long enough for the bunch of you to get in better shape."

"Then what?"

"What do *you* think? We can't stay here and rot. There ain't any too much ground water. Maybe we'll have to hang around for a week before we can stock enough water for the next lap. All the fruit on the island wouldn't last us a month. Our best bet is to collect all the stuff we can and get away as soon as possible. We could make Easter Island in a fortnight with good weather."

Wanda turned up her nose. "I'd rather stay here than spend two more weeks in an open boat. One taste of hell was plenty."

"Well, we can't just go off and leave you!" I exclaimed.

Glenk nodded. "You're right about that. And I'm damned if we'll squat here waiting for *you* to make up your mind."

Wanda said obstinately, "Just the same I'll take my chances on the island while you men get to civilization and send help back. Maybe five people couldn't last long but there's certainly enough food for one person to stay alive a month or two."

The argument halted because we needed our breath to climb a short but steep hill. At the top, we found something else to think about.

The center of the island was a circular plateau about a quarter of a mile in diameter. The usual young growths and stark trunks of the ancient forest covered parts of it. We now had a good view of the peak, or rather, what we had assumed to be the cone of an extinct volcano. At this close range it suddenly became another thing entirely—the ruins of a great building or temple of some sort, ill-defined because buried under a gray-white mound. Scattered off to one side were a number of smaller mounds.

We straggled toward our find. I knew without a word being said that Glenk's greedy soul was driven by visions of loot—I could see the dream of golden sacrificial goblets firing his hot eyes. The island had once been inhabited. The race had reached a stage of culture that made them build statues and structures. Any treasure that they owned in the way of gold, precious metals, gems, or art objects would center around their place of worship or their burial sites, as is the case with most of the earlier civilizations. I knew that such hopes drove Glenk on so strongly that he outdistanced the rest of us.

A restless feeling began to grow on me. It made me uneasy. I didn't know why. The peculiar silence of the island's interior, with the sound of the sea muted by distance, may have had something to do with my worry. The blow on my head plus the letdown after eight days of exposure probably contributed to my state of mind. But most of all, I think it was really the sight of that strange, gray-white mound covering the outlines of the building underneath.

I was wondering why a gray-white deposit happened to coat a particular building while it lay sunk under the sea, and why sediment didn't distribute itself evenly over the whole island.

It is strange stuff indeed that picks out its own site to fall on.

IV. Shining Armor

Glenk was prowling around with a glum expression by the time we caught up with him at the gray-white mound. Seen close by, it lost some of the definite outlines of a building that it had suggested from a distance. Gone was the second mate's dream of wealth, for not the slightest trace of an opening showed, if a temple lay buried beneath the stuff.

Whatever it was, it possessed a most extraordinary shape. It somewhat resembled a vast boulder, a solid block about sixty feet long, forty wide, and thirty high, roughly rectangular. There were several indentations that suggested doors and windows.

On one side a ledge projected much like a porch or altar. The resemblance to a building was uncanny. So was the gray-white stuff, which presented something new in my experience.

Glenk kicked it viciously, in disgust I suppose at not finding gold. Nothing happened. And that scared me, because something *should* have happened.

If you kick a rock, you hear an audible grate or a dull, stony sound. Kick metal and you get a ring or a clang. Kick rubber and it gives to the pressure. But none of these results came about. The only idea I could think of was that it seemed as if he had kicked steel-hard dough, whatever that means.

I felt the wall. It startled me to find it cold and *dry* though sunshine flooded it. Cold and clammy would have been natural—a cold surface sweats to hot air. Or hot and dry would have been all right. But cold and dry under a tropic sun—

"What's the matter?" Glenk asked.

"This stuff—what is it? There's something all wrong about it."

"Bosh. You're seeing things. It's just a big hunk of sunbaked clay or mud."

"It's hard, tough, and cold, yet I think it would give if we hit it with enough strength," I insisted. "Have you ever seen anything like it before?"

Glenk scoffed. "There has to be a first time for anything you see that's queer. Otherwise it wouldn't *be* queer."

"It's more than that. Why does the stuff cling here? It's almost as if a—skin—had developed around a building—"

"Haw—haw—haw!" His booming laughter rolled back at me. I didn't see anything funny, not with that immense mass of strange, pallid stuff in front of me. But Glenk laughed so hard that he gasped, and then laughed some more, while I hoped he choked.

His voice grated on my ears the same way that the touch of the mass had grated on my nerves. It didn't feel right, because it didn't feel like anything familiar, and again a curious thought sprang into my mind. It felt like a dry, frozen jellyfish.

I walked all around the block. When I got back to the starting point, I was more convinced than ever that a temple *did* lie underneath the gray-white deposit.

But what was the gray-white deposit?

I picked up a flat stone with a sharp edge, intending to see if I could chip away part of the surface. Then I saw something that made my hair bristle. I know my eyes bulged. I heard the blood pound like monstrous trip-hammers at my temples.

"Look—look—" I gulped. I wouldn't have recognized my voice as my own. Standing there in broad daylight, I was almost petrified with fear. I admit it. But so were the others.

For the impression of the toe of a shoe had formed where Glenk had kicked the surface a few minutes ago. None of us had seen it form. But there it was. And it most certainly had *not* been there when or immediately after Glenk kicked the stuff.

We must have stood for five minutes in dead silence, our eyes absolutely hypnotized by that indentation. I stared until I began seeing spots all over. I don't know whether I saw the hole close up or not, my eyes ached so from the intensity of staring. But at the end of five minutes, not a trace of the hole remained.

Wanda let out a deep sigh. I turned. I thought she was going to faint. She had the whitest face I've ever seen. I dropped the rock I was still foolishly holding and sprang over to help her. That broke the spell. The others swarmed around us.

Wanda said, "Thanks, I'm all right. It's been such a strain all these days—my eyes were playing tricks—" she snickered a little hysterically "—why, would you believe it, I actually thought I saw that wall move!" She stared up at us with pleading eyes.

"Just an optical illusion," I stated as calmly as I could. "Shadows are apt to play tricks."

"Sure, I saw it too," the thick-headed Glenk muttered.

"That's how group errors get started. That's the way rumors about bleeding images and angel hosts over battlefields are born," I tossed off lightly.

But it all went for naught, because Pete Lapous turned at that moment and let out a sort of squawk or bleat. We all jumped.

Where Glenk had kicked the mass, and where the impression of a toe had subsequently developed, there was now a projecting knob, shaped like the tip of a shoe.

Pete Lapous, grotesque and ridiculous in his long flannels, went legging off as hard as he could, but stopped after a dozen yards when he found nothing at his heels. We yelled at him, got him quieted down. And when we turned our attention on the gray-white surface again, the knob, like the hole before it, was gone. Only the smooth wall met our gaze.

"Take me away from here—back to the shore," Wanda begged. I felt a good deal better myself as she hooked her arm in mine. The good old protective instinct did me a favor then, by exactly counterbalancing the fear that had started growing inside of me. And I considered it a healthy fear, since it put me on guard against an unknown foe.

It upset me to find myself thinking of that gray-white mound as a living enemy. My thoughts were a crazy jumble. I remembered stories I'd read about protoplasm, about fungoid growths, about scaly formations on wrecks, and even about the rust that oxidation produces on iron. I kept seeing the crust of a pie, and every now and then I had an impulse to laugh. If we took the gray-white crust off, what would we find—a temple, or a heap of dried apples? Out of such giddy visions, my perspective slipped back into focus.

"You're very silent," Wanda complained.

"I was thinking that you never can guess what lies under a shell. A pea or a walnut or an egg—or even gunpowder."

She looked puzzled. "That doesn't make sense."

"What does? We get shipwrecked in fair weather in deep water hundreds of miles from land. We can't radio for help. We save ourselves when we should have drowned. We live for eight days in an open dory with raw fish and not enough water and reach an island that isn't on the maps. Nightmare Island—that's what Glenk should have named it if he hadn't forgotten. Or Phoenix Island—down she goes and up she comes. Or Chance Island—you never know what comes next."

I was glad to see her smile. "How about Magic Island? Now you see something, now you don't."

An answer of some sort died on my lips. For I *did* see something then and there. My stride slackened for a couple of steps, before I got on to myself. Wanda felt the lag, asked, "Did you stub your toe?"

"Not enough to matter," I lied.

I heard the pat and scuffle of the feet that followed us, bare soles, and Glenk's shoes. I didn't hear them falter. The others missed what I saw.

"Magic Island—not a bad name. Now you see something, now you don't," I repeated Wanda's words.

She was quick to suspect. "The mounds we're passing—what did I overlook?"

"Nothing. Some mounds cover bones, and some don't."

She dropped the subject. The smaller mounds lying away from the central block were at least twenty feet long. I've heard of Indian burial mounds much larger than those in the States. But it wasn't a bone that caught my eye.

We slid down the hills, threaded our way past the ancient, dead trunks, skirted or plunged through the tangle of green growths. By the time we reached the dory, I hadn't found a way to solve the query in my mind.

Dave Anderson solved it for me. He remarked in his small, quiet voice, "If we're going to stay here overnight, we ought to collect food and firewood. There might be shellfish along the shore."

The second mate growled, "That's what I said when we landed here. You and Lapous scout along the shore. Wanda can watch the dory. I'll hunt for fruit, food, and whatnot. *You*—" he added to me as an afterthought, "can get the makings of a fire."

By tacit understanding, we avoided reference to what we had seen at the gray-white mound. Lapous started poking along the shore northward. Dave Anderson went off in the opposite direction. I didn't think either of them would have much luck, because of the steep cliffs surrounding most of the island. Still, there were a few stretches of beach, and it might be possible to clamber down the bluffs in a couple of places.

Glenk was watching both me and Wanda. I asked her if she felt better, and when she said yes, I struck inland. I looked back once. I didn't trust that Glenk mutt. But he had left Wanda and was pressing into the tangle of vegetation, presumably to locate more nut- and fruit-trees.

As soon as he was out of sight, I circled around to head off Dave Anderson. I picked him because he talked less than anybody else, and I figured he would have sense enough to keep his mouth shut.

He was climbing up along the top of a drop-off when I caught sight of him. I beckoned with my hand. He plodded over, looking neither surprised nor curious, as though it was all part of the day's work.

"Come along with me," I said. "I made a find that's worth investigating. It'll take two to do the job."

He didn't ask questions. He simply followed in my tracks. I began to wonder if he talked so little because he had nothing to say, and was just plain stupid, or whether he knew more than he indicated. Whatever the reason, I never met a more phlegmatic, non-communicative man.

I headed for the mounds around the big rectangle. There were three of the mounds about twenty feet long, and another that was several hundred feet over all, much larger than the gray-white rectangle. The mounds had irregular shapes. Grass covered them. I suppose that the rest of our party considered them so many hills or slopes without further significance. They hadn't seen what I saw.

I led Anderson around one of the small mounds. In back of it, unnoticeable from the path we had followed a while ago except in one spot where the glint of sunlight betrayed it to my eyes, I showed him a chunk of shining, milky metal. It extended into the mound.

We dropped to our knees and looked at the metal. I had expected it to be silver, but it wasn't. It had a thin, bluish tinge, resembled milk glass, and glistened with virginal brilliance. Dave Anderson fingered it without a trace of emotion. For some obscure reason, his placid tolerance nettled me. Excitement was swelling inside of me. I couldn't identify the metal that looked like glass any more than I could identify the gray-white structure a few hundred yards away.

"Get a piece of stone, anything to scoop the surface dirt off. Let's see what's underneath," I told him, and hunted for a sharp-edged rock to use.

There was, we discovered, approximately two inches of clayey silt and sediment covering the mound. Grass bound it together and prevented the rains from washing it away. It had evidently settled on the object during the centuries it lay submerged under the sea. In some places, of course, the deposit was much thicker. Perhaps the caking had been a good deal heavier when the island rose again, but grass seeds had taken root and spread before rains could remove all the encrustation.

At the end of a half-hour of hard work that made us sweat aplenty, we had exposed many parts of one mound, and tapped the other two sufficiently to learn that they duplicated the contents of the first.

That first mound concealed a colossal, crumpled mass of shining armor. It had never been designed for a human form. We guessed that in its original shape it stood twenty or twenty-five feet in height, with a cylindrical body, a turret top, no arms, but three conical lower limbs or appendages that ended in sharp points without trace of a foot.

The body cylinder had been smashed. Inside lay the accumulated sediment of centuries. God knows what once walked around in that gigantic suit of armor. I couldn't imagine what it looked like, whatever it was, and wherever it came from. I realized that it didn't originate on Earth. Neither Dave Anderson nor I could make the slightest scratch on that stainless, eternal metal.

V. Strange Death

While we worked, I had an eerie sensation of being watched. Several times I looked around, but saw nothing. I half-expected the second mate to waddle along, but no one showed up. Finally I hooked my uneasiness to the presence of the gray-white mass off to one side and let it go at that.

"What giants they must have been that wore these suits!" I exclaimed after we had tested the third mound.

Anderson merely twitched his shoulders in a shrug.

I suggested, "Let's try the big one now. Maybe we'll find something to shed a little more light, though I don't see what. I'm baffled already. The remains that turn up only seem to add new mysteries. How did this metal stuff get here? Who made it? What was inside? Where did it come from?"

"Can't say," said my all but silent partner.

We moved over to the main hill, and encircled it to get a better idea of our task. Like the gray-white mass and the metallic formations of armor, the large hill also had an odd shape. It resembled a tear drop, broad at one end with a beautifully curved nose, so to speak, and a more gradually tapered point at the other end. As in the case of the three smaller mounds, it was covered with grass.

One side contained an irregularity, a bulge, a dozen feet out and a dozen high. We tried gouging the grass and clods of soil off. It took us a long time to penetrate a few feet into the bulge. So far as results indicated, we could tunnel through the whole hill, given opportunity enough, without finding anything.

I abandoned that task and asked Anderson, "How about one more try higher up or farther along?"

"Sure."

He scrambled to his feet, wiped some of the dirt off his hands, and followed me away from the bulge. I picked a spot at random —and a few inches in struck the same milky, glistening metal which composed the armor.

We climbed on top of the bulge—and about two inches down struck the metal again.

Dismay and sick disappointment took possession of me then. I dropped the rock I had used for digging. There never was a more heartfelt curse of defeat than the one I uttered.

"What's wrong?" My companion asked in his slow, soft voice.

"Nothing—nothing at all. Just that we'll have to give this up. It's too big for us to tackle alone."

"Sure," said Dave Anderson, and we started back. He ambled toward the sea, obediently going ahead with his previous instructions to hunt seafood.

I flung a last malevolent glance at the gray-white rectangle, where it bulked ominously against the westering sun. On my way down, I loitered, selecting such firewood as was suitable. It didn't matter now if the rest of the party investigated the mounds. We'd only be here another day or two. I was bitter with disappointment, tantalized by a riddle none of us could solve or would have any chance to solve.

I knew in my heart what lay under the great hill. It concealed a half-buried ship, or ark, or cruiser of some sort. It was the vessel the giants came in. Maybe it had wrecked in landing. I don't know. Maybe the bulge was the open door to its interior. Maybe the bulge is a gap that burst open in landing and spilled the occupants out where *they* also smashed on the ground rocks. I don't know that either.

What I do know, and hate to know, is that while this island lay on the sea bottom, sediment drifted in through the opening and filled the interior at least to the height of the rent. Without proper tools, it would take us all working together a week to clear out even a small part of the silt. It would take a month to clear the whole inside even if we had spades and shovels.

There wasn't the ghost of a chance for me to find out the secret of the hill. I believed that it contained the wreck of a cruiser, a space ship. I believed that its interior would disclose fantastic machinery, engines, equipment, foodstuffs maybe, perhaps maps and plans and documents, records of an amazing cosmic voyage—I don't know what all. My imagination was reeling. The thing lay at my fingertips—and I couldn't get at it. The vessel—the queer armor—the gray-white stuff, they all linked up somehow.

I was beginning to get a picture, the picture of a thriving community here at some time in the past, a branch of the Polynesians. I saw a meteor from the skies plunge into their midst. But this meteor was a dazzling silvery streak that smote the ground and burst and spewed out a trio of dead or dying giants from the wrecked starplane. Maybe it spewed other things, too, such as a test tube full of—what? Maybe the natives had a temple, and maybe they built a temple after the cruiser piled up. And maybe the test tube full spilled out and took over the temple.

That sequence would explain the huge, alien statue that stands by the lagoon and faces the rectangle on top of the isle. I could imagine the superstitious natives worshipping the intruder from the skies, and revering it as a deity, the statue erected in the image of the remembered dying giants in armor—until the day of that older earthquake which plunged the whole island to the sea bottom.

Right there my thoughts became a hopeless jumble again, because of the gray-white growth upon the temple. I had been nursing the idea that it was alive in a dim, rudimentary way. The manner in which the impression of a shoe tip had formed a long while after Glenk kicked the wall, and how the stuff had still later thrust out to form a knob like a shoe tip, proved in my mind that it had about the lowly instincts of a worm. I regarded it as an overgrown blob with just a glimmer of life far back in the scale of evolution.

But if it grew on the temple when the pilgrims from afar landed —how could it have survived those centuries under the sea? And if it developed down on the sea beds, a product of Earth's deep marine life, how could it have gone on living and growing when the island sprang above the waves again? How could it live in air one moment and go on living in the sea the next? Was it alive at all, for that matter, and if so, what did it live on? Or was it a vegetable, fungus growth rooted to the soil, a hybrid midway between land life and sea life, so primitive in its nature that it could exist equally well under both conditions?

My brain was looping by the time I got back to the dory. My ideas turned wilder and wilder. I found great vistas opening up to me that I'd never thought much about before.

In my thirty-odd years, I had knocked around a good deal. I had done my share of miscellaneous reading. I had seen queer sights, and had met plenty of tramps no better and no worse than the ones I was marooned with. But we were all up against something new. Right then I'd have traded the kit and kaboodle of my companions for an hour's talk with a professor who had the imagination of H. G. Wells, the brain of Einstein, and talked words I could understand with the assurance of Roosevelt.

The sun had slid far down when I reached the dory. I dumped my load of wood. Nobody paid attention to my soiled hands and tattered pajamas. I suppose we were all worn out from the ordeal and our day-long labors on the island, preoccupied with our own special thoughts. We had a silent dinner on some shellfish that Lapous brought back, along with bananas, coconuts, and oranges that the second mate produced.

I wanted to talk to Wanda afterwards, but couldn't think of anything to say. The discoveries that Anderson and I had made dominated my thoughts. Dave and I hadn't tried to cover up the objects we exposed. Wanda, Sam Glenk, Pete might stumble on those same relics if we held the island for several days. Then we could talk, but until then, I saw no point in pouring a stream of extra worries into Wanda's pretty head.

We turned the dory over at sunset as shelter for her.

The rest of us slept under the stars.

I watched Dave Anderson lower his big frame and spread out. I wondered what went on in his brain. At no time since returning to our makeshift camp had he given an inkling of unusual occurrences, or of being troubled.

I rolled over on my back and stared up at the stars. They didn't look so friendly as the night before. They blazed infinitely afar with riddles and mysteries beyond them. I fancied other starplanes plummeting those gulfs upon tremendous voyages that would dwarf all the Odysseys and explorations of mankind. I speculated on the possibility of Earthmen one day launching rockets to the moon, or landing on the planets, or hurling starships into the depths of space.

A dream of giddy swoops and plunges through infinity beset me. I found myself on a teeter-totter. A roller coaster miles high shot me at bullet speed up to its crest, then flung me into sheer, vertical drops.

I wakened suddenly. It was very dark, and I had the feeling very late at night.

The island vibrated, trembled with a rumble like thunder.

"Get up! Earthquake!" a voice bellowed through the blackness.

I scrambled to my feet. Shadowy forms materialized around me. I swayed, confused, and the island shook again. I was vaguely conscious of the calm sea, the lapping slur of waves against the cliffs. It couldn't be an earth tremor, and yet I distinctly felt the ground sway.

A scream split the air in the distance. I couldn't tell what direction it came from. It sounded too shrill to be human. It screeched again, continuously, higher and louder.

A grotesque figure in flannels plunged by me.

"Pete! Pete Lapous! We can't do anything in this blackness! Somebody's got to stay by Wanda!" I yelled.

His teeth chattered. "What the hell, what the hell, I can't let him get killed, I got to help. I'm scared to death, I tell you, but I got to help!"

It was a pathetic and at the same time a brave person that pattered away from me. I sprang after him, grabbed him by the arm.

"Who is it? Who's missing? Quiet, all of you! Keep your heads!" roared Glenk.

We babbled in chorus—all except Dave Anderson.

"It's Anderson hollering. Shut up and try to get his direction!" the second mate boomed command.

The scream broke off abruptly, completely. The isle stopped vibrating. We listened hard in the dark, straining our ears, but not another sound came. I grew aware of Wanda's tense breathing beside me, caught a whiff of her hair.

I heard restless, uneasy movements around me, while the slow minutes crawled by. We waited in vain for that terror-born scream to rise again, and I for one was glad to be spared another such agonized, frantic, wordless cry. Glenk blew on the almost dead embers, nursed the coals into a comforting flame. Thus we waited, our nerves raw, until the pale light of dawn glimmered above the horizon after what seemed interminable ages.

"The voice came from the peak of the island. You've got the only gun among us. Let's all strike for there first," I demanded of Glenk.

"Bunk!" snorted the second mate. "I'll bet an eyetooth the yelling came from across the lagoon."

"I don't know where it came from. It just filled the air on all sides," Wanda contributed.

"No, no, up there, up there along the cliffs!" Pete insisted excitedly. He pointed toward the route that Anderson had taken hunting for shellfish the previous afternoon.

Glenk waved his hands. "This island covers two square miles. We'd need all day to cover it traveling in a group. We'll have to split up—"

"So that whatever got Anderson, meaning the gray-white stuff, can pick us off one at a time—" I began.

"Forget that nightmare of yours!" he shouted. "For God's sake, can't you think of anything else? Maybe he was just restless and went walking around. Maybe a tree fell on him. Maybe he fell off a cliff. Maybe we missed an animal that scared him. How the hell do we know what happened till we find out? How the hell can we find out unless we cover the ground as fast as possible?

"Maybe he's only knocked out. We've got to find him first before we do anything else. Now scatter, all of you. I'm going across the lagoon. Pete, follow the route that Anderson went yesterday. Wanda can watch here same as before in case he turns up. And *you* go take a look at your damned bogie and if you don't like that, stick around the lagoon while *I* hunt up your pet brainstorm."

I was mad enough to have taken a punch at him but it was no time to fight among ourselves. It would have served no purpose for me to try to explain all that Dave and I had learned the day before. From the mulish temper Glenk was in, he wouldn't listen to reason. I suppressed my feelings and headed straight for the heart of the island.

Scared? The germ of panic dwelt in me. The silent bushes around me, the growing, ghostly light of dawn, the gaunt, forbidding boles of dead trees, and the half-knowledge, half-mystery of what lay ahead all preyed on my thoughts. But I was angry, too, which helped. Angry, because I suspected that Glenk had deliberately given me the dangerous assignment in the hope I wouldn't come back. That would leave him a clear field with Wanda, not counting Pete, who didn't count anyway.

My feet, already sore from previous activity, collected a few more scratches as I plodded inland and upward. I kept my eyes open. Two questions bothered me.

First, why was Glenk in such an evil humor? I figured a lot of reasons before the answer came, so simple that I cursed myself for a dimwit. Anderson had risen in the night and gone away without the rest of us realizing it. Therefore we all, including Sam Glenk, must have been sound asleep. Therefore Dave Anderson could have calmly proceeded to take the gun away from Glenk if he thought of it. Had he? I didn't believe so. True, Glenk hadn't flourished the pistol, but then Dave Anderson, if he possessed it, would certainly have fired in the face of danger. I kissed good-bye to a lost opportunity. I could be sure that there wouldn't be another to relieve the second mate of the gun.

This line of speculation brought up the second query. Why had Dave Anderson stolen away from us? The answer eluded me, since I knew very little about his character. I finally decided that he was as devoid of fear as is humanly possible. His big body had survived the shipwreck even better than Glenk's. He woke in the night. Perhaps he had seen something at one of the mounds that escaped my attention. His reticent soul had decided to investigate it at his own leisure.

I felt a sense of guilt. I was reasonably sure that I had reconstructed the events accurately. But I couldn't get away from the fact that on my shoulders lay the responsibility. I had brought him along to share my find. Whatever the bent of his secretive personality, I had whetted it by admitting him to my knowledge. If only I hadn't—one man alone could not have uncovered those tantalizing objects—we might have left the isle in safety and little the wiser—

The voices died out behind me. The only one I wanted to hear didn't come at all. I suppose Wanda was puttering around the dory, or getting water from one of the inadequate springs.

Going up the last slope to the middle plateau, with the sun now flaming above the far rim of the sea, I imagined many weird prospects ahead. The sight of the gray-white oblong cheated my hopes and my fears. That peak, those mounds were the same—

I paused. The features of the landscape seemed as I remembered them, but with a wrong note somewhere.

The gray-white mass, the enormous hill, the mounds—

There were only two small mounds instead of three.

VI. Red Carpet

I stared incredulously. There was not a trace of the third mound, the one that Dave and I had examined first. I could scarce believe my eyes. Not even on this crazy island did a hill walk away and disappear over-night.

Advancing warily, I kept an eye on the gray-white rectangle. I didn't expect anything definite, but it wouldn't have surprised me much if the whole mass jumped at me. With every passing minute, my inner turmoil increased, and my nerves grew more edgy.

I made my way toward the site of the missing mound. When still at a distance, I caught the glint of sunlight on metal lying on the level ground. I hurried my pace then, in the hope that the metallic shards might offer a clue to Dave Anderson's fate and what had happened to the vanished hill.

They did. The ground, where the hill had stood, bore the powdery outline, immensely broadened and completely flattened, of the shining suit of armor. Some force of inconceivable power had erased the mound, levelled it, hammered it to ground level. I recalled the way the island had shaken in the night, the rumble of thunder like an earthquake—but no tremor in history caused a hill or a building to collapse to paper thinness. This was rather as if the mound had been caught between solid rock, which in fact lay a couple of feet down under the top soil, and the application of titanic pressure.

I suppose the scene registered instantly on my brain. I couldn't have had time to reason it out in detail, because I found Dave Anderson at almost the same moment that I reached the remains of the mound. Behind it, or more accurately, at the point where we had noticed the fragment of protruding metal on the day preceding, there now lay a red carpet.

My skin crawled while I stared at that horrible splotch on the ground, vaguely human in shape, an inextricable mixture of blood, soil, flesh, giving off the unmistakable odor of human pulp. I couldn't bring myself to go close to the red smear. By a handful of yellow strands I made the identification—Anderson was the only one of us with such blond hair.

I turned toward the gray-white rectangular mass with hatred pounding through me, and blind horror. In no way did that huge block differ from its appearance the day before, yet I sensed it as a far more positive entity, a more dangerous and deadly menace. I backed away from it, watching for the slightest motion of the mass, but it stood there squat and ominous in the morning light, as rigid and lifeless as stone.

Well separated from it, I began hurrying back to the shore. I shouted once or twice to Pete Lapous, who ought to be nearer than anyone else, but after that saved my breath. What could possibly be gained by haste? I was reluctant to admit that I ran simply to put distance between me and that monstrous, pallid-hued, rectangular block. In spite of fear, I forced myself to set a slower pace.

I didn't find the others around the dory, not even Wanda. I trotted up the ridge of ground that enclosed the lagoon—and then forgot the horror on the peak. All my resentment against Sam Glenk flared up. I started racing as fast and as silently as I could in the reckless hope of getting him before he saw me.

Why? It didn't stretch my imagination one iota to visualize the whole picture at first glance. Wanda, abandoned by the rest of us, had gone for a morning dip and swim in the lagoon. Glenk's course had taken him around to the far side of the lagoon. When he found no trace of Anderson, he must have noticed the girl, and decided to obtain a little of his malodorous brand of fun while the rest of us rambled over the island.

Wanda was raging, but she couldn't do much against brute power as that massive pig clumsily pawed her and tried to kiss her when she came out of the water.

I almost made it. I would have made it if Wanda's eyes hadn't lighted when she saw me. Glenk was so deep in his own desires that he didn't have time for other thoughts. But her expression warned him, and he swung around to meet me charging in. With a sweep of his arm, he shook her off while she tried to hang on and hamper him. He didn't go for the gun though I now saw its bulge in a pocket.

I landed one solid blow. I hit him with everything right on the chin, and it wasn't enough. I might as well have smashed at a stone wall. It staggered him, but he took it, and wrapped those ape-like arms of his around me.

That, I thought, as the pressure began, was the end of all this mad adventure for me. Glenk squeezed with an iron grip, stuck his head down, and butted against my chin. I could hear Wanda clawing and beating him from behind, but he ignored her. My head tilted back, back, back, and wrenches of pain stabbed my throat. The sky was darkening, reeling with giddy flashes. I listened for the sound of my own neck cracking.

I caught a blurred vision, wondered if I had already entered the realm of phantoms. And then the sharp *thunk*—

But I was miraculously relaxing, and Sam Glenk tottered, slumped like a poleaxed steer. I heaved a deep breath, on the verge of collapse myself, and managed to croak, "Thanks!"

"A pleasure, a pleasure, I want to do it again," crowed Pete Lapous. "I heard you yell five, ten minutes ago. I come a-running. I see no one, try the lagoon. Hah! What a man! Yell a mile, hold on till I come. So then I grab the big rock and *clunk* goes the skull. Ah, so you still wiggle, you great swine? I fix that. I break your skull good this time."

I really believe he would have finished Glenk if Wanda and I hadn't restrained him. Pete yanked the revolver out of the second mate's pocket, and danced away.

There was murder in Glenk's eyes as he came back to life. And paradoxically, his sullen fury seemed directed entirely towards Pete, because Pete had the revolver. If the gun had been lost, Glenk would still have dominated the group. He didn't need the weapon for that. But we needed it, if only to control him. The gun was his symbol of authority. And Pete had it. From then on, I could discount Glenk. Recapturing the weapon from Lapous would be his dominant purpose.

My breath returning, I panted, "We've got to leave the island. Today. Now."

"Can't make it. Not enough water for the trip yet," grunted the second mate.

"We'll have to chance it. I located Anderson—what was left of him." I started recounting the story of my gruesome discovery. A shocked expression came over Wanda, a puzzled look dawned in Pete Lapous's eyes, and Sam Glenk's face mirrored utter skepticism. They couldn't or wouldn't believe. My extra knowledge proved a boomerang. In order to drive home the truth, I told what Dave Anderson and I had uncovered on our private exploration.

I wound up with, "That's why we've got to leave. It's too damned plain that the gray-white monster killed Anderson. I don't know how. I don't want to know. Dump whatever food and water there is into the dory. It's our only chance. Here we're doomed."

The second mate's eyes lighted. The dream of loot again, I thought. He saw the shining armor only as precious metal to be carted off. He turned around, with, "Before I make up my mind I'll have to go up there and see for myself."

"I shoot! I shoot!" The cook volubly promised.

"Shoot and be damned. Part of the story sounds o.k., part of it doesn't. If there's anything on this island with a cash value, I'll be a son of a gun if I'll go off and leave the secret behind. Anderson got trapped by night, if he is dead. This is broad daylight. I can look out for myself."

He swaggered inland toward the peak of the island. Pete flourished the revolver. If he wanted to take a few potshots at Glenk, that was all right with me, but I didn't think he would.

He didn't.

VII. The Super-Structure

"Follow me!" I told the cook and Wanda. I raced for the dory an eighth of a mile away, with them at my heels, and cursed Glenk. He was a brave man, a fool, and scum all rolled up in a barrel of meat. I hated him, but it wasn't in me to push off and leave him to the deadly surprises of the island.

Lapous and I turned the dory over. Wanda pitched in to help. We slid it out far enough so that a good push would launch it. I gave Wanda her orders. "You stay here, put what fruit and water there is aboard, then climb in yourself and wait. Keep an oar handy. Shove off if you see anything you wouldn't want to see."

I started running with Pete toward the heart of the island. She shouted some questions that didn't even register on me.

It was bad going for both of us, barefoot. The bushes ripped at our legs, the rocks bruised and cut our already sore soles. My headache resumed its throbbing from the blow that Santos had swung at me with an oar a couple of nights ago in the boat. Glenk's loving workout on my throat hadn't made me feel better. It was all a mad business—why the devil should I run my legs off to help that stupid ox? But I knew the answer to that one too. The rest of us owned not the ghost of a chance of reaching safety across five hundred miles of ocean without Glenk to pilot us and drive us by his tough will.

Where was Glenk? I estimated that he would reach the summit of the island at the same time that we did. He had the advantage of a five minute start on us, which he would lose because he made his way through more or less new terrain.

It turned out much as I expected. When we emerged on the central plateau, we saw Glenk off to our right half way toward the closest of the two remaining small mounds. Beyond loomed the long hill, and on top of the island stood that solid block of gray-white stuff.

Nothing had changed on the scene, yet I went forward filled with nervous apprehensions. I looked in Glenk's direction, but actually from the corners of my eyes I kept my gaze on the huge oblong mass, the greatest enigma on the island. I was beginning to crystallize a theory out of the jumbled images that floated around under the surface of my imagination.

I said to Pete, "Stay away from Glenk. Then you won't need to worry about his diving for the gun. Watch the gray stuff—it's the real danger."

Glenk went to one of the spots where Anderson and I had dug into the mounds. He discovered the giant armor, excitedly tried to break off a chunk, and when his efforts failed, attempted to drag a whole section out of the hill. Not even his prodigious strength could do the feat.

He worked like a madman for several minutes. He must have believed the metal an alloy of silver or platinum, which it couldn't possible have been. At the end he straightened up and scowled savagely at the buried, unyielding armor. Sweat streaked his face that had already sprouted a ten-day stubble of beard.

I called to him, "Now that you've seen for yourself, admit it's hopeless and let's shove off."

"Not till I get a hunk of this stuff."

"Go ahead. Anderson tried. Take a look at what happened to him. Then stay around as long as you like. It's your private funeral." I pointed to the flattened mound.

Glenk walked over to it. The sight gave him a jolt. I could tell by the way he stared down at the red carpet, and jerked his head up for a hard appraisal of the gray-white oblong. His ruthless, fearless nature lost its moorings for once. I think that the first fear he had known must have fleeted into his life—and out. Glenk's makeup rested on the sort of obstinacy which wouldn't let him admit that he had met his match.

He turned his back squarely on the great mass and strode to the shining armor with a jaunty step. "The hell with your bugaboos. There was an earthquake last night. It woke us all up. Anderson got caught. That's all. The hill smashed down. It finished him and another quake might finish me. I'll take the chance."

"Listen, you damned idiot!" I shouted. "You're getting us all into trouble just because of your infernal pigheadedness. The stuff isn't worth a nickel a ton except as a freak! You can't—"

"Freaks are worth cold cash. Shut up with that I-can't business."

"It's sure death to stay on the island. We can't wait till doomsday for you to shove off with us. Are you coming or aren't you?"

He didn't answer. He made a beeline for the armor under the mound. Judging by his devil-may-care attitude, nothing I could say would influence him. I don't think that anything mattered in his life except his own utterly selfish lusts and motives.

Boiling inside, I called it quits. I was through with Glenk. Back to the dory—

The explosion of the revolver startled me. I jumped in a half-turn at the sound of the shot. Glenk whirled around with the speed of a cat for all his bulk.

Pete Lapous had dropped out of my mind while I argued with Glenk. That scrawny scarecrow, for God knows what reason, had taken a pot-shot at the gray-white stuff. Maybe he had seen movement, or imagined it, or simply possessed a nervous trigger-finger.

He didn't miss. He couldn't have missed at a range of fifty yards.

The picture that registered stunned me. Pete Lapous and Sam Glenk froze with the same paralysis of shock. It must have lasted for many long, precious seconds, and it seemed eternity. My time-sense went awry. I have the memory of a series of separate episodes, each complete in itself, each lasting for a protracted interval. Yet the developments came swift as the wind, caught us unprepared by their almost simultaneous speed.

While we three stood like statues, the outlines of that great mass of pallidly white stuff wavered and rippled. It was like watching a hill flow down to the sea. And yet wavered is not the word—the stuff collapsed, billowed out in a pool, flung itself to the ground.

I cannot express the phenomenal velocity that it developed from inertia, hurling itself in a second or less to the ground, and resting there in inertia once more. I sometimes think that it responded in exact tempo with the stimulus that prodded it. When Glenk kicked it, it leisurely formed a depression. When Pete Lapous shot it, it instantly struck back.

And so the building that it concealed was uncovered to our gaze, and I looked with awe at that superstructure, that skeletonic, gigantic framework of black metallic rods and filaments.

The interlacing network was infinitely complex. The vertical rods at the four corners of the rectangle, forty feet tall, as slender as pencils, rested on similar horizontal rods, and supported others —forty feet long for the width of the structure, sixty feet for its length.

From that outer framework, a veritable maze, a labyrinth, a honeycomb of slimmer filaments and rods criss-crossed the interior of the structure. They presented absolutely perfect geometric forms—an outer rectangle, then an inner cube, then a sphere farther in, and a little farther still a pyramid, and beyond the pyramid a cone, and inside the cone other figures, stranger forms, until my vision blurred trying to follow the tracery of that astounding mechanism to its protected core.

Strange as it loomed, terrifying because of its immense size and the wetly glistening sheen, the brilliant luster of those black rods and filaments, it became a thing of far more evil beauty and power for it seemed to possess a life of its own.

Along each of the outer rods, starting at the corners of the structure, travelled a band of frosty light. Those sixteen rings of silvery black radiance shot along the whole elaborate course of the internal framework and vanished toward the innermost heart, all in an instant. Then, an instant later, the sixteen bands came streaking out at lesser velocity, to slide for a momentary pause against the outer corners. And from there they shot again, as if catapulted, at dazzling speed along their regulated paths.

It was like the ebb and flow of some unimaginable life-force, the pulse and beat of a perfectly functioning organism, a tireless, effortless, unvarying motion. Perpetual motion—how long had it been going on? Hundreds of years—thousands? Ever since the giants landed in their shining armor and set it up—dying they must have been from the crushing impact of their starplane, but one of the three lived long enough to fulfill his mission. And here the thing worked still, without motors or engines or driving apparatus of any sort that I could see, unless the principle lay hidden inside the rods or filaments. The frosty rings of light hurtled on their complete circuit, fading inward, bouncing outward, as they would do till the end of Earth in the far future, I felt with prophetic surety.

What was that living nightmare? That monstrous entity of grayly white stuff and rigid framework? A single organism whose body could detach itself from the skeleton? A dual being—the one an incubator or rather a restrainer, and the other a spore, an egg, a plasmic seed, the one controlling the other until the day of expansion and growth when conditions were favorable in the declining cycles of Earth-life?

The death of the races of man millions of years hence—and then the flowering of the giant-plasm in an environment akin to the conditions on the star-world from which it came—

And what would the giant-plasm hatch? A counterpart of whatever creatures occupied those three shining suits of armor? Or some wholly unpredictable growth that thrived progressively upon a dying planet?

So much registered in the first of those crowded seconds—the collapse of the gray stuff, the revelation of the super-structure.

Then the earthquake, the ground shaking, while my bewildered senses told me that the gray stuff alone caused it—the giant-plasm —it must have weighed thousands of tons, millions of pounds—enormous density squeezed into a fluid solid—

VIII. Flight

The earth tremors continued. I felt them as a continuous shaking underfoot. Even they didn't break the trance that held us all rigid. I realized vaguely that the island trembled upon its foundations. The ground would quaver so long as the pool ploughed ahead with its terrific weight.

The pallid substance had begun to move after the moment of inertia following its collapse in front of the black framework that had supported it. It forged ahead with quick giant strides. Its method of progress hypnotized me.

The puddle had formed a foot thick, a perfect disc. The disc put forth two pincers like the claws of a crab. Those arms curved far forward, inward, and met, at the feet of Pete Lapous. The main body of the pool sloughed up to close the gap to the pincerlike arms.

The ground shuddered and rumbled.

Galvanized into action, Pete turned and sprinted with a yell of frenzied horror.

Again the plasmic mold issued the pincers—and those arcing tentacles closed around Pete, lapped near the mound where Glenk and I were rooted. The main mass surged up, closed the intervening space. As it swept across the spot where Pete raced, the foot-thick mass hit his heels with the force of a pile-driver, spurted him high into the air.

The revolver, jolted from his grip, flew off to one side. Pete curved through the air, his arms and legs sprawling, came down head first. He died instantly—I heard the sharp *crack* when his neck broke.

"Run—the dory!" I shouted at Glenk. Electrified into action as violent as my previous immobility had been complete, I was off and away faster than I ever thought I could run. Even so, I saw the next swift climax, by keeping my eyes turned only a trifle from the diagonal course that I trekked toward the dory.

Sam Glenk sprang for the pistol. In the face of that colossal, amorphous hulk that thundered across the ground, he still must have placed a frenzied faith in the weapon. His hand closed on it.

Again the flat, circular disc of the entity put forward the long hooks that united at the very feet of Glenk. The main body swept forward, over the corpse of Pete Lapous.

The revolver exploded in a burst of rapid fire, and when the shots ended, the pincer-arms had closed with Glenk inside the fatal circle. Then he ran, and on his white face I saw implanted the hope of leaping across the advance tentacles. But while he sprinted desperately, the mass caught up with him and bowled him over. The mass kept driving on, across his legs, across his torso. Blood leaped in a torrent from his mouth, eyes, nostrils, ears. His shriek pierced the air for the fraction of a second. In that brief interval, the ponderous thing smote him, crushed him, splashed him into another thin red carpet.

I plunged down hill toward the beach. As I stumbled and dropped out of sight of the central plateau, I saw that avid plasm sweep after me. On the edges of the path that it took, the earth furrowed up in long waves, driven, forced aside like mush by the inconceivable density and weight of that gray-white entity.

My heart hammered, and my lungs burned as I ran madly for the boat. Now, behind me, swelled the crash of vegetation mowed down, and grinding, roaring concussions as the tall dead trees toppled, sheared off and pulverized by the irresistible progress of that juggernaut. Bushes, trees, hills, rocks—nothing could halt or alter the flow of the gray-white tide.

It lapped so close behind me that pure fright prevented me from turning my head to see how close it was when I broke out on the beach. I saw Wanda upright in the dory, holding an oar ready to push off. Behind me thunderous crashes swept across the sand. I thought Wanda would faint, but she pushed, floated the dory, got it moving out as I pounded across the strip of sand. I saw the fatal tentacles slide forward around me, and dip into the sea.

And then I had splashed out in a convulsive spurt and hurled myself over the side of the dory. There came the sound of a booming impact, and a wall of water swept seaward carrying the dory upon its crest as the main mass of the entity hit the ocean. I struggled erect.

The giant-plasm, partly on shore, partly on the sea-bed, halted its advance, with long twin banks of earth gouged up on the sides of its path. That mighty trench ran backward with undeviating straightness to the peak of the island. And while we watched, the thing drew back from the water. It reversed its direction, began its journey back to the incubator, flowing uphill as easily as it had slid down.

That was the last I saw of it. I must have cracked my skull again when I dived into the dory headlong. The island suddenly reeled away, and upon a vertigo of sickening pain, I floated out to an ocean of blackness.

A constant drone filled my ears when I regained consciousness. I opened my eyes to unfamiliar confines, felt a sense of lightness and motion. Wanda was sitting beside me. I wondered where the chair came from.

"What the heck!" I exclaimed.

"Don't talk," said Wanda. "You'll have to yell to make yourself heard. If you must talk, don't try to talk sense. You're the proud possessor of a couple of brain concussions. You've been out for a good ten hours."

"But where—"

"In a seaplane—amphibian I guess they're called. Simple enough. The owners of the *Reva* grew worried when the daily radio report stopped coming in. After a week of silence, they chartered a plane to search a wide area. It seems the *Reva* carried a valuable cargo. The plane was just getting ready to abandon the search when the pilot sighted that uncharted island, and us. He came down, picked us up, and took off again. That was this afternoon. It's almost dark now. We'll reach the continent tonight."

I craned my neck to peer out the window. I fancied that behind us, far down on the western horizon, on the rim of the Pacific, against the huge red ball of the setting sun, I saw a speck of lonely land. Back there were the suits of shining armor, the relics of colossal beings, the fallen stone statue, the starplane, the black, skeletonic framework and the riddle of the giant-plasm. Those things, and Dave Anderson, Pete Lapous, Sam Glenk ground into clay.

Some day I will return—or will I? I wish I could be present to watch what the giant-plasm becomes in whatever cycle of remote future time is set the hour of its emergence—and yet, would my maddest dreams give me preparation enough?

I was content with the darkness that fell.

DON'T DREAM

JOE HARRIS WOKE up with an explosion of light in his brain. He had a stuffed, groggy feeling, as though he'd eaten a roast ox, washed it down with a barrel of beer, and had a skyscraper collapse on him. The sensation puzzled him. He was rather thin and nervous, chronically tired. He'd never win any medals as a champion eater, and alcohol only made him sick. He hadn't taken a drink in months.

He blinked his eyes open, and the explosion of light gave way to the hazily luminous darkness overhead where New York's glow fogged the stars. The night was so hot and humid that he and Freda had moved the bedding out onto the fire escape.

He tried to drift off again, but only became more unpleasantly conscious of pajamas plastered to his back, a tugboat hooting on the North River, Freda breathing harshly.

Even by night he got no peace from her; she nagged when awake and she snored when asleep. A year of marriage had turned her into an endless buzz on his nerves. He wondered wearily how much longer he could stand it, and whether she would let him get free if he tried.

The tugboat continued its mournful wailing. A tugboat—tugboats—that might furnish the materials for his next daily column. He'd have to talk to a few captains, find out how many tugboats worked the harbor, what the men earned, where they came from. Just plain statistics—he'd need something better, with more human interest—perhaps he could find the oldest captain in service and develop a few sidelights on the changing water front.

Too bad he had to do so much digging around, though; if only the column would write itself! He had a picture of it, "Hundreds of sailors have spent all their lives at sea, without once losing sight of the skyscrapers of Manhattan. These are the men of the tugboat fleet, men like Captain Amos Whangdoodle who, at eighty-six, is still on the job. The job means more than merely nudging great ocean liners into pier—"

A sound intruded on the column that was taking form in his mind. The sound came from inside the four-room apartment. It was a rhythmic, steady tapping or clicking, the sound of typewriter keys in action.

He listened with more annoyance than alarm, as he strove to concentrate on the column. He'd had these ideas before, half-awake in the middle of night, but unless he concentrated or jotted them down, he couldn't remember them by morning.

The typewriter continued its clatter.

He eased himself up to avoid waking Freda and started crawling through the open window. Unfortunately Freda turned over in her sleep and a loosely flung arm batted him. He gave a nervous start, lost his balance, and sprawled to the floor with a thump that banged his nose. Groping around in the darkness, he knocked a chair over and the chair came down hard on some previously sound toes.

Joe let out a yelp that had all the emotional intensity of a frustrated werewolf.

Freda snapped peevishly. "What do you think you're doing, Joe Harris? Stop banging around that way. You come back here and let a body sleep in peace."

Joe felt around for a table lamp and looked into the dresser mirror. His nose was beginning to swell, his toes were on fire.

Freda called: "Turn that light out! It shines in my eyes."

He doused the light and limped off to the kitchen.

Sipping a glass of milk, he wondered if a jury would acquit him if he committed a murder. Freda had been larger than he, a big, blond Svensky when he married her. She hadn't lost weight since. She couldn't, with her fondness for chocolates in the morning, bridge and cocktails all afternoon, every afternoon. And taking it out on him every night. He'd never got quite straight what it was that she had to take out on him, except possibly the mistake of marrying him in the first place.

Wooooo—wooooo—wooooh! wailed a tugboat.

The tugboat reminded him of the column, but he couldn't remember a word of what he had intended writing. It reminded him also of the mysterious clatter of a typewriter.

He wandered into the living room and over to the bookcase-desk in a corner. There was a sheet of paper in his typewriter. On it he read:

Hundreds of sailors have spent all their lives at sea, without once losing sight of the skyscrapers of Manhattan. These are the men of the tugboatfleet, men like Captain Amos Whangdoodle who, at eighty-six, is still on the job. The job means more than merely nudging great ocean liners into pier—

Yes, that was it; word for word exactly as he had visualized the column in his mind—but what had he been going to follow up with? He paced the room with fingertips gently caressing his nose as though to restrain its ripening splendor. It began to come back to him. "New York couldn't have become the port that it is, without the tugboats. Today's ocean traffic couldn't exist and couldn't be handled without the tugboats—"

The typewriter burst into a furious staccato. He spun around with shattered nerves. The machine stopped clicking. He eyed the desk warily and stalked it, ready to run if some ugly little monster should pop out from under.

The sheet in the typewriter had moved up a few lines. The new sentences read:

> New York couldn't have become the port that it is, without the tugboats. Today's ocean traffic couldn't exist and couldn't be handled without the tugboats—

It was a neat trick. It was the neatest trick he had ever accomplished: operating the machine by concentrating his thoughts on it. But he had no time to digest the fact or admire the feat.

Freda's voice broke him up again. She shrilled: "Joe Harris, stop that dreadful racket! I want to get some sleep."

He hobbled slowly out toward the bedroom, everything driven from mind except bloody thoughts of Freda. She'd never let him divorce her. He was too good a meal ticket. He earned only fifty a week now, but his column was beginning to be syndicated, and every new paper that ran it brought him another five-dollar raise.

He wondered how many murderers escaped. There must be quite a number of murders that were never detected. Successful poisons; people pushed off high places on land, or boats on water; you could run a man down with a car and it would look like an accident.

But Freda was an amazon. He pictured himself strangling her, her frenzied struggles, collapse. It was a satisfying but hopeless image—she topped his five feet six by a good two inches, outweighed him by thirty pounds. Shooting would be safer, for him. But it was also messy; a hole in her temple, or forehead, or heart—probably the heart would be quickest and damage her appearance the least.

He felt better. He'd never have the courage to kill anything, and he knew it, but mental scenes of mayhem and manslaughter gave a fair balance to his outward frustrations. He straightened, walked with a less dejected stoop.

Freda might even become a sleepwalker. A somnambulist had to start sometime. She might get up and walk over the railing of the fire escape—

There was as sudden, sodden, horrible *blup* from the areaway five stories down.

Joe ran toward the open window, guided by a huge sign beyond a block of rooftops. The sign flashed, *"Nerves Tense?* LET UP—" More rooftops stretched beyond it, and then an eighteen-story apartment building with lights in three windows, and west of it a wilderness of roofs to the Hudson.

Freda wasn't on the fire escape landing.

A rectangle of light issued from a window on the ground floor. A voice started babbling hysterically. He leaned over the guard rail and saw part of a figure lying in the rectangle of light—pajama-clad shoulders, wheat-yellow hair rippled on cement.

The iron sweated his palms. "Freda," he mumbled, swaying sickly, "Freda, I didn't mean it, why did you—Freda, come back!"

Something flung him against the building wall. He felt a quick rush of air, saw a shimmer of phosphorescence on the bedding.

Freda was lying there. She had come back. He wished she hadn't.

Strangling fingers had made deep purplish bruises on her throat. She had holes in her heart, temple, forehead—if that dark spot *was* a hole over nearly unrecognizable features.

"No, Freda," he gibbered, "if you did it, you did it, you belong down there—"

A pale glimmer cocooned her and she was gone. He heard a sudden, sodden *blup* five stories below.

Somebody's scream blanked out as he fainted.

Four men occupied a room in the Observation Ward at Bellevue Hospital. Joe Harris lay on the bed. The alienist, Fosterbrow, looking down at him, was a long one, bony and semi-bald, with a face like a starved vulture. Detective Henty, on the other side of the bed, hung a hard, square head on an equally hard, aggressive chin, now lowered toward his Adam's apple. Detective Smaltz, looking placid and philosophical, sat in a chair tilted against the wall. Smaltz was the biggest and most substantial of the four.

Henty asked, "Is he coming around?"

Fosterbrow said, "Hard to tell on these mixed cases. Seems to be shock-coma plus a blow on the head. He might wake up in a minute or a week. What'd he do?"

"Killed his wife." Henty mopped his streaming face. "Guess the heat got him. First he chokes her to death. Then he drills her twice in the head and once in the heart. Funny thing is, we didn't find a gun or any slugs. Then he heaves her off a fifth-floor fire escape.

"God, how he must've hated her," he said, marveling. "He wasn't satisfied with all that. He goes tearing down the fire escape, hauls the body all the way up again, and heaves it over a second time. He must've run down and up like a monkey. Leastwise, nobody saw it happen."

Fosterbrow looked dubious. "It doesn't seem possible, for such a little man."

Smaltz called lazily. "Yeah. You can't never tell about these little guys. Get 'em riled and they turn into regular wild cats. You wouldn't think it to look at him, but he's one of these here human monsters, like in the papers."

The unconscious figure groaned, began threshing, and suddenly sat up.

Fosterbrow appraised him, said, "Wait outside for a few minutes, boys. I'll examine him to see he's all right."

Henty hesitated, gave in. "O.K., doc." He barged out with Smaltz.

The alienist had a gentle, soothing manner in spite of his forbidding appearance. He said, "You'll be all right now. Just relax, take it easy."

Joe stared at him wildly. "But where—what happened—"

"You fainted. You're in a hospital."

Joe sagged back, said with dull despair, "I remember. She's dead. I thought things would happen to her and they did." He twisted, clutching the alienist's arm. "Listen, doctor, they can't do anything to me, can they? It wasn't my fault, really. I didn't mean it. I never intended to kill anybody. It's just that something happened to me tonight, something got into me, and things I imagined came true just the way I imagined them. I can't explain it. I don't know how it works, but—" He looked pleadingly into Fosterbrow's eyes, and slowly sank back on the bed. "It's no use, you don't believe me."

"Of course I do. Now, you've had a bad shock. You'll feel better if you lie quiet and don't try to think about it just yet—"

Joe bolted up, muttering balefully, "You don't believe me. Well, damn it, I'll show you—" his voice rose in a hysterical shout—"I'll show you, I'll show you! You're standing right beside me but I've got a picture in my mind of you standing there by the window—"

Fosterbrow was standing ten feet away flat against the window. He pulled out a handkerchief and mopped his forehead. He murmured. "Dear me, now what am I doing here?"

He walked to the bedside, mouthing, "Just relax, and you'll be all right—"

Joe glowered at him. "You still don't believe me? So help me, I'll keep on till you do!"

Dr. Fosterbrow was standing by the window again. His vulture features took on a sad, gloomy resignation. He started walking toward the bed, and almost reached it when—

He was back at the window. He started walking toward the bed, and almost reached it when—

He was back at the window. He stood there, rubbing his bony nose mournfully. He talked to himself. "Nervous breakdown. I knew it would happen if I didn't get a vacation soon. I'd better turn my work over to Peabody."

He started walking to the door, and when he had almost reached it— He was back at the window.

He made the trip five times, and on the sixth his face puckered like a child about to cry from pure vexation.

"Believe me now?" said Joe, bouncing on the bed.

Dr. Fosterbrow didn't answer him. The desire to reach that door had become a mania, an obsession, a single, fixed idea. He wasn't conscious of anything else.

Joe felt sorry for him. Joe said wearily, "All right, doc, you can go now. If you won't believe me, I guess you just won't, and nobody can make you."

Fosterbrow reached the door and put his hand out as though he took it for granted there were fifteen feet of thin air to transverse again. His hand grasped the knob, and he yanked the door open and lunged through.

He caromed against Smaltz and Henty who were talking to a husky orderly.

Smaltz said mildly, "Now, doc, take it easy. He all right in there?"

Fosterbrow said very clearly, and very bitterly, with glassy eyes: "Don't ask me. I say, to the hell with him."

Smaltz and Henty exchanged glances. Smaltz sounded aggrieved. "Now, doc, is that a way to talk? You can say, to hell with him, or the hell with him, but not to the hell with him. That ain't right."

"To the hell with him," Fosterbrow repeated. He started weaving down the corridor. "To the hell with him, to the hell with him—"

Henty jerked a finger at the orderly. "Better get him. Sounds like he's gone completely nuts."

The orderly hurried off.

Smaltz hiked in on the heels of Henty, who hauled out a report book and asked: "Ready to talk?"

Joe Harris, still clad in the faded blue pajamas, was sitting on the edge of the bed. Henty had never seen a meeker, milder prisoner. Joe answered moodily, "Talk? What's the use? You're all like the fellow that just ran out. He wouldn't believe me and neither will you, so there's no use saying anything. Go away and let me alone."

Smaltz said reasonably: "Now, we couldn't do that. We gotta turn in a report, see? All we wanna know is, why'd you kill her?"

"I didn't! That is . . . I don't know . . . you see—" Joe fumbled lamely, and stopped.

Henty prodded him, "Go right on. That's a good start. What did you do with the gun?"

"There wasn't any gun."

"Well, whatever it was that made those holes. What did you use and where did you hide it?"

Joe shut his lips in a stubborn line. A mosquito droned through the iron grille of the window and settled on the back of his left hand. He made no effort to dislodge it.

Henty said: "So you won't talk?"

Joe concentrated on the mosquito, wished it was on the back of Henty's neck.

The insect vanished. Henty slapped himself suddenly, almost knocking himself out with a rabbit punch. "Damn mosquitoes."

Joe spoke quietly, "I put the mosquito there, on your neck. It was on the back of my hand, but I wished it off on you."

Smaltz sighed. "Kinda seems like everybody's gone nuts around here."

Joe insisted, "In my mind I see pictures of things happening, and right away they happen. That's the whole story. It explains Freda's fate— she's my wife . . . was, I mean . . . only I didn't know I could do it, until after it worked on her. That's how I found out."

Henty nodded, too mechanically, and jotted down a few Ines. "Sure, sure. Well, I guess you'll be staying here for a while."

"Oh, no," said Joe. "I don't intend to stay cooped up here."

He stood up and Henty slapped him back on the bed.

Joe rubbed his chest gingerly. "I've had my toes banged up and my nose skinned and my head cracked, and now you wallop me. I'm tired of being pushed around. I wouldn't do this, matter of fact I hate to do it, but you need a lesson. Suppose you go butt your head against the wall—"

Henty dived clear across the room headfirst and whacked the wall like a sack of potatoes. He fell, lay inert for a moment, and began to push himself upright, dazed.

Smaltz clucked, "*Tsk, tsk,* is that a way to behave? You won't never get promoted, pulling such damn fool stunts. Hurt yourself?"

Henty lobbed his head to signify a shaky No.

Joe looked apologetic. "I hope he'll be all right. But you see how it is. I simply visualize something, and it happens—"

Smaltz said, "Funny thing about coincidences—"

"I did that! I made him butt the wall!"

Smaltz nodded affably. "Sure, sure, you and God. Well, they'll take good care of you here. Come on, Henty, let's shove off." He sauntered toward the door.

Joe slid his feet over the bedside again. "I'm not going—"

"You sure ain't." Smaltz wagged a warning finger. "Better behave or they're liable to pop a jacket on you."

Joe said, mildly. "Maybe I can help you out. You're going to make a report?"

"Henty is. My orders are to stick around. Don't get any funny notions—I'll be in the corridor."

"What station are you from?"

"Headquarters. Homicide," Smaltz spoke automatically, and added with an air of faint surprise, "Huh—no more questions, see? That's our business and—"

Joe looked at Henty, who was groggily rubbing the top of his pate. "He doesn't seem in very good shape. I'm worried about his getting to headquarters safely."

Henty sidled hastily to the door. "That's all right, don't you bother yourself thinking about me."

"Oh, but I must," said Joe. "You shouldn't be wandering around the way you are. Might hurt yourself. Tell you what I'll do. I'll give you some assistance. A real big boost. I see you standing by the main desk down at headquarters—"

A section of the wall blew out and a thousand other explosions blended in one sharp and diminishing crackle in the distance, like a whole pack of giant firecrackers exploding at once.

Henty vanished. The hole in the wall was roughly his outline. The same hole extended through a tenement across the street, and it continued, building after building, block after block, mile after mile, straight down to police headquarters. Along the entirety of that colossal tunnel howled a cyclonic wind, a shrieking blast that sucked with it a cloud of dust, plaster, fragments of brick, glass splinters.

The gigantic hole had ripped through apartments and warehouses, factories and fixtures. It had smashed gas and water pipes, floors and furniture and offices. I had pulverized everything in its path—bathtubs and wardrobes, radios and radiators, filing cabinets and kitchen stoves. It clipped an entire row of desks and typewriters from an insurance office as neatly as it took safe and securities and ticker from a brokerage firm.

A momentary illusion of silence, silence only by contrast, followed the deafening concussion. Then the great noise subsided, and was succeeded by a growing, tumultuous clamor, the crazy uproar of panic-shrill voices. Heads—hundreds of them—began to stud the length of the tunnel fantastically. The nearest ones looked toward Joe, and the farthest group peered into police headquarters.

Joe boggled at the Henty-shaped hole in the wall, the Henty-shaped burrow extending all the way to Centre Street. He mumbled dazedly, "I didn't know—I didn't mean it to happen that way—thought he'd just disappear from here and turn up down there—"

The prodigious feat hadn't fazed Detective Smaltz. Apparently nothing could disturb his philosophic calm. He turned away from his scrutiny of the gutted hearts of building, and leisurely pulled out his service revolver. There was a genuine, almost paternal, gleam in his eyes.

He said, "That's powerful stuff you got, whatever it is. I never seen nothing like it. I bet there ain't any other guys in the world could do the same, leastwise not me. I'm just a plain, ordinary dick, and I couldn't come up to that in a million years.

"Well, long as I can't start a thing like that, maybe I can stop it. I suppose they'll break me for this. Might even send me to the chair. Here goes my future, and it's gonna be tough on the wife and kids, but somehow I just don't seem to give a damn."

He aimed the revolver at Joe and fired.

Joe stuttered, "No—don't—the ceiling—"

Detective Smaltz's outstretched arm jerked straight up, and he emptied the revolver into the ceiling. A pained look finally broke down his placidity. "Now, wasn't that a dumb play?"

"Let's walk out of here," said Joe. "They'll need you outside—you know, the crowds and excitement—"

"Sure," agreed Smaltz. His eyes mirrored his internal resistance, but Joe was too much for him. "Sure, come along, we'll go out there."

They went along the corridor, Smaltz ponderously on his number 10's, Joe pattering in his bare feet. There was a guard for the wing containing the psychopathic ward. Joe took his attention off Smaltz and concentrated on the guard.

He promptly learned something else about the extent and limitations of his strange power. The guard passed them. But Smaltz growled, "Make a monkey out of me, hey?" He whirled and swung instantly, so fast that his big fist missed the chin and raked Joe's cheek. Joe staggered and got his mind back on Smaltz.

Smaltz, arm raised for a second punch, lowered the fist at Joe's mental command. But now the guard was released.

The guard growled, "Get back, you, and don't try anything or I'll—"

A voice cut in from behind him. The voice shook with emotion. It belonged to Dr. Fosterbrow, who was hurrying out with his hat jammed askew. "You have my permission to pass that . . . that—" He waggled a finger and shouted, "Get him out of here! Get him out of here!" over and over like a phonograph record stuck in a groove. His eyes were as glassy as before, but one of them had developed a nervous tic of the lid.

Detective Smaltz and Joe Harris walked out.

On the street, Joe said, "You'd better go over there and help." Smaltz nodded and moved on to the swelling crowd that milled and babbled below the Hentz-shaped tunnel.

The time was nearly seven A.M. Other people had run out in their night clothes. Joe could get by in his pajamas all along the route of the tunnel.

He walked to Fourteenth Street amid an ever-increasing uproar of fire engines, ambulance and police sirens, and emergency crews from the public utilities. The crowds grew thicker and thicker. His feet got stepped on. The cement already felt uncomfortably warm from the rising sun, his soles picked up the nasty variety of debris and refuse and animal traces which coat the streets and sidewalks of New York.

He found a store with windows full of men's furnishings on display. He decided on the selections that looked as if they would fit him. A fat man with mean little eyes and a ridiculously small shoe-button nose kept watching him while loitering at a bus stop.

Joe stepped back to the curb and had a vision of the windows shattering. The glass crackled, showered, after the briefest of ghostly-blue radiance enveloped it. He darted to the showcases and grabbed white buckskin shoes, a white Palm Beach suit, socks, tie, shorts, and a basket weave shirt.

He started to scurry off. The fat man looked longingly at the windows, at other pedestrians, and began bellowing, "Stop thief, stop thief, stop thief!"

A couple of men took after Joe. Joe thought, "The fat slob is going to grab an armful, and then he's going to—"

The fat man ran to the window and swooped up a load. Then he stood, rooted to the spot, roaring: "This way, this way! I'm a thief! I'm a thief." He couldn't help it. His jowls quivered with rage and mortification. The two runners abandoned Joe and went charging down on the fat man. A policeman's whistle shrilled out.

Joe ducked around the corner, found a truck parked, and climbed into the cab. He had the shorts on when the policeman made the turn. Joe concentrated on him, and the bluecoat reversed himself, sprinting back along the route he had just traveled.

At seven o'clock that morning, Joe had dreamed of inheriting the Earth. By ten o'clock, he had reached the conclusion that he possessed a wild and diabolically useless talent. He wanted to get rid of it, but had not the slightest idea of how to do so.

He was sitting, in his ill-fitting clothes, on a bench in Union Square. He had decided that the safest place for him was in the midst of the largest possible crowd; and it seemed that all New York was pouring into the district. Traffic had come to a complete standstill. Streets and parks were jammed. Police had begun to rope off the entire area, but hadn't yet made an inroad in clearing out the central throng. Sirens kept up an endless wail.

A general alarm had gone out over the eight-state teletype system. Joe Harris was described as a homicidal maniac whom it would be wise to shoot first and ask no questions afterward.

Joe figured glumly that he didn't have very many hours of life remaining. He could cope with any single cop or detective, but the danger lay in his being shot from behind before he knew it, or encountering a squad of police. While he concentrated on one of them, the others would be perforating him.

He had slouched on the bench for a long time before he became aware of the woman sitting next to him. She was shabbily dressed, and looked half-starved and completely defeated.

She said, "Could I mooch a cigarette, mister?"

Joe, with eloquent silence, turned all his pockets inside out. They contained not a copper, not a cigarette, not a scrap of anything.

She handed him the remains of somebody's discarded paper. "Not much in the want ads. I used my last nickel riding the subways last night—"

Joe pushed his hands deep into the emptinesses of his pockets. He felt personally responsible for the plight of that woman whom he'd never seen before and very likely would never meet again. His luck was running out. All his life he had made it a rule never to pass a beggar, never to refuse a down-and-outer. It was his only superstition, and if it had not noticeably improved his luck, the habit at least had brought him no misfortune.

In the crowd milling past he saw a well-dressed man wearing a ring with a huge ruby. He was a citizen of portly build and prosperous appearance, with an adequacy of chins. He looked as though he carried a roll or a fat wallet. Joe vaguely wished that the stranger would come over to the woman and give her a stake. Even if only alms-by-proxy, he thought it might keep his record straight.

Joe blinked. The stranger gritted his teeth and put up a terrific battle against invisible powers. He sidled toward the woman with all the verve of a pig on the way to a slaughterhouse. He pulled out a wallet and reluctantly passed a ten-dollar bill to the woman. He glowered at her ferociously, and the veins in his neck swelled purple, until Joe hastily willed him to lose himself in the crowd, whereupon he marched away muttering.

The woman started crying.

Joe got up and moved off. He couldn't stand tears. Even the lady with the live locks could have turned him into mush by a little judicious sobbing. Who was that woman of the snake hair, some creature that he dimly remembered from mythology? Oh, yes, Medusa.

A crop of gooseflesh suddenly blossomed along his arms and neck. He felt the eddy of a cold, immortal wind, and upon him the intensity of passionless implacable eyes. The impulse to look aside, to turn around, was overwhelming, but he resisted it, while beads of sweat popped out of his stewing pores.

He heard a peculiar *yip*, a human voice rising in a cry that was abruptly silenced. Joe heard it as from afar, for he concentrated as fast and as hard as he could on returning Medusa to whatever realm she belonged in.

The picture in his mind that summoned her, and the command that whisked her away, occupied mere seconds. Then the chill of apocalyptic air faded, and Joe felt released from some cosmic evil. At the same time an incoherent staccato of voices burst into bedlam all around him.

There had been an orator on a soap box bedeviling the air in plea of this or that ism. He was still on the soap box, arm upraised in a gesture of defiance; and there it would remain till doomsday, and his eyes would always stare stonily over the heads of the crowd at something he had seen, for he had turned into marble.

Apparently no one else had seen the apparition, the return of the goddess with magic locks. No one, that is, except a dachshund waddling along at the hem of its mistress. The dachshund had gone to sniff, and its incipient bark was frozen for all time in lifelike stone.

Joe headed for Fifth Avenue. He blanked his mind of everything except figures and multiplication tables. One and one are two; two times two are four; the square root of three hundred; if A is half as old as B, and B raises forty bushels of wheat on two acres of C's land, and C has borrowed $20 from D, who is the son of A—

Abstractions were safe. As long as he thought of algebraic signs, and symbols that had never had animate life or objective existence, nothing happened. They couldn't be projected, like Henty or Medusa, into life and extensions of life.

Joe wanted to be alone. He was trying to get away to any remote spot where it wouldn't matter what he thought, and where he wouldn't upset the lives of other people. He hurried along, desperately muddled in the wilds of mathematics, and not very attentive to the persons he jostled and caromed from, until he encountered a horse's flank.

The flank was a sleek, black one. It belonged to a spirited nag. The nag was directed by a mounty. And the mounty had as his immediate purpose the forcing back to the sidewalk of any and all who tried to leave the curb.

Joe tried, absent-mindedly. The horse's flank pushed him and the mounty's billy bopped him on the shoulder and a surly voice growled, "Back up there, back up, keep in line—"

The sting of his shoulder brought an automatic response from Joe. He looked at the mounty. The copper had a fish face, the face of a cod with the soul of Napoleon.

"Brass buttons and a billy," said Joe.

"Back up, back up!" The mounty crowded him.

Joe blurted, "It's only the uniform! You'll be a hell of a sight in your birthday clothes. Worse'n Godiva—why, we'd laugh at you and—"

A blue flash zipped over the trooper. His uniform, cartridge-belt, service revolver, all pelted the gutter. He strode the nag, bald as a babe except for the billy on a thong at his wrist. The stick whistled and bounced off Joe's skull. He staggered away in a ferment of stars.

A titter rippled through the crowd, and jeers, and caustic laughter. The mounty went galloping off. Joe saw him in a haze. The swipe of the billy had further addled his senses. But he saw the mole on the mounty's shoulder, and how nakedly ridiculous he looked as he jogged on the humiliating path to his precinct station.

Joe flung himself down on a bed of pine needles on a lonely Jersey hillside. He had been deposited there by a Chicago-bound bus which he had hailed on Eighth Avenue. The driver hadn't intended to stop at Joe's hail, but he did. He had intended to demand a ticket, but he didn't. And he hadn't intended to let Joe off on a secluded stretch in the midst of nowhere, but he did.

Joe was learning that his strange new power had one immensely useful by-product: it obviated the need of cash.

As nearly as he could think it through, now that all thinking was a hazard for him, his wild talent of projection operated in two forms or extensions. He could impose his will on any living person or creature, but only on one at a time. He couldn't blanket all humanity, or even a group; it took his full powers of concentration to direct one man.

The second part was that he'd tapped the source of the apparently unlimited energy or power that caused such results as *poltergeist* phenomena. Called into play, the energy was visible as a bluish glow or glimmer. He had seen it around Freda, had watched it hammer the plate glass window. He could move physical objects by mental command, and thus far had found no limits to the feats he could accomplish.

He learned something else from the paper, a morning extra, given to him by the woman on the bench in Union Square. He had not killed Detective Henty, as he thought. The hyper-energy enveloped Henty in a shell or cocoon. It punched a tunnel through miles of building, but at the same time gave Henty a protective screen, and deposited him unharmed at police headquarters.

According to witnesses, there had been an explosion and a shower of debris that bruised an officer, but that was all, and there was Henty. A hurtling human projectile, he had done all the damage but emerged without injury.

The same energy had operated Joe's typewriter, and been responsible for Freda's fate. It had produced the weird effects that shattered the equilibrium of Dr. Fosterbrow.

It was a marvelous talent, but so far it hadn't done Joe much good, because he couldn't control it. He couldn't simply decide that something should happen, and then watch it happen. The process was automatic.

The moment a picture-action or wish-command flashed across his thoughts, it was translated into action. And, like all mortals, Joe was subject to idle whims and day dreams. No human mind can concentrate for more than a few minutes; he was no exception; and while he could channel his thoughts successfully for varying periods, the instant his fancy wandered all sorts of astonishing and unpredictable events ensued.

He had another object lesson as he was scanning the paper. His eyes lighted on an item concerning a large gold consignment being unloaded from an ocean liner. Quite unintentionally Joe visualized a box of gold bars, and thought how wonderful it would be to own one of those precious crates.

With an eardrum-splitting clap of thunder and a bluish haze, a box of gold bars deposited itself next to Joe. The wind of its passage fanned his face like a gale.

He had pictured the box at its pier, and seen it beside him, in fancy; and, instantly, there it was. It proved to be altogether useless; he had no tools with which to pry off the solid wooden casing, and the box was entirely too heavy for him to budge. He could have summoned tools; but, under Federal laws, the gold would do him no earthly good. In the end he wished the metal away again, and it vanished by the queer route of teleportation.

Of all the potentialities at his command, the one that disturbed him most was the resurrection of Medusa. He could do more than transport human beings; he could project the goddesses of legend. Apparently there was nothing to stop him from incarnating any creature of mythology, any spirit that had ever haunted the dreams of man. He could safely think of the possibilities so long as he confined them to negative terms. "I do *not* want to see the one-eyed Cyclops. I will *not* have Titania and Ygdrasil and Bubastis frolicking around me. I am perfectly content to let Merlin remain wherever he is—"

For the most dangerous part of his talent was not that he could bring Medusa to life, but that Medusa came equipped with all her sorcery; and if he should project any other god or goddess or creature or evil spirit, that being would undoubtedly spring forth with the full power of original magic and special functions unimpaired.

With this unhappy prospect drowsing through his head, Joe slid off into slumber under the shade of a pine.

He dreamed he was astride a great black stallion charging at a furious gallop along a tortuous path cut from the precipices of a colossal mountain range. With ringing hoofs the steed charged around a sharp bend.

The path ended abruptly and the stallion toppled over, falling for miles. Joe followed, tumbling at its heels. The stallion smote earth and bounced, and Joe dreamed that his falling body was cushioned by hitting the steed on the rebound.

Then he woke up, and found himself sprawled on the streets of a strange city at the base of towering mountains, on a great horse relaxing in death.

Stunned, he saw two guards in queer, golden greaves and crested helmets spring from the archway to a building of rose and green-veined marble.

They addressed him in a language of odd musical inflections, and rushed him inside. A great banquet, a victory celebration of some kind, a Lucullan feast was in progress. Many more of the golden-armored warriors lay around the hall in various stages of stupor.

A prodigiously fat man, like a caricature of Bacchus, appeared to be the king or leader. He was lolling with asthmatic wheezes and hiccups, surrounded by a dozen fawning girls. There was something eerie and alien and cruel about the women; they looked, in spite of an almost superhuman beauty, not quite human. Perhaps it was the effect of their supple arms which flowed with the ease and jointlessness of snakes' coils; or the pagan jewelry and cryptic, painted symbols that ornamented them in place of clothing. They spoke the same peculiar language of musical inflections as the guards.

The guards addressed the fat man. One of the women leaned over and whispered with a tigerish smile on her sensual lips. The bulbous ruler twisted a ring on his finger and one of the guards collapsed into a layer of rust-brown dust.

The fat man turned lazily toward Joe. Joe blurted, "No—no!" But the ring began to twist. Joe frantically wished himself back on the Jersey hillside—

A great vertigo overwhelmed him, the swoop of instant passage over unimaginable vistas, the fleeting of vast cosmic spaces.

Joe was standing on the pine-covered hill, a hundred yards from where he had fallen asleep. The diminishing rumble of thunder testified to the reality of his return from —where had he been? He had slept and dreamed; and his dreams had become projected into reality in accordance with his new talent; and he had awakened to the distortions of a dream world made real.

He leaned weakly against a tree with a feeling of panic. Till now he'd only worried about controlling his power while conscious and awake. Never again would he sleep in peace, for he dreamed constantly, often nightmares that were jumbles of illogical and unrelated things. To dream of them was bad enough; but to waken and find them vividly real—

A motorcycle *put-putted* down the road. Joe caught a glimpse of a state trooper and hastily ducked out of sight. He watched the trooper go by. As he watched, a perfectly foolish look began to spread over his features.

He muttered to himself, "See here, Joe, you dope. What the dickens are you worrying about? You don't need to be afraid of the cops. You've forgotten your power—you can use it on the police commissioner. You can make him send out a new teletype order canceling the previous one. Why, you can impose your will on the coroner, and he'll certify that Freda died of heart failure, which is true, in a way. You can have Henty withdraw his charges against you.

"Or if you want to work it another way, you can just tie yourself up, plead guilty—and compel the governor to grant you a full pardon. It's as simple as that. And there's no use berating yourself for Freda's death. You didn't intend it, you wouldn't have wished it if you'd known your power. In fact, it was more or less necessary to make you realize the responsibility you now have."

Joe broke off, started whistling as he walked toward the highway. Part of his problem was solved. Now, if he could only devise some method of controlling his talent—the mental equivalent of a piece of string tied around a finger, something to keep him constantly reminded not to forget—he could turn his power to good use.

But that would be harder; he didn't see how it could be done at all.

While wrestling with the problem, he saw a car coming down the road, a farmer driving a milk truck to the city.

Joe's weary feet reminded him of nearer, more homely things. "I'll hitch a ride," he decided, "and see if I can think out something on the way." Picturing the truck driver stopping to pick him up was no effort; it was a foot-felt as well as heart-felt relief.

Moodily, he considered his problem. The truck stopped, the driver woodenly leaned out and stated, "Ya wanna ride."

"Thanks," sighed Joe, and eased himself onto the seat.

Wordlessly, the driver drove on—and suddenly started. He looked past Joe as though he had materialized from nothingness. He gulped, looked at the man beside him, opened his mouth slowly to say "Hey!" and closed it with a snap. His eyes stared down the road with feverish intensity.

Joe simply stared blankly ahead. "I wish," he groaned to himself, "I had some warning. I wish that, just before I was going to do something, a big gong noise—something to really wake me up if I'm asleep—would go off. The way it is, I'd like to see the devil himself—ulp!"

Joe covered his ears with a gasp of astonishment. The gong-noise had lifted the top of his head two inches off his neck, it seemed. The painful expression faded in a look of relief from horror as he grasped the reasons for the warning.

He noticed the truck driver staring at him. "Hey," said the driver, "do you do that often, or are you all through? If you ain't, this is your stop. And, anyhow, I've heard of guys with buzzes in their heads, but not gongs. I don't like it."

"N-n-no. Not of-often," said Joe. "Very un-often—I mean infrequently. No more—if I can help it. It hurts my head."

"I'm glad of that," said the driver sourly.

IT WILL GROW ON YOU

H E COULDN'T FIND the compass in the center drawer. Maybe he hadn't left it at his office after all. Next he tried poking among the litter of medical journals, cancelled checks, and brochures about new equipment in the top right-hand drawer. Underneath lay his automatic, but no compass; he wondered briefly if it would be worth while to take the .38 along on the hunting trip.

He gave up searching. The time he'd wasted would have bought a dozen compasses.

The bell in the reception room rang, and he became conscious again of the cool, conditioned air inside, of the fever pulse of the city outside that he'd escape tomorrow.

He had finished with all appointments for the day; he had so arranged his patients and operating schedule as to permit him a week's absence; the bell, he hoped, would signify no more than a minor case, or an emergency treatment.

The door opened, and he glanced past the portable examination table. For a moment the nurse, in insufferable white, was framed between many-hued bottles of medicines and rows of surgical tools in the wall cabinets. She blanked out all but small segments of the outer room: the cream leather edge and chromium arm of a chair, the robin's egg blue of a wall, the fat nap of a broadloom in avocado green, the corner of a Haupers original oil painting, *July Moon*.

She closed the door and leaned against it, and her face looked as chalky as her uniform.

"A stranger," she said, "a man in a raincoat—"

"Raincoat?" He stared toward the window, where shadows deepened in the canyon, but the great stone manwarren opposite shimmered as though melting from sunfire.

"One of those swagger coats with a belt." She added foolishly, "It hangs all the way down to his shoes."

"What's the matter with him?"

"He won't say, except that it's urgent."

"Who sent him here?"

"A ship's doctor."

"Strange. I don't know any ship's doctors. You've no idea what his trouble is?"

She hesitated, her lower lip curling inward between her teeth. "His coat flapped ao ho wao coming in. Something is—seriously wrong The moot poouliar thing "

"Very well. Send him in."

She looked faint, as though she would slide down the door and dissolve into something liquid.

"I won't need you," he said. "You may go."

She nodded dumbly and went out, with a kind of sidling motion around the man who entered. Her face was developing a greenish tinge. He stepped toward her, but she shook her head mechanically with an expression of terror and a queer shine in her eyes. A line of sweat beads bubbled on her forehead. He eyed her closely as she pulled the door shut. Perhaps it would be well to observe her condition during the next few weeks.

For a moment his attention was distracted. He heard, or seemed to hear, a faint, muffled twittering like the cry of a bird. He looked toward the window, but there was nothing there, not even a sparrow, on the ledge outside. He cocked his head, straining, but did not hear the sound again. Yet he remained vaguely on edge, and wondered if some small animal might possibly have been trapped between the walls of the office.

The muted closing of the outer door told him that nurse had gone. She had stayed later than usual; he was satisfied to have dismissed her. The patient was an irregular, and whatever the trouble, would be diagnosed, treated, or referred quickly.

The man wore a swagger coat, a tan all-weather that hung to his shoes. His hands were trust deep in the pockets. His face was burnt dark, but the skin stretched tightly across cheekbones and around nostrils and eyes. A curious pallor underlay the tan, a dusty grayness. His eyes held a glow, as though he kept going only by some flickering but intense fire from within.

His voice, when he spoke, also had a strangeness. It was flat and dead, with a huskiness on the edge of exhaustion. It came with the precise slowness of one using an unfamiliar language, or reciting a role from memory. He said, "I am very grateful. I have heard that the best specialists are not always so easy to see—" He hesitated, added quickly. "Your fee, doctor, will be paid at once and in full."

"Be seated. You're rather fortunate. My calendar is generally crowded, but I happen to be going off on a hunting trip tomorrow."

"So? I hope the hunting will be good. Very good." The stranger looked relieved. "That is excellent. I, too, am leaving tomorrow morning. I have booked passage on a ship."

"A sea voyage is an excellent remedy for a good many ailments. What seems to be the trouble?"

The smoldering eyes appraised the examination table. "You could perform an operation here—a small operation?"

"It is not my usual custom."

"But you could do it, in an emergency?"

"It all depends on the circumstances."

A faint buzz distracted him, and he noticed with extreme irritation that a bluebottle fly had somehow got into the office. He supposed the insect must have entered along with the patient, or possibly when the nurse was leaving.

"Excuse me for a moment," he said brusquely, "while I bring the wild life under control. This is most unusual."

He took a sprayer out of a bottom drawer, but when he looked, the fly was nowhere visible nor could he hear the hum of its wings. He did, however, for an instant hear again that same muffled twittering as before, and suddenly the hairs rose along his forearms.

"What was that?" he asked.

"What was what?" said the stranger.

"That sound—like a little animal of some kind—trapped or wounded—"

"I heard nothing—nothing except a fly buzzing around—"

The doctor put his spray-pump aside; but he was positive that twice now he had heard an indefinable sound, a cry the more puzzling because he could not quite identify its nature or origin.

"Yes, it must have been the fly," he agreed perfunctorily. "Now, what did you say your trouble was?"

"One moment, please." The stranger loosened the slipknot in his belt and began to unbutton the swagger coat. "I must warn you to prepare yourself."

"I am always prepared," said the doctor a trifle coldly.

"I did not mean it that way. You must be prepared for a shock—for, perhaps, a very great shock. When Dr. Kelman advised me that you had no equals among specialists in your field—"

"Dr. Kelman? Who's he?"

"He was the ship's surgeon of the *S. S. Maracaibo.*"

"I see. I take it you've recently landed?"

"This very afternoon. I came here straight from the dock."

"I believe you said you intend to board ship again tomorrow?"

"It is imperative that I do so. But a different vessel, of course."

"Hmm. If your trouble is really serious—" He broke off, with a sudden feeling of suffocation as though he had swallowed his tongue.

The visitor tossed his coat aside. Underneath, he wore a white suit, a tropical double-breasted that emphasized his stocky build. The jacket was wrinkled, and soaked with sweat. The left trouser leg had been cut off near the hip, just below the pocket; the seam had been ripped open to his waist and crudely fastened with a couple of safety pins.

Between crotch and knee in mid-thigh stood an enormous bandage; a bulky mound like a camel's hump. It was sight of this bandage that sent a sharp tingle of unease through him, for the covering shook and undulated as though something alive were inside, something that scurried round and round in search of a way out.

The movement ceased almost at once, he had the eerie feeling that whatever was within had sensed itself to be under observation. He reached out to unwind the tape, but the man settled himself in an office chair. He propped his bare leg on the footrest and unfastened a huge safety pin that secured the ends of the bandage.

"Permit me," he said. "I have had some experience with this. It is not entirely—safe."

"But this Dr. Kelman you mentioned—"

"The bandage is not his work. Even a ship's surgeon would not have done such a ragged job. I wound this on, and I will take it off."

"But surely Dr. Kelman—"

"Oh, he tried to help, but unfortunately he—ah—injured his hands."

The stranger did not glance up. His thick fingers worked slowly, tensely, at unwinding the tape. He used both hands, but alternately, always leaving one hand free and half-clenched. It was impossible to tell whether he was preparing to pounce, or to ward off a blow.

"The ship's doctor—Kelman—he did not write out a diagnosis or a recommendation?"

"He intended to. But he disappeared."

"He—what?!"

"It was a strange event." The patient worked more slowly now, for the unwinding tape had grown to a sizable mass. He would pass it down and under his thigh, snatch it swiftly with his free hand and just as swiftly jerk the released hand back, always alert, and expectantly poised, half offensive, half defensive.

"Kelman was a curious fellow, a thin, baldish man with a bad case of indigestion. He claimed he suffered terribly from sinus trouble and hay fever when on land. But on a sea voyage he experienced an amazing improvement. Unhappily, he then developed a chronic state of indigestion which would clear up only when he set foot on land. Between the two evils, the sinus trouble affected him most, so he gave up his shore practise. He took his sensitive stomach out to sea permanently, and became a ship's surgeon. He was a good one, though not for me.

"I saw Kelman last night. He spent an hour or more working on me. It was no use. He could do nothing. At one point the knife slipped and he gashed his hand quite badly. He said he would think about the case overnight and write me a report or prescription this morning. But he seems to have vanished during the night."

"You are positive?"

"The ship was searched in every conceivable place."

"He left no message—no clue?"

"None. The captain will report that Kelman was lost overboard under circumstances unknown."

The doctor asked—and he was unable to keep the growing uneasiness out of his voice—"You think there may have been some connection between your trouble and Kelman's disappearance?"

"I do not know."

"Suppose you go back a little and tell me the symptoms, or the origins, of this—this—whatever it is."

The hands hesitated for a barely perceptible instant; if the doctor had not been watching so closely he would have missed the break in their rhythm.

"I am not entirely sure about it myself," said the patient slowly, without raising his head.

"That often happens. Just tell me what you do know."

"Is it absolutely necessary?"

"Of course it is," the doctor insisted. "A case history is essential to adequate diagnosis and treatment."

"I am afraid that what I have to tell you will not help you very greatly. For some time past I have been on a mission of a most confidential nature."

"Where? You said you had just arrived by boat—"

"I am not at liberty to tell. There are many countries in Central and South America," said the patient stiffly, "and many islands off the coasts. My work required me to visit numerous places."

The doctor thought, a revolutionary agent or a troublemaker if ever I saw one. Aloud, he said, "That is sufficient—the exact spot is unimportant. Go on."

"I have recently spent several months in a rather isolated locality. There was a native girl. We had an understanding—or so I thought. A man's needs are the same wherever he is. If he cannot have what he wants he must take advantage of what there is—you know how it is."

"I can imagine," said the doctor dryly.

"A couple of weeks ago I told her I must leave. She wanted to go with me. That was of course impossible. She must have been careless—or at any rate she had gotten herself pregnant. She was not only very unreasonable, she fought like a wild one. She had a knife in her hand suddenly, and before I could seize it she had slashed both of us.

"She kept screaming something in her own tongue. I caught only snatches of it. It was the effect that her blood was mine, that she was now part of me, and that she would go with me always. Then she broke loose and ran out, but when I got to the door she had already sped into the jungle.

"My worst cut was on the upper thigh. After bandaging it, I got on my horse and rode toward the village, intending to have the wounds cleaned and dressed. I had not gone far when my horse shied at something I never saw. I received a mighty blow from a branch overhead and felt myself falling.

"The next thing I knew, it was dark, and I lay on the floor of my house. I saw ashes of a fire at my feet, and smelled a pungent bittersweetness in the air. There were spots of blood too—much fresher than what we had spilled in the afternoon. I found, also, that I had—changed.

"I had intended to leave soon, but I was forced to go at once. I could not consult the local doctor, for if word went around of what had happened to me, I would be an outcast. My usefulness would be ended. The same reason prevented me from moving on to my next assignment, which was also among rather primitive people. I took the first boat north, hoping that the ship's surgeon would be able to treat me successfully, in utmost privacy, and at a safe distance to sea."

There was silence, except for the soft swish of tape.

"That's a curious story," said the doctor reflectively. "You'll pardon me if I say I hardly know what to believe."

"It does not matter what you think. That is of no importance. All that I care about now is the operation. But it will not be easy. I have told you how Kelman tried, and failed. You see—"

He unwound the last of the tape. A pillow case lay underneath, twisted around the thigh. His breathing had a hoarser sound, a rasp and a catch. He loosed the corners of the pillow case and flung it aside with a jerky but practised motion that left both hands cupped, veins bulging up.

There was a great purplish splotch on the skin. The ankles were rooted in its center, tiny ankles that flowed into the rudiments of feet that merged with the flesh. She could not have been more than a foot tall, a miniature and sinuous Venus, a perfect figurine, exquisitely formed in each minute detail, like a doll, but perilously alive with a vitality all her own. In the light of late afternoon her body seemed at moments nut-brown, then changing to a sort of metallic sheen, the color of old bronze overlain with a patina of verdigris. Her eyes were closed. Her face had the vacant repose of an idiot child.

She opened her eyes and looked at the doctor.

He got up and walked over to the window. There came a foolish little twittering from behind. Some force stronger than his will turned him around. The small horror was talking in a language that he did not know. She was cooing upward at her host with mindless adoration, and straining tautly upon her rooted feet as though attempting to leap into his arms.

"What is she—what is it—saying?" he asked in a faraway tone.

"I do not hear anything."

"Do you know what dialect it is?"

"I do not hear anything." His eyes flickered briefly; the doctor had an impression of having looked—through a curtain momentarily drawn—upon great fires raging in some illimitable void. Sweat was pouring down his cheeks, tears from a face of stone. Only then, and with a shock of pity, did the doctor realize to what extent will power alone kept up the man's outward aspect of strength.

The doctor said, "Just stretch out on the table and relax." He washed his hands thoroughly and put on a smock, but decided against rubber gloves. His palms already felt warm and moist. "We'll have that—growth—taken off right now. It should be a fairly easy and almost painless operation." He laid out a row of scalpels and scissors, sutures, surgical thread, antiseptics. He sterilized the needle of a hypodermic syringe, tested the plunger, and filled the chamber with novocaine.

"Kelman tried everything." The man appeared to be talking to himself. "He wasn't smart enough. He couldn't get rid of her. I don't think anybody can—"

"Nonsense. I'll fix you up in no time," promised the doctor. He thought, "Damn that ass of a ship's surgeon; the fellow was probably a broken-down hack who couldn't have treated a carbuncle successfully, let alone remove an abnormal growth."

He became conscious of a buzz again, and glanced up. The bluebottle fly had returned. It circled over the man on the table. The insect droned lazily off to one side, gathered height, and sailed down past the tawny figurine. It got no farther. A small, supple arm swooped outward, the snared fly made a shriller hum. There was a flash of teeth as tiny as the points of an ivory comb, a dreadful smacking of the rosebud mouth.

The doctor felt as though someone had hit his solar plexus. His breath came out in a whistling sigh, and only with the action did he realize how tense, how stilled he had been.

He walked over to the table and swabbed the two areas of injection with alcohol. He did not glance directly at the alien thing; but its very nearness made him aware for the first time of its evil force, the exotic temptation that it combined with a singleness of purpose and a quality that he could not quite identify—wiliness, perhaps, or wariness, or cunning of a sort.

"This may give you a bit of a twinge," he warned, and lowered the needle. It never penetrated the skin. The whole figure whipped over as if snapped on the end of a lash. The hypodermic was knocked clear out of his grasp, smashed on the floor.

"I begin to see what you mean," said the doctor softly.

He reconsidered his method. This was, he now realized, a problem far more serious than he had expected. Not an operation but a battle loomed ahead. He faced a foe who was resourceful, determined, and of unknown abilities.

"I'm afraid it won't be possible to use a local anesthetic," he admitted. "And I suspect that a general anesthetic might have little effect upon the—growth—"

"Yes," said the patient. "Kelman tried ether. It put me asleep, but it had no effect on—that."

The primary need, the doctor decided, would be to make the creature impotent. That was the core of the problem: to neutralize it, reduce it to an inert state or at least helplessness.

He surveyed the office equipment. There was a wastepaper basket, but of the wire mesh type, useless for his purposes. Next his eyes lighted on the glass shell that protected his microscope. This shell stood approximately two feet high and a foot in diameter at its base.

He lifted the glass cover and warily approached the waiting mannikin. The patient should be able to hold the shell firmly in place over the living doll while he inserted a tube under the edge and turned on the gas.

He dropped the glass casting in position. She stood erect within, barely quivering. "Quick now—hold this," he told the patient.

They almost succeeded. The man slid his hands around the container, and the doctor, releasing his grip, reached for the gas tubing. At that instant the imprisoned girl seemed weirdly beautiful; her features had the delicate clarity of a cameo; her hair, shimmering down her back, looked softer and finer than cobwebs, of a lustrous mahogany hue. Her eyes were hot and glittering.

The patient's hands, dropping along the sides of the shell, had not quite come to rest with a firm hold when she doubled up with the boneless and springy ease of live rubber. She curled her fingers under the rim and jerked. The glass container rose, tilted. The doctor sprang to push it back. The patient bobbled it. The shell tilted around between all hands, then spun free and smashed into countless fragments on the floor.

There was a hint of mockery in the poise of that small, naked, and apparently defenseless being.

The doctor backed away. His feet crunched splinters of glass, and the remnants of the hypodermic. He did not stop to clean up the debris. He withdrew to his desk, opened the top right hand drawer, and took out the automatic.

He balanced the weapon as he spoke, but his eyes never left the passive figurine. "I am a good shot," he said quietly.

"No—put that down."

"I won't miss."

"That's what I'm afraid of," said the patient in a dull voice. He was lying motionless, staring at the ceiling. "You see, I, too, am an expert marksman. I have taken out my own .45 many times in the last two weeks. But I could not bring myself to pull the trigger."

"I have no scruples. I will accept full responsibility."

"Will you? Suppose you don't miss—suppose your bullet goes right through its heart—*but what will you do if it does not die?*"

Slowly with a trancelike motion, the doctor replaced his automatic in the drawer.

A series of desperate expedients fleeted through his mind: of spraying the thing with liquid air till it froze solid and could be snapped off like an icicle; of heaping it with plaster of paris till it was rigid in a solid block; of destroying it with x-ray therapy; of amputating the whole leg at the hip.

His eyes fell on the row of surgical tools laid out, the scalpels that he did not dare use so long as the figurine remained capable of violent opposition. But the sight of the scalpels gave him the clue to a new possibility.

He walked over to the table and strapped the leg down tight at ankle, knee, and waist. He padded the kneecap with cotton and taped it for maximum protection, then taped the entire upper leg as closely as he could approach to the rooted feet without interference. When he had finished, the thigh was covered except for the purplish area in which the living doll grew.

He took a square decanter of whiskey from his cabinet. "Here, drink as much of this as you can stand. You'll need it."

"Thank you, no. I wish to see the end of this—if there is an end."

"I'm going to operate. There won't be any finesse about the job. It will be crude. It will be quick and direct. It will hurt. If it fails, I am afraid there will be nothing more I can do for you. Will you drink? Or take an anesthetic?"

"Thank you, no. Proceed, please."

"I'll be back in a few moments."

He left the whiskey within the patient's reach and walked through the outer room. The Haupers *July Moon* had a strange, unfamiliar look and he scanned it a second time in passing. Had the painting changed? No, it was still a perfect and timeless abstraction, a captured moment of eternity, serene from its dark shadow masses and detached, remote, immortal to the gibbous moon beyond its mysteriously luminous sky. The painting had not altered, but he had. Its mood was alien to him now. Its inward essence was one that would never again be his.

He went out into the corridor. A feeling of emptiness, of vacancy gripped him; some basic part of him had been stolen beyond recovery.

Near the stairs, built into the wall, was a fire-alarm box and a length of folded hose. Beside them hung a short-handled axe with a blade of almost surgical sharpness. He lifted the axe and returned to his office.

The patient did not turn his head. He did not seem to know or to care what the doctor was doing. He had not touched the whiskey.

The doctor said, "Now, grip the sides of the table and hold on hard." He turned the adjustment crank until the table slanted at a forty-five degree angle.

The axe had a good balance. It was both light enough to be aimed well, and with a heavy enough head to give the bite of the blade a strong momentum.

As he tried out the axe in a tentative arc, a torrent of soft cooing and twittering issued from the tiny lips, a sound more dreadful than any cry or protest. She was looking up at her host in an ecstasy of adoration, and her voice was drooling love, the fawning, brainless love of a cretin. That love flowed over and glued the doctor in its mewing fullness. It had nothing of passion or desire; it was merely an endless well of pure, idiot love; it asked for nothing, not even a gentle caress or an affectionate return.

The doctor's hands, which had been so uncomfortably warm, were cold and moist. A hammer began tapping at his temple.

He swung the blade.

The bright edge went through, streaked with red. There was a convulsion of movement from the severed figurine. Perhaps his foot slipped on crumbs of glass—perhaps the little creature somehow deflected the blow—perhaps the swing itself pulled him off balance—for the blade kept going, slashed through smock and trouser, lanced into the flesh alongside his own knee with a stab of fire. He stumbled and the metal edge of the table made a thick, ugly sound against his forehead. The axe slid out of his grasp. He sat on the floor, and when he sagged limply backward, his skull bounced with a sodden thud.

It was very dark when he groaned and struggled up. Waves of nausea and pain made his head a bursting volcano. His leg ached with burning intensity. He looked toward the window. A faint reflection from the streetlights washed the building opposite, but all its apartments were blacked out. By that evidence he knew it must be midnight or later.

He pulled himself to the wall and pushed the switch.

The patient had gone.

A row of small, round spots like dried blood traversed the floor from the table to the area where he had regained consciousness.

The cloth of his suit had soaked up and caked around the deep gash at his knee.

She was standing there, in the wound, the little doll, firmly rooted, tiny ankles blending into the form of feet that merged with his flesh. Her eyes were watching him avidly.

He stretched out his hands with a sudden terrible impulse to seize the thing and tear it out. His hands faltered, wavered, and drew back. He could not imagine what it would be like to touch the creature; he could not bring himself to find out.

He began dragging himself across the floor until he was able to reach into the top right hand drawer of his desk.

The *Southern Cross* had made steady way since morning; the sea had been smooth, the day warm, but the occupant of cabin 39 had not come out for either the noon or evening meal.

He had bolted his door. He had lain in his berth all day with a fever, dozing for hours.

His left leg was swathed in the bandages that he had applied in the doctor's office. It was badly swollen and throbbed maddeningly. But he made no effort to summon the ship's surgeon.

After nightfall he got out the extra bandages that he had brought along. Perhaps he had drawn the first dressing too tight.

With a pocket knife he slit open the bandage along his side and gingerly lifted it away.

A tiny figurine, not yet fully formed, was growing out of the purple patch on his thigh. The figure of a woman blossomed, but with the pale hue of an unfinished foetus.

He was beyond horror. He stared at the little living thing with a kind of deliberate finality. He turned toward the porthole and looked out across the dark waters; he seemed to see an infinite series of progressively diminishing creatures who vanished only at the point of eternity.

He measured the porthole with his eyes, but his shoulders were too broad.

He put the long swagger coat on. It rippled near his knee even after he buttoned it and drew the belt tight. A thin cry, a high but stifled wail came from the blanketed shape, unearthly as the note of an elfin flute.

When he opened the door, a steward was hurrying past. The steward paused. "Are you all right, sir?"

"Quite all right."

"If there is anything I can get you—"

"No. I just thought a short walk would do me good."

"Very good, sir. Good night."

"Good night."

He watched the steward vanish around a turn.

A short walk, he thought; yes, a very short walk. He thrust his hands deep into his coat pockets and began climbing the companionway to the open deck.

STRANGE HARVEST

THE SUN HAD scarcely risen when Al Meiers shoved himself away from the breakfast table and lumbered to his feet. A big, powerful man even for the Shawtuck County region of husky farmers, he had a face like tanned leather and arms whose hair lay swart over muscles like cables. He was all bone and solid flesh. Though past fifty, he strode with the ease of youth.

"That was a good breakfast, maw," he drawled to his almost spherical wife. She smiled out of eyes that had smiled through drought, storm, plague of locusts, and depression.

"Get along with you. Them apples'll never get picked with you aloafin' around here all day."

"Them apples'll be down by night. Hank!" he roared. The harvest hand, dripping of suds and rainwater on the doorstep, hastily smeared his face with a towel.

"There ought to be over two hundred bushel," said Al.

"Maybe more." Hank, a wiry drifter, slouched beside Al as they passed the chicken-coops. Roosters crowed, hens squawked out of their way, and the spring chickens beeped in alarm. Al made a splendid figure even in his dirty overalls, a bronzed giant of the soil.

They passed the pigsty where sows and porkers squealed over a sour-smelling trough. The sun stood just above the horizon, and the warm air held that peculiar scent of late summer—smell of manure, of clover, hay, and wheat, of baked earth and ripening vegetation.

A wagon loaded with empty bushel baskets stood by the barn. Al hitched the horses and took the reins. The team of Belgian Grays ambled down a dirt road.

"It's been a good year for crops," said Al. He jammed tobacco in an old corncob pipe and lighted it without loosening the reins.

"Yeah. Only there's something funny about 'em this year."

"Yeah. They're bigger. Biggest ever."

Hank spat out a hunk of plug. "That ain't all. They kind of shake even if there ain't no wind. As I was sayin' yesterday, I got to feelin' pretty queer when the tomato patch kind of shook when I was hoein' it."

"Giddyap!" Al bellowed. The team clattered faster. He inhaled and blew out a cloud of fragrant smoke. "Uh-huh. I don't know what's got into things. Best weather and best crops we ever had but something's wrong. Last fall the crops started growin' again about harvest-time. The darnnedest thing. It wasn't till October we got all the spuds in and the corncrib full."

Hank looked uneasy. "I don't like it. There been times when I, well, I just didn't feel right."

"Yeah?"

Hank lapsed into moody silence.

"Yeah?" Al prodded.

"There wasn't any wind yesterday but I swear the north clover patch flattened out when I started to mow."

"Yeah? You been seein' things." Al was noncommittal. Hank kept silent.

"I never saw corn grow like this year," said Al after a while. The horses clopped along. "Ten foot high if it's an inch. Fred Altmiller was sayin' the other day that he figured on gettin' a hundred fifty bushel to the acre. Nary an ear less'n a foot long."

Hank moped. "Last time I went through your corn, there was the damnedest racket you ever heard. You'd of thought a storm come up. There wasn't a cloud nowhere. Wasn't any wind."

"Lay off the corn likker," Al jibed.

"Wasn't corn likker," Hank protested. "It's the crops are queer. I'd of bet there was somebody around when I weeded the melons last week. Sounded like voices."

"What did?"

"Why, just everything. Whispers, like the corn was talkin'."

Al snorted. "You're headed for the bughouse. I been farmin' here for thirty years an' I never hear tell of such a story."

"It's so! It's been goin' on all summer!"

The wagon bumped through fields of ripe wheat and oats, lurched around an immense boulder, and rattled up a hill where the cows munched at grass strewn between.

Al agreed with Hank but he wouldn't admit it. The first principle of stolid people is to deny the existence of what cannot be explained and does not harmonize with the run of experience. Ever since the phenomenal post-season growth of vegetables and fruit last fall, he had been wondering. The spring planting, the perfect weather, bumper crops, truly miraculous yields—these blessings were offset by certain evidence that had made him increasingly uneasy. There was the matter of waving grass on still days. He hadn't yet gotten over the way the trees hummed one hot afternoon when he was spraying the apple and cherry orchards.

"Anyway, it's been a good year," he repeated. "Them apples are prize winners. The trees are bustin' with 'em."

The wagon bumped across the hill-top and the horses plodded down. "Just look at 'em, just look—well—uhh," his voice petered out.

Yesterday an orchard of Jonathans had occupied this acre between two small hills.

Yesterday.

Today there was only torn soil and furrows stretching toward the opposite hill.

Al gaped and his face turned a mottled red. Hank's eyes popped. He opened his mouth and closed it. He stared as if at a ghost. He ran a finger around his neck. The sun slanted higher. The field lay bright and newly ploughed. But there were no apple trees.

Al blasted the morning air with a howl. "Some dirty thief has swiped my apples!" he yelled.

Hank looked dazed. "There ain't any trees, ain't any apples, ain't nothing."

Al sobered. "Not even roots."

"No stumps," said Hank.

They stared at the bare ground and at each other.

"The orchard walked off," Hank suggested.

The horses whinnied. The red in Al's weathered face died out. It became a study in anger and bewilderment.

"Come on!" he choked and flicked the horses' flanks with a whip. They plunged down-hill, slewed onto the field, and followed the furrows over the looted soil, across undulating mounds, and straight through a field of wheat. There was a swathe like the march of an army.

"It can't be. I'm dreamin', we're both crazy," muttered Al.

Hank fidgeted. "Let's go back."

"Shut up! If someone's swiped my apples I'll break him in half! The best crop in thirty years!"

Hank pleaded, "Listen, Al, it ain't only the apples. The whole trees 're gone, root an' all. Nobody can do that in a night!"

Al drove grimly on. The horses galloped over a hill to the road and followed it as it wound down toward a small lake between terminal moraines. There they jerked to an abrupt halt under Al's powerful drag.

Al glared. Hank's eyes roved aimlessly around. He fumbled for a chew which he bit off and absently spit out. He tried to loosen an open shirt. He didn't want to see what he saw. "So help me God," he muttered, "so help me God," over and over, like a stuck phonograph record.

Here stood the orchard of Jonathan apples grouped around the pond; a half-mile from its accustomed place, but otherwise intact.

Al leaped out, a peculiar blank expression on his face. He walked with the attitude of a cat stalking prey.

The orchard of Jonathans wavered.

There was no wind.

The orchard looked for all the world like a group debating. Whispers and murmurs ascended, and the branches shook.

Hank leaned against the dashboard. Tobacco juice dribbled from his gaping mouth and watered his new crop of whiskers.

"Come on!" snarled Al. "Get them poles and nets. We're gonna pick apples!"

But he did not need to pick apples. He reached for a luscious red Jonathan hanging low on the nearest tree. The branch went back, then forward, like a catapult. Al ducked. The apple smacked the wagon. Both horses whinnied and raced off. As if that were a signal, the orchard launched into violent motion. A noise like a rushing wind rose. The tree-tops bent and lashed as in a gale. Apples showered the farmers, darkened the air, bounced and squashed painfully from faces and shins and bodies.

The ungodliest yell ever heard in Shawtuck County burst from the throat of a hired hand whose terrific speed carried him after the careening wagon out of the picture, and the county.

Lars Andersen was walking along a path with a scythe on his shoulder to mow some odd plots of hay, early that morning. His Scotch collie bounced beside him. The path went around a vegetable garden and then paralleled a wind-break of elms. Now it is a well-known fact that any intelligent dog will have nothing to do with grass or mere vegetables.

The collie, being a dog of rigidly conventional habits, made a beeline for one of the trees. Whatever he intended to do was postponed. The lowest branch of the tree curved down and not only whipped his rear smartly but lifted him a good dozen feet away. He yelped and tore for home like mad.

Lars had a thoughtful expression on his face as he turned around and headed back. He guessed he didn't feel much like mowing today.

Old Emily Tawber fussed with her darning until mid-morning before laying it aside. "Jed can wait for his socks," she muttered crossly. "I can't cook and sew and tend to the crops all at once, and them watermelons ripe for market."

She put her mending back in the big wicker basket, pulled a vast-brimmed straw hat over her head, and went out in an old rag dress that she used for chores.

She stomped across the yard and through her flower garden to the melon patch. There were about fifty big melons ready for picking. She would pile them up alongside the path for Jed to load and take to market in the morning.

"Land's sakes, I never see such melons in all my born days." Old Emily stuck her arms on her hips and surveyed the green ovals. These were giant watermelons, three and four feet long, weighing a hundred pounds or more. She had been surprised throughout the summer by their growth.

"Well, the bigger they be, the more they'll fetch," she decided and went after the first one.

It must have been on a slope for it rolled away as she approached.

"Well, I swan!" said old Emily. "Things is gettin' to a pretty pass when you can't get at your own seedin's."

She walked after the watermelon. It rolled farther. Old Emily became flustered. She increased her stride. The melon bumped unevenly in a wide circle around the vine-root. Old Emily panted after it and it wobbled crazily always just ahead of her.

Old Emily began to feel dizzy. She guessed the sun was too much for her. She wasn't as spry as she used to be. The world reeled around. The melon kept going, while she paused for breath, then it rolled all the way around, came toward her, and crashed into her ankles. The blow sent her sprawling. This was when peril first entered her thoughts. She staggered to her feet and from the patch.

"Watermelon won't get me," she crooned. "Watermelon run along but he won't get me. Don't let old watermelon get me." This was all that anyone heard her say during the rest of her earthly existence.

The harvester thundered as Gus Vogel gave it the gas and it clattered toward his wheat acreage.

Gus hollered, "With this weather we'll be done come night!"

"If the machines don't break down," bawled brother Ed above his machine's racket.

"Wheat is two dollar 'n' a quarter a bushel," Gus chortled. "I bet we get a hundred bushel to the acre this year."

The two machines rattled along a dirt road that was little more than weed-grown ruts until a sea of tawny appeared beyond the brook and cow pastures.

A full half-section in extent, the field of ripe grain rolled away in a yellow-brown flood shoulder high, the tallest wheat within memory, headed by two-inch spears with dozens of fat grains.

Gus and Ed jockeyed the harvesters into the near corner of the field. Those long rows erect as soldiers would soon go down in a wide swathe. The three hundred twenty acres of wheat were worth over seventy thousand dollars.

Gus roared lustily as his machine lurched ahead and the blades whirred to reap, "Let 'er go!"

As if struck by a mighty wind, the wheat flattened against the ground in a great area that widened as the harvester advanced.

Not a breath of wind stirred. The air hung warm and fragrant, the sunlight lay mellow on ripe grain, meadowlarks carolled morning-songs, and the black crows cawed harshly high overhead. But the wheat lay flat, mysteriously, in a large strip. Beyond this strip, the golden ranks rose tall again, but a myriad murmuring issued from them like voices of invisible hosts. The hair prickled on Gus's scalp. He looked behind him. Not a stem had been cut by the reaper, and the full ears were intact. In a sudden vicious, unreasoning rage, he drove the combine ahead at full speed, and the blades sang a song of shirring steel, and the wheat went down in a racing band farther ahead at a faster pace than he could achieve, and the slicing blades whirred idly over the prone grain.

Then Gus and Ed stopped the machines and climbed out. Gus knelt over and bent his face low to study this extraordinary field. A patch sprang upright like wires, lashing his face. Gus gaped, popeyed. The veins stood out on his temples in purple. Somewhere within him something happened and he pitched to the ground, his face livid, as Ed ran to his aid.

Not least among the remarkable events in Shawtuck County that morning was the saga of the fugitive potatoes.

The potatoes were only a small planting of an acre or so that Pieter Van Schluys had raised. They should have matured in early August but they didn't. They kept on growing and their tops got bigger and greener and lustier. Pieter was a stolid Dutchman who knew his potatoes as well as his schnapps.

"Dere iss someting wrong," he solemnly told his American frau. "Dey haff no business to grow furder. Already yet dey haff gone two veeks too late."

"Dig 'em up, then," said the bony Gertrude. "If they're ripe, they're ripe. If they aren't, you can tell quick enough by diggin' a couple out."

"Ja," Pieter agreed. "But it iss not right. Potatoes, dey should be in two veeks already."

"Maybe if you weren't so lazy you'd of dug 'em two weeks ago."

"Dat iss not so," Pieter began, but Gertrude tartly gathered dishes and pans with a great noise.

Pieter blinked and rose. It was hard to have such a shrewish frau. In this *verdaemmte* America, *frauen* were too independent. You could neither boss them, nor beat them.

He rolled to the door and waddled past a silo to the barn where he took a potato-digger from a mass of tools. He leisurely filled a well-stained meerschaum pipe which had a broken stem, and lighted it. A couple of geese honked sadly as he passed in a cloud of burley smoke.

Pieter paused by the potatoes to wipe his sweating face with a kerchief bigger than a napkin. "Gertrude," he muttered, "she iss no better as a potato."

Having expressed his rebellion, he dug and heaved. The tubers did not come up. Pieter strained, struggled, perspired. The heap of earth grew larger, but no potato appeared.

"Dat iss some potato," Pieter muttered. "Himmel, vat a potato it must be."

Pieter looked at his planting. "Diss iss not right for a potato," he spoke in reproof, and shovelled more soil away.

Had his eyes deceived him? Or had the plant actually sunk? He looked at the vegetable tops with thoughtful disgust. It seemed beyond question that the leafy tops were considerably nearer ground level than when he arrived.

"So?" Pieter exclaimed. "Iss dat how it iss? So!"

He scooped again. He watched with a kind of bland interest at first, then a naive wonder, and finally anxiety. It did seem that the potato was getting away from him. No, that could not be. He must have taken too many schnapps last night. Or it was too hot. He wiped perspiration off his face with a sleeve of his blue denim shirt. The potato was as far below his digger as ever, and surely his eyes did not befool him when they registered that the potato's topmost leaf was now at ground level. Quite a heap of soil lay beside it. The rest of the potato patch stood as high as before. Only this one pesky tuber had sunk unaccountably.

Pieter dug deeper.

The mound of dirt increased. The hole grew larger. The elusive potato continued to slide below his digger. It was maddening. There must be a cave as big as the Zuyder Zee under this vegetable. He might fall into it with the plant!

His slow brain, obtaining this thought, brought him to a momentary halt. But no. Ten years he had farmed here, ten years had harvested. It was very strange. Pieter did not feel quite so chipper as after breakfast, and he certainly had not been jovial then. Pieter became stubborn. The devil himself was in this potato. The devil was leading him to hell. Or nature had gone crazy. Or he had.

Pieter shovelled and scooped, but the tuber dug down like a thing possessed, a mole, a creature hunted. The pile of dirt had spread far by now, and Pieter stood in a deep pit with the potato still below him. He had reached sandy, thin, base soil. He was angry and stubborn. He dug till his arms ached. He panted in Dutch and cursed in English. He muttered, he swore.

"Something iss crazy or I am," he decided and made a halfhearted plunge at the vanishing vegetable.

"You seem to be having some difficulty. Can I be of help?" inquired a polite voice.

A stranger stood on the rim of the hole. The stranger wore old corduroy trousers, a stained work-shirt, and a slouched hat. He had amused gray eyes. A briar pipe stuck out of his mouth. He twirled a golden key idly so that the chain wrapped round and round his forefinger. His face was full of angles, and a peculair mark, not a scar, possibly a burn, made a patch on his left temple. By that mark, Pieter recognized him from hearsay as a comparative newcomer. He had bought the Hoffman farm a mile out of Shawtuck Center on County Road C somewhat over a year ago. He paid cash, and claimed the odd name Green Jones.

Pieter scowled. "Danks, but I vill manage. De potatoes iss hard to dig diss year."

The stranger's jaw fell open. "You don't mean to tell me you're digging potatoes! Way down there?"

Pieter felt acutely unhappy. "Ja."

"You sure plant 'em deep! Why don't you try for those nearer the surface?"

Pieter stared glumly at Green Jones, then back at the potato plant, now a good five feet below ground level, and still going down in the crater he had dug. Damn the potato! Damn the stranger! Damn all this business!

"Ja," said Pieter. "Be so kindly as to help me out."

Green Jones lent a willing hand, heaved while the rosy Dutchman puffed, and helped him scramble up. "Dat vas very good of you," Pieter thanked him.

"Don't mention it."

Pieter marched to the next cluster of potato tops, spat on his hands, and made a ferocious jab at the ground. His digger sank a foot. The tuber sank a foot and a half. Pieter glowered.

"Hawl!" exploded the onlooker. Pieter glared murder. Green Jones chuckled to himself and blew out a cloud of pungent smoke.

"How you did it beats me, but I never saw anyting like it!" Green Jones walked off in great good humor, a lank figure striding down the road, leaving behind him the aroma of fine tobacco, the echo of his chuckles, and a wrathful Dutchman.

"Potatoes!" Pieter muttered. "Himmel, everyting iss crazy mit de heat."

Like the first, this second group of fugitive potatoes seemed to be burrowing into the earth. The magical submersion was too much for him. He reeled toward his farmhouse to drown his troubles in a sea of schnapps.

The incident at Loring's farm was notable for its spectacular brevity. Mrs. Loring wanted to can corn. Lou Loring said he'd haul her in enough for the winter. Between other chores, he went to his sweet corn field about ten o'clock with his daughter Marion.

Marion held a bushel basket and would have followed him down the rows if there had been any stripping.

Lou reached for an ear.

The ear moved around to the other side of the stalk. A weird cater-wauling went up from the whole field and the stalks, standing ten feet high and more, seemed to shake.

Lou hesitantly pursued the ear. The cob returned to its original position. Lou batted his eyes. Marion gave a peculiar squawk and raced pell-mell for home.

Lou swore and reached for another ear. Did the whole stalk revolve? Or did the ear slide away? Was he out of his head? The furious sounds of the cornfield alone were enough to make his flesh creep.

Between the rows of corn, pumpkins had been planted. A few weeds grew, and a sprinkling of wild ground cherries. Lou reached for a lower ear and in so doing almost stepped on one of the groundcherries. The plant leaped straight up and fell a foot away. The roots moved feebly, began to sink in the soil, and the groundcherry rose gradually erect.

What with revolving ears of corn and leaping groundcherries, Lou felt that he needed a day off, to have his eyes examined. And off he went.

The main hangout in Shawtuck Center was Andy's general store. On Saturday night, Andy usually did a whale of an illicit business in Minnesota Thirteen, a strain of corn that eager moonshiners quickly and happily discovered made superior whisky. Weekdays were dead, especially the early days. But the way farmers began drifting in on this Tuesday was a caution. A dozen had collected before noon. Andy did not know what it was all about, but the corn liquor was flowing. There were rickety chairs, empty barrels up-ended, and nail-kegs aplenty to hold all comers.

The universal glumness was a puzzle to Andy. "How's tricks?" he asked when Al Meiers came in.

"So-so." Al twiddled a cracked tumbler, drained it, clanked it on the counter.

"Something wrong?"

"We-ell, no."

"Here, take a snifter of this."

"Don't mind if I do." Al gulped the drink.

"You ain't lookin' so well, Al."

Pieter Van Schluys waddled up.

"Hi, Pieter, why aren't you hauling in?"

Pieter glowered at the speaker. "Dose potatoes," he muttered, "dey iss full mit de devil!"

"So?" Andy perked his ears. An amazing interest developed among the rest of the group.

"Ja. I dig for vun potato and so fast as I dig, de potato dig deeper. Ja. I tink dere iss a hole so big as China under dose potatoes or de potatoes iss, how you say it, haunted, ja, else I am crazy mit de heat."

"I'll be damned," Al broke in, "and I thought I was seein' things. Listen!" He told of the orchard that walked away. Hesitantly at first, this big farmer almost pleaded for belief, and when he saw that the jeers he expected did not come, he warmed to his tale like a child reciting a fairy story.

"That must of been your hired hand went by here like a blue streak in that old jalopy a couple hours back," Andy guessed.

"Yeah. Hank lit out. I don't blame him much. I don't s'pose he ever will come back."

Ed Vogel had a grim face. "I just saw Doc Parker. He says Gus had a stroke when we was mowin' this mornin', but he'll pull through. Only there wasn't no mowin'. The wheat don't cut. It just lies down an' then springs up again. You'd of thought it was alive and knew just what I was gonna do."

"My apples ain't worth a dime a bushel now," said Al. "After they got through throwin' themselves around, they was so banged up they ain't even good for cider."

Ed wore a reflective air that turned to a scowl of apprehension. "Say, if things go on like this, we won't have no crops this year. We're ruined."

Until he spoke, not one of the farmers had fully realized the extent of the disaster that faced them. Each had been preoccupied with his own worry. The fantastic rebellion of nature was a mystery. Now Ed's remark drove home understanding of what they were up against. If this was not all a collective hallucination; if they were as sane as ever and had witnessed what they thought they saw; if they had no more success in harvesting than they had had so far—then they were bankrupt, ruined. They could pay off neither mortgages nor debts. They would be unable to buy necessities. They would not even have food for themselves, or seed for next year's sowing.

"I wouldn't eat one of my leapin' apples for a million dollars," Al Meiers declared, and meant it.

"What are we gonna do?" Ed asked helplessly. "We can't all be batty. Somethin's wrong, but what? No crops, no food, no cash. Crops are bringin' high prices this year, but we're done for."

Andy peered over his shell-rimmed glasses. "Why don't you go see Dan Crowley? Maybe he could help you out."

"Good idea," Al agreed, lumbering to his feet. "How about it, boys?"

"Sure, let's see the county agent."

Gloom hung thick on the anxious group that faced Crowley.

"Take it easy, boys," Crowley advised genially. He was county agent for the Department of Agriculture. He was fat and bald. His nose stood out like the prow of a ship and stubble covered his jowls. He smoked black, twisted, foul stogies that smelled to heaven. His feet were on the desk of his office when the farmers came, and there his feet remained while he puffed poisonous clouds and listened. His muddy blue eyes were guileless. Dan Crowley looked harmless, hopeless, and dumb.

They were deceptive traits. Dan had a good head. He just didn't believe in extending himself needlessly.

"So that's how it is," Al Meiers finished. "I'm ready to move out of the county now and burn the damn' wheat to the ground."

"Now, now, Al, don't be that way. You know I work for you all."

Pieter Van Schluys moped. "Ja. Vat good iss dat?"

"Plenty. Just leave it to me." Dan hooked his thumbs in his armpits and leaned farther back.

"You haff an idea?" Pieter asked hopefully.

"Sure thing. Now run along while I'm thinkin' about this. I'll get it straightened out." Dan was vaguely definite. The farmers filed away.

Shawtuck Center grew more and more restless as the afternoon waned and farmers arrived with newer and wilder accounts of the pranks that nature was playing. Andy's general store buzzed with anxious and angry voices. The population of Shawtuck County was made up almost exclusively of hard-headed Dutchmen, Scandinavians, and Germans who had settled through the Midwest during the great immigration waves of the late nineteenth century. They were a conservative, strong-working, sturdy lot. They clung to past customs, and some of the superstitions learned in the Old Country. The town simmered with tales of witchcraft and hauntings, of the Little People, of goblins and evil spirits.

What caused this strange revolt of the plant kingdom at Shawtuck Center? Nothing of the sort seemed to be afflicting the outside world. And what possible action could he take? He could at least make a field inspection for a special crop report.

Dan went out, climbed into his official car, and headed out of town on County Road A.

The land, under the warm, mellow light of the sun, gave testimony of abandonment, without the voice of any farmer. Harvesting ought to be in full swing, but not a figure tramped the fields, not a reaper moved. Here and there stood threshers, harvesters, wagons, farm implements, and combines, all untended.

Yet the fields, though deserted, were not wholly silent. This was a day of quiet, such a day of stillness and ripe maturity as often comes at harvest time; but ever and again, as Dan drove along, he saw strange ripplings cross wheat and hay fields, watched clover sway, heard a sound like innumerable murmurous faint voices sweep up from grains and grasses and vegetables; and one patch of woods was all an eerie wail, and infinite restless disturbances of flower and leaf and blade set the forest in motion; while the wild chokecherry and sumac nodded in no wind and shook for no visible reason alongside the dirt road.

Dan felt uneasy. All summer there had been little signs, increasing evidence, that a change had come over nature; and now the rapid and sinister character of that change became intensified with its completion. The trees, the plants, the vegetables had mysteriously developed a life and will power of their own. And they had cast off the dominance of man.

Dan drove on through back roads, and twisted over cart paths, weaving in and out around Shawtuck Center during the afternoon. Everywhere he went, he found the same uncanny solitude, the constant whispers whose speakers remained invisible, alfalfa and barley and corn that quaked though no presence was near and rarely a breath of air stirred. The sun was sinking when Dan headed homeward, and it seemed to him that new and deeper murmurs issued from the bewitched fields and the enchanted woods. But he had learned one fact, and it puzzled him.

The phenomena were limited to the valley where Shawtuck Center lay in a bowl of low hills.

Returning to his office, Dan passed a group to whom Pieter Van Schluys was relating again the saga of the fugitive potatoes. "So dere I vass, fife feet down already, ja, and der man, de Jones person, he stand dere and laugh. Himmel, maype it vass funny as a funeral, nein?"

Dan wondered why anyone should be amused by such a strange occurrence. He went thoughtfully into his office and looked at the routine blanks and forms on his desk.

He could well imagine the results if he reported the facts to Washington. "Meiers's apple orchard walked away last night and the trees planted themselves around a pond on the Hagstrom farm because they liked it better there." And, "The Vogels' wheat refuses to be harvested. Kindly advise proper action to take." Or, "Emily Tawber's melons object to being picked. Does she lose her guarantees under the federal Watermelon Pickle Price Support Program?"

No, Dan decided, if he sent in these official messages, he would only be fired and replaced. His only course was to make a further investigation in search of a cause for the bizarre happenings.

He went to the wall and studied the large map of Shawtuck County. It showed the size and location of every farm, the variety and acreage of every crop. He drew a rough circle around the area of the phenomena. At the center of the circle lay the farm of Green Jones. Dan decided to pay Jones a visit.

As Dan turned in at the private road by the mailbox lettered G. Jones, he noticed immediately in the twilight that the land had not been tilled at all. Jones was no farmer. Only lank weeds grew in his fields.

Dan stopped at a gray old frame house guarded by elms and maples. Lights burned in the ground floor windows.

Dan heaved his bulk out with a sigh and lit the inevitable stogy. He rang the bell, and presently a tall, thin man with an angular face appeared at the screen door.

Dan said, "I'm the county agriculture agent. Mind if I drop in for a few minutes?"

Jones replied firmly, "Why, yes, I do mind. I've a lot of work to do and I'm pressed for time."

"So'm I." Dan blew a cloud of reaking smoke at Green Jones. "I have to get off a special crop report to Washington tonight."

"What have I got to do with that? I don't grow any crops," said Jones, frowning.

"Maybe not. Maybe you just help to make other people's crops grow."

A wary look came into Jones's eyes. "What do you mean by that?"

Dan said slowly, "It's like this. There's been queer things going on around here all summer. All year, in fact, ever since you moved in. Walkin' trees an' gallopin' potatoes and God knows what all."

Jones spoke with a tone of bored indifference, "I heard some of those wild rumors."

"They ain't rumors. I went out for a look-see this afternoon. Crops an' everything else that grows have gone crazy all around Shawtuck Center. There's a borderline maybe a quarter-mile wide where things are kind of uncertain, an' after that the trees an' such haven't anything wrong with 'em. So I looked at my map and saw that the center of that circle is right here."

Green Jones straightened up coldly. "Are you implying that I have some connection with these phenomena?"

"Implying? Hell, no, I'm tellin' you."

Jones regarded the county agent with a peculiar, shrewd appraisal. Finally, after appearing to weigh many matters, he shrugged and said, "You win. Nice crop detective work. I suppose I might as well take you into my confidence. I don't want a lifetime's work wrecked in a day." He stepped aside. "Come in."

The parlor was severely furnished. Besides a sofa, several chairs, and a desk, Dan noticed two prints on the walls: one of Burbank, and another of Darwin.

"Have a chair," his host suggested.

Dan sank into a wing-backed piece that promptly collapsed under his weight.

"Dear, dear," Jones protested. "That was a good chair."

Dan eased himself into the more substantial sofa and blew his nose violently to indicate that he was sorry but unembarrassed. Unfortunately, he dropped his stogy which left a scorch on the thick blue carpet amid a fine powder of ashes.

"My beautiful rug," mourned Jones.

"Sorry," mumbled Dan.

"Never mind. It's done."

"An' everybody hereabouts is done for, the way things are goin' now." Dan steered back to his original topic. "Jones, I don't know who you are or how you done it but you sure raised hell with the crops."

Jones slouched against a mantelpiece. From far away came an insidious drone that Dan could not quite identify. His host idly twirled a golden key on a chain. He looked cool, slightly detached, and yet there was a deep passion behind his features. "Right. My real name doesn't matter. I'm a botanist. Some years ago I got the idea that vegetation seemed to show a sort of rudimentary awareness. It couldn't be called intelligence. I noticed how tree roots turned off and travelled considerable distances straight to underground water pipes. Then there is the fly orchid that acts with almost human ingenuity. It attracts, traps, and devours insects.

"I became convinced that there was a kind of dormant awareness in the plant world. It would be a great achievement for science and a possible blessing to man if plants possessed instinct and science could develop it to reason or at least the power of free motion. Then food materials, like animals, could seek a water supply and largely do away with the harmful effects of drought. I worked on that line. I didn't get far until other scientists discovered that ultraviolet rays, even the ordinary illumination of electric lights, could be turned on plants all night long and they grew almost twice as fast as other plants. Physicists found that various cosmic radiations produced definite effects on vegetation and could cause radical changes.

"Two or three years ago, I found that a universal radiation isolated first by Diemann greatly accelerated all activity of plants. I built apparatus to capture and to concentrate that radiation. I turned the intensified radiation loose on some hothouse plants and they grew like mad. I decided to experiment on a larger scale, and bought this farm because it was in a secluded district. For the past year I've been bombarding vegetation around Shawtuck Center with Diemann's radiations. You know the results—abnormal growth, mobile powers, and apparently rational, rudimentary impulses. That's the whole story. Now I've laid my cards on the table."

Dan knitted his brows. "You say the ray makes plants *think?*"

"No, I don't know that it does. All I know is that Diemann's radiations have always been essential for the growth of plants. I proved that by trying to raise flowers in an insulated hothouse. Nothing I experimented with would grow at all without Diemann's radiations. I reasoned that a concentration of the rays, if strong enough, might cause abnormal developments and hasten the evolution of species. I'm only experimenting and recording data as I go along. There seems to be something more than instinct developing, but it's too early to call it reason."

Dan said, "Hmm. Why did everything happen today? That's kind of suddenlike if you've been usin' this ray for a year, ain't it?"

The stranger shrugged. "Yes, but remember, I too am almost as much in the dark as you are. I know the cause of the change but I don't know the how or why or what. I must observe for years to determine these factors. Possibly there was a dividing-line. On one side stood inanimate vegetation, constantly but feebly irradiated. Then my concentration of Diemann's ray built up the change until its influences reached their climax last night and inanimate plants crossed the line to animation."

Dan suggested, "You might be smart if you quit now."

Jones looked aghast. "But my experiment has hardly begun! Think of what mankind may learn as a result of my researches! The whole course of civilization may be affected!"

"Yeah," Dan answered grimly. "That's what I'm afraid of. If this goes far enough, there won't be anybody left. Animals won't get no food except each other an' we won't have much except animals an' they won't last long. If the crops lie down or walk off an' can't be harvested, how're we gonna live?"

Green Jones looked thunderstruck. Dan could not help having a half-liking for him. He was obviously sincere, and evidently had meant well when he began his experiment. It was not wholly his fault that it had worked out differently from the way he expected.

"I didn't realize the change had gone as far as that." The botanist twirled his key, but his mind was elsewhere.

Dan stood up. "Jones, you're in a tough spot."

"Yes?"

"Van Schluys is pretty dumb an' so are a lot of the boys but sooner or later they're gonna start thinkin' like I did about why you were so tickled when he was tryin' to dig spuds. Or they'll pin you down on the map. God

help you when the boys come tearin' out here hell-bent for your hide.
You ruined their crops an' they'll tear you limb from limb."

For the first time, the botanist came all the way down to earth from
his remote dreams, speculations, and theories. His face paled a bit. "That
was a bad mistake on my part, I'll admit." The ghost of a smile hovered
in his expression. "Just the same, it was a sight for the gods to watch that
Dutchman pursue his fleeing potatoes."

"Take my advice and move out while you can," Dan said gruffly.

The botanist seemed unnerved. "As bad as all that? But I can't leave
my experiment unfinished!" he cried shakily. "Besides, how'll I get
away? My car's broken down."

"If your experiment's worth more'n your hide to you don't blame me
for what happens. But I guess this is official business, so I could use my
official car to drive you to the next town if you wanted to leave tonight."

Mr. Jones carefully, moodily, replaced the gold key in his pocket. He
seemed to be undergoing an inner struggle to make up his mind.

"Where is the machine?" Dan asked out of idle curiosity.

"Next room." The scientist's indecision and worry fell away. He
snapped erect. "I've got myself into a jam all right but it's too late for
regrets. I'll take your kind offer. If you'll give me an hour or two, say till
ten o'clock, to collect my data and a few belongings, I'll be ready to go."

"An' you'll turn off the rays?"

"Yes, I promise." His voice was eager, sincere. Dan knew men and
knew that Jones would keep his word.

"I'll be back at ten sharp. Better not let anyone else in."

Dan left, jubilant over the success of his visit. He had discovered and
he had eliminated the menace to Shawtuck County agriculture.

It was eerie driving through the woods. There was neither moon nor
wind. The stirless air lay like a cool and weary sleep over the aging
world; but the autumnal quiet that should have prevailed was missing.
There were great rustlings abroad, and dark movements among the
blacker masses of trees and crops, a continuous ghostly murmur issuing
from the shapes of things possessed. The entire landscape seemed
restlessly alive. There were voices without speakers, and slow creeping
without breeze or visible agency; and Dan felt the impact of dimly
remembered legends from childhood, about haunted woods and forests
where witches resided, the Druids of the trees, the gnomes, and the
Little People who lived under blades of grass and toadstools. It would be
strange indeed if somewhere in the long ago, Diemann's radiations had
been stronger when the world was younger, and all manner of growing
things had then owned powers of life and motion that declined through

the ages, leaving only ancestral memories for record until Jones brought back to nature its ancient gift. They were mysterious and disturbing activities that obsessed Dan as he drove toward town; and he was glad to leave behind him the soft and wailing wide whisper of inarticulate things, as the lights of the town drew near.

Back in his office, having firmly shut the door, Dan cocked his feet on the desk and smoked interminably. A small shaded lamp on the desk kept the room in semi-darkness. The air became stale and bluish with smoke. Through the half-curtained windows, he watched figures drift by; arguing farmers; worried old crones; harassed and hopeless and blank faces, strong ones and weak ones, some dull and others furious, all showing the paralysis, the demoralization that the revolt of nature had produced. Beset by events alien to their lives, they were unable to cope with them, much less understand them. The only refuge lay in herding together and trying the forced gayety of town, with plenty of potent drink, as an antidote; as if the courage of the individual might return through combined strength and association with his neighbors. It was a night of fights, altercations, and bitter argument, and rowdy choruses from Andy's store.

Dan folded his hands on his lap. He had no desire to mingle with them until his task was finished. Tonight would see the end of the strange harvest, and tomorrow he could worry about the crop reports to Washington. The day's work had been strenuous, for him. He dozed, being one of those fortunate mortals who can snatch a cat nap under almost any circumstances.

He could not have slept long. It was only just past nine when he blinked awake. He had a vague impression of some distant and receding roar, echoing through slumber to wakefulness; but all he now heard were the sounds of a few racing feet. The street outside his window was deserted.

Dan regarded the window and the empty sidewalk for perhaps a minute before a thought struck him with such force that he sent the chair spinning away as he crashed to his feet and pounded out.

The street was almost deserted. The tumult of less than an hour ago had subsided. A few broken windows, a picket-door hanging askew, some smashed bottles, and a couple of overturned kegs in front of Andy's store were the only remaining evidence of the crowd. The one person in sight was an old woman with infinitely wrinkled face and slow steps passing the Church.

Dan called, "Where's everybody?"

Old Mrs. Tompkins peered out of ancient eyes. "Eh? They all went out to the Jones place."

"What!"

"Lordamercy, you don't need to yell so. I ain't stone-daft yet. They're gone and much good may it do. Pieter was telling his story and I don't know who it was decided Jones could say a-plenty about these goings-on. I'm a religious woman, Dan, but I tell you if it's this Jones who's the cause of all this grief I'd—"

Whatever she thought was lost on Dan who jumped into his car and sped off toward the Jones farm.

Dan hoped to overtake the angry farmers. He didn't know exactly what he could say or do, but he thought they would at least listen to him. Dan sympathized with their feelings. They had been baffled, scared, and ruined by the perverse results of Jones's experiment. There was a certain justice to any punishment they might inflict on him. But Dan could see the scientist's side too; his passion for discovery in unknown fields; his willingness to experiment, whatever the cause; his primary purpose of aiding humanity and increasing the general good. The experiment had gotten beyond control. Vegetation given a new power, had responded in a far more willful and independent manner than Jones anticipated. He could scarcely be blamed for the curious developments which had occurred. He might have hoped to benefit mankind, but the character of Diemann's radiations had ruled otherwise and given the plant kingdom a new vitality that fought human control.

There were differences and changes in the farmlands through which Dan sped. He remembered well the Hanson grapevines, but they had somehow vanished, leaving only torn earth. And the Ritter chestnut grove—of which no trace remained, save deep furrows.

As Dan approached the Jones place, he felt a sudden tightness in his chest. A crowd of farmers surrounded the house, milling around.

Beam of flashlights and glow of lanterns cast flickering lights and shadows on alarmed faces. The surging mob seemed checked. Then, to Dan's amazement, they all suddenly broke and fled to their autos. They raced away, leaving Dan alone in the moonlight.

An ominous chill came over Dan as he stopped his car. A vast, dark mass, a writhing mound, engulfed the house. Dan got out and stood paralyzed for an instant. Forest trees and cultivated fruit trees, flowers and climbing vines, vegetables of countless variety, bushes and brambles and berries, representatives of all the plant life of Shawtuck County had converged here and overflowed Jones's place. And Dan heard an indescribable sound, a strange, eerie, inarticulate murmur of vegetation.

Now he heard other sounds, the sharp crack and tinkle of broken glass, the splintering of wood, and he knew that the windows and the very frame of the house were giving way. Suddenly there came a cry, a scream for help from within, and he barely recognized the voice of Green Jones. A great shudder convulsed the tangle surrounding the house. There was nothing familiar in the now loud, incessant, and threshing roar of vegetation; a weird tumult such as the wildest gale had never produced.

With unaccustomed agility, Dan leaped to the rear of his car. He habitually carried a variety of new farming aids that he demonstrated as part of his duties, products such as weed-killers, insecticides, fertilizers, and implements. Among these was a portable flame thrower designed for burning out infected fields and blighted trees that he had been showing off in recent weeks. He grabbed it and aimed the nozzle at the heaving mass. A burst of intense flame struck and clung to the tangled foliage of shrubbery and vines and trees. Briefly, then, a sad sound flared up, like a many-bodied, sub-human, voiceless thing crying for life.

Now a great rent appeared in the mass and even the front of the house began to burn. Dan shut off the stream of fire but carried the thrower with him as he ran inside the burning structure.

His bulk was unused to such exertion, but he gave a convulsive leap when he saw the dark branches and vines beating at the side windows of the parlor, and watched a pane smash. He hurled himself against the door to the next room with a force that burst it from its hinges. He looked at a dynamo that hummed a faint drone on the floor near the doorway, its brushes occasionally sparking, and connected with an object that occupied the whole center of the room. It looked like a huge metal box. Its plates glowed with a pulsing and ghostly radiance that shifted between soft silver and the crimson of fire. Near the ceiling above it and completing the circuit by thick cables that pierced the metallic concentration box to whatever mechanism lay within, hung a globe between anode and cathode. The globe swam with blinding mist, a purple, impalpable force that streamed out constantly and almost visibly in all directions. The giant globe had a sound all its own, a peculiar, intense whine, at the upper range of audibility.

The rear window to the room had been burst, and a flowing tide of plant growths had already enveloped part of the machine. Jones lay on the floor, evidently knocked unconscious when the mass burst in. For an instant Dan used the thrower again. The vegetation burned into ashes, and suddenly the huge globe melted with a violent flame of purple and red and silver streaked with blue.

Dan dragged Jones from the burning house. The night air became filled with one loud, prolonged, and mournful wail that faded into an inchoate murmur, an inarticulate whisper, then silence. Gone were the eerie voices and the purposive movements.

Only the crackle of flames and pungent smoke came from the dying house and the dead mass.

Harvesting of crops proceeded normally around Shawtuck Center the following day. The destruction of the machine had also destroyed the newly acquired powers of the plants and fruits and vegetables.

Dan often wondered about that last night. Had the growing things, impelled by some dawning intelligence, converged to destroy their creator, or to encompass and protect him and his machine? He never knew. While Dan watched the burning house, Green Jones must have regained consciousness. He had walked away down the lonely roads of night.

NIGHTMARE

THE NIGHT HAD grown gloomy, and the air moved with the moans of an arising storm, but blacker than that darkness and more sinister than the wind that arose from the west was the house that stood before him. He knew it was deserted and that for years it had been unoccupied—just as he knew that his journey's end lay in one of its rooms. He was alone, and the house waited malignantly; the moans of the wind arose ever higher, and a fearful apprehension steadily grew through the forest all around; the cypresses were shivering, and the sly shape peered malevolently from a corner of the house. The restlessness of terror stirred within the forest to the moaning of the wind, the low-flying clouds above, and the gloom that had become horribly alive.

He looked again at the black house. He knew not whether to enter or to pass on and return in the day. But there were no habitations in all that lonely and desolated realm, save the old house. What he sought lay within—with the guardian. And the sly shape was becoming bolder around the corner of the house, and the night grew ever more sinister as the wind changed its moaning to a louder tone that went rising to a howl. The night was black, and the forest—black the sky, the wind, and the old house itself.

Yet he walked through all that blackness to the house, for the treasure lay within, and the guardian might not be expecting him, unless the sly shape got back to warn the thing it served. He tried once or twice to catch the sly shape, but it ran back of the house and mocked him with a ghastly ghoulish tittering. He could not pursue it far, for the decayed one, and the innumerable fingers of pallid flesh, and all the other servants of the guardian were near. And so he left the sly shape and cautiously walked to the entrance of the house. The hinges of its door had long been rusted, together with the lock. Only a push was needed to open the door, but before giving it, he paused again to look around. The moaning of the wind came ever higher, and all had become so gloomy that he saw nothing save the oppressive darkness. As he pushed open the door and stepped through, he heard far away, above the sound of the wind, the distant howling of some animal. When he had passed the portal, it ceased abruptly. . . .

The hall he had entered was silent and dark. There met his glance when he flashed a light around him only the empty hall, with dust everywhere. But a head rolled from a door on the right, grinned at him for a moment, and rolled out of sight across the hall before he could fire at it. He knew now that the guardian would be warned, but he decided to go on since he had come thus far. Besides, if ever fear obtained the supremacy in his mind, he was lost; the servants of the guardian would pour upon him in a rush. And so he searched the hall again.

He saw then at the far end of the hall a stairway that began on the right, went up a few steps, and turned. He thought for a moment. The guardian was not likely to be on the ground floor because that was too accessible; he must go upstairs to seek the guardian and the treasure. He listened again. Somewhere in the rear of the house he heard a dull bumping for a few seconds; he thought it must be the head thudding up a rear stairway to warn its master. The wind was howling around the house but avoided entering it, so that all within was still.

He walked down the hall toward the stairway, glancing as he passed into the dark room from which the head had rolled. Innumerable burning eyes gazed covetously on him from within, and in mid-air a great clawing arm reached toward him out of the darkness. He walked on without looking back, though there came from behind the pattering of many steps. Oddly enough, the dust on the floor where the head had rolled remained unbroken.

When he reached the stairway, he immediately began the ascent. The moment his foot touched the first step, his mind became a lair of the blackest and most unutterable horror, a horror that crawled through his veins and filled his entire body. And at every step he took upward, the horror in his brain thickened and deepened hellishly. He knew then that the guardian was above, and waiting. But he had to pause a moment, for his legs had grown suddenly heavy when the horror came upon him; he gazed at his foot. A great, fat thing clung to one heel. He reached down to beat it off, but with incredible speed it leaped aside and fled. When it fled, the weight on his mind lessened a little and he began to climb again. But there seized him all at once the fancy that the entire upper floor was filled with corpses from some awful charnel, so that he must stumble through them all to reach the guardian. And ever, as he climbed, the horror grew and grew upon him.

But he staggered doggedly upward, trying to shut his mind to the intruders. He lifted his legs drearily and monotonously, until even this maddened him, and he rushed up the last few steps. He stood before an ancient oblong hall that had nine shut doors; behind one of them lay the treasure and the guardian. He knew not which was the right door, and hesitated a moment. But hesitation meant fear, and fear meant . . . He began to walk down the hall, past the doors on the left. But he had taken only the first step when there forced itself into his mind the thought that a wan *thing* kept pace with him in his rear. And at every step he took down the hall, his belief became more and more a knowledge that the wan *thing* followed him, and drew closer.

As he passed the first door, images of nameless things came pouring horde on horde into his mind; the guardian was aroused and all its legions were emptied into the corridors and chambers of the house. Phantoms wandered into his mind at will, nor could he stop them; the cohorts of death, pale and ghastly, thronged into his thoughts and would not leave, but ever increased; abominations of countless kinds arose in his vision so that he could see and think only of the loathsome servants of the guardian. The house which had been still became filled with sound, but the sounds all were terrible and indescribable—a faint, rushing patter as of rats running through the walls; a low gurgle like that of one who drowned; a dull pat . . . pat . . . pat . . . as if a great toad passed down the hall below; a sibilance, far away, that yet filled the hall with a husky whispering.

And always, as he walked on, the images came crowding thicker, and the sounds grew more unnatural, so that in his mind was the ever-changing course of the phantoms, in his ears the ceaseless sounds of all things damned. He knew that the wan *thing* behind followed closer and grew more bold; he knew that the sounds were beginning to wash in his mind in measure with the welling of the phantoms; he knew that the guardian in a desperate attempt to drive him back mad or afraid was calling in its servants from everywhere and sending them, except for those that kept watch over the treasure, to attack the invader, each in its own fiendish way.

As he passed the second door, he stumbled. He recovered himself quickly, but stumbled again. And though his brain was weakening under the strain that continually increased, he shook aside for a moment the black mists which thickened before his eyes and glanced at the floor. He leaped from his path and instantly was jumping and twisting from side to side in a frantic endeavour to evade those bloated things. There were not many at first and for a few seconds he avoided them. But they rose upon the floor with an awful rapidity; they rose like huge purple mushrooms, instantly, as if the very dust upon the floor quickened into life. They waited for him where they rose. For a time he avoided them and kept on, but they became so thick that when he was no more than half-way to the third door, he stepped on one. And though it sank under his foot, when he went on it remained fastened to his heel, growing fatly as if it fed. He stopped and in a kind of panic tried to shake it off. Almost instantaneously, the floor beneath him was crowded with the things which fastened to him like monstrous leeches. He battered and beat them, but they multiplied so rapidly that he stopped and staggered on.

And ever the horror grew upon him as he passed toward the third door, blotting out of his mind all save the occupants it brought. His feet dragged heavy and leaden; his mind tottered under a mighty blackness that throttled it and pressed it down; his entire body struggled against the attack of the massed legions of the guardian. And when he reached the third door, he knew that what he had sought so long was within; he knew that the treasure and the guardian awaited. For through the closed door emanated an utter malignance, an utter evil that swept upon him in a sea of hatred and malevolence until it seemed that about him surged a blackness of things nameless and indescribable that ravened for him, that filled the hall with innumerable gloating, low whispers. For one moment he stood before the door, as if in doubt; but the awful tide surged upon him, and all the servants of the guardian poured out in a last overwhelming rush. Then, with the bloated things on the floor creeping toward him, with the whispers rising into a husky mocking, with a horde of phantoms crowding rank on rank into his mind, with an unbearable darkness falling heavily upon him, and with the knowledge that the guardian and its greatest servants waited within, he hurled himself blindly forward and burst open—

The Door to the Room.

THE CRATER

I T WAS A land of many silences. He stood just inside the crater's rim and stared downhill toward that colossal, windowless tower of stone which thrust skyward from the pit of the crater.

He found himself wholly unable to recall the ways by which he had come to this singularly sad and depressing valley. He could not remember what lay beyond the crater's rim. He could not even recall what identity, what name, or what personal existence rightfully belonged to himself. Somewhere afar beyond the locked gates of memory lay a knowledge to which he could not return. Nor was it within his power to retrace his steps. Into the crater he must go, toward that vast tower, as in a dream, and drawn on by a compulsion whose force he could neither question nor resist.

Low in the west, he believed, sank the dying sun; there persisted in his thoughts a confused image of a monstrous, bloody-red sphere, like a great burning eye, that hung on the horizon; but he could not now see that sun, except by inference from the somber glow that filtered over the crater's edge. Yet no shadow lay within the slopes, neither from the surrounding rim, nor athwart the tower. The presence of light and the absence of shadow made him uneasy.

As he walked down the slope, he listened to the curious silences. There was a silence that should have been filled by the cry of a nighthawk; another silence that waited for the soft passing of a rabbit; and a silence for the wind to rustle across sand. But if life existed here, it was inarticulate: life that crept away into holes beyond the silences. The naked land seemed as though its poverty had never been able to afford the luxury of one shrivel of grass, or to nourish a tiny lizard. Nor did his progress create a breath of air in that lifeless hush.

The hands that built the tower must have belonged to an age of which no trace remained except the work itself, for nothing else within the crater suggested that it had ever been other than starved, sterile land. Beyond the bloody light about the crater's rim, beyond the lost provinces of memory, danced a tantalizing haze from whose tissue he tried again, hopelessly, to recapture any thread of identity.

He gave up the attempt at remembering while he studied this edifice to which he had been so irresistibly drawn. At its base lay a dark opening into which the dust and sand had drifted, and whose ruinous outlines made it impossible to determine whether a door had once barred entrance. He could not account for his failure to perceive the opening when he had stood at the crater's rim. He felt an impulse to turn and look again at that encircling ridge outlined in liver colored flame, but a stronger compulsion drew him into the tower. On the whole he felt grateful for a reprieve from terror; he had detected, above the eerie silences and beyond the crater, a labored thudding, a fitful, convulsive throb, as though an organ imbedded in alien ground discharged its waning life.

The darkness of the hall in which he found himself perturbed him. There was light, still smoky red, but so faint that he waited till his vision adjusted to it. He became gradually able to see better, but with an illusion that the crimson glow emanated from phosphorescence of his own body.

Down the short, dusty hall began the spiral of a circular staircase that ascended into the heights of the tower, mounting between the outer wall and the stone core. Toward his right lay the entrance to a room. Upon his left lay barren flagstones, the curve of the wall, and one gaping hole at the base where the wind or some animal had long ago burrowed. But he grew aware of the configurations with only dim perception, for his ears listened to a clacking that originated in the room to his right. A thin sound, and brittle, the dry clacking proceeded with a monotony as terrifying as it was austere.

While he watched the entrance to the room, a head rolled out and spun to the middle of the floor. It regarded him intently, with deliberate malice. The head gave him a shock of fright. However, it also gave him a faint suggestion of memory, of pseudo-recognition. He stared back at it while his mnemonic faculties surged, and subsided. The features looked familiar, but he could not think of a name.

The head rolled across the flagstones and over to the gaping hole, where it pierced him with a cold, baleful fixity before it twisted into its den.

He hurried along the hall to the spiral staircase. In passing the room to his right, he cast a furtive glance through the entrance from which the head had emerged. The same strangely bloody light of the invisible sun pervaded the room; but even without it, he would have seen that white audience, their backs toward him, whose clacking chatter appeared directed toward some lecturer beyond his range of sight. A blind horror of that speaker drove him on. He resisted the impulse to venture inside for a glimpse of whatever it was that addressed the throng of attentive skeletons. The dead audience, though the nearest members sat in part profile and must have sensed his presence, ignored him.

The spiral stairs, soaring into mysterious recesses above, gave him no measure of relief or escape. A vagrant thought came to him again and again, persistently telling him that the head sponsored a message which the pale listeners or the fateful lecturer stood ready to interpret.

Like his faint memories of some other world whose enigmas he could not fathom, the head, the skeletons, and the barren land receded into the oblivions of former time and prior experience. The immediate reality of his progress continued, as always, to form the crystal between a sifted past and a vague future.

Yet he found it hard to grasp the meaning of this reality which beset him. Its parts belonged to a coherent pattern, but the design could not be plain, or the meaning, until the lost reservoir of memory aided him. And memory began only with his standing on the inner edge of the crater; of all else that preceded he had but a dim awareness. As he climbed the steps, however, a doubt arose, dividing the haze and confusing him more. Outside the crater there must exist other heads, other skeletons, other towers and ominous suns and fantastic beings, which conformed to the same undeniable logic that attested to the truth of his immediate experiences, and through which he must have passed. But doubt assailed him because his memory did not extend beyond the crater's rim, so that, if only a blank lay out there, the tower and the white audience might be a distortion, a dream from which he could escape—to what far land? If the intense vividness of his climb was all a dream, and if the realm beyond the crater was all a blank, what logic or what wholly unimaginable reality could exist elsewhere?

There was no answer in memory. He kept on climbing the spiral stairs. Perhaps the top of the tower, which extended above the crater's rim, would give him understanding; perhaps a sight of the lands beyond the crater would yield knowledge, or at least open the way to recollection.

The circular steps wound endlessly upward, around the solid core. A silt of dust lay upon the stone, stairs and walls and ceiling. And here the baffling silences again prevailed: a silence for the drip of moisture that did not come; a silence for the clacking sounds that should have crept upward, however muted by distance, from the audience hall below; and, most puzzling by far, utter stillness in place of the echoes that should have marched with his progress. His footsteps made no sound upon the stone. He listened as he climbed, but neither the beating of his heart nor the least sigh of suspiration came to his ears. He listened only to silences that had nothing to occupy them.

It was a mysterious realm through which he mounted, a world with a logic all its own, but frightening because of its dreamlike strangeness, and its hint that beyond the crater lay some other world with a different system of values and symbols. He felt on the verge of making a discovery: that he was dreaming false dreams and would waken; or that he was living an incomprehensible life and would shortly sleep, to dream of more flexible worlds inhabited by more than heads.

The recession of the spiralling stairs below him must have raised him to a tremendous height, but he had no means of seeing himself in true perspective, for the solid core and the outward wall limited his vision to stone, that and the upward curve ahead. For a long time after, he continued his climb, with its monotonous sameness, amid the silences, and accompanied by ghostly light. Illumination of a strange sort moved onward with him: strange in that it died out to darkness at the turn of the stairs above and below, always, and cast no shadow before him or behind. The persisting absence of a shadow distressed him but he could not find a reason for his unease. There had been no shadows ever since he stood inside the rim of the crater. In time he tolerated the lack of a shadow to the same extent that he had accepted the existence of the great tower, the ambiguous head, and the white listeners. They were immediate realities which he had to believe in the absence of any other reality.

Thus he came at last to the top of this seemingly topless tower; and found a new perplexity that almost was disappointment. For here, also, not a window, not a door, not an opening of any kind broke the circular walls of the room in the tower's peak. Though he must by now be far above the rim of the crater, he still had no inkling of what lay beyond.

The contents of the room absorbed his attention. Twin caskets, hewn from stone, rested upon the floor. The lid of one was open, disclosing it to be empty; but from the other, closed and covered with the dust of ages, emerged a dull thumping like the beat of soft fists, and occasionally a thin, weak, mindless cry.

He walked over to the caskets. Whatever was imprisoned in the one to his right did nothing to indicate consciousness of his presence; the tiny thuds and faint cries continued with the same queer, tight logic of all that had happened to him from the moment when he entered the crater. But the sounds that filled the old silences troubled him further: only an idiot child, or a monster, or something of loathsome origin could have dwelt within the casket through the time-lapses that sifted dust so deep upon the cover. He did not try to find out what occupied the casket.

He did, however, turn slowly around when he became aware of being watched. In a semicircle facing him squatted many observers that stared at him with intently bright eyes and fat, pulsing throats: a frog throng, curious and waiting. Their mouths opened, and he listened for the shrill piping of the hylas, but heard only the muffled pounding from the closed casket. Yet he saw the pulses throb harder in those fat throats, and knew that the frogs were talking among themselves in a language to which his ears were not attuned.

The way downward through all the dizzily descending spiral of the gigantic tower, and off to the far rim of the crater, was a long one, a return not within the logic of the realm, even though the frogs permitted.

He turned again and settled himself in the open casket. The lid, closing, washed away the aura of pale light that had enveloped him. His last glimpse of the room showed the moist eyes of the frogs fixed upon him, with the pulses in their throats vibrating to a silent chorus of ecstasy.

In the casket he lay, like a cocoon, awaiting light and heat to emerge into another life; for he would never know what land lay beyond the crater.

THE DELIRIUM OF THE DEAD

IN THE TWENTY-SECOND year of my life, I met Claribel. For the first time in the dark record of my existence, I fell in love with a woman who was young and beautiful, and my days were happy. My life till then had been a gloomy record of hate and melancholy. I lived in the realm of my mind, and my mind was poisoned against the world. For years I walked alone, and I kept a bitter silence in my efforts to avoid the people I hated. I wandered in regions of surpassing beauty, regions which were never defiled by human voice or step, and where the gods dealt in millions of years instead of twenties.

But one day, I met Claribel. I had never before come down to earth. When I saw her, I first realized the existence of a visible world about me. I came out of the shadows of my strange inner realm and in my return to the world I saw objects as physical rather than phantasmal units. And I saw things because I saw Claribel, and seeing Claribel, my mind and its regions were a closed book.

I loved her. I loved her as I never desired anything in the world or out of the world. I loved her with a passion that ran the entire course of human emotion from the physical to the spiritual. I saw her as a material but hauntingly beautiful woman, a girl of soft and exquisite face. I saw her as the perfect and lovely embodiment of the beauty that was my ideal. I saw her as the glory of woman in all her terrible beauty when her face was transfused with the rapture of returned passion. I saw her as a woman and more than woman, as the incarnation of physical beauty and the expression of the unearthly beauty that transcends human grasp, the strange and mysterious beauty that I sought in my dreams. I was idolatrous. I came out of my isolation, and every barrier broke down before this fulfillment of my long-suppressed and long-unassuaged desire. In the burning rapture of finding the physical expression of every dream I had ever had, I forgot even the vestige of my former secretive and secluded life. I had Claribel. And Claribel was all I desired.

I was happy in those days that I knew Claribel, happier than I had ever been. The old record, of my life with its dark and stormy pages was shut, and I was almost content. As far as it would ever be possible for me, I was happy; I could not, like other people, be carefree; my life had been too bitter, and the hate that came of my brooding and morbid introspection had shaken my soul and poisoned my thoughts; but I was happy, and my days were pleasant in their rapid succession.

The spring and summer passed. I idled the days away with Claribel in long walks through the woods, or in drowsy indolence on the river bank during hot days; and in the evenings I made love to her, and stroked her silky hair, and held her lovely and feverish face in my hands, and caressed her soft cheeks and the lids of her strange and dreamy eyes. And we were happy. She too had seen things that the world does not know, and she sometimes whispered of those terrible sights and half-sights which I also had known in other years. But we whispered of these things only till we realized that the night was waning, and that we had each other. And then we would cease our dreaming in the joy of each other, she with rapture in her face, I with delirium in the possession of the one who made me of the world, the one whose beauty was unearthly and perfect enough to draw me from the realm of the unreal to the material world. But I forgot even the world when I was with Claribel, and time did not exist. There was splendor in my dreams for the first time; the fearful images that had possessed my mind gradually faded and gave way to beauty and the things of beauty.

And now I come to bitterness. Into my life entered again the old loneliness and the desolate dreams of before. I hesitate to continue the narrative of those appalling days; I hesitate to fill these pages with the later events of my life. Grief, and hate, and pain, world-weariness and morbid brooding were again my lot. And even I can scarcely recall certain events of the days when frenzy entered my soul and intolerable gloom settled over my spirits.

I loved Claribel, and all spring and summer we were happy.

And on the first dull and melancholy day of autumn, she died. She died of a strange malady that gave no warning and left no record. She died, in all her beauty and in all the glory of her youth. She died, with a smile on her lovely face, and ecstasy still in her mysterious eyes for me. She whispered sweet and dear things even as her eyes were closing. And when they closed forever, I was standing by her side, and swaying.

What time was it? The cold moonlight streamed in through the casement over the figure of one sleeping. A deathly pallor lay on all the white and silent room. And I was mumbling in my desolation and groping for something that was no longer mine. What was that strange white face on the bed? The hair streamed out in long dark waves over the pillow. What was that white pallor over all the room? But there was a whiter face on the bed, and the eyes were closed. What was the dead thing in the sky? Was it the moon, the blind eye of night? There were dead eyes on the bed, and darker night though all the room was ghastly in the pale moonlight. What was the cold silence outside? There was colder silence in the room, and a cold, still face on the bed. And far away, something was beating on the chambers of my brain and torturing my mind. What had happened? But there was a black pall that covered the cold moonlight, and I could not find my way. Over and over, the tolling of a terrible bell, over and over, the dreadful and regular tolling of doom, over and over, a horrible knell that drove me to frenzy. What was this throttling night, and the monotonous and fearful tolling, tolling, tolling of a bell? But there was a white face on the bed, and dark hair streamed over the pillow. And it was quiet. God! How quiet it was! And the moon made cold patterns of light and shadow on the floor and the walls and the bed. And there was a stranger pattern on the pillow.

What time was it? Days had passed, for the figure on the bed was gone. But there was a white moon in the sky, and I walked in a solemn place where many people sleep. Where was Claribel? She was mine, and I had lost her. And I had sunk by a bed with moonrays whitening the room and the still form of Claribel who slept the sleep of lilies, with her pure, white face set in the dark hair that streamed over the pillow. But they had taken her away, and she was mine no longer. What had they done with her? They had taken her to a narrower room, where she must lie forever lonely.

There was no time. The black years of my life stretched out interminably behind me in their long and endless array. And the black years of the future whirled out into infinitude in measureless aeons. And the black year of the present stretched on and on, laboring and slow and incessant, with the seconds dreadful centuries, and the minutes whole cycles, and the hours appalling records of eternity whose end never approached. And I lived on and on, aged and yet enduring longer and more insufferable epochs of my terrible existence. But the moon rode high, and I walked in a place where the people sleep and know not that they sleep. Was Claribel sleeping here? There was a name I found, and there was never another name of these syllable on the tongue of mortal.

And I had my Claribel, whom they had placed in a smaller room that stifled her.

What time was it? The moon, the blind eye of night, hung low in the west like a tired dead thing. The stars were pale. And then I leaned against a stone, and crossed my arms over my face, trembling, and shuddering, and babbling to the night, sick with horror as I remembered the tomb that I had violated and the body I had defiled. And I shook with the most racking pains and stumbled through the night, crazed and sobbing and vainly attempting to forget the shocking rites I had performed in the tomb of Claribel, performed on the body of her whom I had passionately loved in life, and whose love I carried to the grave.

I tossed all day trying to sleep, but my head and eyes were feverish, and I got no rest. Toward night, I dozed, but my sleep was a fearful thing where images of blasphemous and sacrilegious rites raised their obscene heads, a sleep where nightmare after nightmare stormed the chambers of my brain. I saw graveyards and graves opening up all around me and stretching away to illimitable horizons; I saw tombstones mounting like gigantic monoliths to the sky; and everywhere I saw the lovely face of Claribel, lovely in death as she was in life, and I saw other things that brought me wide-awake with my breath coming uneven and heavy while I vainly attempted to shut out the fearful images that streamed through my brain like a running corruption.

I stood by the tomb of Claribel, and the tomb was open. I looked at my hands, and my hands were soiled. And then the horror of the thing swept over me and I turned faint and sick under the dead moon as I realized what I had done. I shook as though my body were trembling in dissolution, I clawed at my face and eyes, I cursed with blasphemous curses the world that gave me birth, I thought of the body of Claribel lying torn and violated in the tomb, and my face set in a terrible mask but the bitter tears burned down my cheeks. Twice had I defiled the body of Claribel as she lay in death.

What time is it? The graves opened up all around me in long and endless array, the tombstones rear their vast white marble to the sky, the dead moon fills the entire heavens in one great blind white eye glaring on a chaos of yawning graves and tottering headstones, and everywhere in the white face of Claribel drifting in the air and on the ground and in the graves with her dark hair streaming out around her, and her body about me wherever I turn.

Christ! Christ! There is blood on the body of Claribel.

PROSE POEMS, ESSAYS, AND MARGINALIA

Introductory Note

The "prose poems" presented the editors with several problems while assembling this volume. The first question was whether they should be dealt with as fiction at all, or relegated to some hypothetical poetry or marginalia collection. Having decided to retain them for the sake of completeness, we then had to decide how to fit this material into the chronology. Several pieces were first published in *Minnesota Quarterly* while he was still a student, others remained unpublished until now. To keep with the chronological organization by publication date, there would have been a clump of prose poetry at the beginning of the book and a second at the end, even though most or all of this material had been written during roughly the same period. Alternately, we could have ignored the matter of dates entirely, and sprinkled them randomly through the collection.

To preserve the integrity of the structure, it was decided to separate this material and organize into its own section, first with the published pieces and then the unpublished. Many readers, Lovecraft included, have found these early, poetic pieces artistically superior to Wandrei's later, more "commercial" fiction. Others, who find the prose a little rich for their tastes, may not wish to attempt to read them all in one sitting.

After the unpublished prose poems, the section segues into a selection of early juvenalia, mostly written as school work. "The Phantom City," "The Kingdom of Dreams," and "Lotus and the Poppy" touch poignantly on the sense of isolation and alienation the young artist felt, and how he escaped it through the creation of a "kingdom of dreams," inspired by his own fantasies and the writings of kindred souls such as Arthur Machen, Clark Ashton Smith, and H. P. Lovecraft. These same writers, along with others such as H. G. Wells and F. Marion Crawford, form the subject of the final essay, "The Imaginative Element in Modern Literature."

One other oddity was included at the last minute: "Cigarette Characterization," which was originally published as one of several "cigarette characterizations" in the June 1934 issue of *Fantasy Magazine*—the same fanzine that published the famous round-robin story "The Challenge from Beyond" the following year. In this case, Wandrei and other writers, including Frank Belknap Long, Jack Williamson, and Arthur J. Burks, were asked to write, in their own literary style, a paragraph describing a lit cigarette. The paragraphs were published without the authors' bylines and the challenge for the readers was to guess who wrote which paragraph.

THE MESSENGERS

L
ONG HAVE I searched in Time and Space, but they are gone. And
long have I travelled to that land, but it is barren.

I had passed beyond the Western Portal, on that day of old, far, far
beyond, and now had come to a desert. Upon the horizon a dying sun
forever sank but set never, and its red rays crossed the forbidding sand
to illume the ruined fanes of a people who have vanished and are
forgotten. And standing there, I looked about. The dull and sombre sky
was watching them, and them, too, I watched as they travelled. They
came, I know not whence, and passed, I know not whither, phantoms that
thronged across the heaven mutely. None other eye but mine could see,
and none other know that they have come and gone. All day I watched
them pass, the Messengers. What wonders did I see! What splendour!
What fabulous riches in that silent-wending caravan! Perhaps they were
the offering of some ultra-stellar king, richer than the richest dream,
who wooed the stately, marmoreal queen of Polaris; or the spoils of an
interplanetary war raging unquenchable among the Titans of star and
star; or the tribute of a captive world sent to the conqueror across the
deep. Illumined by the rays of the westering sun, the envoys and their
burthen passed—richly figured tapestries, gold, and green, and purple,
stuffs woven by the velvet-fingered artisans of Aura; great jewels—emeralds, and rubies, and opals, and precious gems never known to man;
rare perfumes gathered from the flower that blooms only in the inacces-
sible vales of Aldebaran; strangely carven ebony; slaves, and queer
beasts, and indescribable priceless things from emperors and planets of
the remoter infinite. And their passing was like the richly figured tapestry, or like pageantry of the gods.

Often have I wandered in that desert; and often, now, I stand and wait.
But the fires of the dying sun have cooled and become ashen in the long
years that have passed, and the dusking skies brood darker. I wander

disconsolate in the ever shifting sands of the desert, while the ruined fanes are swallowed in the rapid-running sands of time, and the wind whispers lonely across the ancient desert, and the dunes creep and flow as I vainly wait.

For the Messengers have passed.

THE PURSUERS

IN THE BLOODY glow of sunset they came, all hideous in its red rays, while I cowered back watching them. Under the dying twilight in a rapid ghastly rush, they swept across the smouldering sky, fiendish with their alien, malefic hate. Beside them sped unleashed quivering things that sought the ancient trail of the Messengers. Prophetic was the portent of that silent passing in the dull, burning sky, a portent of cosmic evil sent abroad. In the fascination of fear, I watched the monsters rush by, monsters the tongue affords no terms to describe, beasts whose name would sicken horror, loathsome, loathly entities that tore adown the dim-felt trail in fury. And there were some I could not see, that could not be seen, but the air thickened where they travelled, and the shapes were indescribable. In trailing line they journeyed, but they journeyed on the wings of light, an avenging hurricane that stormed after the fugitives. Out of the depths of space they came, and into the darkling deep they rode. The air itself brooded at the phantom passing, and the immemorial desert waited, desolate, for the usurpers of the sky to vanish. But for long hours, the horrid throng hastened on its way, with malevolent faces ablaze and bloody under the bleeding sky. And through all those long hours, I watched the pursuers rush from the unknown and depart, threading the trail among the trackless stellar labyrinth beyond. The lurid eye of the sun stared at them from low upon the western horizon; in the dreary waste of desert and the smoking sky, all that moved was the horde which swept across the heavens.

They are gone, out of the glowing sky into rayless night, questing still the far, stately parade of the Messengers. The sun is lower on the dim horizon, and the empty vault is bleak. And now the cosmic drama is veiled forever.

THE WOMAN AT THE WINDOW

T HE SUN HAD bled for ages over that strange land; old and dying it was now, but still it bled, even as it swung down the final path of its history. The land had grown old with the aging sun; and now it too was exhausted and desolate where it stretched away for long distances under that lurid orb.

A tower rose from out the midst of the land, a tower old and crumbling, a tower of curious architecture and fantastic lines. No man knew when it had been built. It was born with the land, and with the land it was passing away. But it rose yet, in the middle of the red kingdom, and the sun as it sank each evening looked back for an instant on the castle, tall and ancient, that stood amidst the timeless realm. Sinister it was, as it rose, lone and terrible, in the ghastly rays of the sun; more sinister it was, in the utter desolation and solitude of the land wherein it lay; and yet more sinister it was, with its ruined walls crumbling, and its stones falling away, and the red sun coloring it with evil shadows in the day and dreadful shadows at twilight. In the dead night, the castle dreamed in darkness, for the seven moons of old had long ago disappeared into the black void of the starless sky. But at dawn, and during the day, and at twilight, the castle was a visible and evil landmark arising like a mute sentinel or an exiled ghoul out of the level lands around it that stretched far away. In ages, the land had known the touch of no feet. In aeons, not a creature, not a being had broken the silence. Never a step was heard on the sands that wasted away in the desert. Never a sound disturbed the solitude of that horrible realm. Only the castle rose, mute, ghastly, and eternal, bathed in the red of the one huge deathless sun; and its wall crumbled, and the grains fell, but it stood yet, infinitely old and weary.

There was one great window facing the west in the tower, a queerly shaped window with fantastic traceries and odd arabesques figuring its surface. There was none other in all the castle save this one grotesque opening that faced the west. It was a dim entrance to the unknown interior, an obscure and antique opening which alone gave ingress. Every night, the sun paused for a moment on the horizon, and its fixed, staring eye peered across the red waste to the castle that rose like a crimson horror. For a minute at twilight the blood sun paused, and the fantastic pane colored and smouldered and glowed with ineffable evil fires, and curious crimsons ran across its surface until it lighted up wildly as if the interior burst into spectral witch-fire. Dull red was the sky; crimson the sun; the land was old and of a reddish hue; and the castle itself a scarlet spectre at dawn, and a crimson sentinel at day, and a blood-red age-old fiend at twilight with its one red-illuminated window staring at the staring sun.

And when the window began to glow at twilight, and the scarlet rays swept across its surface and turned it into a sheet of blazing red, a strange transparency crept into it, and the window dripping intangible blood limned with a hellish indistinctness the face of a woman peering out. Her eyes were fixed on the motionless sun; in the minute at dusk when it halted, and all the strange land was a study in reds and shades of red, and the sky itself the color of liver and the realm livid with blood red rot in its length and breadth, the face became visible at the window while curious and exceptional rays left the sun and turned the window into fire. But no illumination ever reached the face of the woman who stared, and at the end of the twilight moment, when the crimson fire duskened on the pane, her countenance slowly disappeared into the mysterious and phantasmal gloom that filled the interior. For, even as the sun sent livid waves across the window, her face became visible, motionless and gazing into the west; but eternally dark and indistinguishable though the scarlet rays made efforts to illumine and outline it; and when the baffled sun retreated, the face of the woman at the window was reclaimed again by the guardian shadows that came from the remote recesses of the castle.

It had always been thus. In the youth of the crimson realm when the sun blazed in the bright red of its dawn, the castle had stood, and the woman had peered westward at twilight. In the maturity of the land, when darker colors had erased the orange reds of youth, her face appeared still at eve, unfathomable and shadowed and eternally staring at the spectral sun. And now, in the old age of the immemorial realm, when its cycle was running to its end and the reds were all dark as old blood save for a moment at sunset when the window burned with ruddy scarlet, her countenance still was outlined for a minute, symbol of a mystery that not even the worn out sun could solve. No one ever left the castle. No one ever entered. It was timeless as the realm, and changeless save for the slow corruption of age, and fixed as the many and singular shades of red that were a part of the land. And no one knew whether the woman ever left the window, for she was motionless when the twilight rays outlined her face and motionless when they retreated to the sun.

And now the lurid sun was approaching extinction, and the land no longer lay under hot and painful crimsons but slumbered with suffocating dull reds and dark blood-colors filling the heavens and oppressing the castle and the antique realms that stretched around it. And at twilight, the sun still labored with futile efforts to send its last livid rays into the castle, while the window smouldered and glowed redly. And even yet, the woman at the window became visible, peering with ceaseless and unfathomable scrutiny at the sun, eternally watching, eternally waiting. When the sun was near its final eclipse, her face was still behind the red window, staring westward. When Time lay heavy on the realm and elder prophecies of Doom were nearing fulfillment, her mysterious face even as long peered from the window. And when Night descended on the realm and obscured forever the castle and the window and the sun and all the curious and abominable and insane reds, the rays at twilight left the sun for the last time and colored the window once again with the last glow of that frightful color which dominated the entire land.

And the woman at the window was staring at the staring sun.

THE PURPLE LAND

IN THE MIDST of an immense and silent desert stood a tablet which was perpetually concealed by the purple shadows that dominated all the realm. Forever and forever the desert extended in all directions, yet found no change in the limitless expanse, not in the dead sands, nor in the level sweep, nor in the soundless quiet, nor even in the purple shadows themselves. In the day shown no star, and never a sun or a moon rose to break the enchanted spell; but always, the heavens had been luminously purple, and the stagnant air duskily velvet, and even the vast desert dark and purple like a tapestry under a purple dome. In the elder epochs of times past, the sky and the desert may have been violet; but the succession of years had watched a slow darkening of all the realms as if, like a great fading lamp, it approached extinction. Perhaps, too, in other years of the immemorial land, there had been eyes to watch its purple beauty; but now only one figure walked abroad.

He was swathed in purple robes like a spectre; his face was concealed in purple veils; when he walked, the folds of his robe streamed out behind him in long tatters. Once in great intervals, he came and stood beside the tablet and read it; for it was graven with runes and symbols of a mysterious, antique tongue, and told a strange tale of purple shadows; and there were many differences in the runes as if many different hands had inscribed the legend; and the symbols at the top were so faded and worn that they were scarcely legible. And when he had read this tale of memory, as silently as he came he turned and walked into the purple shadows until the streaming purple tatters of his robe were swallowed in the vast and soundless grave of night and the desert. And each time when he departed, there was one more symbol carven deep in the tablet, as if the history of anterior days were yet incompete, though the face of the tablet was now almost covered.

Then once the stranger walked out of the shadows with his tattered robe flying behind him and read the legend; though now the desert brooded in dark purples of corruption. And it seemed that the heavens and the air were suffocating of purple. And when he turned, he walked slowly and straightly into the immense purple shadows so that his robe did not billow; and far out in the oblivion of the shadows was swallowed. On the sands of the desert was no trace of his steps, nor did he ever return to read the legend.

And on the tablet, the symbols were complete.

DREAMING AWAY MY LIFE

D REAMING AWAY MY life in dreams of death and beauty, questing forever and questing forever vainly her whom I had loved and lost in the buried days of old, came I, on that lost moon, falling far beyond the utmost universe, to the valley where bloom the flowers of death. Then came I there, to that strange realm where passionless eternal flowers dream a passionless eternal dream of death. And lo, the flowers rise beside a silent pool of ebon waters dead. And lo, a stream flows by murmuring like forgetful Acheron. And when I came, the gloom was thick upon the valley, and all was still. But a faint wind had begun to lull the flowers with an eldritch whisper, and from the slow waters rose a low, lone chant. And the flowers in a voiceless antiphony swayed rhythmic: the eldritch wind played upon the flowers of death a dirge, and the dirge was like the cry of a damned thing lost or a lost thing damned, damned and lost through all eternity. And the dirge touched within me some forgotten chord, so that I trembled at the tones. And turning in blind despair, I passed from out the valley.

And as I went, I watched the pall that was the sky above, shifting blacknesses that changed from ebony to jet and pitch to sable, deepening and darkening until the firmament writhed in cosmic torment. For long hours, the skies brooded in their malice and their hate, while I wandered on and on before their sullen blackness should drop out of the deep above and smother me. Yet the towering gloom ever mounted, as if the masses gathered from all the heavens and all the ages; and the masses were hateful. But I wandered on throughout the desolate land. And I was accompanied only by the black skies. And when I had gone leagues and leagues, the skies began to move, and I shivered when I saw the great gulfs above flowing in turbulent motion; and the darkness did not fall, but like a running spatial sea hastened toward the horizon and poured nadir-ward as if into some colossal and stupendous gulf beyond. And the great

torrent of sable rushed with a rapid fury from the skies in a vast cataract
that curtained the whole horizon. The skies were uncovered, and the
door was open. And they began to smoulder until, at last, they were bare
and burning.

I went on, under the glare of that furnace. There was no object in the
sky, but the entire heavens were one flame, hot and dull. And the fires
bent down on the land I crossed. And the land was no longer desolate.
But everywhere under the glowing sky were hot things that rose, languorous and weary. And the flowers grew, tall and beautiful, but weary
under the flame; and the blooms were purple and crimson and orange,
and they exhaled poisonous perfumes that rose to the aching sky; but the
heat of the heavens descended, and the perfumes rose, and the hot
flowers swayed under the fire. There were no trees. There was no forest
vegetation. But the flowers grew along the way, tall, and hot, and tired.
And they looked up at me and sought relief for their suffering. But I had
no black to place upon the gold and purple and orange petals, and the
perfumes of the blooms arose, hot and evil like an exhalation of a poison
that was sweet and scorching. The rocks of that land were red, and
burning; the moss about their base was purple, and suffering; the flowers
everywhere were weary and beautiful. And yet I could not pick them; for
when I touched their petals, they were soft and warm, and the touch of
them made me sick, for it was like a lovely silken corruption whence
arose exhalations that overpowered. And yet I could scarcely remove my
hand from the blooms, for they were like the hot flesh of infants; and
when I caressed them, they clung to my palm; and when I tried to
withdraw, the heads of the flowers swayed and followed in my palm with
the sinister exhalations rising stronger until my hand was beyond their
reach; and then they swayed back, tall, and drooping, and frantic under
the hot sky. And there was flame above, and there was glare below. And
the rocks were molten; and the things that grew were purple and orange
and crimson; and the odors in the air were evil and corrupt and poisonous; and the pools along the wayside were stagnant; and the flowers
around them drank of the water but found no relief; and the pale growths
upon the surface of the pools basked in death under the burning sky, save
where livid lichens grew and sent up dank, poisonous odors. And death
was in the sky, and death was on the land; but the flowers lived, suffering
and hotly beautiful, and died not. They pleaded still, but I caressed them
no longer; for their voluptuous petals and colors and perfume drugged
my senses and brought up memories that I had buried. And so, I went on,
and looked no more upon the tall, languorous flowers; but they were
everywhere, weary and poisonous, lifting their feverish faces to the

burning sky. But the sky had no mercy, and I had pity for them and their soft, spoiled petals no longer.

Then the heavens died. There was neither glow nor fire above, and I could not see the land. But I vaguely kept on, seeking her whom I had lost, and seeking vainly. My steps were aimless, but the land itself was shrouded. And through the darkness I walked, while the heavens lay in their pall, and the air mourned. And there were things in the air mourning too; phantoms, pale and spectral, weeping; shadows that drifted away into the gloom. There were eyes, great, tearless eyes that turned toward the heavens; there were hands, folded in the obscurity; there were faces, faces of pale, fair women weeping in the gloom, lovely phantom faces drifting; and I sought and sought, but none was familiar; and I looked into them all. And they changed, and even as I looked, they were malicious and sinister; the faces were lovely and beautiful, but avaricious; and the eyes were gleaming, and the lips writhing, and the faces gloated. But I could not avoid them nor shut out their sight; and they came closer, with starved faces hungry and seeking. And they were all strange, and I knew them not; and I shrank from the lips that writhed over the gleaming teeth. And the wall of night encircled me with ring on ring of faces intermingled, blending together and separating again. And the innumerable wild faces were consumed with desire, and a savage hunger for flesh to fill the cruel, gaping mouths. And they drew closer in the darkness, and their eyes gleamed spectrally, and their taloned hands were outstretched, and a smile was on the starved lips. And I threw my arm over my head and ran through the night. And a demoniacal outburst of laughter swept from the furies, and they ringed me closer and closer till the burning eyes shone almost into mine, and the hot breath was on my face, and the cruel lips were close and triumphant, and the talons curved towards me. And then, in the midst of all the malevolent faces, I saw one, dim and shadowy, that saw me not, nor sought; nor was it turned towards me. But it was pale and beautiful, and it faded in the darkness. And I ran towards it and followed it, but, faint and far, it passed beyond my vision in the night. And when I looked around, there were no furies. But the night was strangely dead.

THE BLACK FLAME

TERRIBLE SHE STOOD, amid the spaceward pouring gulfs of monstrous flame, immingled with immensities of empty black; untouched and unconsumed with upward surging billows of incandescent splendor rising and rising all around; aloof, supreme, and remote with the awful radiance of abyssal flame in flow and refluence across her alien face; transcendent, with the rapture of flaming chaoses of infinity illuming all her dreadful beauty. And struggling, struggling, ever struggling from the ultimate pits of darkness onward, upward, and for ever toward the radiant goal, through gulf on gulf aeon on everlasting aeon, slowly, tortuously, with panting breath and limbs that fought the titans Time and Space, I rose from farther deeps unplumbed. Age after age, from cosmic darkness through rayless night, I fought my endless way, upheld by one desire, borne on by one aspiration, drawn by one glow, and yet that faint, far glow a universe all of fire and ebony surging in gulfs immense. And so, I came, after stupendous toil through epochs and epochs of time returning in recurrent cycles to her of the immortal loveliness and the terrible beauty in the shifting chorus and response of flame and blackness. But the radiance wherein she stood enshrined and untouched withered like a furious blast from furnaces infernal at my approach, and all my huge labor was in vain; and the gulfs in unison resolved together, flame to ebony and ebony to flame, flowing as one inseparable back to the choral cosmic harmony of dust and dreams. Vainly and vaguely I questioned; but, trembling out of immensity, echoing and reechoing across the now forever undisturbed domain, from realm to realm thrown on across the bleak and blank abyss, all strangely silent now and vacant, came the last bitter echo of a voiceless whisper: "Thou fool! The flame is black!"

THE SHRIEKING HOUSE

GHASTLY ROSE THAT long shriek under the black sky, a terrible sound that flayed my nerves so that I sought—vainly—to cover my ears. But ever the shriek rose louder to the black and silent sky.

"The house is shrieking," I said, turning to the passersby with a despairing gesture.

But they looked at me wildly, and their faces darkened with horror, and they covered up their eyes with their cowls, hastening by.

"The house is shrieking. Can't you hear it?" I said, and my voice was beseeching.

But their faces were fearsome as they hurried by.

And ever the shriek swelled to the dead sky, pouring from the house in one incessant sound that coursed through my brain with a horrible, torturing monotony. And I turned in despair to the street, but there were no passersby, and the street, and the house, and the sky were black, all black, and dead.

Then I knew that the house shrieked and shrieked for me alone, and I went up to that screaming horror and entered. In a moment I was running through the corridors, and with a frightened apprehension, I raced from garret to cellar of the shrieking house.

The house was quite empty.

THE PHANTOM CITY

I HAVE LIVED my life thus far in one of the best residential districts of St. Paul. A home a block to the north and west of the intersection of Summit and Lexington was my birthplace, and in it I have been brought up. With the exception of infrequent visits to relatives in Minnesota towns, I have never left the Twin Cities. My farthest visit was but to Round Prairie, slightly more than a hundred miles northwest of St. Paul; one was to a little town called Waupun just across the border in Wisconsin; the other five or six were to LeSeur, a village seventy miles to our southwest.

Under such conditions, it might be expected that I should make myself thoroughly acquainted with the city; it might be undoubted that I should wander through the streets, making myself at home in St. Paul and Minneapolis, exploring the numerous curiosities that, I am told, can be found. I have not done so. I never shall. Those mysteries and arcana may remain mysteries and arcana always, for all I care. If you enjoy walking through the city streets in all the ugliness of day, do so; if you like the wretched buildings of downtown St. Paul, and the wretched buildings and still more miserable streets of Minneapolis, enjoy them; if you like the hideous noises of automobiles, streetcars, factories, trains, school children, and numerous other things, the constant smells of smoke, gas, and gasoline, the sight of too many unpleasant objects to enumerate, and the beautiful Mississippi with a great variety of detestable things above it, on it, in it, and along it, take as much pleasure as you wish. To me, the Twin Cities are a pestilence on the weekdays, an abomination on Sundays, a limbo in summer and a nuisance in winter, during the day. But I shall always have for St. Paul the highest respect, for if it had been beautiful in my eyes, I might have been content with my lot; if it had offered me pleasure, I should not have created worlds of my own, and I should not have known St. Paul by night.

Years ago, in the spring, I was returning home one night along St. Anthony Avenue. It was after midnight, and the streets were completely deserted. All at once, why, I am not certain, I become aware that I was treading a strange city, one that was new to me. The air was damp, and a cool breeze blew from the south, fresh with a wetness that was singularly pleasant. Water dripped from every house; little streams gurgled in the streets; the air itself was filled with moisture. I had never known that dampness and cool wind could be as enjoyable, and because there was no one out at that time to intrude, I walked for hours in the silent pleasure, listening to the sounds of running water, feeling the damp wind on my face, thinking of the place in Givler's "Dream Flowers"

> Where cool, sad fountains sing
> With drowsy, charnel murmurings.

I had discovered that St. Paul at night was a phantom city, but one which was never the same. That first effect, I regret, cannot come again; but others have come, and St. Paul at night has gained the respect that St. Paul at day has lost.

There is another night that I remember, a night that lifted the city out of the commonplace and raised it to something far above materiality. One autumn, I was out late after darkness. The night was cool and frosty, with no wind. The streets were even more desolate than usual; there was no moon, and everything was still. The city seemed a great sepulchre, with dark house like coffins in the gloom. On Lexington Avenue, the lights burned clear, but no one was abroad. I have seldom known the city to be so quiet. I walked out toward Como road, alone the entire distance, in a stillness that was almost unbroken. Near the outskirts of the city, where there were no lights, the road was strangely dark, and the few houses, deeper shadows out on the walls of night, were almost hidden. Somewhere out on the Como road, I paused and stood for a long time. Little of St. Paul itself could be seen, but a dim glow from its many lights hung over a city that was brooding. The heavens themselves had a rare and unusual appearance that I can describe only as a thin duskiness. Symbols of all mystery, the pale, cold flame of the eternal stars shone frosty in the sky.

But the city was not always pleasant. Many times it had been depressing or even hostile. I remember another autumn night a year or two later, when the full moon was rising above the horizon as I went out. The streets were tomb-like and deathly under the moon, whose rays were neither white nor yellow, but pallid. The leaves had fallen from the trees in that dreary time of year, late autumn before the snow has come. Trees and houses stood gaunt, the tired sentinels of a phantom city. The cold moonlight lay white upon the ground, except when fell the dark and sombre shadows of intercepting things. Pale and sick burned the street lamps. I thought I must be treading the silent streets of some city desolated by an unknown catastrophe, or a world whose life had run its course at last. The houses on Dunlap Street were repellent; toward the city limits, the few old houses seemed empty, the cenotaphs of some forgotten race that had fled. The fields in the nearby country had long been reaped, so that even they were barren. In the sky, the stars shone wan, their flame dimmed by the full moon. And to the north and west and south, were the moon was weakest, an unearthly gray-blackness had come into the sky, a pall broken slightly in paces by faint stars.

THE KINGDOM OF DREAMS

I DO NOT know how I first came to create the Kingdom of Dreams. It may have suddenly flashed into existence sometime when I was feeling unusually disgusted with the world, or it may have had a gradual growth for years with no definite birth. However or whenever it originated, it had from then on an existence more real to me than the material life which forms the existence of most people. The happiest days I spent as a child were in the mythical Kingdom of Dreams.

My first excursions into it were, as I remember, tentative and exploratory, but they steadily became more and more deliberate, and of longer and longer duration, until my life was almost equally divided between a tiresome routine on a place called Earth and a timeless and spaceless wandering through the Kingdom of Dreams. I think my first introductions came externally from the many books I read, but as I became more and more familiar with the empire, I must have assumed the sway myself and moulded it to my own desires, for it was not long until I could enter it at will no matter where I was or what I was doing.

There was no limit to the emerald sea about the isle. It stretched on and on until it vanished, infinitely distant, in the azure horizon. A curtain of haze sometimes hung low upon the horizon, but there was nothing behind it save the ceaseless expanse of waters. My entrance to the Kingdom of Dreams was always by that sea. I found myself steering a boat with one great, white sail, a boat that scudded across the waves with a wild and eager swiftness. A fresh wind blew cool at my back and drove the boat always at that wild speed. The sea was sprinkled with foam; the waves washed rhythmically and filled the air with their eternal murmur, or they lapped softly on the boat when it dipped and skimmed onward, but the sea never became stormy. The scene itself was usually the same: the dome of the sky azure and clear except for a few high, fleecy clouds, the sea freshening under the breeze, and the boat scudding across the waves.

I invariably guided the boat to one spot, a small cove whose waters were crystal-clear and in whose depths grew frail corals amid strange sea-growths. I landed on a spot where the beach was soft and white, let the boat drift as it wished, and set out.

The Kingdom of Dreams was an enchanted isle set in foam-flecked seas of emerald, but an isle which I never completely explored because nothing ever showed itself twice to me. I could not find again the things I once had seen. Nothing existed in the Kingdom except that which was beautiful; but nothing whose pleasure has once been tasted can longer be beautiful, and so the realm was forever unexplored though I travelled there long hours. All that I saw became lost immediately, a fading memory before the new and unexperienced pleasures I found to take their place.

I remember one of the first—perhaps the first—of my wanderings. I found myself walking along a road paved with a smooth, black stone. Ahead, under the glare of a burning sun that was yet not uncomfortable, rose the spires and domes of a city that shone like molten brass. The air was still and hot; no sound save the musical hum of some insect broke the silence. I went up to a massive door that guarded the entrance to the city. No keeper was there, but none was needed, for at my approach the door separated in the middle and the halves slid into the walls with a brazen clang. When I had passed through, they flew together again with another metallic ring.

Quaint and curious houses, all joined together, lined the street down which I was passing. I entered none though they looked deserted. But the houses gradually became bigger and queerer until I was walking between oriental edifices crowned with spires and minarets. The rows ended, the street abruptly turned—and I found myself before a mighty palace all built of crystal and marble. I went up to the castle; the doors opened silently even as I approached, and I passed in without halting. The doors closed behind me. Instantly, two black leopards padded up to me from either side of the doors and took up their station with me. I walked down the marble floor of the hall with the sleek leopards, who crept a little ahead and to one side of me.

And then I began to explore the palace, led by the watchful leopards. For hours I wandered through its never-ending succession of halls, each filled with strange treasures; for hours I passed into room after room, regretting even as I passed that I could not linger; for hours I reveled in the hoards of the castle until I seemed to be watching a continually shifting pageant of the gods. There was a long hall filled with countless many-colored silken tapestries that rustled softly as I passed. There was a chamber fantastically wrought from one enormous emerald that blazed with its own secret fire; and in that chamber was naught save a teakwood chest filled with perfect stones from the heart of the jewel. Remote from all the rest I found a little, dark room that had upon a table of ebony a priceless flask of wine made by unknown hands long ago and left aging in this room ever since. I tasted it, and its very taste was pain for I knew that when I left, the room would be lost to me forever. And so I replaced the flask of blood-red wine that I might always recall with greater joy the pleasure I had not experienced. I found a hall of splashing colours wonderful, of gold and green and purple, of ruby, jet, and blue, that melted and blended in a restless prismatic splendour. And in an isolated crypt I came upon a nameless, fearful instrument playing the nameless, fearful anthem of Antares, a melody from which I fled, frantically trying to stop my ears, until I had fled the castle, fled the isle, and fled the sea.

LOTUS AND POPPY

I HAVE SPOKEN already of the Kingdom of Dreams, the result of my first excursions into the realm that I discovered long ago, so early in my life that I cannot remember its origin. My wanderings in it were the precursors of those that I later made in stranger realms and farther skies. It was the first of the magic empires that came under my sway, and though in time it bowed before greater creations, I shall always remember it as the primal of the domains that have been mine. Why these lands came into being, I do not know; their origin is now obscured, if there was a period when they did not exist. But I do know that they have been realities to me, and that I have spent in them more time than in this world.

My life has been one singularly aloof and removed from contact with other people. This withdrawal was not of my will, originally; the earlier years of my life passed in the usual fashion. But scarcely had I begun to attend school when, at the age of seven or eight, I was advanced a year ahead of the other pupils. This, coupled with the fact that I had entered school about a year sooner than is customary, took me away from the friends I knew and into a group which was foreign and remained so. It was in years older than myself, and regarded me not as an equal but as something of indeterminate status. I was out of my element and marked for that reason. And the neighborhood in which I lived was no different.

There are not many substitutes for playmates, but I tried whichever my mind discovered, and because I already had a liking for books, I soon found that I had in my hands the secret, the key to the unknown. Books had for me a fascination that other things did not possess; they contained all that I had not; they held within them mysteries that I longed to know; they opened the way to lands undiscovered and unexplored; they offered me the sceptre of Infinity, themselves my servants. And so, what seemed once a misfortune gave me what I should otherwise have lost.

There came, almost at this very time, an event that completed the change. What it was I shall not say, for I do not wish to recall it. But my life, which until then was divided between reading and living in the usual sense, became entirely mental, entirely in worlds I created myself, remote from human contact. I turned to imagination as I had never turned before, and lost myself deliberately across the border. At intervals I read and read for months with an unappeasable thirst; I delved into old and little-known volumes, as well as those more famous; I removed myself so completely that speech was of rare occurrence, and, when I did talk, was composed of a peculiar phraseology that resulted from taking the prose I read and attempting to make it conform with current slang and mannerisms.

At first, I could not, like Clark Ashton Smith, command:

Bow down: I am the emperor of dreams.

Imagination, when I first discovered it, was beyond my control and would not shape itself as I wished. It was years before I could say:

Surveyed
From this my throne, as from a central sun,
The pageantries of worlds and cycles pass;
Forgotten splendours dream by dream unfold,
Like tapestry, and vanish.

The realm I had entered with doubt and hesitancy was so overwhelming and transcendent that those early visions passed uncontrolled and for long uncontrollable.

There is a mighty music in a certain kind of prose; there are poems haunted by a wizard imagery; and this was the prose and poetry that I sought. I was not studying prose values, of course, nor did I then know that the greatest prose and poetry ever written was that completely removed from life in its ordinary physical forms, that which was timeless; it was instinctively that I rejected the most powerful literary myths. The authors I read were Poe, and Bierce, and Machen, Swinburne, Clark Ashton Smith, Park Barnitz, and Baudelaire, Thomson, Blake, Keats, Saltus, these and all such others that I could find. Their work was pure literature, prose and poetry in their highest and most enduring forms. I did not realize it then, but I did realize that their writings gave me an ineffable pleasure.

Arthur Machen has said that those who quest in Eternity will have done most of their dreaming before they are eighteen. I do not know. But

in my own earlier years dreaming was to me the breath of life and
something more than life, the realm of the mind my abode, and world-
making my occupation always. It was the books I read that fanned the
flame and sent me searching in farther heavens. The discovery of Poe
was the greatest literary event of my life; *The Hill of Dreams* for months
made the reading of other books wearisome; *The City of Dreadful Night,
Can Such Things Be, Shadows and Ideals, The Book of Jade,* these and a
handful of others were the volumes I admired. I began to dream, and to
dream on larger and greater scales until sometimes existence itself
became an unreality before what was to me reality.

Then, indeed, could I like Givler watch "The lamps of Eternity whiten
and die;" then could I mark "The systems vanish one by one;" then could
I listen to the song of the stars and the comets. My true domains passed
forever from those of actuality to those of romance: fabled Atlantis, and
Ultima Thule, and Avalon beyond the horizon. All portals were open
before me; all things were under my control. I listened to the murmuring
waters of Acheron, and drank of Lethe; I quested for the deathless
amaranth; I tasted the blood-red poppy and the lotus of oblivion; I sailed
on the shoreless and bottomless seas of Saturn; I plucked the death-
flowers of the moon; I watched the flaming many-colored suns of alien
skies in farther universes; I travelled down the disappearing path of
Time to epochs where Time itself was lost, to Futurity when the abyss at
last was dying; Eternity and Infinity lured me on to remoter lands and
greater conquests. But it was not until I found *Ebony and Crystal* that I
was satisfied, and not until I obtained *The Star-Treader* that I appreciated
the cosmic scale of my universe and roamed beyond even its outposts.

UNFORGOTTEN NIGHT

I REMEMBER HOW I tossed and rolled, unable to sleep, on that night long ago. I remember how the slow hours passed, bringing only a growing restlessness. I remember how my nervousness grew upon me, stronger and stronger, for I knew that I *must* go out. And I recall how late—late in that night I arose, dressed, and went out. Yet I do not know what I saw when I first left the lonely farmhouse; I do not know what I saw in the later hours of that strange walk. I remember but one scene, clear and ghastly, which has obliterated all else.

I had come to a pause on a short bridge that crossed a dark, stagnant pool. Behind me lay a narrow road, thick with the moon's pallor. On either side stretched a forest, still and fearful, a forest that was not solid but somewhat open near the road so that I looked into its depths and fancied I saw things move. But across the bridge, the entire country spread before me until its low hills faded into the night. There were no trees on the other side of the pond, but only grass or occasional bushes among the rocks and boulders strewn through it. I glanced up once—and once only. A huge wan moon was creeping across the sky, casting a deathliness on all it touched. A few haggard wisps of cloud hung motionless and leprous in the air. To the south the heavens were dimly and darkly luminous, but to the north they were completely empty with a sinister, a malignant blackness. The stars were shining coldly, but their whiteness intensified the ebon horror of the skies.

Nothing lived in all that utter solitude. There came no sound from the forest; no murmur rose from the dead waters beneath; a maddening and appalling silence crouched upon the land. And the stealthy silence seemed only to deepen when the low and rhythmic cadence of my steps again fell upon the road.

SANTON MERLIN

S ANTON MERLIN WAS the epitome of a master of the black arts. In
Amenti, he could have superseded Thoth, for he had the wisdom
of thirty centuries added to the knowledge and accumulated lore
that made Thoth the god of magic. Had he ever turned loose the ancient
and long-forgotten forces over which he had gained control, had he ever
evoked them from astrology, necromancy, and the kabalistic rituals by his
own secret incantations, there would have come again to earth, but in
reality, what Breghuel the Elder engraved centuries ago. All the saintly
would have been blotted out, and all that was pure defiled in a perpetual
sabbat.

He was tall and slim, of an extreme and almost deathly pallor; but his
unnatural paleness was subordinate and accentuating to his eyes.

The man himself, and all his soul and mind were enclosed in those
eyes. They were larger than is usual, but deep-set and surrounded by
dark rings, the rings not of dissipation, but of profound research in a field
which has been neglected for hundreds of years. They were strange and
haunting eyes, and they had properties of a kind I have never found
elsewhere. I have watched them for half an hour, and only seen a white
face with two dark circles; and I have then seen them begin to glow and
melt until they gleamed blackly liquid, hinting of mysterious rites and
forbidden knowledge. It was as if he had been thinking of sorcery,
became aware that he was watched, opened up his eyes in a blaze of hate
to lay some hypnotic spell upon the intruder, and then, contemptuous of
wasting his time on a minor subject, had withdrawn again into his mind.
Yet it did not seem that he dropped his lids, but that his eyes possessed
some extraordinary power by which they could at times let through the
light of the mind, and at others shut up Santon Merlin within himself.

His hair was thick and so dark as to appear almost black; it was
neither combed nor unkempt, but shoved back as if from running

his hands through it while absorbed in some rare Latin work on demonology.

Neither his lips nor any other part of his face stood out. To be sure, you knew in a vague way that his forehead was high and pale, that his lips were thin and had a sardonic droop, but these were noticed only inasmuch as they intensified the overwhelming supremacy of his eyes.

His very presence suggested the nature of his studies. When he entered a room, something heavy and blighting seemed to creep in with him, an effluence of utter and transcendent evil. Before a beholder knew anything about Santon Merlin, there arose in his mind thoughts of witchcraft, the occult sciences, and outlawed rites in secret places. In a violated crypt, with a brazier before him lighting up hieroglyphs and symbols marked on the floor, with a yellowed manuscript between his hands, and with his eyes burning feverishly while he murmured an incantation, he could have taken the place of the Prince of Darkness.

On his left hand, setting off his long and tapering white fingers, he wore the one stone that was adequate, a ring set with a great emerald. Like Santon Merlin, it was dull and lustreless under an unfavourable light; but in the proper environment the jewel glazed into flame as mysterious and sinister as he who possessed it.

CIGARETTE CHARACTERIZATION

THE DEAD WHITENESS of that evil cylinder, with its tip glowing and dying and reddening again, might have been rationalized on the basis that after all, it was merely a cigarette being smoked; but it hung in the midair, and he suddenly realized, as it began to creep toward him, that there was no one else in the tomb, and no possible way for anything else to be there, unless it had lived there all these centuries that the lair of the worm had been sealed.

THE IMAGINATIVE ELEMENT IN MODERN LITERATURE

F**ANTASTIC AND WEIRD** literature will always be with us; it will exist through Eternity, or until, millions of years in the far distant future, the world is a dead world plunging madly, coldly, lifelessly through the black reaches of space, until the human race has passed into shadowy oblivion and dust Why are we here? Where did we come from? Whither are we going? What created life? What happens after we die? What are the secrets of Time, and Space, and Matter, Life, and the Universe? These are questions that the mind of man, groping blindly in all-enshrouding gloom, has sought always to pierce. And so long as they remain unanswered, so long will the fantastic and supernatural in literature exist, a means of partially satisfying the craving desire that cannot be appeased as yet by the light of knowledge.

Tales of things beyond our understanding have thus always existed. They may be traced back through the centuries to the witchcraft and magic of the Middles Ages, to the delusions of ignorance in the Dark Ages, and to the myths come down from eras so old that they are forgotten, save for the distorted myths themselves.

You can imagine our precursors in the dawn of time, even, speeding fearfully through the dank gloom of hot jungles that reared their strange and giant growths from slimy, steaming pools and swamps; you can imagine those beings, dimly afraid of the unseen forces even then, fleeing through the forests from the imaginary terrors surrounding them. In that long dead day the childish minds of the first men were already peopling the darkness with phantoms and unknown things even as the child of today is frightened at the same terrors of night.

There are, in general, three main types of imaginative literature: the simple ghost story, the horror story, and the pseudo-scientific romance.

Each of these types has evolved along definite lines, and each places limitations and restrictions on the writer. The ghost story should be fairly short, usually under 10,000 words in length. It is too apt to be tedious if longer, and usually cannot be developed properly if it is too short, i.e., under 3,000 words in length. The horror story, likewise, should be short, and ought never to exceed 5,000 words. Horror is a quality that depends in effectiveness on brevity, on gripping the reader in a rapidly rising intensity of terror that reaches its apex quickly, and on leaving an indelible image with him by the cessation of the story immediately after the climax; the shorter the story, therefore, the better, and the more effective the impression. The pseudo-scientific romance, however, usually demands book-length. So much explanation is needed both to lend an air of realism and to inform the reader of the working of unfamiliar machines and apparatus that a short story will not suffice. Then, too, a series of impressions and incidents generally occurs in this type. The writer of such a story, therefore, has fewer restrictions, and much greater leeway, than the authors of the other two.

These are the main divisions, although they may, of course be subdivided into more exact groups—a fact that is especially true of the last type, due to the fact that science has no limits, and applies to everything. In the following paragraphs, therefore, I shall discuss each type in turn.

The ghost story is the simplest and oldest type of imaginative literature. It is the oldest, for it may be traced back to the biblical account of Saul's visit to the Witch of Endor, an account that Byron once said was the best ghost story every written. It is the simplest because it entails none of the involved technicalities of the pseudo-scientific romance, and none of the careful, delicate structure of the horror story. Artists like Blackwood, however, sometimes combine the two, as in "The Empty House." Mr. Crawford has done the same thing in "The Dead Smile."

Ghosts have, until recent years, been the main-stays of weird literature. From the first crude fragments of long-dead centuries to the more finished tales of Hawthorne, Irving, Bulwer-Lytton, and the Brontës, the ghost story has held possession of the imaginative field, with the exception of Poe's experiments in madness and horror.

Ghosts were conventional; hence, ghost stories have always enjoyed a tremendous vogue. Countless tales of this type were written, thus, in past years; but in spite of the competition of past centuries, the best supernatural tales belong to the first twenty-four years of the twentieth century.

Can anyone ever forget Ambrose Bierce's "The Damned Thing," or indeed, his *Can Such Things Be?* He was not appreciated in his own time, but he is now getting the attention he should have gotten while alive. Mary E. Wilkins-Freeman, however, met with no such arbitrary fate; *The Wind in the Rosebush*, in spite of its five horrific illustrations, was a deservedly popular book. Mr. Crawford's *Wandering Ghosts* was likewise acclaimed with joy upon its appearance, and "The Upper Berth" has taken rank as one of the great ghost stories, in fact, one of the most gripping tales of horror, that has ever been written.

More recently, Algernon Blackwood, master of the occult, has taken place as one of the best authors of the supernatural. Every short story and novel that he has written since the appearance of *The Empty House* in 1906 deals with some phase of the invisible world: *John Silence, The Listener, The Lost Valley, Incredible Adventures, The Wolves of God*, and others.

E. F. Benson, however, is the latest writer to investigate the unknown. *Visible and Invisible* appeared five or six months ago, but it contains three stories, "And the Dead Spake," "The Horror-Horn," and "Negotium Perambulans," that are already taking place as masterpieces. I give this book the highest recommendation to those who delight in the supernatural.

I know of no one able to read who has not enjoyed a tale of the invisible realm. The question of what comes after death is so intimately and basically connected with everything permeated with the strange, intangible substance called "life" that everyone is interested in stories which have for their theme life after death. Most people seem to have a great fear and horror of death as the absolute cessation of existence in any and all forms. I believe that many people devour ghost stories, and even believe in spirits, because they want to be, nay, ask and beg to be, convinced that there *is* a life after this existence ceases. Terror and madness would probably be the lot of countless thousands were it proved beyond all possible doubt that when a person dies, he *dies*, physically and spiritually, always and forever.

But enough of spirits.

A horror story is a much more delicate piece of artistry than the ghost for two reasons: first, the impressions must be arranged carefully in a steady movement toward a searing climax, that reaches its peak only in the last paragraph, or sometimes in the last three; second, a reader does not, for his own sake, want to be too strongly impressed with terror; hence, the writer must cope with antagonism from the start, must build so cleverly that in spite of himself the reader is swept along in fascination. A good horror story, for these reasons, is a much scarcer, but much more meritorious, thing than a ghost yarn. It is perhaps for this reason that few writers have attempted the problem in recent years.

Mr. Crawford's "The Upper Berth," however, may aptly fall in this category; it is a gripping, terrible narrative that will never entirely erase itself from the memory of one who has read it. Up to the time I read Mr. H. P. Lovecraft's awful tales of horror and madness, "The Upper Berth" was the one tale that impressed me most. I shall never forget it, but neither shall I ever forget the prose—a prose that verges sometimes on poetry—of Mr. Lovecraft. "The Rats in the Walls" is a work of such gripping horror that when the climax is reached your fingernails are gone. You may try to forget it; yes, you *may* try, and you may *try.* You may have an easier task with "Hypnos," "The White Ape," "The Hound," "The Picture in the House," or "Dagon," but you will never entirely forget any of them. They must be read in their entirety to be appreciated, however, for they are so carefully planned in rising waves of terror that a selection would be ineffective. They are tales that strike at the roots of sanity, but they are tales of a master-hand.

The third and last class of weird literature is one that has grown to a considerable extent only in recent years. There had been no incentive for the pseudo-scientific romance up to the middle of the nineteenth century. Then the immense strides science was taking, however, began to pen a new field for those interested in the progress of the race, and Jules Verne stepped forth as the first scientific "dreamer," a dreamer, though, whose "fancies" have already become over seventy-five percent true, according to a recent article in *Science and Invention.*

In the opening years of this century another writer, who at first was a scientist, leaped into international fame by the production of a series of brilliant scientific fantasies and romances. I refer to Mr. H. G. Wells and his *The Food of the Gods, The Invisible Man, The First Men in the Moon, The War of the Worlds, Thirty Strange Stories, Twelve Stories and a Dream, Tales of Space and Time, The Time Machine, When the Sleeper Wakes,* and *The Island of Dr. Moreau.* If anyone wishes to read a description of the world thirty million years hence, a description that is the most impressively sombre I have ever read, I recommend *The Time Machine,* and more especially the chapter entitled "The Further Vision." There are other passages in the same book that have a rare beauty, a fascination of almost painful intensity. The one person in literature whom I most admire and worship is Mr. H. G. Wells.

Other recent writers have turned out scientific fantasies, some of which are really enduring. Ray Cummings has given us *Around the Universe*; Abraham Merrit *The Moon Pool* and *The Metal Monster*; Garrett P. Serviss, the famous astronomer, *The Conquest of Mars* and *A Columbus of Space*; and Milo Hastings, *The City of Endless Night*. Some of these writers have looked far into the future, and some not so far, but all of them, in seeking to pierce the veil have written works that are not for us to judge, but rather they of the coming centuries.

For some reason or other, there seems to be a strange dearth of imaginative poetry at present. Very few poets seem inclined to touch a subject that offers a limitless field for theme and mode of expression. However, I have recently obtained a copy of a limited edition, *Ebony and Crystal*, by a California poet, Clark Ashton Smith. It is not an attractive volume, for it has detestable red covers and a poor binding, but, oh! the gems that lie within!

There is a fantastic beauty, an exotic strangeness in all his poetry; a wild and morbid strain of madness, horror, and nightmare imagery riots through the lines in unearthly fascination. It is with an almost quivering sense of ecstasy that you read the weird poetry of Clark Ashton Smith.

OF DONALD WANDREI,
AUGUST DERLETH, AND
H.P. LOVECRAFT

In *The Penguin Encyclopedia of Horror & The Supernatural* there is an interesting, but also strangely curious entry on Donald Wandrei. After a half page of text detailing Wandrei's importance to the field, contributor Don Herron ends his essay with the following paragraph:

> Today Wandrei occasionally sends out a limited state broadside of a new poem, and iconoclastic letter-essays that denounce many of the organized forces behind the modern fantasy movement—a movement he, as a founder of Arkham House, was instrumental in setting in motion. In 1984 the World Fantasy Convention conferred on Wandrei a Life Achievement Award, which he declined.

For most of those involved in the field of fantastic literature during the 1970s and 1980s, that very nearly sums up the career of Donald Wandrei. Soon after his death in 1987 *Studies in Weird Fiction* released a special Donald Wandrei edition. Included in this were essays by Dennis Rickard, S.T. Joshi, Marc Michaud, Steve Behrends, and T.E.D. Klein. A piece by Don Herron, too lengthy for inclusion in that issue, was published later. While all of the articles were tributes to Wandrei, most also shared a common trait. Specifically, they tended to call attention, not just to Wandrei's work in the field, but also to his efforts as a litigator and pamphleteer. Klein, for instance, writes about the subterfuge he had employed to gain entrance into Wandrei's house and then describes his host as "periodically throwing back his head and screeching, crowing, with triumphant laughter, talking about things 'falling into place' . . ." Hardly an attractive depiction of one of the founders of the modern fantasy movement. Even the more flattering portraits produced by

Michaud, Rickard and Herron couldn't seem to avoid at least some discussion of Donald's litigations or such events as the Necronomicon Press/Collected Letters hoax of 1977.

To one reading those essays, and others like them, the implication was obvious: Donald Wandrei, a youth of unlimited potential, had become, in his declining years, a paranoid crank. This image, once established in people's minds, was hard to shake. Especially when those active in the field were continually bombarded with stories that seemed to bear this out: reports of Wandrei's latest missive condemning the organizers of the World Fantasy Convention, tales of mail from Clark Ashton Smith laying unopened in the Wandrei living room for twenty years, details of conspiracies so unrelated as to appear delusional.

Indeed, there was some level of truth to this image. Before meeting Wandrei for the first time, this author was heavily coached by mutual friend John Koblas in what *not* to say in his presence. Arkham House was forbidden, as was H.P. Lovecraft, Kirby McCauley, and a number of others. The list seemed endless. Unfortunately, in a wide-ranging conversation—and those with Donald Wandrei tended to be just that—such lists are bound to be incomplete. Thus, during this meeting, the author committed a *faux pas* of sorts by mentioning Gerry de la Ree. After a brief rant, mainly centering on booksellers who mail stick-on labels to authors in order to reap a higher profit from collectors, the conversation returned to normal and all was right with the world.

This is mentioned here for a reason, for much of Wandrei's later reputation was based on exaggeration and hearsay. One of the publishers of this book, for instance, knew Donald Wandrei for nearly a dozen years but never asked him to sign a book because of his alleged hard-feelings towards Arkham House. Only after Don's death did he learn that Wandrei had no aversion whatsoever to signing books, provided, that is, that they were for personal, rather than resale purposes. So it was with the list of "things not to mention." It wasn't that Donald Wandrei minded talking about H.P. Lovecraft, Arkham House, or his brother Howard, it was just that he refused to be questioned and preferred to speak on such subjects only when he chose to. Nor was this reticence a product of senility or old age. Rather, it was a trait that was lifelong, an outgrowth of Wandrei's secretive nature.

In dealing with the bigger picture—Wandrei vs. Arkham House, his feud with the World Fantasy Convention, etc.—the situation is, or at least was, a bit more cloudy. Only now, years after Donald Wandrei's death, with many of his papers in institutions where they are available to researchers, can some sense finally be made of the last two decades of his life, and of his role in the publishing house that he helped to form.

For the first part of this journey we will rely on the narrative of Donald Wandrei himself. Produced as an affidavit during his lawsuit with Arkham House, the following is both one of the briefest and one of the most detailed descriptions of Wandrei's personal and business relationships with H.P. Lovecraft and August Derleth ever produced. It is published here, in an only slightly abbreviated version, for the first time.

❖ ❖ ❖

My first direct communication with H. P. Lovecraft of Providence, R.I., came in a letter from him addressed to me and dated December 12, 1926, in reply to an inquiry by me. I had become an ardent admirer of Lovecraft's stories, for their outstanding literary distinction, as they were being published in the magazine *Weird Tales*. In a 1926 issue, the magazine published a letter from Lovecraft highly praising the fantastic poetry of Clark Ashton Smith in a book titled *Ebony and Crystal*. I could find no record of this book or author at the St. Paul Public Library; and the St. Paul Book & Stationery could find no listing in any book index or catalogue. I then wrote to the editor of *Weird Tales*, inclosing a letter to be forwarded to H. P. Lovecraft, asking the name of the publisher and price of the Smith book. Lovecraft's letter to me was in reply to this request. His letter was of equal literary status with his stories, and gave me Clark Ashton Smith's address in Auburn, California. I immediately wrote to Smith, inclosing payment, and received a reply and the book, which enthralled me fully as much as Lovecraft's stories. A lifelong correspondence and friendship with both authors developed; and I still retain the complete correspondence of both H. P. Lovecraft and Clark Ashton Smith to me, in the original envelopes, intact with postmarks and postage stamps.

I had begun selling work of my own to *Weird Tales*, first a story "The Red Brain," then a group of poems published over a year's time under the running head: *Sonnets of the Midnight Hours*. I decided to hitch-hike my way east in the summer of 1927, to meet the editor of *Weird Tales*, Farnsworth Wright, in his Chicago office, and to get firsthand information of book publishing in New York. When I wrote of my plans to Lovecraft, he invited me to visit him in Providence, and gave me the names of his friends in New York where he had previously lived in 1924 to 1926. A full account of my stay with Lovecraft is given in my memoir, *Lovecraft in Providence*, published in *The Shuttered Room and Other*

Pieces, by H. P. Lovecraft and Divers Hands, Arkham House, Sauk City, Wisconsin, 1959. In New York I met and established lasting friendships with the members of what Lovecraft called his "old gang": James F. Morton, Samuel Loveman, Frank Belknap Long, Everett McNeill, George Kirk, H.C. Koenig, Vrest Orton, Reinhardt Kleiner, Seabury Quinn, Wildred B. Talman, and Arthur B. Leeds.

During the two weeks that I stayed in the roomy old house in Providence, R.I., where Lovecraft lived with his aunts Mrs. A.E. Gamwell-Phillips and Mrs. Edith Clark, Lovecraft took me on numerous walking tours of Providence locales and antiquities, and on excursion trips to Salem, Boston, and Marblehead. Frank Belknap Long and his parents, Dr. and Mrs. Frank B. Long, also arrived on a vacation trip to New England, and another visitor was James F. Morton. Still another visitor was W. Paul Cook, printer-publisher-author who had already published under his imprint, *The Recluse Press,* Samuel Loveman's long poem *The Hermaphrodite,* and Frank Belknap Long's collection of poems, *A Man From Genoa.* After reading new poems of my own that I had been writing during my stay at Lovecraft's house, Cook offered to publish a book of my own poems, which came from his Recluse Press the following year, 1928, under the title *Ecstasy.* Lovecraft also told me he was corresponding with a gifted young author named August Derleth from my neighboring state of Wisconsin, in Sauk City, and that I ought to correspond with or meet young Derleth. Lovecraft showed me two new tales he had written in longhand, "Pickman's Model" and "The Horror at Red Hook," but that he dreaded the job of typing them. I offered to take these tales back to St. Paul with me and type them for him free of charge. He agreed, and I later in the year made the typed copies and both stories were then sold and published in *Weird Tales.* On my return trip to St. Paul, I again stopped in Chicago to see Farnsworth Wright, where I gave him a glowing account of my stay with Lovecraft, and told him of the two new Lovecraft stories that I would be typing.

After my return to St. Paul, I received a letter from August W. Derleth dated October 11, 1927, in which Derleth referred to his corresponding with Lovecraft, and his varied interests as a student at the University of Wisconsin in Madison. The letter was so full of literary flavor that I replied, and another lifelong correspondence and friendship developed. I still retain the entire correspondence from Derleth to his death in 1971, intact and in the original envelopes with postmarks and postage stamps.

In 1928 I graduated from the University of Minnesota and returned to New York where, with the good offices of Vrest Orton, I obtained a job as advertising manager for the book publishing firm of E. P. Dutton & Co.

The fiction editor of the firm was Martin Yewdale, with whom I had frequent contact, and I tried to interest Yewdale and Dutton in publishing a book of Lovecraft's stories, but my efforts met with failure. Yewdale insisted there was little book market for a collection of short stories, even less for a book of horror-fantasy tales, and none at all for fiction from "the pulps," a term used in the publishing trade for newsstand magazines like *Weird Tales* that were printed on a coarse grade of woodpulp paper as distinguished from "the slicks," a term used to describe magazines like *The Saturday Evening Post* which were printed on a higher grade of paper with a smooth coated or glazed surface.

During the year-end holidays of 1928, Lovecraft came to New York and stayed at the Longs' spacious apartment on West End Avenue. I renewed friendship at gatherings of the Lovecraft "old gang" at the Longs, at Samuel Loveman's apartment in Brooklyn, and saw Loveman's even more extensive than Lovecraft's accumulation of watercolors, pen drawings, and small stone sculptures by Clark Ashton Smith. I accompanied Lovecraft and Kleiner on a visit to Everett McNeill's quarters, and went on long walking tours of Lovecraft's favorite old sections of New York, with Kirk, Kleiner, Long, and Leeds, and with Lovecraft and Long to museums and to the Poe cottage at Fordham. Lovecraft told me that Cook had finished printing the sheets of Lovecraft's tale, *The Shunned House*, for what was to have been Lovecraft's first book publication from Cook's Recluse Press at Athol, Massachusetts, but that Cook's wife had suffered a nervous breakdown, the printed sheets were folded but not bound, and that it might be necessary for Cook to move away from Athol because of his wife's poor health. I told Lovecraft to persuade Cook to leave the sheets of *The Shunned House* for storage and safekeeping with Lovecraft in Providence, until Cook had permanent new quarters and could resume printing and publishing.

For personal reasons, I resigned my job at Dutton's in the summer of 1929 and returned to St. Paul to do postgraduate work at the University of Minnesota towards a Ph.D. While in New York, I had made friends with an author named T. Everett Harré. Harré told me he had been offered a job editing a new magazine to be called *Mystic Magazine,* with Fawcett Publications, headquartered at Robbinsdale, Minnesota, a suburb of Minneapolis, but that he had turned it down. Harré told me to try for the job myself, and wrote me an introduction to the managing editor of all the Fawcett Publications. In September, 1929, I went to the Fawcett offices in Robbinsdale, and looked at layouts and dummy of the new *Mystic Magazine,* but it was obviously intended as a rival of MacFadden

Publications *Ghost Stories* for which Harré was writing in New York. I declined the job of editor, but said I had a young author friend named Derleth in Wisconsin whom I thought would be ideally suited for the job. Derleth had already published several supernatural tales in *Weird Tales* and was in touch with the best authors. Fawcett's asked me to notify Derleth for an interview if he would come to Minneapolis, and I promptly wrote to Derleth at Sauk City. The very next day August Derleth presented himself at the Wandrei residence at 1152 Portland Ave., St Paul, the first time we had met. I gave Derleth details on how to get to the Fawcett offices in Robbinsdale, he returned to the waiting car of the friend who had driven him to St. Paul, and proceeded at once to Robbinsdale where he immediately accepted the job editing *Mystic Magazine*. Derleth returned to Sauk City for clothing and personal belongings, then came back to Minneapolis, and rented living quarters.

August Derleth edited *Mystic Magazine* from October, 1929, to March, 1931. He not only edited it, but often told me with relish that he also wrote many of the articles in each issue under different pen names, thus more than doubling his income. He was a frequent and welcome guest at our house, invited to every party, and guest of honor at our family Thanksgiving dinner in November, 1929, where he enjoyed the first turkey he had ever been served. He met all of my friends, and was always regarded more as a family member than a visitor.

By 1931, the Great Depression had become so serious that magazines and entire publishing companies went into bankruptcy. It was evident that *Mystic Magazine* would cease publication, and rather than wait the inevitable day, Derleth resigned his job and returned to Sauk City in March, 1931.

Before Derleth left, I told him of my intention to see what I could do about reproducing some of my brother Howard's fantastic pen-and-ink drawings in color, in book form. Derleth of course knew Howard at our house, and had seen some of Howard's drawings that I had had framed, and which hung on our walls. These drawings of a nightmare world in intricate detail were like nothing ever before seen in the history of art. Derleth agreed such a project ought to be tried. In the past, I had read stacks and been a page boy at the St. Paul Public Library in 1923–1924, and had watched the binding and stamping of covers of hurt books in the bindery room. In 1928, four fellow students and I had gotten together and published a book called *Broken Mirrors,* with woodcut illustrations laid in, during our senior year at the University of Minnesota.[1] My father, A. C. Wandrei, an attorney, had given up his private law practice for a position as classification editor at the West Publishing Co., law book publishers of St. Paul. On occasional visits to his office, I had become acquainted with the printing operations, since the firm had its own printing presses and bindery in the same building, including the use of pure gold-leaf for letter-stamping of book covers. In 1931 I took a large drawing in color and some smaller, simpler, and earlier black-and-white drawings of my brother to the Webb Publishing Company, a big general publisher also in St. Paul. The officials there said they had no equipment that could reproduce Howard's large drawing in full, and that any reduction would only produce blurred masses instead of fine detail. They suggested I might try the George Banta Printing Company of Menasha, Wisconsin, but this was too distant for my purposes. The smaller drawings could be reproduced, however, with some reduction, by line-cuts that would not blur or fuzz on a short run. I then chose five of Howard's drawings, wrote poems that fitted the mood of each drawing, rounded out the work with additional poems, and the result was *Dark Odyssey*, a book of poems by Donald Wandrei with five drawings by Howard Wandrei, published by the Webb Publishing Company in 1931, a copy of which went on to Derleth.

In 1932, I abandoned all thought of completing my work for a Ph.D. There were no academic jobs anywhere. The Great Depression was at its worst. I returned to New York, and got a job doing publicity-promotion of new technological processes for Lockhart International. I was also selling stories to *Weird Tales* and a new magazine *Astounding Stories*, put out by Clayton Publications. Clayton, however, went into bankruptcy, but the title and ownership of *Astounding* was bought by Street & Smith Publications, who resumed publication of it in 1933, and whose editors wrote me asking for new stories. In the autumn of 1932 I went to Providence again and spent a week with Lovecraft. He had become discouraged and was doing little writing, for Wright of *Weird Tales* with incredibly bad judgment had been rejecting his stories.

Wright rejected two of Lovecraft's Longest stories, *At the Mountains of Madness* and *The Shadow Out of Time*, which I read in typescript and considered not only among the best Lovecraft ever wrote, but among the greatest tales of supernatural horror ever written by any author, including Poe. Lovecraft also told me that Cook had left Athol and moved twice in search of quiet surroundings for his invalid wife, and that the printed sheets of *The Shunned House* had been boxed and left with Lovecraft for storage.

When Street & Smith wrote me in 1933 about their ownership of *Astounding Stories* and resumed publication of it, I went to their offices and met the new editors, F. Orlin Tremaine and Desmond Hall. Thereafter I regularly sold science-fiction tales of mine to *Astounding,* and detective stories to *Clues Detective,* another Street & Smith magazine also edited by Tremaine and Hall, as well as mystery stories to *Black Mask* owned by the Field & Stream Publishing Co., and *Argosy* of Munsey Publications. In the spring of 1933 I received a letter from Clark Ashton Smith informing me that a young friend of his, Helen Sully, was coming to New York on a vacation tour, and asking me to be her host and guide. I wrote at once that I would gladly do so, and when Helen Sully reached New York, I entertained her at parties at my studio apartment, introduced her to Frank Belknap Long at whose apartment she was also a welcome guest, and to other available members of Lovecraft's "old gang," including Samuel Loveman. We took her to museums and on sight-seeing tours. I was fascinated by her descriptions of Clark Ashton Smith and his surroundings in Auburn, California, and determined to save money for a trip to California to meet Smith. From New York, Helen Sully went to Providence, where Lovecraft was her host, and she thus became the first person ever to have direct, personal friendship with both Lovecraft and Smith. Thereafter she maintained a steady correspondence with Lovecraft, and like Derleth, Long, me, and many others, retained all her letters from Lovecraft. At the year-end holidays of 1933, Lovecraft again visited New York, staying with his friends, the Long family. In a party for Lovecraft at my own studio at 84 Horatio St., I set up my camera and tripod and showed one of my other guests, Dorothy Chamberlain, how to take a picture of Lovecraft, Long, and me. This photo I later furnished to Derleth, who reproduced it in *Thirty Years of Arkham House,* published by Arkham House in 1970.

In the spring of 1934 I returned to St Paul, and made my first visit to Sauk City, with my mother, on a morel-hunting trip. The hospitality of the Derleths who made room for us in their house was unrivalled. My mother and Mrs. Derleth became immediate friends. On field trips to the woods and hills, my mother and I showed August where and how to find morels during their season of May, and at the Derleth house my mother showed Mrs. Derleth how to cook and serve them. From that time on, August arranged his writing schedule every year so as to leave the month of May free for him to spend all available time in the woods gathering fresh morels, and preserving the excess by drying on long strings of carpet thread needled through the hollow stems of the morels, a technique that my parents had invented and which we had demonstrated to August. Later in 1934, my brother, Howard, told me he intended moving to New York, and asked me to find an apartment suitable for us both.[2] Several years previously he felt he had developed the fantastic and intricate genius of his large pen-and-ink drawings in color as far as he could, and had then developed to a fine art the ancient oriental technique of making batiks, a process employing a tool called a tjan-ting used with dyes and hot waxes to create paintings on silk. Howard invented an electrical Tjan-ting that enabled him to control the design outline from pen-point delicacy to quarter-inch width. He had also begun selling fantastic stories and detective tales to *Weird Tales, Detective Fiction Weekly,* and *Astounding Stories,* but under various pen-names because of editors' fears that two different Wandrei names would confuse readers. Before returning to New York, I took a train to Auburn, California in the autumn of 1934 and spent a week with Clark Ashton Smith, thus becoming the second of the only two individuals ever to have in-person friendship with both Lovecraft and Smith.[3] Smith's aged parents were still living, in the old hillside house outside of Auburn; and with Smith I visited the Sullys, Helen and her widowed mother, in Auburn, and on an outing we all took snapshots which are still in my files. I then returned to New York by sea, on the *Pennsylvania* of the Panama-Pacific Line. In New York I found an apartment large enough for both Howard and me at 155 West 10th St. I notified Howard, who then came to New York and we shared the apartment through the following year, both of us writing stories for the magazine markets.

One day in the summer of 1935, when I brought a new story of mine to Tremaine, he asked me if I had a science-fiction novel that would break into three installments to run in three consecutive issues of *Astounding.* He said he urgently needed such a novel, that he had the space open but nothing to fill it. I told him I had no work of such length, but had recently read two new and outstanding short novels by Lovecraft. Tremaine asked me if I would write to Lovecraft and find out if these were still available. I wrote such a letter the same day, but I was afraid Lovecraft might not send me the stories if I told him my full intentions; and I merely said I was anxious to read the tales again, and had a new friend who also wanted to read them. Lovecraft sent me the two typescripts, "At the Mountains of Madness" and "The Shadow Out of Time," by return mail, and I promptly took them to Tremaine's office. So urgent was his need, with *Astounding* ready to go to press, that he merely asked me if the longest of the two, "Mountains," which was just the right length to break into three installments, had enough basic science to qualify; and on my assurance that both tales had solid science behind them, Tremaine wrote out payment vouchers for both stories without even reading them. He asked if the checks should be made out to me, so that I could deduct an agent's fee, but I refused. I said I was acting solely as a friend, had no intention of ever being an agent, and instructed him to mail the full checks directly to Lovecraft. This was done, and so swiftly that Lovecraft was amazed to receive payments for the two stories a day before my letter of explanation reached him. He replied asking me if he should send me an agent's fee for my efforts, but again I refused, and wrote back that I had simply acted as a friend, and because I wanted to see the two novels in print where I could read them again and again. This was a completely unauthorized and unorthodox method of handling literary property, but I succeeded because of my continuing friendship with both Lovecraft and Tremaine.[4] The checks were a windfall of $700 or $800 for Lovecraft, and enabled him to fulfill a lifetime's dream of visiting and exploring historic colonial sites in Charleston, South Carolina, and then proceeding to Dunedin, Florida, to spend the winter months with R. H. Barlow and his parents who had a distant kinship of 6th or 7th cousins to Lovecraft. On this extended vacation, Lovecraft used my apartment at 155 West 10th St. as his temporary headquarters in N.Y., occupying the spare room and having his mail forwarded in my care, both on his way to Charleston, and on his return from Dunedin. My brother had married Constance Colestock and the two then had their own apartment. In a party that Howard and Connie had for Lovecraft, he saw many of Howard's pen-and-ink drawings, and thereafter in letters to various correspondences referred to Howard as the greatest genius of fantastic art that the world had produced.[5] Excerpts from these letters are included in the forthcoming Vol. V of Lovecraft's *Selected Letters,* of which Arkham House has already published Vols. I, II, and III.

In 1937 I was on a visit to St. Paul when my brother Howard wrote me of Lovecraft's death. I sent a letter to Derleth immediately, and suggested that we put together an omnibus collection of Lovecraft's stories and try to find a publisher. Derleth had also received word of Lovecraft's death from Howard, and wrote me the same suggestion, our letters crossing in transit in the mail. I then wrote to Derleth suggesting that we also start obtaining and copying all possible Lovecraft letters, that it was my conviction that Lovecraft's fame would ultimately rest fully as much on his letters as on his tales, that I regard Lovecraft as probably the greatest of all letterwriters in English-American literature, and that to my direct knowledge Derleth, Howard, I, Frank B. Long, Clark Ashton Smith, Helen Sully, and Lovecraft's two aunts, Mrs. Clark and Mrs. Phillips-Gamwell, both of whom I had known during my visits with Lovecraft in Providence, had all retained every letter ever received from Lovecraft, and very likely many or most of his other correspondents had preserved their Lovecraft letters. Derleth agreed, and asked me to notify all of my own correspondents and Lovecraft friends of our double project. This I did. Lovecraft had named R. H. Barlow as his literary executor, and we secured from Barlow written authorization for us to publish and copyright Lovecraft tales, letters, poems, etc. Lovecraft had also given specific authorization to six persons to use all story ideas in his notebooks, and to use all his Cthulhu mythology, these six individuals including Clark Ashton Smith, Frank B. Long, Derleth, and me. I myself, however, have never made any use whatsoever of this prerogative.

In 1938 and 1939, Derleth made two trips to New York, at which times he was entertained by Howard and Connie at their apartment, and met such members of Lovecraft's "old gang" as were still available, including Long and Loveman. I accompanied Derleth to the offices of Scribners, book publishers, where we talked with Bill Weber of their editorial staff. Weber told us that Scribners decided to reject the Lovecraft omnibus, which we had titled *The Outsider,* for the same reasons as Duttons ten years earlier. I accompanied Derleth to Providence, where we visited Mrs. Gamwell at Lovecraft's residence. Barlow had already removed the majority of Lovecraft's literary effects, including his notebooks, complete file of *Weird Tales,* and the fantasy books of his library, as well as the still unbound sheets of *The Shunned House.* There still remained, however, a residue of Lovecraft's early writings on astronomy, other juvenilia, and related memorabilia. We told Mrs. Gamwell that we had already begun depositing Lovecraft material in the John Hay Library of Brown University in Providence, including all files of Lovecraft letters that the correspondents who owned them agreed to deposit and did not wish returned after they were copied by us. Mrs. Gamwell agreed to let us deposit the residue with the John Hay Library, which we did. We went to the John Hay Library and talked with the librarian, and made certain the Library would welcome the continuing deposit of Lovecraft material.

After the Scribners rejection, *The Outsider* was rejected by Simon & Schuster. Derleth's account of our efforts appears on pages 1–4 in his preface to *Thirty Years of Arkham House,* published by Arkham House, 1970. When he wrote me of his idea of publishing the book ourselves, I went to Sauk City and we discussed it in detail. We needed a name, and I suggested various combinations of parts of our last names, like "Der-Wan" and "Wan-Der," but these had little appeal to us. We then thought of using something from Lovecraft's own Cthulhu mythology, including "Cthulhu," but the name was too awkward. We then tried finding a place name in Lovecraft's stories, and we both simultaneously seized upon

"Arkham," and added "House" just because we liked the sound and appearance of "Arkham House." Several years later, Derleth had the brilliant idea of adding an insignia or emblem, and this he did in the form of the little haunted house design which thereafter became the trademark of supremacy among books of fantasy. We discussed whether to have the new firm operate from St. Paul or Sauk City, but agreed on Sauk City because Derleth had started to build a house with much larger space than the Wandrei premises in St. Paul. I was familiar with printing and publishing companies in St. Paul, but remembered the high rating given by the officials of Webb Publishing to the George Banta Printing Co. of Menasha, Wisc. Derleth and I drove to Menasha and toured the Banta plant, explained our project, and thus Arkham House was born with publication of *The Outsider and Others,* by H. P. Lovecraft, collected and Copyrighted by August Derleth and Donald Wandrei, in 1939. We had stationery printed with the firm's letterhead: ARKHAM HOUSE, Directors August Derleth and Donald Wandrei, and some of Derleth's letters to me in the years 1939 through 1945 are written on this letterhead. I told Derleth that if the new firm succeeded, it was my hope to find living quarters in Sauk City and do my writing and the Lovecraft editing there.

From 1939 through 1941 I was in St. Paul, with occasional trips to Sauk City where I watched Derleth's house being built. The Nazi-Hitler invasions of Poland, France, and Russia made military service inevitable, and I was inducted into the Army in March, 1942. Since my future was uncertain, I told Derleth to keep all profits from *The Outsider,* from a second Lovecraft omnibus, *Beyond the Wall of Sleep,* which we were preparing, and from any further Lovecraft collections or selections, including the Lovecraft letters, entirely either to pay typing costs for copying the letters, or to finance other Lovecraft volumes, or to insure the continuity of Arkham House. My father died at Thanksgiving in 1942, when I was stationed at Camp Adair, Oregon, and I received an emergency furlough home. I also, in 1943, managed to receive a long week-end pass that enabled me to travel to Auburn, California, and visit Clark Ashton Smith; and in late 1943 received a regular furlough that enabled me to include Sauk City and Derleth. He told me *The Outsider* was out of print, and I immediately shipped him the 80 remaining copies of 100 I had originally bought, and these he used to fill orders as long as they lasted.

In 1944, I had been transferred to Camp Shelby, Mississippi, and my unit was being prepared for overseas duty. I had another furlough home, but stopped first at Sauk City, and Derleth told me to put together a collection of my stories for Arkham House. This I managed to do, and got *The Eye and the Finger* to him for 1944 publication. I told him that in the event of my becoming a war casualty, he should retain all royalties on *The Eye and the Finger* and continue the Lovecraft projects and Arkham House as exclusively his.

My unit, the 65th Infantry Division, was sent to France in December, 1944, assigned to General Patton's 3rd Army, and entered combat through southeast Germany into Austria where we met the advancing Russians at the river town of Schmieding. In November, 1945, my unit was returned to the U.S. and I received my discharge papers and Honorable Certificate.

When I returned to St. Paul, I found that my brother, Howard, and his wife, Connie, had separated, and they were subsequently legally divorced. I made several trips to Sauk City in 1946 and 1947, and in 1947 Derleth and I thought it wise to obtain an assignment of copyright to us jointly from *Weird Tales* for all Lovecraft stories which had been published in various issues of that magazine. This was done. In 1947–1949 I was again in New York, writing for National Comics Magazines, after a chance street encounter with an old friend of my earlier science-fiction years in New York, Mort Weisinger, who had become the general editor of some eight or ten of the firm's publications.

Early in 1950, my mother underwent major surgery, and I returned to St. Paul. My mother recovered, and in November, 1950, I drove to Sauk City first to see Derleth, then drove west to Auburn, where I again saw Clark Ashton Smith and took him to Thanksgiving dinner, and then went on to Los Angeles. I maintained an extensive correspondence with my brother Howard who was then in St. Paul, and retained all of his letters a major portion of which are now being edited for Arkham House publication.[6] In February, 1952, Howard joined me in Los Angeles, for a ten day stay in my apartment, after which we drove to Texas, Mexico, and back to St. Paul. In the summer of 1952, Howard and I both went to New York, where I took some of his art work to the Museum of Modern Art in an effort to interest the officials in his pre-eminence as an artist, but again met with failure.

At the end of 1952, my brother, Howard, my mother, and my sister all were hospitalized at the same time with catastrophic illnesses or surgery or both. Eventually, all three returned to the house, and I was able to go to Sauk City. Derleth and I then drove to Baraboo, to the law offices of the older Judge Hill,[7] where we signed an agreement, witnessed and notarized, covering the Lovecraft copyrights and giving to the survivor the full ownership of the copyrights.

Derleth had made a second visit to St. Paul in 1947, staying as a guest at our house. He asked for a novel by me, and I revised an old and unfinished work which was published by Arkham House as *The Web of Easter Island* in 1948. Derleth also reminded Howard that he had asked Howard in 1944 for a collection of Howard's stories but had never received anything but a list of possible titles. That was the last time Derleth saw Howard, for Howard was hospitalized again with another massive breakdown in August, 1956, and died, in early September.[8]

August Derleth made another trip to St. Paul in 1957, giving a series of lectures at the University of Minnesota, and he was again a guest of our house during the week of his stay, as was his driver, Alice Conger, who was also a long-time friend of mine from my many and often prolonged visits to Sauk City. I told August I still hoped to transfer my writing-working-publishing to Sauk City, but could not say when, in view of my mother's and sister's declining health, and the fact that Howard's will had named me has his executor, and I was still in the midst of sorting his lifetime accumulation of notebooks, diaries, files, magazines-of-publication, and other literary and art works.

❖ ❖ ❖

Why Wandrei chose to end his affidavit in 1957 is unclear. It is also unfortunate, in that a continuation may have answered a number of questions and shed some light on the direction that his later life was to take. Without such a document, one is left to piece the facts together from correspondence, reminiscences of friends, and legal documents related to his lawsuit. Before such a task is begun, however, there is a need to elaborate somewhat upon Wandrei's own statement, and his role in the operations of Arkham House prior to the death of August Derleth.

As the affidavit and other documents make clear, Wandrei was intimately involved in Arkham House prior to his induction into the Army. Aside from the initial set-up, this involvement was primarily centered upon H.P. Lovecraft, his manuscripts, and Lovecraft letters sent to Wandrei and Derleth by correspondents, most of which were then painstakingly retyped by Wandrei. After 1942, Wandrei's involvement was much diminished until at least 1956. During this period Donald was often far away from the upper mid-west, in New York, California, or the military. When he was home in Minnesota, however, he often travelled to Wisconsin by bus or car to visit his partner and assist in whatever way he could.

When Howard Wandrei passed away on September 9, 1956, Donald Wandrei found another reason to reinvolve himself in the affairs of Arkham House. Derleth had previously announced a collection of Howard Wandrei stories entitled *Orson Is Here*. Now, Donald envisioned an expanded schedule for his brother's work that would include Howard's correspondence with Derleth, as well as an expanded version of *Orson Is Here*, to be entitled *Time Burial*. Little, if anything, was done on either project until 1959 when Donald, reeling from his older brother David's sudden death from cancer, began work in earnest.[9] Indeed, the 1960s saw a tremendous expansion in Wandrei's involvement with Arkham House. His own books, *Poems for Midnight* (1964) and *Strange Harvest* (1965) were published, complete with Howard Wandrei artwork. Donald also took an active role in the preparation of future books by old friends Clark Ashton Smith, Frank Belknap Long, and Carl Jacobi. Likewise, the first volumes of H.P. Lovecraft's *Selected Letters*, which Wandrei had begun compiling as early as 1937, began to appear.

On July 4, 1971, August Derleth passed away, and the future of Arkham House was left very much in doubt. As in the deaths of his brothers, Derleth's passing devastated Donald Wandrei, and he resolved to carry on by assisting the estate of his late friend in any way that he could. For over a year, Wandrei made weekly pilgrimages to Sauk City to assist in the disposition of both Derleth's estate and Arkham House.

He provided a friend, a St. Paul bookseller, to produce an appraisal of Derleth's library. Later, and especially after the deaths of his mother and sister in 1972, he made regular pilgrimages to Sauk City to help dispose of the backlog of unpublished Arkham House material. While the extent of this work may never be known, it is certain that it was substantial, and that it included the readying of several books for publication, the writing of dustjacket copy for Brian Lumley's *The Caller of the Black*, and the production of at least one catalog. Don's main expressed purpose in this was to help those running the estate to "learn the ropes."[10] To this end, Donald Wandrei worked closely with Forrest Hartmann, lawyer for Arkham House and the Derleth Estate.

Later, allegedly at Hartmann's instigation,[11] he made the decision to exercise his right of first refusal and purchase the company outright.[12] To this end he even allowed his literary incomes (most of them from the Lovecraft copyrights) to accrue in an Arkham House account on the understanding that they would be applied against the purchase price. Then, in April of 1973, he surprised everyone by publicly renouncing his right to purchase Arkham House and launching a legal crusade that, both directly and indirectly, would forever sully his reputation among fans and aficionados of fantasy.

Ironically, while Don's actions, especially his missives of the late '70s and early '80s, did much to damage his reputation, the main damage was caused by his unwillingness to make his case; to discuss publicly, and coherently, the real nature and basis of his claim against Arkham House. Because of this, serious misconceptions about the case and its outcome were allowed to grow in the minds of those who tried to follow it from afar. These misconceptions live on. Even today most discussions with a long-time fan of Arkham House will elicit two views of the Wandrei lawsuit: (1) that it was an attempt to regain control of the company; and (2) that Wandrei eventually lost his case. Both, as we shall see, are quite wrong.

The exact trigger that set off what we shall call *Wandrei vs. Derleth Estate* is unclear, although at least one person remembers it as occurring due to a chance remark made during a meeting to finalize Wandrei's purchase of the firm[13] (the initial Articles of Incorporation for Arkham House, filed on December 21, 1972, list Donald Wandrei as sole proprietor). In any event, at some point between December of 1972 and April of 1973, Wandrei decided to initiate the break, and his motivation was clear, even if the underlying reasons for his actions were never fully enunciated. After a year and a half of working with Hartmann in the operations of Arkham House, and also occasionally assisting the Estate in regard to the Derleth library and literary properties, Wandrei had decided that Hartmann was a man who was not to be trusted. This represented a complete reversal of Wandrei's earlier position. Just a year earlier he had broken off contact with an old friend for expressing the very same views that he would later adopt.[14]

Having decided that Hartmann needed to be removed, Wandrei initiated a multi-part strategy of which the public "Renunciation" was only the first step. Within a week of his "Renunciation" (on April 21, 1973), Wandrei had also filed a claim against Arkham House for payment of sums due him, and contacted the Wisconsin State Attorney General's Office regarding the validity of August Derleth's Will. Shortly thereafter, he hired a second, Wisconsin-based attorney, to pursue his claims in Sauk County Probate Court.[15]

Hartmann was surprised and taken aback by these actions and, at first, tried to settle. Wandrei, however, seemed to have no interest in any settlement that did not include the removal of Hartmann as both lawyer to the Derleth Estate and as chief of operations for Arkham House.[16] In fact, Wandrei's goals in taking action against the Derleth Estate are best summed up in his Renunciation, and again in a letter sent to his old friend, the author and journalist, Harrison Salisbury.[17] In the Renunciation he says:

> I do this for the purpose stated by my beloved friend August Derleth himself in said whole Clause B: so that the maximum value may be realized for his children's benefit and the proceeds of such sale divided among them.

In the letter to Salisbury, his viewpoint regarding Hartmann is much more overt. Moreover, he states that he intends to:

> . . . expose Hartmann as one of the most ruthless and contemptible con-men of this century, and certainly the worst perpetrator of fraudulent plans, schemes and operations past, present and future that I have ever heard of against a publishing company and against entire Estates.

He then goes on to provide a hint of both his short term strategy and his expectation of a quick and legally significant victory:

> The whole affair is so fantastic that I expect it to establish legal precedents. I rather expect it to boil to a head in the next couple of weeks after a series of bull's eye bombs I've been dropping without advance notice to anyone.

Wandrei's overall plan to achieve his goals is open to some speculation. However, it appears that, by renouncing his claim on Arkham House, and then immediately enforcing his claim to full ownership of the Lovecraft copyrights, he was trying to create a situation in which Arkham House would *have* to be sold, with all of the proceeds from that sale (Wandrei estimated the value at between $100,000 and $150,000) going directly to April and Walden Derleth. His concurrent challenge of Derleth's Will, and Hartmann's execution of same, may have simply been insurance to prevent Hartmann from continuing as lawyer for the Estate once control of Arkham House had been removed. In any event, Wandrei's plan, whatever it was, proved a dismal failure. Within two months Wandrei's hard line had forced Hartmann into taking a hard line of his own. Specifically, he went from referring all requests for information on Lovecraft literary rights to Donald Wandrei[18] to denying that Wandrei had any share in such rights at all.

He even went so far as to amend his Inventory of the Derleth Estate, moving the Lovecraft copyrights and related literary rights from the category of "Joint Property" (with Donald Wandrei) in the original September 1972 version to "Personal Property" of August Derleth in the

July 1973 version. Wandrei responded by challenging the amended inventory in April of the following year.

On Christmas Eve 1974, Judge Harland Hill issued a Memorandum Decision that should have settled the matter once and for all. At issue was the ownership of copyright to the works of H.P. Lovecraft and, in deciding the case, Judge Hill broke these into five distinct categories.

The first of these[19] were "works copyrighted solely by August Derleth." In large part these were Derleth's own "posthumous collaborations" and their ownership was never really in dispute. They became the sole property of the Derleth Estate.

The second category was "books jointly copyrighted by August Derleth and Donald Wandrei." Generally speaking, this covered editorial copyrights on eight books, all of them originally published by Arkham House. Not surprisingly, these were found to be the joint property of Wandrei and the Derleth Estate as "tenants in common."

The third grouping was that of forty-six stories whose copyrights had been reassigned to Donald Wandrei and August Derleth by *Weird Tales Magazine*.[20] On November 8, 1955 Derleth and Wandrei had signed a survivorship agreement specifically relating to these stories. Judge Hill's ruling validated that agreement and awarded sole ownership of those rights to Donald Wandrei.

Category four dealt with all of the H.P. Lovecraft literary rights not covered in the first three sections. The key document governing Judge Hill's ruling in this area was something that has since come to be known as the "Morrish/Lewis bequest." In simple layman's terms, H.P. Lovecraft willed his estate to his aunt, Annie Gamwell. Gamwell, in turn, willed her estate to Ethel P. Morrish and Edna W. Lewis. In a short, one paragraph document dated May 2, 1941, Morrish and Lewis granted Donald Wandrei and August Derleth a "free hand," not just to publish the works of H.P. Lovecraft, and collect earnings from same, but also, "to receive royalties, sell second serial rights, and, if necessary, first serial rights in connection with such publication." As the stories covered by this section were specifically *not* covered by the Wandrei/Derleth survivorship agreement of 1955, Judge Hill awarded ownership of materials in this category to Donald Wandrei and the Estate of August Derleth as tenants in common.

The fifth category, which originally included only those H.P. Lovecraft letters ear-marked for use in the then unpublished Selected Letters Volumes IV and V, was found to be covered by the above, and was thus the joint property of both parties.

One would think that this would have ended the matter. Unfortunately, it did not. Over the next dozen years the battle continued, as Wandrei's lawyers fought to obtain an accounting by the Estate for all fees paid to Arkham House for rights to H.P. Lovecraft material. Wandrei, meanwhile, had entrusted the management of his share of the Lovecraft rights to his agent, Scott Meredith. To protect himself from counter-actions taken by the Estate, he also had the Meredith Agency set up an Escrow account into which all proceeds could be deposited and held until a final settlement was reached.

It was during the first half of this period of stalemate that Donald Wandrei acquired the reputation for eccentricity and paranoia that was to haunt him, not just for the rest of his life, but beyond. While Wandrei was not one to share his motivations with anyone, it can be fairly observed that his actions during this period were driven by two main factors. The first of these was that the battle with the Estate (aka Hartmann) had become, almost from the beginning, personal. On July 3, 1973, Hartmann sent a letter to Ramsey Campbell that included the following paragraph:

> On a sadder note, I must report that Donald Wandrei has gone through a complete personality change and is no longer with Arkham House. Moreover, he has been doing some rather wierd [sic] things lately and should you ever receive any correspondence from him, I would appreciate being advised. This is particularly sad when you consider that Don is one of the top men in the field even though he is at retirement age.

Wandrei, upon receiving a copy of this letter, was incensed. He wasted little time in reproducing it and mailing copies out to various friends and opinion makers within the fantasy field. He also wrote a letter of complaint to the Wisconsin State Bar Association.[21] After July of 1973, Hartmann was far more circumspect in his written statements.

Wandrei, while scrupulously avoiding comment on the real facts of the case, was far more outspoken. The results, when taken outside the context of the real issues involved, did not work to Wandrei's benefit.

The second driving force behind the tone of Wandrei's missives and correspondence of this period was what can only be described as paranoia. Yet, it is a paranoia that is understandable under the circumstances. Having prevailed in court, Wandrei found himself unable to obtain redress. Worse, his arch-enemy, Hartmann, the man whom he had sworn to drive from the field, seemed to be winning on all fronts. Arkham House continued to publish under Hartmann's legal guidance, *Selected Letters IV* & *V* as edited by "August Derleth and James Turner" were released in versions that Wandrei believed had been adapted from his own compilations.[22] Also, several trusted friends had, in Wandrei's view at least, "gone over to the enemy." The most notable of these was Kirby McCauley who, as an aspiring agent, had managed to develop a close working relationship with Forrest Hartmann and Arkham House. Thereafter, everything that McCauley did was examined in the context of his relationship with Hartmann and, usually, viewed in conspiratorial terms. This, in turn, explains Wandrei's later condemnations of the World Fantasy Convention and Conan Properties, both of which were started by McCauley, as well as his occasional mailings regarding such McCauley clients as Stephen King and Peter Straub.

By the early 1980s, Wandrei's frustration and bitterness had grown to such proportions that they tended to spill over into other areas of his life. Relations with old friends sometimes soured as a result. Wandrei even began to question the friendship of the late August Derleth, a man who had been like a brother to him since their first meeting in 1929. Now, consumed by hatred of his former partner's lawyer, Don often found himself asking how Derleth "could not have known" about Hartmann, sometimes even half-convincing himself that Derleth had been "in on it" from the beginning. Of course, that was foolishness, and even Wandrei knew it. Still, his passionate dislike of Forrest Hartmann cannot be underestimated, a dislike best illustrated by the following poem written by Donald Wandrei at the height of his legal troubles:

EPITAPH

In this box be the matter of Forrest D. Hartmann
For his clients be trayed and be judged by each smart man;
Now he's taken his case and Brief waivers as well
For the grilling prepared by his betters in Hell.

Wandrei's obsession with Hartmann and the Derleth Estate had another basis beyond those items discussed above. During his early work with the post-Derleth Arkham House, and again when he was negotiating to buy the firm, Donald Wandrei had brought a number of items of personal property with him to Wisconsin. These items included Wandrei's own copyright records and certificates and the manuscripts for *Time Burial, Colossus,* and the cycle of letters between Donald and Howard Wandrei that we now know as *The Circle of Pyramids.*[23] Not only were these items not returned to Wandrei after he had backed out of his plan to purchase Arkham House, they were retained by the Estate and even used against him. In 1980, for instance, Hartmann offered up an out of court settlement that was interesting, to say the least. In exchange for fifty percent of the monies held in escrow by the Scott Meredith Agency, Wandrei would have been expected to give up all claim to future Lovecraft royalties, as well as monies already collected through agencies other than Scott Meredith (i.e., by Arkham House directly). As a "sweetener" Hartmann further offered Wandrei the return of his personal property and to forego any action for "defamation."[24] Wandrei, needless to say, declined. He filed a replevin action seeking return of his property and, on May 18, 1981, most of the items listed were turned over to his attorney.

The return of his property seems to have had a noticable and positive influence on Wandrei's attitude. While still steadfast in his determination to see the case through to a successful conclusion, his obsession with the matter—and with Hartmann—declined markedly during this period. Ironically, part of Wandrei's improved state of mind may have been due to an unrelated and near-tragic event. On January 26, 1982, he was savagely beaten in his own house by a burglar. His injuries were severe, requiring both hospitalization and an extended period of recuperation away from home. Long-time friend and former Derleth secretary Kay Price credits much of Wandrei's improved mental state after 1981 to the increased social contacts and improved diet necessitated by his period of enforced convalescence. Whatever the cause: the return of his personal property, his potentially deadly encounter with a burglar, his hospitalization-enforced social contacts; there can be little doubt that the "screeching" and "crowing" Wandrei caricatured by T.E.D. Klein bears little resemblance to the Donald Wandrei of the middle 1980s.[25]

While all of this was going on, the wheels of justice were grinding slowly and inexorably toward a conclusion. After innumerable delays and postponements, the retirement of Judge Hill and his subsequent death (after a brief return to the bench, specifically for the purpose of bringing the case to an end), a new judge was assigned to the case.

The matter into which Judge Sverre Roang was assigned on April 5, 1983 was one which had undergone no appreciable change since that December day in 1974 when Judge Hill had issued his initial ruling. Judge Roang, to his credit, wasted little time in moving the case along. On May 5, 1983, a hearing was held. Over the next several months, briefs were filed by both parties. The positions of the litigants were clear. Wandrei's lawyers asked for an accounting, or perhaps multiple accountings, of Lovecraft copyrights pursuant to Judge Hill's 1974 decision. Hartmann, for his part, stuck to a position he had been using successfully since the early days of the case. In layman's terms, he had simply refused to provide an accounting until such time as the court ruled on two legal questions he had posed:

(1) Does anyone have the legal right to collect royalties on literary property in the public domain; and

(2) When a story collection includes only one or more stories under copyright protection, can the holder of enforceable copyright claim the entire income on the story collection?

To say that these questions were curious is an understatement. Firstly, they are hypothetical, unsupported by either documentation or specifics. Secondly, their implication—that the Lovecraft copyrights were no longer valid—directly contradicted many other actions taken by the Estate.[26] In 1976, for instance, when George Wetzel expressed a similar opinion in an article written for *The Miskatonic*, editor Dirk Mosig sent it to Arkham House for review. Hartmann's response was swift and unequivocal. He informed Mosig that publication of such an article *could* result in legal action. The grounds: libel against the honesty and integrity of August Derleth.[27]

In any event, the two questions posed by Forrest Hartmann did not dissuade Judge Roang from moving the case along. On April 11, 1984, he issued a twenty-four page Memorandum Decision that essentially recapitulated the original 1974 ruling of Judge Hill. On the matter of copyrights, Judge Roang brushed aside the Estate's questions by deciding that the accounting could proceed, and that if necessary, ruling on copyright status could be handled at a late date. Furthermore, the court had, "discovered nothing of real factual import in the present record to establish a positive finding that a public domain status does actually exist." Moreover, as many of the monies involved were derived from foreign sales, Judge Roang pointed out that U.S. Copyright law had no extraterritorial effect and that "a determination as to the existence *vel non* of U.S. copyrights and the propriety of receiving royalties from literary properties found to be in the public domain in the U.S., would not affect these foreign royalties." Judge Roang also made much of the Revised Wisconsin Probate Code of 1969, with which he had been intimately involved, and which sets a number of time limits to which the representatives of estates are expected to adhere. The fact that a final judgment on the Estate had still not been rendered in 1984, a full thirteen years after August Derleth's death, was not looked upon favorably by the Court. Even more disturbing to Judge Roang was the fact that, in his opinion, a "complete inventory and detailed accounting as to all tangible and intangible literary property" had not yet been filed. Under normal circumstances, Section 858.01 of the Wisconsin Probate Code would have required such an accounting to be completed within six months.[28]

Finally, after years of apparent inaction by the Wisconsin courts, the matter of *Wandrei vs. Derleth Estate* was heading to a close. Judge Roang's Order for a complete accounting spurred movements toward an out of court settlement. In January 1985, Forrest Hartmann journeyed to St. Paul where he met Rudy Low, Donald Wandrei's primary lawyer, for the first time. Over the next few months, more meetings were held and, eventually, after many months of negotiations, an out of court settlement was reached. Judge Hill's original decision, with its five-part division of rights, was an accountant's nightmare. To simplify matters it was decided that all monies received from Lovecraft rights would be treated the same, regardless of whether they derived from the *Weird Tales* reassignment of 1947 or the Morrish/Lewis bequest of 1941 (Derleth's "posthumous collaborations" and other materials in this class were, of course, not affected). To this end, the lawyers decided on a simple percentage-based division of all monies. Under this agreement, finalized in early 1986, Donald Wandrei was awarded a 53% ownership stake in all Lovecraft copyrights. The remaining 47% became the property of the Derleth Estate. These percentages were also used to calculate the division of all monies paid for Lovecraft rights between the death of August Derleth and the date of settlement.

At last, it was over. Although one cannot help but note an ironic footnote to the closing of this chapter of American literary history. Earlier it had been mentioned that Donald Wandrei established an escrow account through the Scott Meredith Agency for the purpose of depositing monies derived from the Lovecraft copyrights. With a settlement reached, Meredith prepared to close the account and send checks to the principals, minus a five percent service charge. Wandrei and his lawyers raised no objection. Hartmann, however, was not so inclined. In a letter dated June 2, 1986 he threatened the Scott Meredith Literary Agency with legal action if full payment was not received within ten days.

The outcome of this matter is unknown.

There is an old saying that no one ever wins a fight. In the case of Wandrei's battle with the Derleth Estate, that is undoubtedly true. The long, bitter struggle had irreparably damaged Donald Wandrei's standing within the fantasy and science fiction communities. His reputation forever marred by misperceptions of his goals and intents. Likewise, Wandrei's relationship with old friends had also suffered. Indeed, the most hurtful to him was probably the loss of April and Walden Derleth, to whom he had once been something akin to a favorite uncle. Nor was the financial recompense all that noteworthy in the final analysis.

Three lawyers, employed concurrently over a fourteen year period, eventually become quite expensive. In Don's case, this expense (up to April 7, 1986) ran to the not insignificant sum of $107,901.[29] On April 30, 1987, less than six months before his death, Donald Wandrei finally closed the door on his lawsuit against the Derleth Estate by signing over thirty percent of his Lovecraft rights (sixteen percent of the total) to long-time family attorney Rudy Low in partial payment for legal services rendered.

Nor did the Estate go unaffected. April and Walden Derleth not only lost their "uncle" Donald, they also found themselves heirs to an Estate saddled by massive legal expenses. One source, close to both April Derleth and Arkham House, places the legal cost of Wandrei's challenge at somewhere in the neighborhood of $80,000.[30] Wounds thus opened heal slowly. Even now, more than ten years after a final settlement, and with the passing of Donald Wandrei and the departure of all of Arkham House's previous staff, there still remains a level of discomfort whenever questions about the lawsuit are raised. However, it is encouraging to note that a new anthology scheduled for publication by Arkham House in 1998 is expected to include a story by Donald Wandrei—the first such to be published by that imprint since the death of August Derleth in 1971. Perhaps this is as sure a sign as any that the ghosts of *Wandrei vs. Derleth Estate* have at long last been laid to rest.

In discussing Wandrei's role in the publishing house that he helped to found, it has been necessary to confront the question of the protracted litigation that consumed the latter years of his life. Hopefully the airing of the facts will help to set the record straight, allay some of the most egregious rumors, and allow Donald Wandrei's actions to be considered within their proper context. But it is important not to repeat Don's mistake by focusing too much on this unfortunate period when assessing his contributions to the field of horror fiction as a whole. Wandrei's real legacy was not that of a litigator, pamphleteer, iconoclast, or eccentric hermit. In dwelling on those images, we forget the seventeen-year-old poet who opened a correspondence with H. P. Lovecraft and Clark Ashton Smith, the young, successful writer of pulp fiction, and the loyal friend who, with his partner August Derleth, strove with singular perseverance to place Lovecraft's fiction into book form. In launching Arkham

House Publishers of Sauk City, Wisconsin, Donald Wandrei and August Derleth not only preserved the writings of H. P. Lovecraft and a host of other authors, but essentially birthed the specialty press boom of the mid-to-late Twentieth Century and, in so doing, forever changed the history and development of the American Horror Story.

❖ ❖ ❖

The matter of *Wandrei vs. Derleth Estate* is a complicated one and this article, despite its incompleteness due to limitations of space, would not have been possible without the assistance of a number of persons and institutions. Firstly, thanks should go to the Minnesota Historical Society, whose Wandrei archives provided the main documentation upon which this article was based. Additional documentation, some of it quite crucial, was provided by Peder Wagtskjold and the Estate of Eric A. Carlson of Duluth. The author would also like to thank Kay Price and Peter Ruber, whose insights and reminiscences helped shed some light on the possible motivations of the principals. While this information has been used sparingly (or not at all, as in the many cases where supporting documentation could not be found) it was invaluable in leading the author toward an understanding of several key points. Lastly, thanks are given to those who have agreed to read and comment upon this article prior to publication; most notably: April Derleth, Philip J. Rahman, and Paul Bolin.

D.H. Olson
Minneapolis, MN.
March 16, 1997

FOOTNOTES

1   The other authors were: Francis Bosworth, Karl Litzenberg, Gordon Louis Roth, and Harrison Salisbury. The woodcuts were provided by Leo Henkora.

2   This was Howard Wandrei's *second* move to New York.

3   Wandrei had apparently forgotten about E. Hoffman Price.

4   Wandrei's memories of this event conflict directly with those of Julius Schwartz, who also claims to have sold both stories. A likely solution to this mystery, postulated by S.T. Joshi in his *H.P. Lovecraft; A Life* (1996), and seemingly supported by some of H.P. Lovecraft's surviving correspondence, is that both individuals, independently of one another, each sold a single story to Tremaine at roughly the same time. In fact, a November 6, 1935 letter from Don to his father gives the full story—without the time induced distortions that later crept in. In this version Wandrei clams credit for "The Shadow Out of Time" (at $280) while Schwartz is given responsibility for "At the Mountains of Madness" (at $350; less $35 commission).

5   In a letter to Barlow, Lovecraft noted: "One of the latter was Wandrei's younger brother (who has a yarn in the current *WT*)—a weird artist of astonishing skill and genius. Some of his demoniac sketches almost knocked me over with their inspired potency and masterful technique. This kid has gone farther in his art than any of the rest of us in our writing—it can certainly be only a question of a few years before he is recognised widely as a leading figure in his field." (*Selected Letters IV, p 341.*)

6   The Circle of Pyramids (unpublished).

7   James Hill was Derleth's lawyer, and a founding member of the firm in which Forrest Hartmann would later become a partner.

8   Untrue. Howard Wandrei, accompanied by his brother, is known to have visited August Derleth in Sauk City during the latter half of 1952.

9   Both were eventually produced in preliminary, photocopy form. Neither was ever published by Arkham House.

10   Telephone conversation with Kay Price December 10, 1996.

11 Ibid.

12 Section One, Paragraph B of August Derleth's Will.

13 Telephone conversation with Peter Ruber, January 3, 1997. Another issue may have been the "Memorandums of Agreement" mailed to Arkham House authors in early 1973. While the exact role of these documents in Wandrei's decision making are unclear, an April 3, 1973 letter from Wandrei to Hartmann indicates that they were a factor.

14 Telephone conversation with Kay Price, December 10, 1996.

15 Eventually Wandrei's legal team would grow to include three lawyers: Kenneth Stevens of Baraboo, Wisconsin, Rudolph Low of St Paul and, later, Stuart Hemphill of Minneapolis.

16 Ironically, Wandrei's suit may have worked against his cause. According to sources within Arkham House, April Derleth was already giving serious consideration to having Hartmann removed as lawyer to the Estate. The attorney she had chosen, however, is alleged to have backed out once legal papers had been filed.

17 Letter, Donald Wandrei to Harrison Salisbury, May 2, 1973.

18 Letter, Forrest Hartmann to Andre Lamarre, May 14, 1973.

19 For the sake of clarity, the ordering here differs from that of the actual ruling.

20 This assignment, dated October 9, 1947, was recorded by the U.S. Copyright Office on December 5 of that same year.

21 The Wisconsin State Bar Association declined to act. In a letter dated January 24, 1975, Michael G. Price, Assistant Grievance Administrator, informed Wandrei that there was, in his opinion, "no basis" for an investigation by that body.

22 Regarding the division of labor on Lovecraft's Selected Letters, Donald Wandrei appears to have been responsible for the initial transcription and selection of Lovecraft's letters. Derleth completed the editorial process while preparing the books for publication. It is unclear how the late August Derleth and James Turner divided co-editorial duties on volumes IV and V.

23 There is also some evidence to indicate that Arkham House may have had additional Wandrei material as well, including some Howard Wandrei artwork. Donald lists these items in his 1980 "Outline for Replevin" but, in an August 12, 1980 letter to Kenneth Stevens, Hartmann denies any knowledge of them. They were later found and turned over to Wandrei's attorneys.

24 Letter, Hartmann to Kenneth Stevens, August 4, 1980.

25 For another, differing perspective on the burglery and its effects on Donald Wandrei's mental health see page xv of Helen Mary Hughesdon's introduction to this book.

26 The issue of Lovecraft copyrights is a complicated one. Undoubtedly some of Lovecraft's work (those published in amateur, uncopyrighted journals) is in the public domain. The status of other materials has also been called into question by various Lovecraft scholars. The most recent such exploration of the issue may be found in the final chapter of S.T. Joshi's H.P. *Lovecraft: A Life* (Necronomicon Press, 1996). While Joshi makes a powerful circumstantial case for expanding public domain status to much of the Lovecraft canon, he does so with no reference whatsoever to the issues raised in the Wandrei/Derleth estate litigation.

27 Letter, Hartmann to Mosig, March 5, 1976.

28 Hartmann's position, enunciated in his May 7, 1984 letter to Judge Roang (objecting to a draft version of the "Findings of Fact, Conclusions of Law and Judgment/Order" requested by the Court) was that such an inventory had indeed been filed. The Court appears to have disagreed.

29 In actuality, Wandei's cost may have been much higher as he appeared to have made ongoing payments to Kenneth Stevens throughout the 1970's and 1980s.

30 Phone conversation with Peter Ruber, January 3, 1997.

DON'T DREAM

First Edition
1997

Don't Dream by Donald Wandrei was published by
Fedogan & Bremer, 4325 Hiawatha Avenue, #2115,
Minneapolis, MN 55406. Two thousand copies
have been printed from Century Old Style
by the Maple Press Company.